Wilhelm Adolf Lampadius

**The Life of Felix Mendelssohn-Bartholdy**

Wilhelm Adolf Lampadius

**The Life of Felix Mendelssohn-Bartholdy**

ISBN/EAN: 9783337095178

Printed in Europe, USA, Canada, Australia, Japan

Cover: Foto ©Raphael Reischuk / pixelio.de

More available books at **www.hansebooks.com**

# CONTENTS.

NEW AND ENLARGED EDITION.

# THE LIFE OF

# FELIX MENDELSSOHN-BARTHOLDY

BY

## W. A. LAMPADIUS

TRANSLATED BY

## W. L. GAGE

# TRANSLATOR'S INTRODUCTION.

Not long after Mendelssohn's death in 1847, Mr. Lampadius of Leipzig, a young man full of enthusiasm for the composer, and thrilling with the recollections of his career and his character, wrote a sketch of Mendelssohn, which, translated by the present writer and supplemented by the reminiscences of Chorley, Rellstab, and Benedict, has been for more than twenty years before the American public, and has been reprinted in England. Meanwhile, a large number of other works, many of them of great value and interest, have appeared; some of them letters, some reminiscences; and what may be called a Mendelssohn literature has sprung up in connection with his beloved name. Chief among these writings have been his nephew Hensel's large work, "The Mendelssohn Family," the two volumes of "Letters," and the consummate and exhaustive sketch in Grove's "Musical Dictionary," written by the editor himself. Meantime, Mr. Lampadius, the author of the original sketch, is still living in Leipzig, and has supplemented his earlier work with one much more elaborate and complete, a copy of which he has sent me with the request that I should translate it personally, and give it to my countrymen. This I have done, undertaking the task in much the same spirit in which Lampadius has written : a strong, indeed, overmastering affection for Mendelssohn, as a man of such engaging qualities, so pure, and balanced, and sound, that I feel even more strongly than before, that to cause men to know him (quite apart from his music) is to make them acquainted with one of the sweetest and noblest spirits of our time.

5 )

It will be seen that the author has given not only analyses of Mendelssohn's works, minute details regarding the time and place when his compositions were produced, a narrative of the events of his career, and glimpses of his family and friends, but also copious extracts from his letters, including those already published in volumes before our people. These I have retranslated in order to avoid a violation of copyright. I might have omitted them, with a sensible diminution of the size of this volume. But, remembering that the author has as his aim the giving of a complete view of Mendelssohn as a man, in a work whose excellence must lie in its completeness, I was sure that it would greatly maim the life, and injure its effect as a biography, were it to be assumed that it must be read as a mere introduction to the Mendelssohn "Letters," and "The Mendelssohn Family." We want, of course, one book large enough to hold all that one *needs* to know regarding this gifted man, and yet piquant enough to stimulate the reader to go on into yet larger reaches of knowledge. It seems to me that Mr. Lampadius has attained his end, and though I have, here and there, exercised a certain liberty of condensation, it has always been most sparingly used.

W. L. GAGE.

# THE LIFE OF

# FELIX MENDELSSOHN-BARTHOLDY.

## PART I.

### THE MENDELSSOHN NAME. — FELIX' CHILDHOOD AND YOUTH, 1809–1829.

IT is a fact not sufficiently explained by Darwin's theory of descent, that, as a rule, the full intellectual power does not pass over from the father to the son, but rather from the grandfather to the grandson.

Felix Mendelssohn-Bartholdy's grandfather was Moses Mendelssohn (born as the son of a poor Jewish school-master in Dessau, on the 6th of September, 1729; died on the 4th of January, 1786, in Berlin), a pioneer of the new and better time, a profound philosophical thinker, and, at the same time, one of the noblest representatives of true humanity. He served as the type of "Nathan the Wise" in Lessing's play of the same name. Born in the most narrow conditions, and outgrowing at the age of scarcely five years the instruction of his father, he followed his teacher, Rabbi Fränkel, from Dessau to Berlin. Struggling with the bitterest poverty, he raised himself by his own power to a height of cultivation which enabled him, not only to free his people from the oppressive yoke under which they were crushed, but also to make him a co-laborer with Nicolai in his "Library of the Fine Arts," and thus to be of the greatest service to the new epoch which Lessing brought in to German art, literature, and science.

In his own independent philosophical writings, in letters, conversations, and æsthetic treatises, especially in his two leading works, "Phædon," or "The Immortality of the Soul," and "Morning Hours," or "Addresses upon the Existence of God," he revealed his deep religious nature, but without any ecclesiastical relations, as a follower of the great Leibnitz, and a pure deist.

It may not be passed over in a biography of Felix Mendelssohn, that his grandfather possessed a lively interest in music, and a fine taste for it, and that he himself practised the art in his earlier years.

Moses Mendelssohn was married happily to Fromet Jugenheim, the daughter of a merchant in Hamburgh; although, at first, she was indifferent to him, he won her in spite of his deformity (he was slightly hump-backed), and from the marriage sprang six children, who survived him : three sons, Joseph, Abraham, and Nathan; and three daughters, Dorothea (afterwards celebrated as the wife of Frederick Schlegel), Henrietta, and Recha. The second son, Abraham, was Felix' father.

Abraham Mendelssohn was in no respect an insignificant man. In addition to his great skill and activity as a merchant, which soon assisted him to the possession of large wealth, he had many striking traits of mind and character, which not only made him the object of the highest veneration in his family, but also enabled him to have a very clear judgment with regard to music, without possessing the understanding of what is technical in it. He was equally conspicuous for a tender and unchanging love for his wife, and a self-sacrificing spirit for his children, whose education he conducted with the greatest care; and in addition to all this, he was a good German patriot; but in mental productivity he followed neither

his father nor his son, as he himself says with fine irony :
" Formerly, I was the son of my father, now I am the
father of my son ; " and from London he wrote in June,
1833, at a time when Felix had already become famous
in England, in a letter to his wife: " You will be very
glad to read how much Felix is. loved and how highly he
is regarded here ; I feel it most distinctly *par ricochet*,
and the aged Horsley intended to pay me a great com-
pliment to-day when he said to me that he considered
me fortunate to be the son and the father of a great man.
' Where is the cat ? ' I thought to myself, and perhaps
should have been a little disturbed at it if I had not
thought the same thing myself, and had not often made
fun of myself that I am nothing but a dash between the
father and the son."

Of Abraham Mendelssohn's youthful life, little is
known.  In the year 1803, we find him cashier in the
well-known banking house of Fould at Paris.  He was
so well pleased to be there that he fancied he should
never be happy in any other place.   " I would prefer to
eat dry bread in Paris to living anywhere else," he wrote
in one of his letters.

On a journey from Paris to Berlin, he made the
acquaintance of Leah or Lilla Solamon, a beautiful,
lively, and finely educated girl, the possession of whom,
according to the opinion of his sister Henrietta, who
lived in Paris at that time as the teacher of the daughter
of Count Sebastiani, would be an extraordinary piece of
good fortune ; such a woman as this, she thought, he
would seldom, perhaps never, find again.

Abraham Mendelssohn wished to have her share his
fortune in Paris, but the mother of the girl declared that
her daughter should never become the wife of a clerk,

and so he gave up his position in Paris, associated himself with his brother Joseph, and settled in Hamburgh, where, with his young wife, he took possession of a pretty little estate on the Elbe and close by Neumühlen, which soon after became his property. Thus Leah Solamon became the mother of Felix Mendelssohn. Her maiden name, it will be observed, was not Bartholdy; this name the brother of Leah had assumed on the occasion of his acceptance of Christianity. He had been the Prussian consul-general in Rome; he was a man who stood in high honor, had a fine sense of art, and built for himself the well known house bearing the name of Casa Bartholdi, which he had caused to be greatly embellished by the German artists Cornelius, Veit, Schadow, Overbeck, and Schnorr. He was, nevertheless, not a man of great wealth. His mother, a rigidly orthodox Jewess, would not pardon her son for becoming a Christian. When once Felix' sister, the gifted Fanny, had played especially well before her grandmother, the old lady said that, as a reward, she would give her whatever she should ask. Fanny replied, " Then forgive Uncle Bartholdy," and the grandmother, touched at this unexpected request, consented to a reconciliation with her son for Fanny's sake. This was the origin of a very strong attachment to the uncle, and a long correspondence.

. In a house behind St. Michael's Church, Abraham Mendelssohn's first three children were born; the eldest, Fanny, who has been mentioned, saw the light November 15th, 1805; Felix, February 3rd, 1809, and Rebecca, April 11th, 1811. Paul, the youngest child, was born October 30th, 1813, in Berlin, whither the family had fled before the imperious sway of Davoust, who had become suspicious of their thorough German sympathies.

At the national rising in 1813, Abraham Mendelssohn stood with his whole heart on the side of Germany, and with his own means paid for several volunteers. In recognition of his services to his country, he was appointed Civic Counsellor.

That the name, Felix, was chosen as a happy omen of his son's future, is revealed by his entire life. Scarcely any mortal has ever been born under a more happy star than he.

His father took the name, Bartholdy, at the instance of his brother-in-law, after resolving to have the children trained in the Protestant faith. Although himself neither an orthodox Jew, nor a believing Christian, he caused them to become united to the Reformed Church. His religious point of view, which, according to our conceptions, was rather a moral than a religious one, he has given in a remarkable letter to his sister Fanny after her confirmation in the year 1820, from which we quote : —

" You have taken, my dear daughter, an important step in life, and from my heart I wish you joy in it ; nay, I feel myself compelled to think earnestly over many things which have not yet been talked of between us. If there be a God, what kind of a God he may be ; whether a part of ourselves is eternal, and after the other part has vanished, whether it lives on, and where, and how. All this I do not know, and therefore, I have not expressed an opinion of it to you ; but I know that in me, and in you, and in all men, there is an unchangeable leaning to all that is good, true, and right ; that there is a conscience which warns us and guides us when we depart from the true way. This I know, this I believe ; I live in the strength of this, and it is my religion. This I could not teach to you, and no one can learn it. Every one possesses this who does not purposely and meaningly deny it, and you would not do this, I know; for you have the example of your mother, that most noble, most worthy woman, whose whole life is the fulfilment of duty and love, and a desire to promote others' welfare. We have trained you and your brothers and sisters in the Christian faith, because this is the faith of the most cultivated men, and contains nothing which can estrange you from the good, rather much that will aid you to be obedient, to be patient, to bear with resignation what you have to bear; not to speak of the Founder of this faith, known to so many, but followed by so few."

It is wonderful that amid such relations, and under the influence of such views, the father of Felix Mendelssohn could have impressed so deep and thorough a Christian faith in him as is exhibited in his oratorios, cantatas, motets, and spiritual songs, and which has made him, after Bach and Handel, one of the greatest religious composers of all time.

Felix, as a boy, must have been exceedingly beautiful. Upon a well-proportioned though small body, reposed a fair head with a high forehead; the eyes large, dark, and brilliant, the nose with its fine curve, the lovely mouth, the dark brown locks falling freely upon the shoulders, and beautifully encircling the face. No wonder that women and girls, as, for example, in Goethe's house, when they first saw the eleven year old child, fell in love with him, and fondly caressed him; but his spiritual beauty was no less than his physical. He was a "wonder-child," in the best sense of the word; an eager desire to learn, precocious power of production, —these were his gifts, coupled with a noble and beautiful modesty. His musical talent came to maturity at a very early period.   The father gave him the best teachers who were to be found.   He chose as private tutors for the two oldest children, Fanny and Felix, Heinrich Heyse, afterwards distinguished as a philologist, and father of the poet, Paul Heyse; and to this man Felix was indebted for that thorough classical education which enabled him to prepare, in the year 1826, an accurate translation of Terence's " Andria " for Goethe's use.

On the 11th of October, the great poet thus wrote to Zelter: " Thank the good and active Felix for the ex-ceedingly beautiful copy of his first æsthetic studies.   His work shall be given to the lovers of art in Weimar, as a great and enduring delight during the long winter eve-nings to come."

This classical training formed, also, the basis for two master-works of Mendelssohn — the music to Sophocles' " Antigone " and " Œdipus in Kolonos " — of which we shall speak later.

Felix' first teacher in music was Ludwig Berger, a fine and genuinely German artist, equally skilful as pianist and as composer, a graduate of the school of Clementi, afterwards trained by John Field in St. Petersburgh, and living after 1815 in Berlin.   In counterpoint and in musical composition, his instructor was the skilful Zelter; after these, Moscheles formed a third; com-mencing his services in 1824, he not only gave the last touch to Mendelssohn's skill as a pianist, but remained to the last his most intimate friend.

As I have said in another work, and in language which I may venture to repeat, Berger planted the young tree; Zelter dug around it, and protected it from the wind, in order to allow its roots to strike down deeper; but there was yet wanting the skill of the gardener who should carefully cherish it, protect the tender blossoms from the frost, and bring its firstfruits to the enjoyment of the great world.  This was Moscheles.

The results of these three teachers were indeed wonderful.  Even in his eighth year, the lad played the piano with remarkable ability.  In his ninth year, he gave publicly the "Concert Militaire" by Dussek.  On the 28th of October, 1818, he played at a concert, a trio for the piano and two horns.  In the year 1820, Felix' father submitted his latest fugue to a Mr. Leo, who played it through, and found it written in a good and genuine style, but difficult.  The father writes in a letter to Fanny : " The fugue has pleased me well.  I could have scarcely fancied that he would write a piece betraying so much study and persistence.  It is possible that music will be his calling."

The uncle, Bartholdy, could not agree to this, and wrote to his brother-in-law : " I do not feel in accord with you in the matter of assigning no positive career to Felix. Had he such a career, it would do no injury to his musical capacities, about which there can be only one opinion.  I cannot conceive of a musical professor as a man fully established.  That is no career, no kind of a life, no goal.  At the beginning, one is just as far on as at the end ; perhaps, indeed, farther.  Let the boy have a regular course of study ; let him pursue his curriculum at the university, and then enter on an official career. Art will then be his good friend and comrade.  As far as I read the signs of the times, we never needed people of thorough education more than now.  If he is to be a merchant, then let him go early to the counting-room."

Happily, the father did not follow this advice.

His skill in discerning the qualities of true composition

developed itself as early as his ability to play the piano. This came to light first in his discovery of the value of a beautiful concerto by Sebastian Bach, which Zelter had, perhaps, never known ; and at the same time his friends became conscious of that wonderfully fine ear which detected instantly the quality of tones the most unlike, and perceived at once the goodness or the defect of the human voice. At the same time, he was developing an unprecedented power of composition, and fulness of musical ideas. When not yet twelve years of age, in September, 1820, Felix composed, within a few weeks, his first opera, named "The Two Nephews," to which a certain Dr. Kaspar had contributed the text. It was first given in the Music Hall of his father's house, No. 3 Leipsic St. (of which we shall have frequent occasion to speak), and was received with the greatest applause.

A year later, he had written two operas, and half completed a third ; in addition, he had already composed a four and five-part psalm, with a great double fugue, for the Berlin Singacademie, six symphonies, a quartet for the piano and stringed instruments, a cantata, six piano fugues, and numerous exercises, sonatas, and songs. To this general notice might here be added some words from the mouths of his teachers, Zelter and Moscheles ; unfortunately nothing remains to us from Berger.

Zelter wrote, among other words, to his friend Goethe: "The young fellow plays the piano like the devil, and Felix is always at the top of the heap."

In the autumn of 1821, Zelter announced to Goethe that he and his pupil would soon visit him: " I want to show your face to my Doris (the daughter of Zelter), and to my best pupil, before I leave this world."

When this visit, of which a more full account will be

given below, had taken place, Zelter wrote to Goethe, under date of February 8th, 1824: "Yesterday evening, Felix' fourth opera was given entire, together with its dialogue. There are three acts, which, in connection with two ballets, occupy about two and a half hours. The work has been received with great applause. Viewing it from my weaker side, I cannot restrain my wonder that a boy, who is, at best, but fifteen years of age, has made such extraordinary progress. Everywhere you find what is new, beautiful, peculiar, unique: spirit, flow, quiet harmonious tone, completeness and dramatic power; it is massive, too, as if the work of experienced hands. The orchestral part interesting, not oppressive, not wearisome, not merely an accompaniment. The musicians like to play it, and yet it is not exactly light. What is familiar comes and goes, not as if taken for granted, but rather as appropriate and welcome. Liveliness, jubilation without haste, tenderness, love, passion, innocence. The overture is a wonderful thing. It makes you think of the painter who takes a pinch of color and tosses it upon the canvass, spreads it with his finger and brush, and so brings at last a whole group to light, so that one becomes more and more surprised, and confesses that it is a true work of art."

How happily this comparison lends itself to one of Mendelssohn's later works, the "Overture to the Hebrides," that excellent picture of Scottish landscape, and old Scotch legends. "I do indeed," continued Zelter, "speak like a grandfather. I know what I say, but I will not say anything that I cannot prove. The applause came first from the people who played and sang, who certainly are good judges of the matter that they sing and play."

Ignatius Moscheles communicated in an extract from

his diary the following: "In the autumn of the year
1824, I gave in Berlin my first concert. I was then
acquainted with the Mendelssohn family, and soon
became intimate with them. On the occasion of my
first visit to the house of the parents, I made the acquaintance of the 'wonder-child,' Felix, and could not
help loving him. Even his youthful productions were a
complete earnest of his later brilliant renown. His
parents besought me repeatedly to give him instruction on
the piano; and, although his earlier tutor, Berger, was
not offended at this, I hesitated to try to put in leading-
strings a genius so independent, which could easily, perhaps, have been brought from the path which God had
marked out for it; yet at last I yielded to their repeated
requests, and gave him lessons. At that time he played
almost everything that I could play, and took every hint
with the quickness of lightning. My 'E-major Concerto'
he played almost at sight, and my 'Sonate Mélancolique'
he played particularly well, and with delight."

Further hints give us an interesting insight into the
Mendelssohn family, at that time coming to the height
of its renown.

On the 14th of November, in the year just mentioned,
Moscheles was present at the birthday festival of Felix'
sister Fanny. A symphony of Mendelssohn was played;
he himself gave Mozart's "C-minor Concerto," and, with
his sister, a double concerto in E-major, written by himself. Zelter, and many members of the royal Kapelle,
were present.

On the 28th of the same month another musical performance took place in the Mendelssohn mansion; a
symphony in D-major was given by Mendelssohn. He
played his piano quartet in C-minor (Opus 1.), and his
sister Fanny a concerto by Sebastian Bach.

On the 15th of December, a festival was held in commemoration of Mozart's death. His requiem was given,
Mendelssohn accompanying it on the piano.

On the 12th of December there was a Sunday morning concert, in which Felix gave his F-minor quartet,
and Moscheles played with him, for the first time, his
piece—afterwards to become so celebrated—"Hommage
to Handel." An album piece, composed by Moscheles
for Mendelssohn — "Allegro de bravura" — he played at
sight. Soon after this Moscheles went to England.          .

On the 15th of November, 1826, he celebrated the
birthday of Fanny with Mendelssohn, in Berlin.

The 19th of November of this year must have been a
very memorable epoch in the history of Mendelssohn's
musical cultivation. He played for the first time, on
that event, his newest composition, the "Overture to the
Midsummer Night's Dream," the work which first bore
the full mark of his genius, and which has lifted his
name to universal renown. He gave this in a four-hand
arrangement for the piano, his sister playing with him.

On the 23d of November, Moscheles produced the
first group of his *études*. A symphony and overture
was given by Mendelssohn, the leading theme being
taken by the trumpet. He also played a *capriccio* (probably Opus 5), which he gave in a spirited manner, but,
as it were, in a humor half of self-mockery.

We now turn back from this digression to a regular
delineation of Mendelssohn's life. His visit to Goethe,
already touched upon, was an epoch in his career. He
laid in it the foundation for that relation to the great poet
which lasted until Goethe's death, and showed himself
in the fullest sympathy with that noble spirit, who stood
forth as the representative of not alone Hellenic and

genuine German culture, but also of all that is fine, classic, and true ; and opposed to all that is small, imperfect, and weak.

The visit took place in the first days of November, 1820. In addition to two letters of Mendelssohn himself, in which we have an interesting account of the event, Rellstab, the great musical critic of his time, has given us the following accurate and lively picture of this visit : —

" The piano was opened, the lights placed upon the desk, and Felix was to play. He asked Zelter, to whom he showed himself devoted with the greatest love and confidence, 'What shall I play?' 'Well, whatever you can that is not too difficult.' It was at last arranged that he should improvise freely, and he asked Zelter for a theme. The old man seated himself at the piano, and with his stiff hands (he had several lamed fingers), gave a very simple air in G-major. There were perhaps sixteen bars. Felix played it entirely through, and then while practising the triplet figure with both hands, made himself securely master of the theme, so that he could not easily be moved from it; then he broke immediately into the wildest allegro; from the gentle melody there sprang a tempestuous and yet recognizable leading figure, now appearing in the bass, and now in the upper notes, growing powerful, exhibited with beautiful contrasts, and yet always rushing forward. Every one fell into astonishment. The little hand struggling with the great masses of sound, proved itself master of them all, even the most difficult combinations. The runs rolled, and purled, and flew with the swiftness of light, a stream of harmonies rushed forth, surprising contrapunto passages

developed themselves, and meanwhile the melody remained distinct, and could be seen and traced in all the
stormy sea of tone.

"The young player had the tact not to prolong this too
far, and so the surprise remained even greater then if
he had been longer.  Silence reigned all around as he
took his hands from the piano in order to let them now
quietly rest.

"Zelter was the first to break the silence, 'Well, I
think you have been dreaming of kobolds and dragons.
That time, indeed, you did drive everything before
you.'

"Goethe was filled with delight; he caressed the little
artist, took his head between his hands and stroked it
in a friendly manner, and said lovingly, 'Well, we
have not done with you; you must let us hear you play
something else before we decide entirely upon you.'
'Well, what shall I play?' asked Felix.

"Goethe was a great lover of Bach's fugues.  It was,
therefore, suggested that he should play one of these.
The boy gave it without any preparation and with
complete security.  Goethe's joy and delight increased
with every new development.  After this he requested
him to play a minuet.  'Shall I play the very finest
there is in the world?' he asked with sparkling eyes.
'Well, which would that be?'  Felix played the
minuet from Don Juan.  Goethe remained standing at
the piano always looking on, delight flashing in his
eyes.  After the minuet was played, he demanded the
overture to the opera.  This the little player roundly
refused to attempt, remarking that it could not be played
as it stands, and he dared not change it.  He asked to
be allowed to play the overture to Figaro.  He began

with a surprising lightness of touch, security, roundness and clearness in the runs, with it all he brought out the orchestral effects so skillfully, and made so many fine points clear in his instrumentation that the effect was wonderful. Goethe became more and more lively, more and more friendly, he even began to joke with the spirited and excited boy. 'Up till now,' he said, 'you have only played a little to us that you know, now we will see if you can play something which you do not know. Now I will put you to the test.' He went out, and after a few minutes came back with several pages of manuscript notes in his hand. 'There is something from my own collection, now we will try you. Do you suppose you can play this?'

" Goethe laid the sheet, covered with clear and small notes, upon the desk. It was Mozart's writing. Felix' countenance glowed visibly at the sight of the name. With perfect security he played the manuscript at sight, although not one to be easily read. The skill was as great as if he had known it for years, so secure, so clear, so well considered.

"'Well, that is nothing; others can do that. Now I will give you something that will gauge you. Take care of yourself now!'

"In this jesting tone he brought another leaf and laid it on the desk. That one indeed had a remarkable look. You could scarcely tell whether they were notes, or whether it was a page lined and spattered with ink in countless places. Felix burst into a laugh of wonder. 'Is that writing? Is a man able to read that?' he called out. Then suddenly he grew earnest, while Goethe uttered the question, 'Now guess, if you can, who wrote it?' and Zelter, advancing to the instrument and looking over the shoulders of the lad, said : ' That is Beethoven's, one could see that a mile away.  He always writes as if he used a broomstick for a pen, and then brushed down the fresh notes with his sleeve.'

"At the name of Beethoven, Felix became visibly earnest, yes, more than earnest ; a holy awe was disclosed in his features.  He looked upon the manuscript without turning away his eyes, and then a visible gleam of surprise spread over his features.  This all lasted only a few seconds, however, for Goethe allowed no time for preparation, he would have his proof sharply tested : ' Did not I say to you,' he cried, ' that this would catch you ?  Now try and show what you can do.'  On this, Felix began to play.  It was a simple song, but the notes had been so rubbed out and scratched out that it required a wonderful skill to read them at a glance.  On the first playing, Felix often had to correct himself, laughingly striking a false note, and then instantly correcting himself with a 'not so.'  Afterwards, he cried : ' Now I will play it to you as it should be,' and the second time he did not fail in a note. ' That is Beethoven,' he cried, as he fell into the true melodic movement which revealed to him the characteristic of the great master.  ' That is Beethoven alone ; I should have known it.'

"With this last trial, Goethe surrendered.  Indeed, it did not require so much as this to put the brilliant gifts of the boy in the brightest light."

That this visit of the young Mendelssohn in Goethe's house exerted a delightful influence upon him, need not be said.  Under date of February, 1822, Goethe wrote, beginning in his cool and measured way, to Zelter: " Say also a good word to Felix and his

parents. Since your departure my piano is silent; a
single attempt to waken it again would almost miscarry."
But the bond which was knit between them was soon
to become strong. Zelter gave continual intimations
to Goethe of the wonderful talents and fruitful activity
of the boy; and Goethe's interest mounted ever higher
and higher.

How great his delight had been in Goethe's presence,
and how profound his emotion in consequence of being
there, appears from the two letters written to the
family in Berlin, which are not to be passed over
without some quotation.

In the first, written in Weimar, November 6th, 1820,
he says: " Now, listen, all of you, all; to-day is Tuesday.
On Sunday came the sun of Weimar. In the morning
we went to church, where the Hundredth Psalm, by
Handel, was given in a half-and-half manner only.
Afterwards I wrote to you a little letter of the fourth,
and then went to the hotel, where I drew the house of
Lucas Cranach. The hotel is The Elephant. After
two hours, came Professor Zelter, saying, ' Goethe is
there; the old gentleman is there.' At once we went
down the staircase, and to Goethe's house. He was in
the garden, and came directly round the corner. That
is not wonderful, dear father; it would have been just
the same with you. He has a very friendly, nice
manner, yet I do not find him at all like his portraits.
He showed me then his interesting collection of fossils
which his son has arranged, and kept saying to himself,
' H'm, h'm, I am very much pleased.' Afterwards we
walked for an hour in the garden with Professor Zelter;
then dinner. You would never take him to be a man
seventy-three years old; you would not consider him

more than fifty. After dinner, Miss Ulrika, the sister
of Goethe's wife, begged a kiss of him; and I did, also.
Every morning I receive from the author of Faust and
of Werther, a kiss; every afternoon, from Goethe, as
father and friend, two kisses. Only think of it! In
the afternoon I played for Goethe more than two hours,
partly fugues by Bach, partly my own improvisations.
In the evening, we all ate supper together, Goethe
among us; he generally never takes an evening meal.
Now, my dear, coughing Fanny, yesterday morning I
brought your songs to Madame Goethe, who has a pretty
voice; she will sing them to the old gentleman. I told
him that you had made them, and asked if he would
like to hear them. He answered, ' Yes, yes; indeed I
would. They will especially please madame.' A good
omen! To-day or to-morrow he shall hear them."

In the second letter, dated Weimar, November 10th,
Felix writes, among other things, " Every afternoon
Goethe opens the piano, with the words, ' I have not
heard you to-day at all; now make a little noise;' and
then he is accustomed to take his place near me, and
when I am there I generally improvise at the end; I ask
for a kiss for myself, or I take one without permission.
You have no conception of his goodness and friendliness,
and just as little of the wealth which this polar
star of poets possesses in minerals, busts, copper-plates,
statuettes, great drawings and the like. His figure does
not seem to me imposing, he is not much taller than
father; yet his bearing, his speech, his name, they are
imposing. His voice has a wonderful ring, and he can
shout like a hundred warriors. His hair is not yet
white, his walk is firm, his address gentle.

" On Tuesday, Professor Zelter wanted us to go to

Jena, and from there to Leipsic.  On Sunday afternoon,
Adela Schopenhauer (the daughter) was with us; and,
contrary to his custom, Goethe spent the whole evening
with us.  The talk turned upon our journey, and Adela
resolved that we should all throw ourselves at the feet
of Professor Zelter, and beg for a few days' grace.  He
was hurried into the chamber; and now Goethe broke
out, with his voice of thunder, scolded the Professor for
wanting to take us to the old ' nest,' ordered him to
keep still, and, without permitting a word in reply, he
bade us go to Jena and come back again.  We assailed
Zelter so from all sides, that he had to give in to
Goethe's will; and now Goethe was thanked on all
sides; they kissed him on hands and mouth, and whoever could not come near him, caressed him and kissed
his shoulders, and, had he not been at his own home, I
do believe that we should have accompanied him to
his house, as the Roman people accompanied Cicero
after his first oration against Cataline.  As for the rest,
Fraulein Ulrika threw herself upon his neck; and, as
he is very polite to her (she is exceedingly handsome),
all this worked favorably to the result.

" On Monday, at 11, there is to be a concert at Frau
Von Henkel's.  Now, if Goethe says to me, ' My little
fellow, we have company at 11, and you must play
something to us,' do you think that I can say no?"

Felix' mother sent this letter of her son to her gifted
sister-in-law, Henrietta, in Paris.  She expressed her
delight and astonishment in the following words: " How
can I thank you enough, dearest Leah, for the pleasure
which you have given me in this beautiful letter?  You
are indeed a happy mother.  I have no words to
express what I feel in reference to this gifted, sensitive,

gentle, natural, fiery-hearted, magnificent boy. If I should try, I should only utter nonsense. He is an artist, in the fullest sense of the word. Such high faculties, in connection with the most gentle and noble spirit! If God preserves his life, his letters, after long, long years, will make an epoch. Preserve them as a sacred trust; they are consecrated by all that is most child-like and pure. How delightful it must have been to see the boy so open and approachable with the noble old Goethe! What we in our youth so often dreamed of,— how delightful it must be to live in Goethe's neighborhood,— Felix has experienced to the full. The qualities of his good father have ripened to an extraordinary talent in the son."

How nobly have these prophecies of Henrietta been since fulfilled!

On the 6th of July, 1822, Abraham Mendelssohn, accompanied by his wife, his four children, their tutor Heyse, Dr. Neuburg, some servants, and two charming spirited girls from Frankfort, besides Marian and Julie Saaling, entered upon a journey of pleasure to Switzerland. This journey, which exercised a very favorable influence upon the father's outward circumstances, must also be regarded as having no less an influence upon Felix' physical and spiritual development. As they made the journey in several carriages, a little adventure occurred at the outset which is worthy of mention. They wanted to make a side excursion to the Hartz, and so went from Berlin by way of Potsdam and Brandenburgh to Magdeburg. In Potsdam, on the departure of the carriage, Felix was forgotten, and his absence was only noticed in Grosskreuz, the first station beyond Potsdam. Heyse drove directly back to fetch him ; but the courageous Felix had already started, running at the outset in order to overtake the carriages, and, as he did not succeed, marching on in company with a strong peasant girl, both of them breaking stout sticks to help them on the way.   He had the intention of going on thus as far as Brandenburgh, but at a short distance from Grosskreuz Heyse found him.

From the Hartz the journey proceeded by way of Göttingen to Cassel, where they enjoyed a lively season of intercourse with Louis Spohr; then on to Frankfort, where Aloys Schmitt arranged a little company for a musical performance, about which Fanny speaks very disdainfully in a letter : " You cannot believe how these dear people have cracked and confounded my ears, for they would accompany poor Felix in his quartet.   My only pleasure on the occasion was to study the countenances.   Then I had to play something myself ; and now don't let me talk about it, bid me keep still, the accompaniment was dreadful.   I, trembling in every nerve, was so upset, that out of sheer anger I would like to have cudgelled them all.   I pass this all over, else I get myself in too great a heat."

Among the pupils of Aloys Schmitt then present was Ferdinand Hiller, a pretty boy of ten years, with free and open countenance, afterwards well known as one of Felix Mendelssohn's most intimate friends. From Frankfort the whole merry caravan proceeded by way of Darmstadt and Stuttgart to Schaffhausen, and so on to Mt. Gothard.   The journey from Altorf to the foot of the Gothard and back is described by Fanny in one of her graphic letters.   From there they proceeded by way of Interlaken to the Wengern-Alp, and so on to Lake Geneva.   From there an excursion to Chamouni,

and then the return journey with a prolonged stay in
Frankfort and Weimar.  In Frankfort they made the
acquaintance of Schelble, the leader of the Cecilia Society, an acquaintance which was later of special value to
Felix.  They made a stay in Weimar, and went to
thank Goethe for his exceeding kindness to Felix on the
occasion of the visit with Zelter.  With reference to this
visit, Henzel tells us, in "The Mendelssohn Family,"
"Goethe was never tired of listening to Felix when he
sat at the piano, and he talked incessantly with the
father almost exclusively about Felix.  One day he expressed himself on the occasion of his being irritated at
some little matter, 'I am Saul, and you are my David.
When I am sad and downcast, then come to me and
cheer me with your harp.'  One evening he asked Felix
to play a fugue by Bach which the young wife of Goethe
pointed out.  Felix did not know it by heart, but he
knew the theme, and he drew it out in a long fugue passage, improvised, of course.  Goethe was delighted,
went to the mother, pressed her hands with great
warmth, and exclaimed, 'He is a heavenly, precious
child.  Send him to me very soon again, that I may re-
fresh myself by him.'"

We must speak of this Swiss journey and its delightful close in Weimar, following our leader Hensel, a
little more in detail, because it was of such importance
in determining the whole development, spiritual and
physical, of Mendelssohn.  The impressions of the
grand Alpine world imprinted themselves deeply on the
soul of the thirteen-year-old boy, so that Switzerland
ever remained his favorite land; and years after, even
after he had seen Italy, seven years later, he gave his
decided preference to the Alpine region.  Interesting, too,

is what Fanny writes about the effect of this journey on the physical development of her brother : "We could see the unmistakable marks of this journey after our return.   He had grown taller and stronger.   There was more expression on his face ; his hair, which now had been deprived of the long fair locks, contributed no little to change his appearance.   The age of childhood had gone ; his form had taken on something manlier, which was as becoming to him even as his childlike beauty. He was different, and yet just as fair as before."

In the year 1822 we must relate further, that in spite of this great journey, Felix composed no less than twelve different works.   First, the Sixty-sixth Psalm, for three women's voices.

Second.   Concerto for pianoforte in A-minor.

Third.   Two songs for men's voices.

Fourth.   Three songs.

Fifth.   Three fugues for the piano.

Sixth.   Quartet for piano, violin, violoncello, and bass viol in C-minor, composed in Geneva.   (His first printed work).

Seventh.   Two symphonies for two violins, violoncello, and bass viol.

Eighth.   An act of the opera, "The Two Nephews."

Ninth.   Jube Domine in C-major.   Written for the Cecilia Society in Frankfort.

Tenth.   Violin concerto for Edward Rietz.

Eleventh.   Magnificat with instruments.

Twelfth.   Gloria with instruments.

Assuredly an imposing productiveness for a boy of thirteen years.

In the same year Felix appeared publicly for the first time in Berlin, in a concert of Pauline Milder.   In the

same time also falls the establishing of the Sunday Musical Concerts, already mentioned, which were visited by
such numbers of foreign musicians. Among these, in the
year 1823, was Frederick Kalkbrenner, a celebrated piano
player and composer from Paris, of whom Fanny wrote :
" He has heard much of Felix' work. He has praised
with taste, and has blamed with freedom, and yet with
great and tender delicacy ; we often hear him, and we seek
to learn of him. He unites the most varied qualities in
his playing ; precision, clearness, expression, the greatest thoroughness, and an almost inexhaustible power and
endurance. He is a very clever musician, and possesses
an astonishing grasp and insight. Aside from his talents
as a musician, he has a fine, amiable, and highly-culti-
vated mind, and no one can praise and blame more
agreeably than he."

In August of the same year, Abraham Mendelssohn, in
connection with his two sons, Felix and Paul, made a
journey to Silesia. In Breslau they heard the celebrated
organist Berner, of whose playing Felix gives a lively
picture in a letter. In Reinerz he himself played in a
concert given for the poor. He was to give a concerto
by Mozart, but as this could not be brought out, in consequence of deficient accompaniment, Felix improvised,
amid great applause, upon themes by Mozart and Weber.

We must now speak of a circumstance which exercised
the greatest influence upon the musical and intellectual
and spiritual faculties of both Felix and Fanny Mendelssohn. It was the purchase, in the year 1825, of the fine
mansion with garden annexed, Leipsic Street, No. 3, a
house which till then had been in the possession of the
Reck family, had fallen a good deal out of repair, and was
much neglected ; but it contained large, high rooms, ad-

mirably adapted to theatrical and musical entertainments. A garden of seven acres adjoined the house, filled with magnificent old trees, of which some are standing yet ; the building having, since its purchase by the Government, become the place of meeting for the upper Prussian Parliament.   The court of the house was occupied by a garden pavilion, one story high, holding several hundred people ; and, separated as it was from the garden by moveable glass partitions, it afforded, therefore, a delightful and attractive outlook.

In these rooms there was developed gradually a most stirring musical life, separated from the tumult of the street, and favored by immediate contact with nature. Here the Sunday concerts took place, at which gradually assembled all the culture of Berlin ; men of eminence in all departments, musicians, painters, sculptors, poets, actors, scholars, found their entrance to this house and its circle of friends.   I may mention of musicians the following : Weber, Spohr, Zelter, Paganini, Henselt, Gounod, Hiller, Ernst, Liszt, Schumann.   Of painters, Cornelius, Ingres, Horace Vernet, Magnus (who painted the best portrait of Mendelssohn, now in the possession of his daughter, the wife of Professor Wach, in Leipsic), Augustus Kopisch, Verhoeckhoven, Kaulbach, and Von Schwind.   Of singers, Milder, Novello, Lablache, Grisi, Pasta, Unger, Sabatier, Schröder - Devrient.   Of actors, Rachel, Seydelmann.   Of sculptors, Thorwaldsen, Rauch, Kiss ; and of architects, Schinkel.   Of poets and authors, La Motte Fouqué, Brentano, Bettini von Arnim, Heinrich Heine, Ludwig Robert, H. Steffens, Paul Heyse.   Of men of science, both the Humboldts (who as youths had listened to the addresses of Moses Mendelssohn), Hegel, Gans, Bunsen, Jacob Grimm, Lepsius,

Bockh.  Of mathematicians, Jacoby, Dirichlet, Ranke, and Ehrenberg.

These and many other celebrities beside, William Hensel, the celebrated husband of Fanny, whose reputation as a portrait painter stood very high, sketched in an album, which is most interesting in its contents, gathered, as the faces often were, without the consciousness of their possessors, during musical entertainments or amid animated conversation.  A thorough, fresh, rich, and poetic life unfolded itself in this family circle, and in the friends closely related to it.  Among these, chief of all Karl Klingemann is to be mentioned, one of the most intimate friends of Felix Mendelssohn, known as the author of several admirable songs, of which Mendelssohn set many to music ; as, for example, the noble spring song, " Es brechen in schallendem Reigen," and the song, " Ringsum erschallt in Wald und Flur ; " the slumber song, " Schlummre und traüme von kommender Zeit," and many others.  He was also the composer of the vaudeville, " Die Heimkehr aus der Fremde," which Mendelssohn composed for the silver wedding of his parents.  Afterwards he was transferred to London as Secretary to the Hanoverian Embassy, where he became Mendelssohn's true Pylades, and on his arrival there, in 1829, did for him the most immediate duties, and took care of him after he had been overturned in a gig, and had injured himself so seriously in the knee that he was compelled to remain two months longer in England.  In all this he showed him the most self-sacrificing love and care, judging from his correspondence with Fanny, with whom he stood in relations of very intimate friendship.  Among other friends are also to be named Louis Heydemann the jurist, and his brother ; William Horn, the son of the celebrated physician, and himself a physician; Edward Rietz the violinist, and the gentle Marx, at that time editor of the "Musical Journal" of Berlin, a glowing admirer of Beethoven, and afterwards his biographer. This circle was joined by Hensel after his return from Italy. He got his lodgment in it by means of a spirited drawing of the "Wheel," for this was the name given to the initiated. Felix represents the hub, clothed in Scottish costume, making music to which the dolphins are listening; the spokes are Fanny and Rebecca, sisters of Felix, embracing each other, and holding a leaf with notes in their hands, and ending below in the form of otters. Besides them are a great number of persons connected with their circle, and displayed in all possible forms of dress and touches of character. Outside there stands a stranger, fastened to a chain whose end Fanny holds, just on the point of throwing himself at the wheel.

This charming symbol could not fail of its end; the wheel opened and took Hensel in.

Besides these persons, the home circle embraced some very lovely girls with whom Fanny and Rebecca were especially intimate, nieces and granddaughters of the old lady who occupied the garden-house connected with the mansion. The soul of this whole circle was Fanny herself, to whom we owe the first place in the delineation of Felix' youth, and to whom, therefore, I dedicate a special page.

Fanny, the oldest child of Abraham, saw the light, as already remarked, November 15, 1805, in Hamburgh. She was, therefore, about three and a half years older than her brother; and being just as handsome, full of talent, and spirit, and amiability as he, she could not fail to exert the strongest influence upon him. "Down to the present time," she wrote, in 1822, about Felix, " I possess his entire confidence.  I have seen his talents develop step by step, and I myself have contributed something to their development; he has no musical confidant before me, he never commits a thought to paper without laying the first copy of it before me.  For example, I knew his operas by heart before a  note was written down."  Besides being his counsellor and greatest admirer, she  possessed  a wonderfully thorough  musical education ; she  was quite equal  to her  brother in the command of the piano ; she  possessed a most extraordinary  musical memory,  and even  a  unique talent for composition.  Her father, although  in his scheme of life he placed the wife and mother before the artist, yet, recognizing the great  talents of his daughter, he had her trained in thorough-bass and musical composition.  She proved herself the possessor of these talents, partly by the music which she  herself played at the  Sunday morning concerts, and  partly  by her management of the musical forces, choral and instrumental, which she assembled, and by means of which she  gave great and important works.  For example, she writes, herself : " I have, in the previous month (June, 1824), given a beautiful fête, Iphigenia in Tauris, rendered by Decker, Bæder, and Mantius ; it was, indeed, so perfectly rendered that you cannot conceive of anything finer."

A year before, she had also given Gluck's " Orpheus and Eurydice," but before all these, she devoted herself to Bach, and so laid the foundation for the possibility of that splendid and never-to-be-forgotten representation of the great " St. Matthew Passion," on the 11th of March, 1829.

When Fanny was seventeen years old, she made the

acquaintance of William Hensel, a noble man of fine feelings, then twenty-eight years old, and a genuinely artistic nature; the son of a poor country parson in the neighborhood of Berlin, he had first intended to study mining engineering, but his whole nature drove him to art; at first, indeed, to poetry, but afterwards exclusively to painting. His father died while he was a youth, and so the care of his mother and sisters fell upon him; he discharged this duty with the greatest self-sacrifice, worked day and night, even drawing sketches by the light of a tallow candle, with which some calendars and diaries might be embellished. With no less eagerness, he offered his services to his country, and served in the war of 1813; he was a brave soldier, was wounded several times, and was carried to Paris. At the conclusion of peace, he remained some time there, in order to prosecute his study of art amid its museums.

In Berlin, he became known as the author of the illustrations of "Lalla Rookh," which were undertaken at the command of the Grand Duchess of Russia, when Nicholas, the Grand Duke, was visiting Berlin. These sketches gave such pleasure that they were painted by order of the King. Being put on exhibition in his study, they were seen by Fanny, who had gone thither with her parents to enjoy the view of them; he became a suitor for her love, and gained it, but it was to be a long time before he reached the fulfillment of his hopes. He received an _honorarium_ from the Prussian Government for these pictures, and an order for a copy of Raphæl's "Transfiguration." This copy is now to be seen in the gallery at Sans Souci.

Hensel went upon this to Italy for five long years.

Fanny's mother did not permit an interchange of letters, as, according to her view, a man ought not to think of marrying before his circumstances should permit him to do so. She herself undertook the task of correspondence, certainly not an edifying one to the young man; but after his return, in 1829, there was a family engagement, and the wedding followed, October 3. The young pair received the garden-house as their dwelling, and there passed most happy days.

As the fruit of this union, in the summer of 1830, there was born a child, very weak, and two months before the time, whose life was maintained in infancy only with the greatest care. He received, at baptism, the name of the great Sebastian Bach, whom Fanny so devotedly loved. (Even as a child of thirteen years, she could play by heart four preludes by Bach, to the amazement of her father.) This son is the compiler, now living, of the well-known book, " The Mendelssohn Family," that invaluable work, for which all the friends of Mendelssohn cannot thank him enough; for he has contributed in it, not merely the most precious materials for a thorough biography of Mendelssohn, but he has afforded an insight into the life of all the members of the family, and given us the enjoyment of the best society which the age can afford, in the richest and noblest form.

Before we return to the youthful history of Felix Mendelssohn, we must speak a little further of some events which belong to the history of the life passed in the house No. 3 Leipsic Street.

The summer months of the year 1825 were a kind of unbroken festival, full of poetry, music, ingenious plays, spirited musical travesties, and all kinds of

delineations. In the garden pavilion lay always ready
a sheet of paper with pen and ink, so that they could
dash down any of the drolleries which came through
their heads; and this garden journal was continued
in the winter, under the name of " The Tea and Snow
Journal," and contains all sorts of charming things,
serious and jocose. Even older persons, such as father
Abraham, Zelter, and Humboldt, did not scorn to make
their contributions, or, at any rate, to enjoy the tasteful
and delightful life of the house.

The writers who exercised the greatest influence upon
the spirit and fancy of the inner circle, were, chief of
all, Jean Paul and Shakespeare. One might indeed
wonder how two characters so opposed in nature could
work harmoniously upon the genius of these two young
people; but what was felt in Jean Paul was his humor
and his depth of feeling, which, at that period of life,
exercised a not unsound influence. Felix continued to
have this delight in Jean Paul even in his later years, as
we find in a letter written February 4th, 1843, in which
he sends to a Leipsic friend the " Siebenkas," and
recommends it with the words: " I believe the fairest
hours of one's life are those in which one can enjoy
such a splendid work as that." But the greatest poet of
all time, Shakespeare, whose acquaintance the young
people first made through the incomparable translation
of Schlegel and Tieck, made an impression, upon a
spirit ready to feel his power, that need hardly be told.
It was not alone the tragedies, even the comedies and
the fantasticalities of the great Englishman exercised
their influence upon him, and among these, chief of
all, the " Midsummer Night's Dream."

We must bear in mind that these Mendelssohn

children were looking out every night, through the old lofty trees of the great garden, upon the moon which transfigured them, in order to understand the origin of the magnificent overture.

In the further course of the youthful history of Felix, we must now touch upon the journey which his father undertook, in March, 1825, to Paris, in order to bring back to Germany the aunt Henrietta. He made use of the occasion to introduce his son to one of the greatest musical authorities living, Cherubini, the director of the Paris Conservatory, and to get his impressions whether Felix possessed a sufficiently decisive calling for music to make it worth while to develop his capacities further. Felix played to him and Balliot his B-minor quartet, and laid before him the "Kyrie" for five voices and orchestra. Cherubini's answer could not be otherwise than decidedly favorable. There was then in Paris a great number of distinguished musicians, Hummel, Moscheles, Kalkbrenner, Pixis, Rode, Balliot, Kreutzer, Rossini, Paër, Meyerbeer, Plantade, Lafont, and others; but there was so much that was little and spiteful and envious in these men, there was such an eagerness for effect and such superficiality, that Felix did not care to become intimate with them; besides, they had no acquaintance with the great German masters. He expressed himself in several very interesting letters about these Paris musical matters, uttering his opinions with sharpness and a good deal of violence, but not without arousing the opposition of his mother and his sister.

On his return, they visited Goethe again, and the latter writes, among other things, under date of May 21, 1825, to Zelter: "Felix produced his latest quartet to the astonishment of everyone ; the personal dedication of this elegant work has pleased me greatly."

In June, he sent to the lad what Zelter calls "a beautiful love letter."   It ran as follows : —

"You have, my dear Felix, given me rare pleasure, in the precious package which you have sent me" [the *de luxe* copy of the B-minor quartet, with the dedication to Goethe]. "Although previously unannounced, it yet surprised me. The engraving of the notes and the title page, even the magnificent binding, compete with one another to make the gift a perfect one. I have, therefore, enjoyed not only the well-clothed body, but also the beautiful, strong, rich soul ; and you may imagine the delight and wonder with which I regard it. Accept, therefore, my heartiest thanks, and let me hope to have the pleasure soon of admiring your astonishing gifts here in person. Remember me to your excellent parents, to your gifted sister, and to the admirable teacher. May the memory of me remain bright in such a circle.

"Yours faithfully,
"J. W. GOETHE."

WEIMAR, *June* 18, 1825.

In the same year is found also the composition of one of the most admirable of the works of Mendelssohn, one which even now maintains its full value for all lovers of music, the "Octett" (Opus 20), prepared as a birthday present for Edward Rietz. It is composed for two first and two second violins, two violas and two cellos. A wonderful composition, not only by the contrapuntal arrangement of the voices and the harmony, but also by the tender grace and brightness which breathe their charm through the whole work. In its four movements "there is no trace, even in the andante," as Reissman well says, "of the dreamy, soft sentimentality such as is seen in many of Mozart's works ;" but, on the other hand, there is found especially in the scherzo a trace of that airy, elfin world, which we may view as the precursor of the " Midsummer Night's Dream " overture.

Mendelssohn endeavored to compose a piece suiting the passage from Faust : —

> " The flight of the winds, the veil of the mist,
>   Are lighted from above :
>   A breeze in the leaves, a wind in the reeds,
>   And all is vanished."

and it is a real translation of the words into music. Fanny remarks, in speaking of the "Octett," "I see everything in the poem which was before his mind. The whole. piece is played staccato and pianissimo, the tremolo passages standing alone. The light flashing trills, all is new, strange, and yet so attractive and so familiar, one feels oneself so near to the spirit world, and so lifted up to the clouds, that one almost is tempted to seize a broomstick in one's hand and follow the merry troop ; at the end the first violin fades away into the lightest sound, and ' all is vanished.' "

Before we now come to the consideration of the " Midsummer Night's Dream " overture, the composition in which Mendelssohn's individuality is most fully developed, we must speak briefly of the youthful work whose appearance took place in 1824 ; namely, his fourth opera, the first and the only one, with the exception of the fragment of the " Lorelei," which was publicly represented, "Camacho's Wedding." Mendelssohn's friend, Edward Devrient, who, since the year 1822, had lived in very close relations with him, had undertaken to compose an opera for him, and to that end chose as his text the episode of Olind and Sophronia, in Tasso's " Jerusalem Delivered." But Felix found this too serious and earnest to undertake it. He himself had already chosen a theme for a comic opera from Cervantes' " Don

Quixote," to which his friend Klingemann had furnished the text. If one reads it in the original, one sees that there are very attractive materials, suggestions for solos, full of feeling; lively choruses, and especially attractive and brilliant ballets. The substance of the story is briefly this: The fair Quiteria, daughter of the rich Carrasco, is loved from her youth by a shepherd endowed with all the splendors of body and mind; but, as he is very poor, Carrasco forbids him the house, and promises his daughter to the rich Camacho. The wedding is to take place with all possible luxuriousness, and with beautiful allegorical representations, when Don Quixote with his knight appears in the village, and is informed by two students of the on-go of things. He at once resolves to help the unhappy lovers to their rights. Basilio, clothed in a long black coat, with flame colored stockings, and a cypress wreath in his hand, in one half of which is concealed a dagger, appears just at the moment when the wedding festivities are in full move, and, after a touching address to Quiteria, plunges the dagger in his side so deeply that half of it appears beyond his back, and covered with blood. Don Quixote springs to the rescue, takes Basilio in his arms, and finds that there is life still in him. Basilio begs with weak and half-extinguished voice that Quiteria would give her hand as wife to him while dying, otherwise he cannot give her absolution. Don Quixote finds this a very natural request, and reflects that Quiteria can, as widow, yet be joined with Camacho. Quiteria signifies her approval, the priest who is present gives Basilio his blessing; but scarcely has that taken place when Basilio springs up, lively and sound. He has only concealed the dagger under his coat, and plunged it into a tube filled with blood; but the contract already blessed by the hand of the priest cannot be annulled. At the outset, there is a violent controversy, then an assault upon Basilio; but the noble knight of La Mancha brings the thing to a quiet conclusion. Camacho expresses himself satisfied, as he sees that Quiteria does not love him, and is noble enough to permit the wedding festivities to run their quiet course, which, however, the lovers will not permit.

One sees, at a glance, that the material is attractive and piquant enough to afford the young musician a fine opportunity for the composition of a comic opera. Felix worked at it from July 24 to August 25. In the following year it was placed in the hands of the manager of the Royal Theatre, at the express wish of Mendelssohn's mother. Count Bruhl was good natured in its acceptance; but Spontini, who, as chief musical director, had the most decisive voice, treated the work with depreciating coldness. He said to Mendelssohn, pointing at the tower of the French church directly opposite: "*Mon ami, il vous faut des études grandes, grandes comme cette coupole.*" At last, in the beginning of 1827, the preparations for the representation began, in consequence of Count Bruhl's insistance. Numerous difficulties were encountered, even during the last week's rehearsals. The singer who was to take the part of Don Quixote was taken ill of jaundice; the choir director protested against the time as premature, saying that the choruses were not thoroughly learned; yet the opera was performed on the 29th of April, of the same year, yet not in the opera house, Mendelssohn preferring the more modest theatre as more appropriate to the nature of the work. The house was

very full, the applause of personal friends cordial; and
yet, whether owing to the want of dramatic life, or
whether with all its wealth of melodies Mendelssohn
had not breathed into it the true spirit of the comic;
enough to say, the result was not a decisively successful
one.   Mendelssohn, although called to the stage, did not
appear, and was obliged to be excused.   He was very
much cast down, and went home late, and disturbed.
A repetition of the piece was afterwards demanded, in
spite of many hindrances, but it did not take place.
Mendelssohn would hear nothing about it, and said that
the fault of the failure was not his, but that of the
manager.   The work was severely reviewed in Saphir's
" Schnell-Post," by a student who had been received
very kindly in the Mendelssohn family, a fact which
wounded Mendelssohn greatly;  he felt then what he
often said to Devrient later, that " the greatest praise in
the foremost journal does not delight one so much as the
most worthless criticism, in a low, dirty sheet, troubles
and saddens one."

Yet such an occurrence as this, in the life of a mere
boy, could not suppress Mendelssohn's activity or spirits
for any great length of time.   He had already composed
his overture to the " Midsummer Night's Dream,"
that work in which, casting off the dust of the schools,
he has displayed so fully and strongly his ingenuity,
his fine feeling, his light and graceful humor, his own
individuality, that the work has become a standard.   We
have already stated that the first conception of the work
occurred to him in the summer of 1826.   Mendelssohn
told Ferdinand Hiller, when playing the overture to him
in Frankfort in the year 1827, with what pleasure he had
busied himself over this work for a long time;  how that,

in the hours which were free during his attendance at the university at Berlin, he used to practise at the work on the piano of a lady who lived near the university. "I have hardly done anything else," he says, "for a whole year;" and "really," Hiller adds, "he had not lost his time."

As has already been narrated, Mendelssohn played this work before Moscheles with his sister Fanny on the 19th of November, 1826, for the first time, in a four-handed arrangement for the piano. Soon afterwards it was given with full orchestra in the garden hall. In February, 1827, he produced it in the city of Stettin, among several of his compositions, and it was received with very great applause.

A work such as this, which has made the circuit of the world, and has wrought with a charmingly attractive power upon the minds of musicians everywhere, does not need to be analyzed in close detail. It is the most splendid illustration of a poem which, perhaps, without Mendelssohn's music, would have remained understood by but few who are now enabled to appreciate it. There are, I suppose, still extant, some idiots like a certain bejeweled nobleman who was present at its first representation in the new palace in Potsdam, and who said at dinner to Mendelssohn, with reference to his music, "What a pity that your fine art is wasted on such miserable stuff!" But such expressions as these are, of course, only exceptional; to most people the beauty of the music and the beauty of the poem are both equally and mutually illustrative.

> "Splendor of the glorious night,
> Thou my sense dost conquer quite:
> Wondrous world of fairy song,
> All thy old renown prolong!"

This celebrated quatrain of Ludwig Tieck might well

serve as a motto to Mendelssohn's music for the "Mid-summer Night's Dream."

A few hints may perhaps be given here for a better understanding of the work. The poem of Shakespeare does not emanate from his youthful period, as some have thought it necessary to assert in order to excuse its apparent juvenility, as they view it, but was written in his most mature period, in 1598, and was probably a token of homage which he offered to his friend the Earl of Southampton, on the occasion of his marriage to his beloved Mistress Vernon. The germ of the first sketch was, according to Tieck's remarks upon the play, probably an epithalamium for the newly-married couple, in the form of the so-called "Masque," in which Oberon and Titania and her fairies wish and prophesy good fortune to the bridal pair. The comic by-play, the scenes of the chorus, form what may be called the anti-masque, and around these two the later scenes of the play are grouped. Southampton was married contrary to the will of Queen Elizabeth. She appears to be the royal "vestal, over whose heart Cupid's arrow, recoiling, falls upon the tender flower, once milk-white, but now purple with love's wound, called by maidens, 'Love in Idleness;'" the "wonder-flower, whose juice, dropped upon the sleeping eyelids, makes every creature, be they man or woman, madly dote on whom they next may see." Puck must bring this flower at the command of Oberon, who at once charms his wife Titania with it, so that she must fall in love with Bottom with the ass's head. Puck receives, moreover, a commission to anoint the eyes of an Athenian therewith, in order to bring him back to his first love; but he, purposely or not, makes a mistake in the person, and so causes no end of confusion between the two pair of lovers, whose disenchantment can only be set right by a new enchantment. The double action corresponds to the real title of the play, "Midsummer Night's Dream;" that is, the "Dream of St. John's Night." This time was employed in England, as almost everywhere in Europe, in all kinds of innocent superstitions and nonsense, to win the love of husbands or wives, to procure prophecies of marriage, and the like. Certain herbs and flowers were said to have a special charm on this night, and be able to work with peculiar power. The heat, at that time of year, it was thought, wrought with such strange effect upon the fancy, that the most singular dreams and all sorts of foolish humors came to men; and hence we have the title of this romantic masterpiece, in which all of Shakespeare's imagination, all his humor, are brought into play; and every kind of folly and every kind of jovial delight are tossed to and fro with careless and delightful ease. There is a real and solid foundation to the play, given by the marriage of the Duke of Athens to Hippolyta, the Queen of the Amazons. A most charming contrast to this is formed by the rough wit of the honest journeymen of Athens, who present the play of " Pyramus and Thisbe," and so in this varied treatment there are four separate themes in the music of the "Midsummer Night's Dream," and all of these four are wrought together in the most graceful and happy way in the overture: the fairy world, in a charming and airy movement; court life, with its refinement and polish, in which we can almost distinguish the duke and his bride; the joys of restored love; the wholesome and rough humor of the honest workmen, who give the last touch to the whole by the delicious travesty over which they preside. The very opening of the piece, the first five measures,

contains the most original and delightful commencement
of which it is possible to conceive.   The first and second
flute are heard in the first measure with sustained tone
in E-major.   Then, in the second, one hears the two
clarionettes in B-major ; in the third, the bassoons appear
in A-minor.   In the fourth, which is carried over into
the fifth, we have the first and second horns in E, and
then a full, strong chord in E-major.   A light whispered
tone, as of a gentle breath, grows into the strength of the
full power of all the wind instruments, and so gives to
this unknown realm of the elves and fairies a kind of
superhuman grandeur.   In the sixth measure we have the
entrance of the violins, which, for the next sixteen measures, with their sixteenth notes pianissimo, give a conception of the most delicate fairy tones, followed by a wonderful heptachord, with a sustained tone in B ; the first clarionet and the second horn meanwhile pausing for an
instant, but then taking up the tone still more strongly,
and giving us a powerful B-major.   We have then
a similiar, but shorter pause, with the piano passage
as before ; then the great leading theme sounding out in a
clear E-major, passing into prolonged manifold modulations toward the close, and softening into a charming
melody in octaves ; a musical expression for the pangs of
love's yearning and love's joy.   This is interrupted by a
transition to B-major, produced by a sustained fortissimo in
the drollest contrast ; further on are passages which remind
one of a country dance, and which represent the rough
journeymen ; then comes again the heroic element, manifested by the sound of the duke's hunting horns awakening
the slumbering lovers in the forest ; then again a short
*entr'acte* of dancing fairies ; and, still further, the lament of
Hermia, deserted by her sweetheart in consequence of the

mistake in the magical draught.   She is followed by the
fairies in a passage of five measures, in which recur that
same delightful elfin brightness and charm with which the
whole began.   It would lead us too far, and even then would
give no clear picture of the music, were I to follow the
analysis to greater length ; enough to say, in closing, that
the end of the piece passes into a pianissimo and a constantly diminishing tranquillo in octaves, becoming slower
and slower, and then closing with a light drum roll ; with
accords of all the fairies, the piece vanishes into sweet
and charming silence.

This delineation, weak as it is, may give some little idea
of the richness in fancy and spirit, in knowledge and
delicacy, with which our young composer, at the age of
seventeen years, followed the work of the great Shakespeare.   Seventeen years later, the whole of the music of
the "Midsummer Night's Dream," with all its most
charming *entr'actes*, songs, and melodrama, was composed, of which we shall have occasion to speak at the
appropriate place.

We now turn from our consideration of this first work of
the seventeen-year-old boy, to speak of the further progress of his life.   After the performance in Stettin of the
overture, with other of his compositions, Felix had the
misfortune to be overturned in the post-carriage on
the return journey.   He suffered very little inconvenience
from it, but rode in the extreme cold for an hour on one
of the post-horses, and got help.   Here would be a fitting
place to speak of Mendelssohn's physical accomplish-
ments, as well as of his culture in other departments.
Subsequently to the year 1825, he had practised gymnastic
exercises of all sorts with great eagerness and pleasure.
His father had erected a small gymnasium in the large

and fine garden of the house, in which Felix soon became master of all the best known exercises. He also took great pleasure in riding, and, with his friend Devrient, was delighted to use the horses belonging to the old keeper of the king's stables. In the next summer, 1826, he began with passionate delight to practise exercises in swimming. For a little society of swimmers, to which also Klingemann belonged, the latter composed " Swimming Songs," which Felix set to music, and even tried to practise in the water. Felix was also an exceedingly light and graceful dancer. In addition to these corporeal exercises, he made no less progress in his mental and artistic development. He was especially devoted to drawing, in which Professor Roesel afterwards became his teacher, and carried him to a high degree of perfection. The public have already seen excellent specimens of his work, especially in the landscape-sketches in his " Letters of Travel," and also in those to Devrient. As a boy, he possessed a pleasant alto voice, which he cultivated, as did Fanny also, under Zelter's training; as a youth, he had an agreeable though rather light tenor voice, which afterwards became of great use in the study and direction of his great works. In the violin his teacher was his friend Edward Rietz, who died unfortunately too early. Felix, too, was exceedingly fond of the viola, especially in his quartets. After Easter of 1827, Mendelssohn matriculated at the University of Berlin, at the same time that his former teacher Heyse became professor. As evidence of his preparation, he submitted his translation of the " Andria" of Terence, prepared under the direction of Heyse.

In the years 1827 and 1828, he heard various professors; but he took the greatest delight in Ritter's geographical lectures. In addition, he listened to Gans, to Lichtenstein,

and Hegel, of the last of whom Zelter wrote to Goethe:
" Hegel is now lecturing upon music ; and Felix follows
him very easily, and knows how to reproduce all his
personal peculiarities in an exceedingly näive manner."

One can easily imagine how Hegel's abstract nature,
his dragging everything that was at hand, and that he took
for granted, into his system, and his dry, disagreeable
manner, must have amused the young man, already
master in the art on which the professor was discoursing.
From this time university friends began to come to the
Mendelssohn mansion,—Droysen, afterwards so celebrated
by reason of his historical works, at that time a young
teacher and song writer whom Felix and Fanny liked
very much to hear ; the two brothers Heydemann ; Dorn,
afterwards capellmeister and composer ; Kugler, half
student and half painter ; Schubring, a student, and Bauer,
a theological candidate, both of whom used to take part
in musical practice at the Mendelssohn house,—and remained his friends to the last.   He carried on an active
correspondence with them, and it is generally known
what a large share these two theologians, especially the
first, had in arranging the text of St. Paul and Elijah.
In addition, Edward Rietz belonged to the circle of intimate friends ; Klingemann, too, who not long afterward
left Berlin and became Secretary to the Hanoverian
Embassy in London ; and Marx, author of the work upon
" Color in Tone," and who later contributed valuable
hints towards the structure of the " Midsummer Night's
Dream" overture,—its first conception, indeed, was given
by him.   Marx exercised a great influence upon Mendelssohn, not entirely to the delight of the father, who feared
the effect upon Felix.   He accompanied Felix upon his
first visit to Munich, and afterwards the two friends

parted, because Mendelssohn would not give Marx' Oratorio of "Moses" at one of the Rhenish festivals.

During the Whitsuntide holidays of the year 1827, on account of some exhaustion of body brought on by the production of his opera, and through severe mental occupations, Felix had a rest of some days, upon the estate of Sacrow near Potsdam. There he wrote and set to music the song which afterward formed the foundation of the A-minor quartet. In the summer of the same year, he undertook, with some friends, a pleasant vacation journey to the Hartz Mountains, Franconia, Bavaria, and the Rhine. In Hensel's book will be found an exceedingly graphic and delightful description of a mistake in the way leading to the Brocken, brought about through a drunken guide, and of the extremely primitive night quarters in the village of Budenbach, a kind of "nest" in Franconia. In Baden-Baden Mendelssohn played and improvised in private concerts, in conjunction with Robert, Haizinger, and Fraulein Neumann. The manager of the faro bank was in a rage against him. He asserted that he had enticed away a great multitude of people from the *roulette* table by his playing, and that this was against his contract; and he carried it so far as to take away the piano. "At once Robert and Haizinger entered into a conspiracy against him, and procured a very fine instrument in another hall. Robert and Haizinger read a new comedy, the latter appearing to especial advantage and receiving much applause. Later, there was music: Haizinger yodeled Austrian; Fraulein von W. ' peeped' Italian; Madame N. sang with her husband fifty verses of Fidelio; I, meanwhile, drummed *études* by Moscheles, which gave special delight in Baden; I also improvised, and the people were delighted."

In Heidelberg Mendelssohn made the acquaintance of
the great jurist and musical connoisseur, Thibaut. Under
date of Sept. 20, 1827, he writes to his mother: " ' Oh
Heidelberg, thou beauteous town, even if it has rained
the whole day,' say the bumpkins; but I am a bursch, I
am a kneip genius; what does the rain trouble me ?
There are still left grass, musical-instrument makers,
journals, kneips, Thibauts, — no, that's a lie, there's only
one Thibaut, but he counts for six. There is a man! I
have a regular naughty boy's joy, dearest mother, that
I did not make this acquaintance out of simple regard to
your letter of to-day; for even yesterday, that is, twenty-
four hours before I received it, I talked with him a couple
of hours. It is wonderful; the man knows little about
music, even his historical knowledge of it is considerably
limited, he treats it almost exclusively out of mere instinct.
I understand more about it than he does, and yet I have
learned no end of him; for he has thrown a light on the
old Italian music for me, and has really set me aflame
with its glow. There is a spirit and warmth with which
he speaks; I should call his really a flowery language. I
have just come from him; and, after talking a great deal
about Sebastian Bach (of whom he knows not the best
and the deepest, for in Sebastian everything is found),
at last he said, in parting, ' Good-by; and we will knit
friendship to Louis de Vittoria and Sebastian Bach, just
as two lovers exchange promises to look at the full moon
at the same time, and so believe themselves not far
apart.' "

After Mendelssohn had, on his return, spent some
days with the uncle at his estate on the Lese, and had
gone with him to the Cecilia Society in Frankfort, he
returned about the middle of October to Berlin, strengthened in body and mind, and with new zest for work.

This renewed impulse to activity soon brought forth beautiful blossoms. I must first remark that already, in the winter of 1825, Mendelssohn composed a brilliant overture in C-major for the orchestra, which afterwards took the name of the " Trumpet Overture," in consequence of the trumpet call which is in it. It was first given in a concert of the violin virtuoso and composer Mærer, and then again in the great garden-hall of the Mendelssohn mansion ; in 1828 at the Dürer festival, and in 1833 at the musical festival at Düsseldorf. Mendelssohn did not consider it ready for publication, and therefore allowed himself to use the " Trumpet Call " in the overture to " The Hebrides," begun in 1829. It must have been published very late, for it appears in the Breitkopf-Härtel Chronological Index as Opus 101. As further productions of Mendelssohn's muse, Fanny states, in a letter to Klingemann dated Dec. 25, 1827, that he had prepared a symphony as a Christmas present for their sister Rebecca, written for the same instruments that Haydn wrote his for, and that it was brought out in the family circle, which found it an extremely humorous thing. In Christmas, 1828, there was another produced, which was also exceedingly pretty and universally acceptable. But, besides these productions of his youthful humor, there were other very beautiful and serious works ; Fanny speaks especially of a production of this sort, a four-voiced chorus, with small orchestra, based upon the choral, " *Christi du Lamm Gottes.*" She says, " I have played it a few times ; it is extremely beautiful. Felix has lately been applying himself especially to church music ; on my birthday, Nov. 15, he wrote for me a piece for nine voices, for chorus and orchestra, on the words, ' Thou art Peter, and on this rock I will build

my church;' but in Latin." It is the same work of
which Felix speaks in a letter to his mother, dated Heidelberg, Sept. 20, 1827, and is a composition on which
he was then engaged. It formed the initial point for
his intimate acquaintance with Thibaut, who had already
spoken, in his " History of Music," of a certain " Thou
art Peter." The next important work which he undertook was a great cantata, the text by Lewezow, composed for the Dürer festival in Berlin, and given in the
Singacademie, April 18, 1828. Devrient indeed thinks
it was without results; but Fanny is of an entirely different
opinion. " Felix," she writes, " has in six weeks written
a great cantata for chorus and full orchestra, with arias,
recitatives, and all kinds of matter. You can imagine
that this slight work has no value for him. In the beginning he raged so over it that he wanted to burn up the
whole thing, in his usual way; but, as the rehearsals
went forward, the choruses were sung splendidly by the
Academy, and he began to take more pleasure; and the
wonderful decorations of the hall and the liberality of the
arrangements completed his joy. On Thursday evening
was the general rehearsal, which went off considerably
confused and unsatisfactory; but Felix remained calm all
the while, and was sure it would go well, and it did go
magnificently. Felix' C-major trumpet overture, beautifully played, opened the festival. Then followed an address three-quarters of an hour long (somewhat tedious).
Then the cantata, which lasted a good hour and a quarter.
The solos were sung by Milder, Stürmer, Turrschmiedt,
and Devrient; everything went so perfectly, and the reception of it was so satisfactory, that I cannot remember
any pleasanter hours. At the dinner which followed,
Mendelssohn's health was drunk by about two hundred

persons. Zelter and Schadow took him by the hand, and the latter addressed him heartily and proclaimed him solemnly Honorary Member of the Society of Artists, from which he should receive a diploma. Yesterday the whole day was spent in visits of congratulation."

Here I close my account of the second occasional composition of this year. In the middle of September, 1828, there was a gathering of physicians and naturalists in Berlin, and Alexander von Humboldt arranged, at the command of the King, a concert in the hall of the Royal Theatre. Ladies were excluded. The choruses consisted of the best men's voices in the city, and Humboldt, no great musician himself, had limited the numbers considerably. The orchestra became a curious assemblage; there were only bass viols, cellos, trumpets, horns and clarionets; Mendelssohn wrote the music for the occasion to a little cantata composed by Rellstab. There was a tenor solo with chorus, Devrient tells us, which made an agreeable impression; but when he goes on to say that " special musical occasions were not able to incite Mendelssohn to his best, he rushed through them so quickly, in a kind of machine style," I cannot entirely go with him. I recollect, for example, the overture to " Ruy Blas," not to speak of others.

Between these two special occasions, which I call so because the composer wrote to order, there appeared a second characteristic piece, which flowed directly out of Mendelssohn's genius, the overture known as " A Calm Sea and a Happy Voyage" ("_Meeresstille und glückliche Fahrt_"). The name overture is not directly appropriate; it should rather be called a tone picture, for it is a portrait of nature and of emotions. We do not know, indeed, what it was that incited the young composer

to enter upon this new style of creation. It is wonderful
that he could compose it, he who had never seen the
ocean. It is as striking a proof of the power of his fancy
as Schiller's portrayal of Alpine scenery in " William
Tell." It could not be possible to delineate more beautifully and more vividly the dull stillness of the air at the
outset ; the jubilation over the first breeze, the constantly
increasing strength of the wind catching the sails of the
ship, the merry rush onward through the agitated waves,
the arrival in the harbor. The key-note of the whole
was given by the well-known poem of Goethe, bearing
the same name, whose text Beethoven had already used
characteristically in a piece for choir and orchestra. It
was a bold undertaking for Mendelssohn, who unquestionably knew this composition of the great master,
and undertook to follow him ; but his success was most
happy and unmistakeable. Fanny gives us, in a letter
to Klingemann, dated June 28, 1828, an account of its
origin. " Felix," she says, " is writing a great instrumental piece, ' A Still Sea and a Happy Voyage,' after
Goethe. It will be worthy of him. He is going to bring
together in it two pictures standing in contrast to each
other." Edward Devrient, in his " Recollections," says
further : " In this time falls the composition of his second
characteristic piece, ' A Still Sea and a Happy Voyage,'
which in the opinion of his admirers called out almost as
great a sensation as the ' Midsummer Night's Dream.' If
in this the striking grasp and delineation of the complete
poem was to be wondered at, in the new composition it
is the capacity of translating to us the impression which
the aspects of nature in themselves make. The concerts
in the garden-hall, in which this piece was given, were
true festivals for us. The violoncello solo in the ' Happy

Voyage' was always a signal for jubilation and greetings among the young friends."

The remarks of both of these prepossessed witnesses, the sister and the friend, contain much that is true; but they do not hit the form or the inner nature of the work. The adagio commences the "Meeresstille" in D-major quietly in four-fourth time, passing into prolonged accords, in which you can really seem to see the deep blue and motionless ocean before your eyes, and runs on for forty-four measures, at the end of which the flute signal sounds (Reissmann called it "The boatswain's whistle metamorphosed"); and then, with a wonderfully beautiful accord of diminished sevenths of the wind instruments, we have the first breath of a fresh breeze charmingly portrayed; and so the "Happy Voyage," in the *allegro multo vivace*, continues unbroken to the end. Lovely pictures appear repeatedly following each other: we see the bright sky, the proud and beautiful ship cutting the foaming waves and displaying its full sails; we see the land coming nearer and nearer, and the opening harbor; we not only see, but we feel and hear, the wind with its rising breath, the jubilation of the happy mariners, and, after reaching the end, the joy and rejoicings. During the last thirty-six measures we see the ship entering the harbor, we see the anchor thrown, we hear the cry of welcome with which the people on the shore greet the new comers, and even there are not wanting the salutes at the end, indicated by the kettle-drums on the ship and on the shore; and so, from the last three measures *fortissimo*, we pass to a *diminuendo* and *pianissimo*, into the expression of thankfulness for the completion of the happy voyage, and thus the music closes with a hush of peace. Devrient's description does not, therefore, entirely cover the case. The music not only paints the impression which nature makes upon us, but also it indicates all those moods of mind and feeling, of expectation, of joy, of jubilation, of thankfulness, which gives such a sense of reality to human life and the world in which we live, and which forms such a contrast to the world of dreams and visions, which always appears distant and cold. I am sorry not to be able to give the date when this work was completed, and when it was first played; probably in the year 1830, in one of the winter concerts of the Philharmonic Society in London. Mendelssohn himself, who could never do enough to perfect his best works, writes about this in a letter to Schubring, dated Düsseldorf, Aug. 6, 1834: " The ' Meeresstille ' I have entirely re-written this winter, and I believe it is about thirty times better than it was before." I myself heard it given under Mendelssohn's own direction, in Leipsic, in the first Gewandhaus concert, Oct. 4, 1835. It gave exceptional pleasure. The musical critic of the "*Allegemeine Musik Zeitung*" says, " The ' *Meeresstille und glückliche Fahrt*,' by Mendelssohn, was as successful as one would expect, from what it had been before, and what it had grown to be in its new form;" and how often have I enjoyed, with ever fresh delight, this beautiful piece from that time to this.

Yet the fruitful muse of Mendelssohn did not content itself with this one work, but went on producing more and more. Fanny writes to Klingemann, under date Dec. 8, 1828, on the occasion of mentioning her birthday festival: "Felix has written three things; a ' Song without Words ' (of which he has lately produced a number of beautiful ones), another piece for the piano, and a great work, with four choruses, on the words, '*Hora est jam de somno surgere*.' The Academy will give it. I will gladly respond to your request to inform you further about Felix' new works; but, speaking in general, he becomes undeniably clearer and deeper with every work. His direction is more and more firm, and he goes straight to the goal set clearly before him. He is complete master of all his resources, and so he extends his realm from day to day, like a field-marshal, dominating all the materials which lie at his hand."

Having given this account of the gradual growth of our young composer's works, and having brought it to a kind of termination for the time, we must speak of him in his greatness as director, and see how in his youthful years he grew in this new capacity in a wonderful and masterly way, as was first displayed in the public performance of the " St. Matthew Passion " of John Sebastian Bach. The delineation of this event, which was to form an epoch in the whole musical world, is one of the chief features in Devrient's well-known volume of " Recollections." I will make such use of it here as is necessary to give completeness to my narrative. Devrient himself had a very important part in the whole affair, and without his encouragement his young friend would scarcely have conceived the thought of bringing this work to the public eye. The first germs of the undertaking date from Felix' youth. Old Zelter used to gather around him, on Friday evenings, a little company of the Singacademie, and their task was to learn difficult works of the earlier composers. Under his leading they used to sing from time to time what Zelter called, in his rough way, " bristly bits " from

Sebastian Bach, which gave an idea of him as only a kind of unintelligible genius, with immense mathematical capacities, which he employed in fugue writing. The Singacademie really knew only a few of his motettes, and practised even these but seldom. In these Friday-evening exercises Fanny and Felix sung alto, and Zelter used to allow them occasionally to accompany this and that piece on the piano, until at last Felix undertook the whole work of accompanying. In this way he made the acquaintance of some works of music which Zelter considered as a sacred treasure, to be hidden from the world; and among these some passages out of Bach's " Passion Music." It was his glowing wish to possess the whole of the " St. Matthew Passion," a wish which his grandmother gratified at Christmas, 1823. She procured, not without difficulty, permission to have a copy taken. Edward Rietz, Mendelssohn's teacher on the violin, and at the same time his friend, conducted the whole affair in a masterly manner. Felix displayed his gift to Devrient at the Christmas festival, with a countenance full of veneration and delight. The sacred work became afterwards to him the fondest object of study.

Since the winter of 1827 Mendelssohn had been gradually collecting around him a reliable chorus for the purpose of practising rare music. In the winter of 1828–29 he took up his beloved " Matthew Passion." He was soon engrossed in the work; he set his conception of it so skilfully and at the same time so modestly before the singers that the characteristic features of this difficult music very soon got a ready hearing and interpretation. Edward Devrient had a great desire to sing the part of Jesus publicly; but the difficulties connected with a public rendering of the piece, which requires a double chorus and orchestra, were very great; there was also the fear of difficulties with the Singacademie in procuring the building, and respecting the co-operation of the society and the unapproachability of Zelter on the whole matter. The question arose, Will the public be inclined to give a whole evening to Bach, the unmelodious, mathematical, dry, and unintelligible Bach? Mendelssohn's parents shared this fear. He himself replied with jest and irony to the pressure of his friends that he would undertake the direction, ridiculing the idea that such a boy as he should be at the head of so great an enterprise.

On an evening in January, 1829, they had run through the whole of the first part of the work, Bauer taking the part of the Evangelist, Kugler taking the leading bass passages. Everybody was delighted with the beauty of the work. That night Edward Devrient, in the silence of his own thought, came to the conclusion to bring the whole work to the public eye. His wife encouraged him in the scheme, and· he could scarcely wait for the morning to come. Going to Mendelssohn, at eight o'clock, he found him still in a deep, death-like sleep. His brother Paul shook him again and again, and called out, " Felix, wake up, it is eight o'clock!" but it was a considerable time before Felix roused up enough to say, as if dreaming, " Oh, stop that! stop that! I tell you it is nothing but nonsense." But at last he got his eyes open, and, seeing Devrient at his bed, he called out in his friendly tones, "What, Edward, what brings you here?" Devrient: "I have something very important to talk over with you." Paul conducted him to the next room, where Felix took his breakfast of bread and coffee. Devrient bade him hurry through, because he did not want to interrupt him in his eating. At the end, he exclaimed abruptly, " I have during the night resolved to bring out the ' Matthew Passion' in the Singacademie, before you go to England." Mendelssohn, laughingly: " Who to direct it?" Devrient: " You." Mendelssohn: " Oh, pshaw ! But I will help you with the music." Devrient: " Come, come ; I really mean what I say, and have thought it thoroughly out." Mendelssohn: " Come, old fellow, you seem to be solemn ; let us hear what you have to say." Devrient: " Well, we recognize the ' Matthew Passion' as the grandest and greatest of all German works, and we ought not to let it rest until we have brought it to the light, and have seen it work upon an audience " (Felix could make no reply to this) ; " and you, and nobody but you, can undertake it, and therefore you must." To which Mendelssohn replied, " If I could see it carried through, I certainly would."

Devrient now opened his plan of operations. Zelter owed them something for their ten years' work with him in the Singacademie, and he would like to do a service to them both, and he would be the man to procure the hall, and the permission and the co-operation of the Singacademie, in bringing out the " Passion Music." Mendelssohn's parents and Fanny coincided in Devrient's plan. It would be a great delight to them, if, before Felix' entrance upon the world, he could perform this great and memorable task. The father had many fears that Zelter would oppose, but Devrient was of good heart.

Felix now thought out a little clever device not to compromise himself and the undertaking. The chorus rehearsals should take place with a somewhat increased number of the company usually singing in his own house ; no particular object should be announced ; members of the Singacademie should come in according to their pleasure and inclination. They might thus gradually increase the number, and thus steadily they might advance towards the goal which he had so earnestly in view. If everything fell out right, well and good; and the whole thing might be given up, if necessity required, before they began to talk about the public concert.

Devrient has given such a vivid and dramatic picture of their interview with Zelter, that I cannot refrain from placing it before my readers.

"Thus prepared, we advanced to the room where old Zelter sat in the lower story of the Singacademie. At the door Felix whispered to me, 'Now, if he is rough, I am going away; I cannot bring myself to jaw with him.' 'Rough he will be, certainly,' I answered; 'but the jawing part I will undertake.'

"We knocked at the door, the rough voice of the master summoned us loudly in. We found the old giant in a thick cloud of tobacco, with his long pipe in his mouth, sitting before his old piano, holding the swan's feather in his hand with which he was accustomed to write, and having a sheet of music paper before him. He wore his short, sand-colored jacket, his breeches bound just below the knee, coarse woolen stockings and embroidered shoes. His white hair was thrown back upon his head, his countenance wore its habitual expression, with its harsh, common, and yet strong features, directed towards the door; and he called out, as soon as he recognized us through his glasses, in his friendly way, 'Well, see there! So early, and two such nice young people. Well, you are doing me an honor. Come in and sit down.'

"On this I began a well-considered address about

our admiration of the work of Bach, whose acquaintance
we had made in the Friday evenings under his direction.
We had gone on with them in the Mendelssohn mansion, and now we wanted to make an attempt, with
his assistance, to bring Bach's great work to the public
knowledge, and we wished not only his assistance, but
also that of the Singacademie.

" ' Yes,' he said, leaning forward and throwing his
chin into the air, as he is accustomed to do when he
speaks with great emphasis, ' if that can be possible;
but to do that requires more force than we command
at this day.'

" Then he began to enlarge upon the difficulties and
demands of the work. ' We need a Thomas school for
the choruses, such as there was in Bach's time; we
need a double orchestra; and the violins of our time
do not know anything about music, do not know how
to handle a bow. All these things have been long
talked over and thoroughly weighed; and, if these
difficulties could be so easily got rid of, all four of
Bach's " Passions " would have been given over and
over again.'

" Zelter grew warm, laid down his pipe, and began
to stalk about the room. We had all arisen; Felix
pulled me by the coat, for he gave the thing up as lost
already. I answered Zelter that we, especially Felix,
had weighed all the difficulties, but that we did not
think they were insuperable. ' The Singacademie
already has an acquaintance with Sebastian Bach, has
drilled the choir so admirably, that it already knows
how to take every difficulty. Felix has learned the
work thoroughly, thanks for his [Zelter's] direction
in it. I am burning with desire to sing the part of

Jesus, and we might venture to hope that the same enthusiasm which moves us will very soon reach to the members of the society.'

" Zelter grew more and more fierce. He had thrown out, here and there, expressions of doubt and depreciation, at every one of which Felix had pulled me by the coat, and gradually approached the door; and now the old gentleman blazed out, ' That I should listen to you patiently! Other people count for nothing. Worthy good people hesitate to undertake this work, and now a couple of young smutty-noses [the reader must pardon the characteristic and dirty word] think that they can do it, — that to give Bach is only child's play!' "

It is wonderful that Devrient was not frightened away and silenced by this tirade; still he was resolved to carry it to the very last. He goes on to relate: " This bull's-eye shot he fired off with extreme energy. I had hard work even to keep back my laughter. Zelter had a free pass for all sorts of grossness, and for the 'Passion Music' of Sebastian Bach, and for the honor of my old teacher, I put up even with this. I looked around at Felix, who was standing at the door, the handle in his hand, and who motioned to me, with a wounded and pale countenance, that he should go. I intimated to him that we must remain, and began again with good courage to set the thing forth; that, although we were young, we were not so entirely immature, since our master had already inspired us to undertake many difficult enterprises; that youth was the time for such undertakings, and that he must consider it a good thing if he had two pupils whose aim was nothing less than the very highest that he could teach them.

"My expositions now began to take visible effect. The crisis was over.

"'We only want to make a venture, to see if the thing can go through; and we would like your assistance just so far. Then, if it did not succeed, we could all of us let the thing drop without any public talk.'

"'How do you think you are going to do this?' he asked, still standing. 'Do not you see the difficulties? First, there is the management that must consent; there are a lot of heads and a lot of minds, and then there are women, too; you have to get them. You cannot bring all these things together.'

"I replied to him that the management was already friendly; that the chief singers had already practised in Mendelssohn's house; that I believed we could reckon with certainty on the use of the hall, and the co-operation of the members of the Academy.

"'Yes, the members, the members of the Academy, the members. There is exactly where your difficulty begins. To-day you have ten of them to your rehearsal, and to-morrow twenty of the ten will stay away.'

"We had, of course, a laugh over this, for it showed us clearly that the battle was won. Felix explained his plan about the preliminary rehearsals in the little hall, spoke of the gathering of the orchestra, which Edward Rietz should lead; and, when Zelter at last could make no more objections, he gave in, and said, 'Well, I wont say "No" to you; I will help you wherever I can. Go on, in God's name; we will see what comes of it.'

"So we thankfully took our departure, and as good friends of our old sturdy bear. 'We are through,' I said, at the house door. 'But see,' said Felix; 'you are a regular rascal, you are a perfect Jesuit!'—'All to the glory of God and Sebastian Bach,' I answered; and we went out in jubilation into the winter air, thinking that our hardest step was accomplished.

"Everything else went on easily; the management fell in to all our wishes, asking only fifty thalers for the use of the hall. The rehearsals began on Friday, Jan. 22, 1829, directly after the engagement of Fanny to Hensel. Already, at the first rehearsal in the little hall, the number of participants had doubled; and so it grew from one rehearsal to another. The copyists had difficulty in supplying all the copies that were needed; and, by the time the fifth rehearsal was reached, we had to go into the great hall of the Academy."

What Devrient says respecting Mendelssohn's talent, which had already become great, as director, is interesting in its relation to his method of study and direction: "In order to fix the attention of the singers and hold it, Felix often, in the very first rehearsals, took, not scattered bits, the lighter parts of the piece, but grasped a definite group, for the purpose of giving the sense of the whole; practised the choruses with the greatest exactness, until their expression was complete, and this communicated to the singers a perfect conception of the whole work. His explanations and hints were short, to the point, and as full of matter as they were of youthful modesty.

"The great rehearsals were lifted into prominence by Zelter's presence, and the authority which that presence gave; but, so long as the orchestra was not present, Felix was obliged not only to direct, but to accompany the work on the piano; an undertaking of extreme difficulty, by reason of the rapidity with which the passages fold over one another and inter-play with one another.  He had to do all the playing with his left hand, while he did his directing with the right. In his whole life he probably never had a task more difficult than this.  When the orchestra came, Felix placed the piano between the two choruses, having one of these behind him, and the other, consisting mainly of *dilettanti*, before him.  This difficult situation Felix commanded with a composure and security which would have been striking if he had directed at ten festivals.  The delicate and unpretending manner in which, by the movement of his hand and head, he reminded them of the shading in expression; the composure with which, at the general rehearsal and at the final concert, he held the great mass in steadfast and even movement, scarcely nodding, as if he were saying, ' Now, it is going well,' and let his baton fall, and listened with his bright and almost glorified face, an expression which beautified him especially when he was conducting, until at last he found it necessary to resume the use of the baton, — all this was as lovely as it was astonishing."

How exact this delineation of Mendelssohn as director is, I must myself confirm as eye and ear witness, for I was present at at least four great oratorios and all the preceding rehearsals, as tenor chorus singer, and stood scarcely three steps from him.

When it became time to invite the solo singers, both the friends, Mendelssohn and Devrient, made the rounds.  Felix, childishly enough, wanted that both should wear the same costume, blue coat, white waistcoat, black necktie, black trousers, and light yellow gloves of deerskin, then in fashion.  Their invitations

had the best success; the four leading singers of the
opera readily promised their co-operation. Their appearance at the rehearsals gave a new charm to the
study of the work. Aside from the greatness of the work
itself, everybody was astonished at the richness of the
melodies, the deep feeling and the passion, things that
no one had before supposed were to be found in Bach.
The pressure to the concert surpassed all expectations;
there were at the first concert only six free tickets, of
which Spontini had two. About a thousand persons
could get no tickets; and, therefore, there was an
earnest application for a repetition. Spontini, becoming jealous, endeavored to prevent this; but Felix
and Devrient secured a command for it from the Crown
Prince, who took an active interest in the affair. On
Saturday, the 22d of March, Bach's birthday, this second
representation took place in the presence of an audience
still more crowded than before; every place, even in
the vestibule, as well as in the little rehearsal room
behind the orchestra, being occupied. Both representations, the first on the 11th, and the second on the 22d,
of March, were given in the interest of a sewing school
for poor girls, and both had a complete success. The
impression made by a chorus of between three and
four hundred voices, the admirably drilled orchestra,
the presence of the best singers in the opera, produced
a powerful and overwhelming effect. Stürmer sang the
part of the Evangelist; Devrient, Jesus; Baeder took
the part of Peter; Busolt represented the High Priest
and Pilate; Wappler was Judas; Schatzel, Milder, and
Thürschmiedt, took the soprano and alto solos admirably.
Devrient says, what is worth noting, in speaking of his

own delineation of Jesus: "I knew before that the impression which the impersonation of Jesus would make would be decisive of the reception of the whole work, and everything came just as I would have it. I was conscious that the thrills which ran through me would be shared by the hearers, in their silence like the silence of death. Never have I beheld an assembly so touched with holy awe as on this occasion were both artists and hearers." And what he sang so piously certainly did reach every heart. Fanny confirms the impression in a letter to Klingemann, March 22. "What we have been so long dreaming of as a possibility has now become actual fact. The 'Passion' has come to life again, and has become the possession of the living men. The crowded hall presented an aspect of a church; there was the most perfect silence, there was, too, the real spirit of worship in the assembly; all that could be heard was an occasional irrepressible expression of deep feeling. What is often said untruly of an undertaking of this sort can be said in this case truly, that there was indeed an especial depth of feeling, there was a universal interest; and every one did, not only his duty, but many did even more than that."

The influence of this performance in giving an impetus to the new musical movement is immeasurable. It was the first step towards making the master works of Bach and of Beethoven, until then almost unknown, the possession of the world. "Mendelssohn gave his life to the work of restoring these authors to the knowledge of men; and, if they have become the property of the German nation, it is in large part to be ascribed to him."

Mendelssohn could not wish for any more joyful result of his efforts. Adorned with these new laurels, he, a youth of twenty, could now go forth into the world, to which the liberality of his father prepared the way, and see wide open before him a new theatre for his manifold activities.

## PART II.

I am reminded, in writing the above title, of Goethe's "Wander Years;" and, indeed, I have selected the term "Years of Travel" as a reminiscence of Wilhelm Meister. The hero of Goethe's romance, after wanderings of all sorts in the realm of feeling, and in the company of his son Felix, suffers a long separation from his beloved and noble bride, in order to become worthy of an undeserved · happiness; whereas, our Felix, accompanied by the blessings and the love of his parents and brothers and sisters, furnished by the generosity of his father with means for all the comforts and conveniences of travel, enters upon his journey in the great world, in which, though always in the purest and noblest manner, he should enjoy to the full, intercourse with nature, art, and distinguished men. On this journey he was to gain materials for his most important works, to which he had indeed begun to give a fixed form in his mind; he was to practise his art industriously as virtuoso; he was to take a distinguished place in the best society; and, even if the final result of all these journeys should be no other than his own patriotic resolve that Germany should be the scene of his action, yet foreign lands, and especially England, were to secure to him his first great triumphs, and give him consciousness of his power, though without the least injury to his lovely modesty.

The period of these years of travel extends from 1829

to 1833, although not without some interruptions, by reason of a long stay at Berlin.

The first journey of Mendelssohn to England, to which a protracted excursion to Scotland was conjoined, may indeed be said to be a kind of prelude to his "Wander Years;" for he passed the winter of 1829-30, between November and May, in his father's house at Berlin. But in this prelude there lay the most important germs, which should afterwards unfold in the life drama of the young artist. England, where Handel had gained his great renown, where Haydn had been received with such lively interest, where Von Weber had given his "Oberon," written exclusively for a London audience, as well as where he had directed, in 1826, the representation of his "Freyschütz and Preciosa," was a land adapted in the highest degree to bring a nature so rich as Mendelssohn's to its maturity, and to give it prompt recognition. As early as 1827 Mendelssohn's father had sought Moscheles' advice, in London, whether he would consider it well that his son should travel; Moscheles' reply could only be in the affirmative. The father considered it more suitable that this journey should begin at the close of Felix' university course. In the spring of the year 1829 the hour had come when the young artist could make his first independent flight into the great world. Before we follow him thither, we will cast a glance upon his productivity up to that time. Before his journey to London, Mendelssohn had composed the following : three quartets in C-minor, F-minor, and B-minor, for piano, violin, and violoncello; two sonatas, the one for the piano and violin, the other for piano alone, E-major; two symphonies in C-minor and D-major; the great overture in C, with the trumpet theme; four separate operas, among them the still extant " Camacho's Wedding ; " two groups of songs, each consisting of twelve numbers (Opus 8 and 9); various " Songs without Words ; " the two cantatas for the Dürer festival ; the two great works, " Overture to Midsummer Night's Dream," " A Still Sea and a Happy Voyage," as well as the " Octet" and the two symphonies before mentioned.

He brought over to England, in manuscript, for his teacher Moscheles' inspection, a religious cantata based upon the choral in A-minor, a " Hora " for sixteen voices, and his first stringed quartet in A-minor, for which he laid the foundation in a song written near Potsdam, for Whitsuntide, 1827. After the giving of Bach's " Passion," Mendelssohn wrote to Moscheles, in London, giving him an account of it, and announcing his prospective journey thither. Moscheles had already made the direction of the Philharmonic Society in London acquainted with the extraordinary talents of this young man, and arranged everything for Mendelssohn's reception. His friend Klingemann had also been diligent in preparing for him a quiet home. On the 10th of April, 1829, Felix, accompanied by his father and his tenderly loved sister Rebecca, came as far as Hamburg, whither Fanny sent him a charming parting letter. He had to remain for at least several days in his native town. The journey across to London was not at all agreeable, being long and stormy. Only on the 21st of April could he announce to his " Dearest Father " and his " Dearest Becky " his arrival. The letter is so characteristic that I must cite a portion, at least, of it here : —

" Having arrived in good order in London, I have nothing to do before telling you at once about my coming. Our journey across was not pleasant, and was very long ;

for only to-day at twelve o'clock have we landed at the
Custom House. From Saturday evening to Monday
afternoon we had the wind absolutely in our faces, and
such a storm that the whole crew became sea-sick. We
were obliged to lie still for some time, once by reason of
a thick fog, and another time in order to do something to
the machinery; even last night the anchor had to be
thrown at the mouth of the Thames, in order not to strike
against other ships. Add to this that from Sunday
morning till Monday evening I passed from one swoon
to another, merely out of vexation at myself and everything on board the steamer; bitterly hating England, and
especially my 'Calm Sea' overture; finding all manner
of fault with the watch, and asking at Monday noon if
we could not yet see anything of London, to which the
man on duty replied, in an indifferent manner, that we
could not think of such a thing till Tuesday noon. And
then, to speak a little of the bright side of things, seeing
the moonlight on the water last evening, hundreds of
ships playing around us; then in the morning sailing up
the Thames between green meadows, smoking cities,
with twenty steamers running a race, swiftly leaving behind all the skiffs in the river; and, at last, the tremendous aspect of this monster city."

In a letter just as dramatic he pictures the impression
made by London upon him, as upon every one who
sees it for the first time. In this second letter, dated
April 25, 1829, he writes: "It is horrible, it is madden-
ing! I am wholly turned upside down! London is
the most immense, the most complicated monster that
the world bears up. How can I crowd together in one
letter what I have experienced in three days? I can
scarcely number the leading things; and yet I do not

keep a diary, and I will not try to set down in order all, but only just the things that come to hand. I am swept around as if in a whirlpool; and, in the whole of the last half-year in Berlin, I have not seen so many contrasts and so many varieties as in these three days. Just go with me from my home down Regent Street: see the splendid broad avenue filled on both sides with pillared halls (unfortunately to-day all enveloped in thick fog); see the shops, with their signs as high as a man's head; and the omnibuses, on which human beings tower up into the air; see here how a long row of coaches is left behind by the pedestrians, because it has been stopped by some elegant equipage; see there how a horse rears, because the rider has some acquaintances in yonder house; see how men are used to carry round advertisements on their backs, on some of which are announcements of the artistic performances of trained cats; see the beggars and the negroes; and the thick John Bulls, each with his two pretty thin daughters on his arm. Oh, those daughters! But do not be disturbed, there is no danger from that quarter, neither in Hyde Park, filled with their beauty, where yesterday I drove with Madam Moscheles in a very fashionable style, nor in the concerts, nor in the opera (though I have been at them all). The only danger is at the corners and at the cross streets; and I often say to myself, in a low tone, and in a voice that you know well, 'Now look out for yourself, not to get run over in the confusion and whirlpool!' I only give it like a calm historian, otherwise you will get no conception. But, if you could only see me sitting at the splendid piano which the Clementis have sent to me, to be mine as long as I stay; could you see me at the pleasant chim-

ney-fire in my own ' castle,' see my shoes and my grey
stockings and my olive colored gloves (for I have to
make visits by and by), and close at hand my immense
bed as high as the sky, in which I can lie in all directions, cross-wise as well as up and down, with the
motley curtains and old-fashioned furniture; if you
could see my morning breakfast of tea and toast, the
servant girl in hair-papers bringing me just now my
new hemmed black tie, and asking for orders, to which
I reply with a nod backward in the polite English
fashion; if you could see the elegant street, veiled in
fog, and could hear the pitiful cries (just now a beggar
is singing his song down there, but he is almost out-
shouted by the people who have things to sell); and
could you see how full the whole city for two miles
from here is of all manner of confusions and sights
and distractions, and then remember that you, after
that, have not seen more than a quarter of London,
you would not be amazed that I am half crazy. Well,
I must not exaggerate, but this is strictly historical."

Next to the charming view which these genial sketches
give us of the quiet, pleasant home of the poet, and
the tremenduous rush and stir of London, the impression
interests us most which he gives of his first acquaintance
with Italian opera and with Malibran.

While still wearied with the journey, he yet allowed
himself to be taken by Klingemann to an English coffee-
house (" For," he says, " everything is English here ").
There he naturally read the " Times," and found in it
the announcement of " Othello," with the first appearance of Madam Malibran. After, with Klingemann's
help, he had made the necessary *toilette*, in which the
grey stockings and the black tie played a leading part,

he went to the Royal Theatre, where, for half a guinea, he procured a seat in the pit. He pictures the house in a terse and happy manner: "Grey house, wholly furnished with purple stuff. Six rows of boxes, one over another, with purple curtains, out of which ladies' faces look, with great white feathers, with chains and jewels of every kind; an odor of pomade and perfume coming from every quarter, and giving me a headache. In the pit, all the gentlemen in ball costume, and with freshly curled side whiskers, and every place completely full." With regard to the representation, he says further: "The orchestra very good, directed by Spagnoletti. In December I will take him off to you, and kill you with laughter. Donzelli (Othello, full of bravura), sensibly dressed, shouts fearfully, sings almost always a little too high, and nevertheless has no end of *haut gout;* of which I may instance that, in the last terrible scene, wherein Malibran is at the top of her voice, Othello allows the conclusion of the recitative to become quiet and soft, and at last so faint as to be hardly heard. Malibran, a young and beautiful woman, with splendid figure and with *toupee*, full of fire, force, and coquetry; costume very admirable and novel, partly imitated after Pasta; with all this she plays beautifully, and has especially good passages; only here and there she passes beyond all limits, and becomes ludicrous and disagreeable. Yet I want to hear her again, but not to-morrow, because Othello is to be repeated, and that I only want to hear when Sonntag appears in it, who is expected about this time."

About two months later he heard the two great artists together in "Don Giovanni," Sonntag singing the part of Donna Anna, Malibran that of Zerlina. Of this representation he writes to Devrient, June 17, 1829: " I have recently seen " Don Giovanni," as given by the Italians: and it is comical, I assure you. Pelligrini sang Leporello, and acted like a monkey; put a *finale* of ten Rossini clap-trap measures to his first aria, played the mandolin solo *deh vieni* very delicately with the bow, gave us some additional embellishments the second time, and closed with an immensely high tone. I cried '*Da capo*,' out of sheer rage. Malibran took Zerlina in a thoroughly stupid manner, as a wild, coquettish peasant girl. She has immense talents. How Sonntag sings Donna Anna you can imagine."

In spite of the criticism and blame, which is mingled, in this judgment upon Malibran, with enthusiastic praise, the reader can yet see the lively interest which the great composer felt in this extraordinary *artiste*. Mendelssohn's father feared, for a short time, that this interest would assume the form of an intense passion, and hurry his son into some indiscretion; but he had no reason for it.

The young artist soon gained a distinguished social position in London. Devrient writes, in his " Recollections:" " Felix made a great stir in London; the musicians and connoisseurs were amazed at his youthful mastery. The leading circles were struck with the fact that he took no pay for his performances, and would not attend wherever money was offered him; in other words, he claimed his right to belong to society. He was amazed at the gulf which was fixed between *virtuosi*, invited to those circles, and society itself. He could not forgive it, when he saw Malibran cast out, as a hireling, from the salon where she had been, as an *artiste*, the object of such attention."

Mendelssohn gives us an exceedingly amusing account of a visit which he paid one day to Dr. Spurzheim, the phrenologist. He tells us, in one of his letters, " A pretty young woman with whom I then was, having a great desire to know whether she had a special inclination to steal, or to commit any other similar indiscretion, it came about at last that the whole company fancied that it would be nice to have a phrenological examination. One was found to be very good-humored, another fond of children; this lady spirited, that one avaricious; and so my young friend insisted on venturing in. But, as the doctor could not examine her head while her hair was done up, she was obliged to let it down; and, as she was really very pretty, and had to do it up again before the mirror, we all thought phrenology is a very fine thing, and praised it accordingly. Of course, it was found that I have great talent for music, and am gifted with imagination. Afterwards it came out that I am fond of money ( ! ), a notable friend of order ( ? ), and take a great delight in children; but that in music I am especially strong. Well, that did not end it, for on Tuesday I was obliged to have my whole head done up in plaster, — skull, face, and belongings, — in order to make a mask ; and now I shall be able to sit in judgment on Hensel as a painter. "

Still more interesting is the account which we take from a letter of the 15th of May, touching a share which our young composer took in two entertainments given in the highest circles, to which unquestionably his fame and his distinguished bearing gave him entrance. Concerning the first of these he writes : " Monday evening, ball in Devonshire House, with the Duke of Devonshire; a splendor like that of stories of the East; everything that

wealth, luxury, and taste could invent, was to be seen
there.   I came in a carriage for a considerable distance,
but afterwards preferred to go on foot.    Entering the
hall, where the Duke received in a kindly way, I heard
people coming behind me on the staircase ; and, as soon
as I looked round, I perceived to my amazement that it
was Wellington and Peel.   In the chief audience-room,
instead of a chandelier, there was a broad, thick garland
of red roses ; it was some fourteen feet in diameter, and
seemed to swim in the air, so carefully concealed were
the delicate strands which held it.    Upon this garland
burned little candles by hundreds ; on the walls were portraits of life size, by Vandyke; and around the room,
close to the wall, a platform, on which the old ladies sat,
each overloaded with pearls and all kinds of jewels ; in
the middle the young girls danced, among whom I saw
heavenly figures ; the orchestra played ; the rooms adjoining were visible, their walls covered with Titians, Cor-
reggios, Leonardos, and pictures from the Netherlands.
On the floor, fair forms moved to and fro ; and I, meanwhile, quietly passed from place to place, unknown and
unmarked, able to see and enjoy all, — it was one of the
pleasantest evenings that I ever had in my life."

A no less interesting picture does he give us of a great
entertainment at the palace of the Marquis of Lands-
downe, in which a special point was made of paintings and
antiques : " The poor man had opened his hall of antiqui-
ties, and received there.   A great arched room, at whose
extremities are two platforms, and two rotundas lighted
from above ; in the rotundas purple niches, in every one
of which stood a grey antique statue, in a threatening atti-
tude.   At the feet of these the old ladies sat in a half-
circle, while in the middle of the hall the people crushed

hither and thither.   In the adjoining room a newly-pur-
chased landscape by Claude Lorraine was set up, a " Sun-
rise over a Harbor."   The staircase is so placed, that,
as in the Hamburgh houses, one can look up and see the
roof; and this staircase was thickly beset with flowers,
from which lying or sleeping statues peeped forth.    I
had not believed it possible that such beauty exists in our
time.   These entertainments cannot be called ' parties ; '
they are high festivals and solemnities."

We now turn our glance to Mendelssohn's activity in
London.

It has already been remarked that Moscheles had called
the attention of the Philharmonic Society to the extraordinary talents of his young friend.   Mendelssohn must now
play at one of the last concerts of the season, on the 30th
of May, in the Argyle Rooms, his first appearance in
London.   There should be given under his direction one
of his earlier symphonies (C-minor or D-major), and he
himself must personally play Weber's " Concertstück."

What he says about a rehearsal for this concert in a
letter of May 26 is too interesting and too characteristic
to be passed over in my account.   " As I entered the
Argyle Rooms for the rehearsal of my symphony,
and found the whole orchestra assembled, and about
two hundred spectators, mostly ladies, but all strangers
to me, and as they were then playing Mozart's ' Symphony' in E-flat, and were afterwards to take up mine,
I began to be, not anxious, indeed, but much excited
and strained ; so, while the Mozart music was playing,
I walked a little on Regent Street, and looked at the
people, and then when I returned everything was ready
and waiting for me.   I mounted to the orchestra, drew
my white baton out of my pocket (one which I had

had made expressly for me, — the man who made it
thought I was an alderman, and wanted to put a crown
on it), and the first violin, F. R. Cramer, showed me
how the orchestra was arranged, that the farthest must
stand up in order that I could see them. After he
had introduced me to them, and we had bowed, some
laughed a bit that such a little fellow should take
the place of their powdered and peruked conductor.
[Mendelssohn directed from an elevated desk, and not
from the place of the first violin, then a novelty in
London.] Then we began ; it went very well for the
first time, and pleased the people, even in the rehearsal.
After every piece the whole public applauded, and the
whole orchestra (the violins beating their instruments
with their bows and the others stamping with their
feet), after every movement. After the close there was
immense enthusiasm, and as at the conclusion there had
to be a repetition, because it had gone poorly, they
made the same demonstrations again. The directors
came to me at the orchestra, and I had to go down
and make no end of bows. Cramer was delighted,
and overwhelmed me with praise and compliments. I
made the round of the orchestra, and had to shake hands
with two hundred people. It was one of the happiest
moments of my whole experience, for in a half an hour
all those strangers had been transformed to acquaintances
and friends."

Respecting the concert, Mendelssohn adds : " The
success of last evening's concert was greater than I
had permitted myself to dream. They began with the
symphony ; then old Mr. Cramer led me to the piano
like a young lady, and I was received with loud
and long-continued applause. They wanted the adagio

again, but I preferred to thank them and go on, for
fear of being tedious; but the scherzo was demanded
so vehemently again, that I had to repeat it, and at its
close they applauded continuously, and kept it up,
applauding and shaking hands until I left the building."

The "Times" thus reports this first appearance of
Mendelssohn in its number of June 1. "The Sunday's
programme announced Mr. F. Mendelssohn's first public
appearance in London. This young professor is, we
believe, a grandson or nephew of the celebrated Jewish
philosopher, Moses Mendelssohn, and has gained distinguished reputation in Germany, not only as a pianist,
but as a composer. On Saturday he brought out a
'Fantasie,' a composition by Carl Maria Von Weber."
(The "Times" doubtless refers to the well-known
"Concertstück.")

A most touching letter of Fanny's, dated Berlin, June
4, and written to Klingemann, tells us of the joy of the
Mendelssohn family when Felix' great success was first
announced. And Mendelssohn himself, in an exceedingly bright and entertaining letter, written June 7,
gives an account of his part in this concert, as well as
an excursion in the country as far as Richmond, which
he made partly on foot, for his refreshment. At the
close of this letter he mentions a strange task which
had been laid upon him, and about which he had
laughed in his sleeve for two days. At the request of
Sir Alexander Johnston, Governor of the Island of
Ceylon, he was to compose a song, with which the
natives were to celebrate the day of their emancipation.
Mendelssohn found this so comical an undertaking that
he made himself merry over it, as over the unicorn, of
which only one of its kind in London is possible.

Mendelssohn won a still more eminent success at his second appearance in the Argyle Rooms at the concert of the celebrated flutist, Drouet, on the 24th of June, in which Garcia and other celebrated singers took part. Mendelssohn played the E-flat major concerto by Beethoven, whose performance had been regarded by English masters as an impossibility. He gained immense applause by his playing, but still more by his overture to the "Midsummer Night's Dream," which he produced for the first time in London, and whose direction he himself assumed. It was received with a stormy *da capo*. This overture made again the initial for a concert given in aid of the Silesians who had been injured by inundation. This concert was given on the 13th of July, in the Argyle Rooms, and mainly at the instigation of Mendelssohn. Sonntag was the leading performer, but Moscheles and Mendelssohn took part in it, playing a concerto of the former, in E-major, for two pianos. The first conception of this benefit concert sprang from a letter of Nathan Mendelssohn, the youngest brother of Abraham, who lived in Silesia, and who had communicated to his brother tidings of the great misfortune of his fellow-countrymen. Felix grasped the idea with much fire, and won over Madame Sonntag, who had already expressed a willingness to sing for the benefit of the Dantzic people, upon whom a similar misfortune had fallen. But she had now lost her interest in the affair, and it required great effort on Mendelssohn's part, and even some diplomacy, to secure this end. The other musicians laid difficulties in the way; they prophesied, in consequence of the advanced summer, an empty hall; they called attention to the cost of the undertaking, and the impossibility of covering it; but, after the reception of a letter from his father, containing a copy of his uncle's communication, he determined that it should and must succeed. "The concert must be given," he says, in a letter to his uncle Nathan, dated July 16. As soon as it was announced, a multitude of distinguished personages, among them the dukes of Clarence and Kent, Prince Leopold of Saxe-Coburg, princes Esterhazy and Polignac, promised their patronage. All the distinguished singers in London were drafted into the enterprise, and induced to sing without pay. Many instrumentalists pledged themselves to Sonntag, and there was no name of brilliance which was wanting for the programme. All at once the thing became fashionable; and from this moment its success was certain. Extremely interesting is what Mendelssohn writes in a letter to the family in Berlin, about the first rehearsal and the playing of Moscheles' double concerto in E : " Yesterday we had the first rehearsal in Clementi's factory. Madame Moscheles and Mr. Collard were present as listeners, and I amused myself immensely, for the people had no conception of our musical nonsense, and how we took one another off. Moscheles played the last piece with immense brilliancy; he just shook the runs out of his sleeves. When it was through, they all thought it was a pity that we had no cadenza, and so I hit upon a place for one in the last *tutti* of the first part, where the orchestra has a *fermate*. Moscheles must, *nolens volens*, compose a great cadenza. We had no end of nonsense to-day, whether the last little solo should remain, because the people would be still applauding. ' We want a bit of *tutti* between the cadenza and the final solo,' said I. ' How long then will they applaud?' asked Moscheles. ' Ten minutes, I dare say,' I replied. Moscheles bargained it down to five. I promised to furnish the *tutti*; and so we have regularly gone to work to cut out, hem, embroider, pleat, put in marmaluke-sleeves, and tailor up a brilliant concert. To-day is rehearsal again, and that will be a picnic, for Moscheles brings his cadenza, and I my *tutti*."

Respecting the concert itself, Felix writes to his uncle Nathan: "As I stood, before the beginning of the concert last Monday, in front of the Argyle Rooms (which the owners gave without charge), and saw the multitude streaming in, and as then, soon afterward, I entered the orchestra, and saw it filled with elegant ladies, all the loges occupied, even the ante-rooms crowded, I became indescribably merry, and it seemed to me a pity that there is no better concert room here, and that so many must be turned away. We received between two hundred and fifty and three hundred guineas, which I have placed in the hands of the Prussian Embassy, and which will be sent to Silesia."

Very entertaining, too, is what Mendelssohn remarks upon certain passages printed on the back of the programme; how Sonntag had received applications from distinguished personages in her own country, that the King of Prussia had personally asked her to sing; communications respecting the ravages of the inundation, translated into English from the personal observations of eye-witnesses; all these things really could be traced back to the simple letter which uncle Nathan had sent. Then he goes on to say: "The concert was unquestionably the best of the whole year. There was no time for an aria; the multitude of singers could only be employed in quartets and the like, and yet the whole lasted nearly four hours. Sonntag sang six times; Drouet played the flute, and Moscheles gave a concerto of my composition with me on two pianos; there was my overture to 'Midsummer Night's Dream,' etc., etc. Well, enough of this; the best is that it has gone by, and has been a success."

The 17th of July in the same year brings us an exceedingly amusing sketch. To the family in Berlin he writes: "The concert for the Silesians was magnificent, the best of the season. Ladies were even scattered around among the double basses. When I came into the orchestra, the Johnston ladies, who had a place between the bassoon and the bass horn, asked me if it were a *good place to hear*. One lady sat upon the kettle-drum, Madame Rothschild and another distinguished lady camped upon benches in the ante-chamber; in fact, the whole affair was extremely brilliant."

After these musical achievements, our young hero well deserved time for rest and refreshment. He found this in a journey by way of Edinburgh and the Scottish islands, as far as the Hebrides. On this journey he caught the impulse which gave rise to several of his most important works, especially to the so-called "Scotch," or "A-minor Symphony;" the "Overture to Fingal's Cave," or "The Hebrides;" and the "Reformation Symphony." In the last week of July he set out, going with his Pylades, Klingemann, from London to Edinburgh. This city, with its beautiful and open situation, clear, although sharp air, and grand environment, the view towards the blue sea, immeasurably broad, covered with white sails, and dotted with black steamers and craft of all kinds, pleased him extremely. "How shall I describe it to you? When God himself takes to panorama painting, the result is something immense. Few Swiss experiences can make the impression this does, all is so strong and serious here. To-morrow there is a contest of the highlanders on the bagpipe; they have already come, bringing, like warriors, each his beautiful girl upon his arm; and they have a stately look as they march around, with their long red beards, their motley mantles, and plumed hats, their naked knees, and their bagpipes in their hands. Their course takes them before the half-ruined grey castle on the meadow, where Mary Stuart once lived in her splendor, and where she saw Rizzio slain. It seems to me that time passes very fast, when I see such a bit of the past brought so near the present."

The Scotch ladies interested and pleased him no less: " Time and space come to an end, and everything sweeps back to the refrain, ' How friendly the people, and how good is God in Edinburgh.' The Scottish ladies are well worth notice; and, if Mahmoud follows father's counsel, and becomes a Christian, I will become Turk, in his place, and settle down here."

Very weighty, in its relation to the development of Mendelssohn's genius, is what he writes at the close of his last letter from the Scottish capital, on the evening before his journey from there, July 30. " We went, in the deep twilight, to the palace of Holyrood, where Queen Mary lived and loved. There is a little room to be seen there, with a winding staircase leading up to it. This the murderers ascended, and finding Rizzio in a little room, drew him out; and three chambers away is a small corner where they killed him. The roof is wanting to the chapel, grass and ivy grow abundantly in it; and before the altar, now in ruins, Mary was crowned Queen of Scotland.

Everything there is in fragments; and, in the dampness and under the open sky, I believe I have to-day hit upon the beginning of my Scotch symphony. "

We have here, then, a key to the comprehension of this most important of Mendelssohn's pure instrumental compositions; we discover the meaning of its earnest and serious character, which continues even to the last thirty or forty measures of the last movement. There is a struggle of elemental human passion, the tragedy of life, in this symphony. There is a vein of saddest melancholy, although in the closing passage the sun of peace does break through. Yet it was only the germ which was planted on the occasion of that visit to the old half-ruined palace. Mendelssohn carried it round with him for many years, and it was completed only in Berlin. The symphony was given for the first time in Leipsic, on the 13th of March, 1842, at the nineteenth Gewandhaus concert, was repeated at the twentieth, and was given in London at the Philharmonic concert on the 13th of June of the same year. In both Leipsic and London the work was received with great applause.

From Edinburgh, the journey which was begun July 21st was continued by Stirling, Perth, Dunkeld, and the Cataracts, as far as Blair-Athol, from which they went by foot over the mountains to Inverary, Glencoe, and the slands of Staffa and Iona. Here they had to remain a few days, because Sir Alexander Johnston had given them a letter of introduction to Sir Walter Campbell, the lord of the last-mentioned island. From there they went up the Clyde to Glasgow, then to Ben and Loch Lomond and Loch Earn, Ben Vorlich, Loch Katrine, and then onward to Cumberland. Mendelssohn had also a letter of introduction to Sir Walter Scott, at Abbotsford; the

travelers did indeed see the great novelist, and spoke with
him for a moment; but he was just on the point of leaving the place.   Mendelssohn was very little edified with
this visit; and, after Klingemann had set it out in very
poetic fashion in a letter to the family in Berlin, Mendelssohn appended the following sarcastic words: " Here
Klingemann simply lies."

From Abbotsford the two friends went, as above narrated, to the Highlands as far as Blair-Athol.   They suffered much there from the unfavorable weather, yet retained their good spirits ; wherever they stopped, Mendelssohn drew, and Klingemann dictated verses for his drawings.   Mendelssohn writes from Blair-Athol, Aug. 3 :
" To-day is the most dreary kind of rain ; but we help
ourselves out, and so it goes well, but well is certainly
bad enough.   The whole earth is wet through, and regi-
ments of clouds are stalking through the sky.   Yesterday
was an extremely beautiful day : we went on foot to see
rocks and waterfalls and beautiful valleys, with their
rivers and dark woods, and the heath, with its red flower ;
we drove in the morning in an open single carriage, and
afterwards went on foot twenty-one English miles ; I
drew a great deal, and Klingemann hit upon the happy
thought that it would be very nice to append some lines
of doggerel to every sketch of mine, and we have kept
up doing this all Saturday and to-day.   It has turned out
splendidly ; he has made some wonderfully pretty things."

Mendelssohn pictures the scene graphically in a letter
written on the evening of the same day, and in a tavern
on the bridge at the Cataract: " The storm is howling ;
outside the house the winds whistle, the doors and the
window-shutters are rattling below ; whether the noise
comes from the rain or from the storm one cannot say,

because both are raging together. We are sitting here
quietly by the chimney-fire, which I fan and see it then
flash up ; as for the rest of the scene, the hall is large and
empty, and on one side you can see the moist drops run
down, "etc.

Mendelssohn read here Jean Paul's " Flegeljahre,"
which he had brought with him. In his copy of this
book Hensel had drawn for Mendelssohn portraits of
Fanny and Rebecca ; and Mendelssohn writes : " The
sisters look out from the pages at me strangely. Hensel
has a talent, he can see faces and he can fix them ; but
the weather is wretched. I have discovered a way to
sketch it, and have washed in the clouds and drawn the
grey mountains, and Klingemann puts verses underneath. "

The Hebrides formed the terminal point of the journey ;
or, rather, Staffa and Fingal's Cave. Mendelssohn wrote
regarding these on Aug. 7, 1829, to the sisters in Berlin :
" In order to show you what a strange sensation has come
to me on the Hebrides, I jotted down the following,
which came into my mind. " Then comes a wonderful
bit of score for violin, viola, double-bass, celli, trumpets,
and kettle-drums, the first great theme in B-minor, the
beginning of the subsequent " Hebrides " overture. Mendelssohn's most intimate friend, Ferdinand Hiller, who
lived with Mendelssohn in Paris from December, 1831,
to April, 1832, says of this : " Mendelssohn has brought
with him also the sketch score of the ' Hebrides ' overture. He told me how the thing came to him in its full
form and color on his view of Fingal's Cave, and he also
informed me how the first measures, containing the leading theme, had come to his mind. In the evening, he
with his friend Klingemann was making a visit with a

Scotch family.   In the salon stood a piano ; it was Sunday, and there was no possibility of having music.   He employed all his diplomacy to get at the instrument one moment, and then, having done so, dashed off the theme out of which the great work grew.   It was completed at Düsseldorf, but only after an interval of years. "

As an appendix to that bit of the score, Mendelssohn writes further, from Glasgow, August 11 : "All that lies between, — a most fearful seasickness, Staffa and its neighborhood, travels, men, — Klingemann has described ; and you must excuse me if I make my account brief.   The best thing which I have to communicate is in the lines of music above."   He writes from Glasgow, Aug. 13 : " Here, then, is the end of our journey to the Highlands, and the last of our double letters. We were very jolly together ; we have lived through many merry days, and we are as happy as if the storm and wind, of which the papers have doubtless told you, had never existed ; but we have had it, I assure you, weather that would break trees and crack rocks."

On Loch Lomond the travellers experienced a wind so boisterous that their little boat was in great danger of sinking, and Mendelssohn made himself ready to swim ; yet they came safely through, and reached a shelter for the night, although one very destitute of attractions. After a very lively picture of the ten days' wanderings, and of the quiet and solitude which they had gained for themselves by it, the letter closes : " No wonder that the Highlands are melancholy ; but, when two young fellows go through them as merrily as we did, laugh on the slightest occasion, and draw and poetize together, groan with one another and at the world, when they do not find anything to eat, and annihilate every eatable that they find, and sleep twelve hours a day, — why, that changes matters. It is an experience we shall never forget in our lives." What a charming picture of the genuine humor of travel!

After a rapid passage from Glasgow to Liverpool, the two friends separated, Klingemann going, on the evening of Aug. 19, back to London, Mendelssohn to Holywell. "The Scotch journey," Mendelsohn writes, "is over; it has passed very quickly, and we are all quiet again. We must now separate from each other, but we have a fine time to remember." He was prevented from going to Ireland, as he had proposed, by a severe rain-storm. In place of this journey he allowed himself to loiter about in England, although reproaching himself somewhat for his careless ease; yet he felt that many good things would come into his head, and that he should doubtless renew his love of composition if he allowed himself rest. He visited Chester, and then Holywell. Between these places he made the acquaintance in the post-chaise of a sturdy Englishman, by the name of Taylor, owner of several important mines in England, and a delightful residence, Coed-du, not far from Holywell. This gentleman invited Mendelssohn, without knowing more of him than his name, to visit him; and Mendelssohn complied. He drove on the next morning to Coed-du, but found only the mother and the daughters at home. The letters in which Mendelssohn communicated this first friendship to his sisters, in Berlin, and the later letters, in which he described a journey of several days through Wales, are among the most delightful which have come from his pen. Under date of Dec. 7, he writes: "My stay with the Taylors was one of those events which I shall never lose from memory; it will always be a flowery spot, a kind of oasis, with meadows and wild flowers and murmuring of brooks over the pebbles. We became real friends, I venture to think; at any rate, I acquired a great liking for the young ladies, and I think they liked me, too. We were extremely jolly together, and three of my very best piano pieces I owe to them."

He refers in this passage to the composition, for the eldest of the sisters, of an impromptu, suggested by a bouquet of pinks and roses; over the music he drew a graceful sketch of a nosegay. For the youngest daughter, who one day met him with her hair full of small, yellow, open flowers, and asserted that they were trumpets, he composed a dance, to which these yellow trumpets contributed their part; and to the middle one he dedicated a song called "The Brook," because, while they were riding together, a rivulet pleased them so much that they dismounted and sat by its side for a while. (Three caprices for pianoforte, Opus 16.) They were indeed beautifully bright days out of which these tender blossoms sprang. Even while visiting there, he busied himself with more serious compositions. "My violin quartet I shall soon send over to you finished; and, in order to complete my ' Reformation ' symphony, I recently went down five hundred feet under the earth; perhaps not without results." He refers to a visit to Mr. Taylor's mine, with perhaps an allusion to Luther, the miner's son.

" The ' Hebrides ' matter, " he also writes, " is also going on for the golden wedding [of his parents, to be celebrated Dec. 22]. I am brewing all kinds of liquors. " And, further on : " My quartet is in the middle of the last movement, and I think will soon be ready ; also the organ piece for the wedding [of his sister Fanny and Hensel], to occur Oct. 3. My 'Reformation' symphony I purpose to begin, if God will; and the Scotch symphony, and all the 'Hebrides' matter, is building itself up step by step. A lot of vocal music I have also in my head, but I cannot now tell you what and how." Mendelssohn doubtless refers in this to the vaudeville, the "Heimkehr aus der Fremde" which Klingemann wrote, and with which he meant to surprise his parents at their silver wedding. On Sept. 11 he writes regarding this: "To-day breakfasted with Klingemann; our idyllic vaudeville gets on famously, it begins to have some form and shape. I think it will come out handsomely, and you will be splendidly introduced, Hensel. Do not have any fears about the singing, that will all be cared for." [Hensel was so poor a singer that everything which was for him had to be written on one note; and yet Mendelssohn could not contain his laughter, because Hensel never hit this one note right.] Well, all this merry preparation for good times to come was through at last; and the good times came, but not without much hard discipline and trial, without which the life of no mortal is complete. He was beginning even now to long for his beloved ones in Berlin again. He hoped to be present at the wedding of his dear sister Fanny; when, on a drive with one of his London friends, he had the misfortune to be overturned in a gig, and so severely dashed to the earth that he received a serious injury in his knee. He was compelled to lie perfectly still a week; and he writes to his sister Fanny, Sept. 25: "My head is perfectly dead with this long lying in bed, and with this absence of thoughts." And it was only on the 6th of November that he began to take drives with Klingemann. During

the period of his confinement, he had to struggle with the
saddest thoughts.   He had his cloak and his cap, he tells
Devrient later, hung by his side, to be a kind of comfort
to him ; but he often doubted whether he should ever use
them again ; and, much as he loved London, the thought
of dying there was exceeding bitter to him.   His friend
Klingemann nursed him with touching devotion during
the whole time of his illness, and his young friends overwhelmed him with delicacies of every sort.   Even Goethe,
who learned of the accident from Zelter, expresses his
tender sympathy in a letter to the latter : " And now, I
wish to know whether you have favorable news respecting our good Felix.   I take the greatest interest in him ;
for it is extremely painful to see the life of an individual
of whom so much is expected, and who is making such
constant progress, brought into abeyance.   Tell me something comforting about him. "   Happily, Zelter was soon
able to comply with this request.   But very touching and
noble is the manner in which this young man of twenty
years communicates with his beloved sister, in a letter
dated Sept. 25 : " But it is even so ; and when one sees
how all the little things of life which one pictures to himself are annihilated by the reality itself, one stands before
the real crises of life in veneration and humility ; yet by
veneration I mean cheerful, joyful, and full of hope.
Live and labor, marry and be happy ; build up your life,
that I may find it fair and beautiful when I come to you,
and that will be soon ; only do you remain the same.
Then let it shake and rattle outside as it may ; for I know
you both, and I know you to be good.   Whether I call
my sister ' fräulein,' or ' madame,' signifies little ; the
name is nothing. "   Truly the words of a man rich in the
knowledge of life and thoroughly mature, the blessing
at once of a priest and a brother.

In order to perfect the restoration of his health, Mendelssohn spent some time in Norwood, Surrey, with his old friend. Attwood. In a sleeping apartment stood a music desk, in which he found laid away carefully some English compositions of varied character; but further research brought to light a precious treasure, the score of Von Weber's " Euryanthe, " in three stout volumes. He studied it with great delight, but he also found occasion to exercise his critical talent upon it. Yet he sums up with the words : " It is beautiful music, and it seems to me simply wonderful to find such a work here in England, where no one understands it or can understand it, where Von Weber was shamefully treated, and where he died. Imagine my feelings at having his darling work in my hands. I have also Cherubini's ' Requiem, ' and other things ; and so the time passes very agreeably."

Mendelssohn spent several delightful days in London, receiving all manner of attentions at the hands of his friends. " I can call the last fourteen days in London the happiest and the richest that I have ever enjoyed. "

He took great pleasure in communicating to his friend Horn all the great impressions which he had experienced in London. He was especially happy in the circle of German friends, Rosen, Mühlenfels, Klingemann, and Kind, whom every evening he assembled around him at his fire, and with whom he talked till the hours waxed late ; and so he could not end this fair period in England without a measure of grief, as, on the 29th of November, he stepped on French soil. A few days later he arrived at Berlin, rather strained, indeed, with the journey, and nervous, and walking with the aid of a stick, yet joyful to meet his friends once more, among whom were the newly married pair, and his friend Devrient with his new wife, all comfortably established in the Mendelssohn mansion.

He now entered on the rehearsals of the vaudeville already alluded to, and which was now complete, save the putting of the last touches to its instrumentation.  I am strongly tempted to enter on an analysis of this delightful and characteristic work, which was written for the entertainment of his father and mother on the occasion of their silver wedding.  It certainly is, youthful production though it be, and little known though it is, one of Mendelssohn's most characteristic works.  It was given with signal success, and to the delight of a large company of people.  It contains fourteen numbers, all different, and all full of Mendelssohn's youthful freshness.

Unexpected hindrances threatened to prevent its production at the only time when it was seasonable ; namely, the silver wedding already mentioned.  The rehearsals were completed, and everything was entirely ready, when Devrient was ordered to be present at the palace of the Crown Prince, to sing at a concert given there.  Mendelssohn was so excited at this interruption to their plans that he began to talk English, and kept it up incessantly.  His father ordered him to bed instantly, and a good night's sleep of twelve hours restored him.  Happily, the court manager of festivities, Count von Raedern, was able to arrange affairs so that Devrient's duties at the palace were abbreviated, and he was able to take his part in the vaudeville.  I must mention, incidentally, the fact that Hensel, whose ear was notoriously bad, could not strike the "F" written for him, although prompted on every side.  This made, perhaps, the greatest fun of anything that occurred during the evening.  Mendelssohn was actually obliged to bend down over his manuscript, in order to conceal his laughter. But what was the most surprising thing was the dramatic talent revealed in the work. Mendelssohn was pressed to allow it to appear on the public stage, and even his mother desired it greatly; but he refused. It seemed to him a violation of filial piety, to give to the public what was intended simply for his parents and the circle of their nearest and dearest friends. Through his whole life it was withheld from a larger audience; but, after his death, this could no longer be. I was present, some years subsequently to his decease, at a representation of the vaudeville in a private circle in Leipsic, in which the duty was confined to me of reading the connecting text. But the whole beauty of the work was revealed when it was presented in the Leipsic Theatre, Nov. 4, 1883, on the anniversary of Mendelssohn's death. The programme consisted of this vaudeville and the overture to the "Hebrides," the "Walpurgis Night," and the *finale* from the uncompleted opera "Lorelei," all splendidly given. I must say I was completely swept away by the beautiful instrumentation, the charming themes, the dramatic life and individuality of a composition written by our dear composer while even in his youth; it showed us how much the more it is to be regretted, that, although Mendelssohn was incited to it on all sides, he never composed an opera; indeed, he never found any text that entirely suited him. Perhaps he was too exacting in his demands. His friend Devrient, who had given to Märschner " Hans Heiling," and to Thalberg " The Gipsies," could not satisfy Mendelssohn; and Karl von Holtei, with whom he once entered into negotiations respecting the text of an opera, once said, correctly: " Mendelssohn will never find an opera text that suits

him ; he is altogether too clever for that." Mendelssohn's
father once said, half in sport, half in earnest, "I am
afraid Mendelssohn will be as unfortunate in finding a
wife as he is in finding the text of an opera." This
fear, however, was happily never realized ; although the
father did not live to see the happy marriage of his son.
It is to be called an even tragic fate, that, after Von
Geibel, the most prominent poet of the time, had furnished him with the beautiful text of the "Lorelei,"
Mendelssohn's premature death prevented him from
writing more than the fragment already mentioned ; but
that fragment is an earnest of what the work would have
been.

Of the mutual family life of the Mendelssohns, the
Hensels, and Devrients, during the winter of 1829–30,
in which, of course, music played a leading part, there
is, with the exception of some songs, nothing to mention
save the completed piano score of the vaudeville, which
he wrote out with his own hand, and gave to Therese
Devrient to be her exclusive property, and the partial
completion of the above-mentioned "Reformation"
symphony, which he produced in all its parts at once,
letting it flow from his mind as a molten stream of
metal flows into the mold. Yet he declared this kind
of work altogether too severe to be continued for any
length of time. It must be mentioned, as a circumstance
of importance, that, at the beginning of the year 1830,
Mendelssohn was elected Professor of Music in the
University of Berlin. He declined the honor, however,
and directed the choice to his friend Marx, who accepted
it. I myself can speak from personal recollection of the
practice in music under this gifted man, who, although
not popular at the outset, nevertheless by his diligence

and skill at last succeeded in drawing together a large number of students.

The year 1830 may be indicated as the epoch on which, in the fullest sense of the word, Mendelssohn entered upon his grand career. It was the commencement of his wide and important travels by way of Weimar, Munich, Salzburg, Vienna, Gratz, and Klagenfurt to Venice, and thence onward to Bologna, Florence, and Rome, where he made a protracted stay, ending with Naples. He then turned back by way of Lago Maggiore, through Switzerland and by way of Munich, Paris forming the terminal point of the long journey. The day of his departure had been fixed in March, when an unexpected hindrance intervened, through the illness of his sister Rebecca, who was seized with measles. The physician ordered her to be completely separated from the rest of the family. Felix was inconsolable at this separation; he wept and moaned like a child, and, indeed, despaired of ever seeing his sister again, anticipating, in the event of his departure, the worst possible consequences; but the next day the physician brought a report, which Mendelssohn announced to his friend Devrient with a kind of desperate cheerfulness: " I have the comfort of knowing that in a few days I shall have the measles too. Do not come to see me, therefore; but, as Hensel would say, ' *Noli me tangere.* ' " So the pain of parting was postponed for the present; and there followed an active interchange of letters between the two friends, which they flung at each other across the court. Mendelssohn wrote, for example, among other things, in his overflowing cheerfulness: " I have burned and torn to pieces what I have written down to now, but the rest can remain alive; namely, How beautiful God's world is! Write to me very soon. I have been trying to play the first *étude* of Cramer, with my hands crossed. I am now practising on the flute the 'Institution of the Lord's Supper,' from Bach's 'Passion.' I am working very moderately, like a Kapellmaster, for all the world. Do you know when Easter comes? Is it Sunday or is it Monday? For, if you believe you are going away before I do, you are immensely mistaken. We shall probably go at the same time, but alas! in various directions. I see there is nothing sensible growing out of this letter, and so I will close; but tomorrow perhaps you shall have more. Your (with my own hand) Felix Mendelssohn Bartholdy. "

By the middle of May both brother and sister were completely restored, and Felix could enter on his journey in perfect health; but I must mention a little circumstance communicated to us by his friend Devrient, touching his departure, which gives a glimpse into the extreme tenderness and affection of his nature. "The parting was not easy to either of us, but Felix' gentle soul was the more moved of the two. As I said 'good-by,' and he had conducted me to the staircase leading to the court, I, who do not like embraces among men when they part, was simply shaking hands with him; he started to go, when, turning abruptly round, his countenance full of expression, and with tears in his eyes, he said: 'I think you might at least give me an embrace.' This, of course, I did with a full heart; and so the dear young man went his way. "

It cannot, of course, be my object to follow the gentle artist step by step on his future wanderings. The first volume of Mendelssohn's letters, published by his brother Paul, in Berlin, 1861, and now in the hands of all the admirers of Mendelssohn, gives us so perfect a picture of his inner life, that it would be a thankless task to make any extracts from it.   But I must cite what Goethe writes to Zelter under date March 31, 1821 : " Before mentioning anything else, I have to announce that I have received a most precious and long letter from Felix, dated Rome, March 5, which gives me a perfect view of the life of this admirable young man.   For him now there is no need to fear that he will not break through all the waves and all the flames which barbarism may put in his path."   I shall strive in this account merely to indicate the important features of these years of travel, in so far as they contribute to make a picture of the collective life and work of the artist; of course, what I do must remain a mere outline sketch.   The first pause of the journey was at Weimar, whither Mendelssohn went with extra post, on the 19th and 20th of May.   He was received in the most friendly manner in Goethe's house, where he was compelled to make a long stay, protracting his visit to a full fortnight, and receiving a genuine artist's consecration before taking his flight to the land " *wo die Citronen blühn.*"   He gives us in the three first letters an extremely entertaining and interesting account of his visit with this great poet, and with the lovely ladies, who formed, as it were, his court.   He was with Goethe almost daily, dined and supped with him constantly ; had to tell him about Scotland, Hengstenberg, Spontini, and Hegel's " Esthetics ; " had to play a great deal to him, among other things the " Three Caprices, " already mentioned, which he had written in honor of the three pretty young girls in Coed-du (Opus 16 in his " Works").   The latter gave great pleasure.   He was also enabled to give Goethe a conception of the gradual development of music, as revealed in its various epochs.   Very interesting is what

Mendelssohn tells us, how Beethoven affected Goethe. He writes, in his second letter: "At first he did not care to hear Beethoven; but I said to him that I could not share that feeling, and played to him the first movement of the C-minor symphony: that moved him powerfully. His first exclamation was, 'I do not call this being simply touched, I call it being amazed. It is immense.' Then he began to mutter to himself, and finally, after a long time, broke out: 'That is simply immense. Why, I should almost be afraid the house would fall in; and what would come, if a number of men should play it together?' At the table, when we were talking of other things, he would break out in the same vein."

Goethe thanked him in the most lively manner for his efforts to make him at home in the realm of music. He gave the leading painter of Weimar a commission to paint Mendelssohn's portrait for him, for which he had to sit several times; and he gave to the young artist a sheet of his manuscript of "Faust," written underneath, with his own hand, "To my dear young friend, F. M. B., the strong yet delicate master of the piano, in grateful remembrance of pleasant May days, 1830. J. W. von Goethe." He gave him, besides, three letters of introduction to friends in Munich, and begged him to write to him from time to time. Mendelssohn did so, sending his first letter from Munich. On the day of his departure from Weimar, June 3, Goethe wrote to Zelter: "At this very moment, ten o'clock in the morning, under the clearest sky and the bright air, our dear Felix is departing with Ottilie, Ulrika, and the children, having spent fourteen delightful days in the practice of his charming art. He goes to Jena, in order to delight our friends who are there, and to leave there,

too, a recollection which cannot fade. I have greatly
enjoyed his presence with me, for I have discovered
that I have not lost my relations to music; I hear it
still with pleasure and sympathy. I love to trace its
history, for who can understand anything without knowing its origin and history? Felix has the happiest
conception of this gradual progress in his art, and a
wonderful memory of the pieces in which he shows the
growth of music. Beginning with the time of Bach, he
has brought before me Gluck, Haydn, and Mozart; he
has given me a definite sense of the great masters of
*technique* of our time, and enabled me to feel the
worth of his own productions; and so he has gone from
me with my best blessing. Say all manner of good
things to the worthy parents of this extraordinary young
artist."

From this time on, Goethe and Mendelssohn stood
in uninterrupted correspondence till the death of the
former; and he took the greatest interest in the charming and affectionate and extremely interesting letters
which his young friend sent him. On the 4th of
January, 1831, he thus writes to Zelter: "Felix, whose
happy stay in Rome you announced to me, must everywhere be received most cordially. A talent so great,
connected with a nature so buoyant and tenderly affectionate!"

I ought not to pass over Mendelssohn's stay in Weimar,
without mentioning that, on the 25th of May, he promises
his sister Fanny to send her very soon a copy of the
symphony which he had prepared there, and which
would soon be publicly given in Leipsic. He charged
her with collecting opinions respecting the title it should
bear; whether it should be called the Reformation

symphony, the Confession symphony, a symphony for a
Church Festival, etc.    It is the well-known "Reformation" symphony, already alluded to.    Whether it was
subsequently given in Leipsic is unknown to me; at any
rate, it is not one of Mendelssohn's most important
works.    I heard it two years ago, in Leipsic, but I
cannot say that it made any remarkable impression upon
me.    The song, "Eine feste Burg ist unser Gott," set
in the upper register of the wind instruments, is indeed
carried out with great contrapuntal skill, but it cannot
be said to be very striking.    The work lacks movement,
and, without injuring Mendelssohn's reputation, it may
well fall into oblivion.

From Jena, Mendelssohn traversed the Thuringian
principalities, whose various kinds of money and tedious
post-carriages caused him much annoyance; and, travers-
ing Coburg and Nuremburg, came to Munich, the second
great station of his journey.    He does not appear to
have stopped in Nuremburg at all; for Goethe writes
about Mendelssohn's departure from Weimar on the 3d
of June.

On the 6th of June, Mendelssohn writes from Munich
to his friends in Berlin, that, although arriving almost
dead with fatigue, he thought it his duty to go at once
and see "Fidelio," about which he reports in full.    His
stay in Munich lasted several weeks; for we find that
Linz was the next station, and that he writes from there
Aug. 11.    No wonder that Munich attracted him, with
its South German life, finding as he did there every sort
of musical interest, and love and honor on all sides, such
as he had scarcely dreamed of before.    His friend Marx,
who met him there, probably not casually, tells us, in
an exceedingly interesting and attractive letter written to

Fanny, how delightfully Felix' Munich life was passing.
I cannot refrain from inserting a characteristic passage
of some length taken from this letter : —

" What we have thus far done and are doing is quickly
said, We reign.   I have issued my edict that I am to be
his viceroy, and I have received homage without any
change of countenance. . . . In all seriousness, you can
get no conception of Felix' position here, he cannot
write the hundredth part ; and I, with the best intentions,
cannot either.   Of course, we have presupposed that his
musical talent would have recognition here ; but now he
might play the poorest music in the world, and everybody would fall into raptures.   He is treated as a
favorite child is in a house ; he is just the centre of
every circle ; from early morning everything revolves
around him.   Yesterday, for example, I was writing,
and Felix was asleep ; and there comes a billet from a
certain Betty whom I know, written in the tenderest
tone, and asking that Felix would come, not to dine at
3 o'clock, but at 12 o'clock, or in the afternoon, or in
the morning ; whenever he came he would be welcome,
etc.   Then the door opens again, and now enters a
messenger from a Count Krotzchy (or Krotzschi, or
something of that sort, only no reasonable man), and he
brings a bouquet of violets from Fräulein So-and-so ;
who is followed by the first piano teacher of Munich,
who would like to take a lesson, — has given up his own,
so long as Felix is here ; then the compliments of
Peppi Lang (oh, how much I have to tell you about her,
a girl not yet 16 years old), and she ventures to request
that he will not take it ill if she sends him a little token
of remembrance (eight charming songs).   Fräulein
Delphine Schauroth (at least sixteen) has composed for

him during the night a ' Song without Words,' and begs
to ask that she may come to see him, not at half-past
ten, but, if possible, even earlier; and so Count Witt-
genstein must cool his feet on the pavement waiting
for half an hour. Counsellor Maurer, Kapell Master
Stuntz, Maureth, and others, appear, not to mention
the dryer visits and engagements; for example, ' Mr.
Von Staudacher, with whom Mr. Mendelssohn has
already promised to dine, and he ventures to hope,' etc.,
etc. Then comes Bärman, with a confidential note that
Staudacher's people have arranged for two entertainments in order to please him. You will consider this
really imperfect list as mere fun on my part, but I tell
you it is the jolly truth."

It is hard to break off from the delineation of this
delightful passage in Mendelssohn's life, full of affection
coming in to him from all sides. It is a striking commentary on what I have already said respecting the
charm of his personality. Marx adds: " Who can set
down all the details, the thousand leaves that refuse to
be counted on the tree of joy and love? Only in the
grand whole can it be seen how the universal interest in
Mendelssohn appears in the smallest boughs and shoots
of that tree."

Mendelssohn appears to have entered into relations
of peculiar intimacy with the two young ladies whom
Marx mentions in his letter, Delphine Von Schauroth,
and Josephine Lang, generally known as Peppi. Fräulein Delphine was of noble birth, and a very accomplished pianist. Mendelssohn himself writes about her
in a letter to Fanny, dated June 11, 1830, — a letter
full of brotherly tenderness and respect. " Yesterday,
grand *soiree* at P. Kerstor's; ministers of state and

counts ran to and fro in it like the hens in a farm-yard. Artists, too, and other people of culture. Delphine Von Schauroth, who is adored by every one here, and rightly, received the attentions of every class. In the first place, her mother is a baroness, and she is an artist, and thoroughly educated, too; in fact, I just lay at her feet. We played a four-handed sonata of Hümmels, with universal applause; to which I gave in and laughed and clapped also, and touched for her the A-flat key at the beginning of the last movement, because her hand was too small to reach it; till at last the mistress of the house called us away, and sat us down side by side, and made them drink our healths. But really, what I want to say is this, that the girl plays extremely well; and the day before yesterday we performed together for the first time, and she made a very strong impression upon me. When I was hearing her yesterday morning, and was in amazement at her playing, all at once it occurred to me that in our house at Berlin, in the rear part of the same, there is a young lady who has certain ideas of music in her head, as many, in fact, as a good many other heads taken together; and I thought that I would send her a letter, and I would even go so far as to enclose my love. Well, you are the lady; and I say to you, Fanny, that at certain passages I could only think of you; for I must be honest, although down here in South Germany lying is very much the fashion. You are one of those who know what God must have thought within himself when he invented music: no wonder that people are delighted with it. And you can play the piano, too; and, if you want a greater admirer than I am, you can paint him, or you can get somebody to paint him." [An evident allusion to her husband, the painter Hensel.]

This outburst of brotherly tenderness and devotion gives us a most charming proof how little Mendelssohn's recognition of talent in others could extinguish his fond memory of his sister. We have also, in proof of this, two other letters from Munich, one dated June 14, containing a " Song without Words," not to be found in his collection of songs without words, and of which I must say, not to be compared with the published collections; the second dated June 26, also to Fanny, containing his congratulations on the birth of her first son ; and as a musical expression of it, a tolerably long " Song without Words," in B-minor. It appeared later, somewhat changed, as No. 2 in the second group of those songs. Of this one Mendelssohn says: " If you do not like it, I cannot help it; it came to me so, as I received your letter, half anxious, half joyful." And I must confess that the impression that this song makes is indeed one more of care and anxiety, than hearty joy at the news of the good fortune of his beloved sister.

On the 27th of this month we have another letter, in which Mendelssohn again comes back to Delphine Von Schauroth : " As for me, I go day by day to the Gallery, and twice in the week to Fräulein Von Schauroth, where I make long visits. " Whether, as the story of the time went, he wrote for her the beautiful song (Opus 19, No. 6), " Bringet des treuesten Herzens Grüsse, " which he composed in Venice, I leave undetermined ; but he certainly paid her homage real and earnest in dedicating to her the pearl of his concertos, the G-minor concerto for orchestra and piano, that true type of Mendelssohn's grace, imagination, and fire. He had, if I may anticipate a little, begun this composition in 1831, while on his journey, and probably in Rome. On the return he brought it with him, and it was first played in Munich Oct. 17, in a concert given for the poor. The hall was crowded, there being eleven hundred present, and the applause most lively. He took it with him to Paris in December of the same year, where it was splendidly played by Franz Liszt at the house of Erard. In April, 1832, he showed it to his friend Moscheles, in London, and he himself played it twice there with the greatest success, May 28 and June 18. In Leipsic Mendelssohn made his debut as solo player, with orchestra, Oct. 29, 1835, and on this occasion gave this concerto. It was afterwards repeatedly given by him, as well as by other artists; and finally, to crown all, it was played by Delphine Von Schauroth, to whom it had been dedicated, Feb. 4, 1870, on the hundredth anniversary of the dedication of the Gewandhaus. What recollections must have pressed through the heart of the aged *artiste* on this occasion!

But Mendelssohn seems to have taken a still deeper interest in Josephine Lang, a lady then very young, who had already exhibited remarkable talents as singer and composer. We have already called attention to her in Marx' letter; but the interest which Mendelssohn felt in her appears still more marked in a letter written Oct. 6, 1831, on his second visit to Munich, while on the return from Italy. This is one of the finest which have come from Mendelssohn's hand. After speaking, in the opening, of his great comfort and contentment in the city, of the preparations made for the concert in behalf of the poor, to be given by him, the first part of which was to begin with the C-minor symphony, and to close with his G-minor concerto, and whose second part should begin with the "Midsummer Night's Dream" overture, and end with a free improvisation by Mendelssohn, he goes on to speak of the great pleasure that he had taken at a private concert in his own house, and one also given by the Queen.   Then he comes to Josephine Lang (it is obvious he alludes to her, and to her only, by the letter L).   " I have forgotten to add that every day at 12 o'clock I give a lesson to the little L. in double counterpoint, four-voice composition, and the like; and I see very clearly how stupid and confused most of our books and instructions are in these matters, and how very clear the thing is when it is plainly taught. . . . She is one of the dearest creatures whom I have ever seen.   Imagine to yourself a gentle, small, pale girl, with noble but not handsome features, so interesting and so piquant that one can hardly look away from her, all her motions, and every word, full of ease and freedom.   She has a gift of composing songs, and of singing them, too, such as I have never heard before.   It is the most complete delight which it has been my lot yet to enjoy.   When she takes her place at the piano and begins to sing, the tones are different from all others; the whole music has a movement all its own, and in every note there is the deepest and finest feeling.   When she strikes the first note with her gentle voice, every one is still and is held powerless and motionless as she sings.   If you could only hear her voice, so innocent, so free from self-consciousness, the outflow of her inmost soul, and yet such perfect quiet!   Last year, when I saw her, she had even then all the gifts of an artist, and she had written no song in which you could not distinctly see the traces of talent.   M. [probably Marx] and I were making a good deal of a stir among musicians at that time; but no one would believe that such gifts lay concealed in her.   Since then she has made very great progress.   Whoever does not feel the

power of her songs now, all I can say is, he has no feeling.   Perhaps I will send you soon, dear sisters, some of
her songs, which she has written out of gratitude to me ;
she claims that I teach her what really she receives from
nature alone. "

The warm interest which Mendelssohn felt for this
gifted and gentle being, and which is manifested in
this lovely manner, he cherished for many years, perhaps even to the end of his life.   Towards the close of
1841, Josephine was engaged to Professor Köstlin, in
Tubingen.   He received the news of her engagement
accidentally, while attending a concert in Berlin.   He
sent his congratulations to the professor, in a very hearty
letter dated Dec. 15, 1841, full of impassioned language
about two groups of songs which Josephine had sent him
six months before, and for which he, " the most wretched
of letter-writers, " had never yet expressed his thanks.
He further laid upon the young husband the following
injunctions :  " In God's name, keep her to composition ;
it is really what she owes to us all, who are continually
on the search for something new and good.   She sent
me once a collection of various composers, and at the
same time a few things of her own, and wrote deprecat-
ing comparisons between hers and those great master-
works.   Oh, Gemini !  Those great master-works and
those illustrious names do look rather small by the side
of this bright, fresh music.   Well, all is, keep her to
composition ;  keep her to composition.   And if I have
anything yet to add, it is, carry the joy of your engagement over into the years of your wedded life.   That is,
I wish for you what I have for myself, and for which I
cannot enough thank God day by day."

I do not know whether Professor Köstlin followed this

injunction, and whether the final wish was ever carried out to the full ; but, from a second delightful letter of Mendelssohn to him, dated Leipsic, Jan. 12, 1843, we learn that Felix was chosen as godfather for the first-born child, and that he accepted the honor with very great delight, although at that very time he was in the heavy sorrow occasioned by the loss of his own mother.

In connection with Mendelssohn's first stay in Munich, we must not fail to allude to his presence at Ober Ammergau, on the occasion of the " Passion Play. " This Edward Devrient describes in a communication dated July 25, 1830. What impression this simple and effective portraiture of the sufferings and resurrection of Christ, as given amid the striking scenery of Bavaria, and by the modest country people, had upon Mendelssohn himself, unfortunately we do not know ; certainly, the man who had been foremost in bringing Bach's Passion music to the knowledge of the public, could not remain unmoved by such an event.

From Munich he went to Salzburg, thence to Ischl, and across the Lake of Traun to Linz, and from there direct to Vienna. Respecting this portion of the journey we have very little information. No one of the works which we possess tells us anything concerning his stay in Vienna. We have a few letters of Devrient written thence, and a letter from Venice to Zelter, No. 38 in the collection of Mendelssohn's letters from Italy and Switzerland ; but this gives us little idea of his journey. The letter from Linz to his mother, beginning with the words, " How the travelling musician had his dark day in Salzburg : A fragment from the unwritten diary of Count F. M. B., " pictures, in his characteristic humor, his ill fortune with certain drawings which he had intended for her, but afterwards destroyed.  Then he describes being caught in the rain on the Capuchin Mountain; a projected visit to the convent at the foot, which had to be given up on account of the want of small change; and also all kinds of minor hindrances in the Custom House, postal and passport matters, as was then too often the case in Austria; and finally he mentions the misfortune of not recognizing a very lovely old lady, who had wished to greet him on the journey, and had even extended her hand to him in the confidential manner of assured friendship.  This was the Baroness Pereira, a very intimate friend of the Mendelssohn family, then on her way to Gastein with her two sons.  Mendelssohn felt such keen regret at not having recognized her, and of appearing with some rudeness, that at first he resolved to follow her, but as last concluded it would take him very much out of the way, and that possibly his effort would be in vain. He was obliged to give the matter up, and go sorrowfully enough to bed.  Yet this small misfortune does not seem to have left any traces of a special misfortune; for he writes, at the close of the letter, "Next time I will tell you about this region, and how pleasant my journey of yesterday was, and how Devrient was right in recommending just this road.  Traunstein and the Falls, and the Traun itself, are magnificent, and in general this is a very pleasant world to live in.  At any rate, I am glad that you are in it, and that the day after to-morrow I shall get letters from you.  Dear Fanny, I am now going to compose my ' Non nobis,' and the A-minor symphony."  (This is the first time since he left Scotland that he mentions this important work.)   "Dear Rebecca, if you could only hear my song, ' Im wärmen Thal,' [from the beautiful song, Opus 19, ' In weite Ferne will

Ich traümen], with my cracked voice, you would find it almost too rich for anything. You would do it much better. "

The next letter is dated from Presburg, Sept. 27, and is to his brother Paul. Mendelssohn had gone there in order to be present at the coronation of the Austrian Crown Prince as King of Hungary. The crowd of Magyars, at that time not filled with that hatred of the Germans which now possesses them, the splendid Hungarian countenances, the many slender figures in their varied costumes, the magnates with their Oriental luxury, and the peasants with their fearful barbarism,—these all interested and exercised an imposing impression upon the young artist. Before this excursion to Presburg, it would seem that he turned back to pass a short time in Vienna. It is an object of wonder that the home of Haydn, Mozart, Beethoven, and Schubert, does not seem to have impelled him to any special creative activity. It appears that the driving life of the city and its unbounded jollity was very little in sympathy with his feelings at that time. He does not appear even to have had much delight in the performances of the opera at the Corinthian Gate Theatre. In a letter to Devrient, Vienna, Sept. 16, he writes: "I have been happy and merry, but have made very little music even within my soul. If Vienna were not such a dreadful hole that I have been compelled to creep away by myself and write church music, I should have almost nothing new to tell you; but I have been able to complete the second number of a choral for instruments, and probably the day after to-morrow shall finish the whole affair; then I shall begin a little ' Ave Maria ' for voices alone, which already I have in my head. In the choral, which I shall send to you as soon as it is done, you will find an aria for you; be so good and sing it in an under voice. Hauser complains, with a curse, that my solo basses and songs lie too high; but I insist that they suit you: and, if I myself sing the whole circle of my songs most wretchedly, yet there comes out of it an advantage which will be flattering to you."

In a later letter from Lilienfeld in Styria, Mendelssohn writes further: "The choral has long been done, and the 'Ave' also. At the first favorable opportunity I will send both to you. A song has also been born; but, as it amounts to nothing, I reserve that for myself. I have been living for some days with Hauser, who treats me with the greatest kindness; he has given me, for a souvenir to take on the journey, a little book of Luther's 'Hymns,' which I will set to music.

He writes to Zelter: "Before my departure from Vienna, an acquaintance gave me Luther's 'Spiritual Songs;' and, as I ran them through, they came to me with new power, and I think I shall set several of them to music this winter. I have already begun here with the choral 'Aus tiefer Noth,' and have also a Christmas song, 'Vom Himmel hoch,' in my head; also 'Wir glauben all an einen Gott,' 'Verleih aus Frieden,' 'Mitten Wir in Leben sind,' and finally 'Eine Feste Burg,' are beginning to take shape. I think I shall compose all these for chorus and orchestra. I beg you to write me what you think of this plan, and whether you approve my retaining the old melody; of course, not holding too rigidly to it, and, for example, treating the first verse, 'Vom Himmel hoch,' in a very free manner as a grand chorus. Besides these, I am at work on an overture for orchestra; and, if I can begin upon an opera, I shall be well pleased. In Vienna I composed two little church pieces, one a choral in three movements for chorus and orchestra, ' O Haupt voll Blut und Wunden,' and an ' Ave Maria' for eight voices *a capella*. The people around me were so fearfully light-minded and worthless that it really drove me into a spiritual frame of mind, and I behaved among them like a theologian. For that matter, the very best musicians, pianists included, do not play a note from Beethoven; and, as I was expressing the opinion that there was something in both him and Mozart, they said: ' So you are a lover of classical music?' — ' Yes,' I replied."

Before we leave Vienna, we must speak of a very strong friendship which Mendelssohn made there with Franz Hauser, which lasted to the end of his life. We are indebted for our account of it to the well-known composer, Edward Hanslick, who, in his exceedingly interesting book, " Auf satze uber Musik und Musiker," has given us a picture of the bond between Hauser and Mendelssohn, which he regards as one of the strongest and most enduring friendships he had ever known. He says, at the beginning of the passage narrating it: " Of the forty-seven letters of Mendelssohn to Hauser now lying before me, the first is of date April 16, 1830, the last Sept. 27, 1848, and, therefore, shortly before the death of the writer. During this long time in which the friends very seldom saw each other, and when they did, only for very brief periods, there was between them an uninterrupted interchange of the most tender correspondence. Mendelssohn's letters not only show the warmth of his feelings and his fine cultivation, but they also demonstrate how worthy the receiver of his letters is of our veneration and regard."

In the first of these letters, Berlin, 1830, he speaks of

Bach's "Passion," touching upon its production in Berlin, and its possible production in Vienna. A few months later Mendelssohn was Hauser's guest in the Bärenmühle. He writes from Rome, in 1831 : "You have sent me again the divine choral of Bach, and written yourself, and the whole is neat and pretty, and yet has a learned look, as my room used to be in the Bärenmühle." Some months later he writes from Genoa : " You have no idea how often I think with gratitude of you, and always of you in the library with the four windows ; you made the time very pleasant for me, and so long as I live I shall thank you for it. I would give so much to see a man that is a man, and hear a voice that is a voice, and some music that one can call music ; here in this cold Italy nothing of the kind exists."

This desire to have a personal meeting with Hauser again was not only actually realized in Munich, in 1831, but later was in a certain measure made complete in Leipsic, in 1834, to whose theatre Hauser was called, and where, in conjunction with the young soprano Lydia Gerard, and the tenor Eichberger, he formed one of the trio dear and unforgetable to all Leipsic lovers of music. It may be mentioned that, on the occasion of Mendelssohn's first visit to this city, when he heard the Gewandhaus orchestra for the first time, he was a guest in Hauser's house.

On the journey from Leipsic to Düsseldorf, Oct. 6, he passed by Cassel, and there visited Maritz Hauptmann. Regarding this visit, he wrote to Hauser, in a letter which bears the stamp of his lively disposition and of his complete and warm-hearted grasp of the characteristics of another artist : " Hauptmann I visited the

next morning; and, to my delight, I can say to you that
he is one of the most pleasing and delightful personages
whom I have ever met. In the first place, he is thoroughly good and earnest, and a true musician. And
then, in the next place, he has a nature which is calm
without coldness, which is superior without any crooked-
ness; just such a character as I like. I felt myself
really at home with him: when we had one opinion
about anything, that was pleasant; and when we differed
in our opinions, that was pleasant, too; in short,
you have not said too much about him, and I am
indebted to you for the day on which I made his
acquaintance. There is only one thing which I regret
in him, — a certain resignation to his own life and
character, which appears when he speaks of his compositions. These seem to me to be lacking only in a
want of sufficient insight and sympathy with his surroundings: they do not appear to have deeper faults.
But I was very sorry to find this want, and I should be
only too glad if I could stay with him for a while and
help him; for, as we were talking about his ' Mass,'
and I was speaking plainly about what pleased me in it
and what did not, and as I was begging him to go to
work and make a better one, which should not have the
faults which had occasioned him more trouble than they
would any one else, he became more and more earnest
and interested, just as if it were a new thing that one
musician should take an active interest in the affairs of
another. He promised me to write a new ' Mass,' and
I really believe that he was serious in it; but I greatly
fear that when his doubts come again, and when he gets
into the same old surroundings, he will fall back into his
one humor, or else forget the whole affair. Yet I shall

write him, and remind him of his promise; and it will be a fine thing if I really incite him to compose a new ' Mass.' "

Through Mendelssohn's influence, Hauptmann was appointed, at Windlig's death, Cantor of the Thomas School and Director of Church Music in Leipsic, which office he entered upon Oct. 2nd, 1842, and held until his death, Jan. 3rd, 1868. He was equally eminent as a theorist and as a composer; in the latter capacity he was like Mozart, in the perfection of form and in beauty of melody. It need not be said that he was a master of harmony and counterpoint, and that he stood among the first six teachers of the Leipsic Conservatory.

After this short digression, we will follow our beloved wanderer on his way.

From Vienna, Mendelssohn, after a short stay in Styria, went to Gratz, in order to visit a relative there. With both the city and the relative, an ensign, he does not appear to have been especially edified. He calls Gratz a tedious hole, wearisome to stupidity; a judgment in which few will concur, for Gratz is a university town, and certainly has a wonderfully beautiful situation. He could not forgive his relative, the ensign, for taking him to the theatre to see Kotzebue's " Rehbock," which he calls one of the lowest and most worthless of all the things that Kotzebue had written; and yet the ensign found it nice and piquant. Mendelssohn says that it had so much *haut gout*, or *fumet*, that a cat could hardly endure it. He tells the story of his journey from Gratz to Klagenfurt in a very droll manner: " Arising at four in the morning, and taking a carriage with a single horse and an old guide, and again next morning rising at four and creeping on with the speed of a pair of oxen, that was indeed a test of patience for a young man eager to hasten into Italy." In Klagenfurt, where he arrived in the evening, thoroughly tired, he had the satisfaction of finding that the post-carriage had been delayed two hours by snow on the Sommering Pass. This he took in company with three Italians, who wanted to talk all night; and journeyed on, arriving in the morning at Resciutta, where he bade farewell to Germany for a long time. Yet the landscape remained monotonous, and certainly he had a very uncomfortable introduction to Italy; for only when he reached Ospada-letto did the charms of the great Italian Plain first display themselves. He remained over night at Udine, and next morning, which was Sunday, he journeyed on amid pleasing views on every side, arriving in the evening at Treviso, where was an illumination. He did not tarry there, however, but went on to Mestre, and, taking a boat there, in the quiet of the evening was carried over to Venice.

The vivid pictures which he has given of the little details respecting his entrance into Italy, are among the finest of all the Mendelssohnian letters. The first, dated Oct. 10, 1830, to his friends in Berlin, begins with the words: "This is Italy; and what I have always placed before myself as long as I can remember as the highest joy of life, has now come to me, and I am entering upon it."

In the two letters to his family and to Professor Zelter, he says very little of the impression which the City of the Lagoons makes upon him by reason of its position, its canals, and wonderful architecture, its partly fallen palaces, and the grand Place of St. Mark; it is the great works of painting which he found there, that seemed to have interested him the most. We may not wonder at this; for we must bear in mind that his brother-in-law was a celebrated painter, and that he himself had much skill in the art of drawing. Titian, Giorgione, and Pordenone, were the masters in whose paintings he most delighted. In a letter to Zelter he says respecting this: "I hasten now hour by hour from enjoyment to enjoyment, and am always looking forward to what is new and unexpected; yet even in these first days I have discovered works in which I have lost myself, and on which I spend hours every day. There are three pictures by Titian,—'The Presentation of Mary as a Child in the Temple,' 'The Ascension of Mary,' and 'The Entombment of Christ;' then a picture by Giorgione, representing a girl with a zither in her hand, deeply sunk in thought, and looking out so earnestly from the canvas; and others that I will not mention. [He doubtless alludes in this to the celebrated picture, bearing the name of the "Lute Player," in the Manfrini Palace.] These pictures alone are worth the journey to Venice; for the strength, the resources, and the religious devoutness, of the men who wrought them, come clearly into view the moment one looks at them. And I am only sorry that I find almost no music here, for, of course, I do not reckon as music what the angels are playing in the 'Ascension,' as they surround Mary and utter their jubilations, one of them beating on a tambourine, a number of others playing on curious crooked flutes, while another is singing. Nor can I reckon as music that which the zither player evidently has in her thoughts. I have heard the organ played only once, and that execrably."

Mendelssohn goes on to tell us that, in the Church of the Franciscans (he is in error, it should be the Church

of San Giovanni a Paolo), while thoroughly carried away
by Titian's altar piece, " The death of St. Peter the
Martyr, " he heard the tones of the organ, which at first
pleased him, but which afterwards drove him from the
building; "for, although divine service was going on, the
man played this," — and then follow six measures of an
extremely trivial *allegro con fuoco* in D-major, to which
Mendelssohn adds " At cetera animalia " and yet Titian's
" Martyrdom of St. Peter " was standing close by during
this. He adds: " I did not take any particular pains to
make the acquaintance of the organist. " After some
depreciating remarks respecting modern Venetian art,
music, poetry, painting, and architecture, he continues:
" I cling to the ancients, and I only try to find out how
they did their work. I have been very active on my own
music, and am often in a musical vein. " It was the
" Hymns " of Luther on which he was specially engaged.
Before leaving Venice we must not fail to allude to the
delightful picture which Mendelssohn gives us of the two
master-pieces of Titian, " The Entombment of Christ,"
and " The Ascension of Mary. " They afford us a
glimpse not only into his appreciation of art, but of the
depth of his religious nature. After speaking half-
humorously of the picture by Pordenone, he goes on : " If
I am to talk about Titian, I must be in a serious vein.
Up to this time I have never fancied that he is so felicit-
ous an artist as to-day I find him to be. That he enjoyed
life in its beauty and fulness is shown by the picture
in Paris, and all this, of course, I have known ; but
he knows, too, what pain is in all its depths, and he
knows, too, what life in heaven is ; his divine ' Entombment, ' and the ' Ascension, ' testify to this. Words will
not permit me to tell you how Mary hovers upon the

cloud and even seems to shimmer in the air; all that she feels of greatness, anxiety, devotion, — all this you grasp at a glance. And then the three angel's heads on the right side! The acme of all that I have ever seen; pure beauty, so unconscious, cheerful, and devout. But no more. I am becoming poetical, or I shall be, soon, and that is not natural with me; but I shall go to see these pictures every day. And yet I must say a word about the ' Entombment, ' which you all know in copper-plate. Look at it and think of me. The picture is the completion of the great tragedy, so still and grand and heart-rending. There is the Magdalen holding Mary in her arms, as if in fear that she will die of grief; she wants to bring Mary away, but she herself looks round once more, as if desiring to impress the Master's countenance upon her memory forever, and as if seeing him for the last time; it is past all description. And then John, his countenance full of grief, and his thoughts fully occupied with Mary, newly committed to his care; and Joseph, devout and preoccupied with the burial; and the Christ lying there in his peace, having endured to the end. Add to this the glorious coloring and the dark mottled sky. It is a picture which one must take away, and which one can never forget. I do not believe there is much in Italy that will so take hold of me. . . . Titian was a man whom one must be edified by, and that will I be, and rejoice that I am in Italy. "

From Venice, which he left Oct. 17, our friend went probably by way of Padua and Ferrara, to Bologna, in order to see the " St. Cecilia " there, and thence over the Appenines to Florence. It is a pity that he has given us no description of the impression which the venerable old city of Bologna made upon him, with its extensive walls

and numerous palaces and churches.    His letters take us
directly from Venice to Florence, whence the first was
written, bearing date Oct. 23, the later ones on the 24th,
25th, and the 30th.

In the letter of Oct. 24, he gives us a delightful account
of the prosecution of his journey from Bologna to Florence.    In order to get a little better acquaintance with
the Appenines, Mendelssohn engaged the services of a
vetturino, and a carriage with a single horse.    He did
not find the Appenines as beautiful as he had pictured
them to himself; he had supposed them to be a mountain
chain, heavily overgrown with wood, and delightfully
picturesque; but he says: " They are only a long row
of hills, dreadfully white and bald, the little green there
is upon them not refreshing to the eye, wanting in dwelling houses, almost no brooks and waterfalls; here and
there a broad, dry bed of a stream, with a little rivulet at
the bottom, and no end of rascals on every hand.    At
last I got thoroughly wearied out with being cheated,
and, when I discovered that they were fleecing me without any inducement excepting for the pleasure of it, I
roundly determined that I would pay only for what I absolutely had, and after this I got along. "

What he says about his vetturino is so amusing that I
venture to cite it here.    " Yesterday evening I was splendidly quartered again; I had bargained with the driver
for eating, sleeping, and everything; the natural result
was that the rascal put me into the meanest hotels of all,
and left me to starve there.    Late in the evening we came
into one of the little taverns where there was a degree of
dirt that no pen can describe; the stairway was full of dry
leaves and wood for the fire; it was cold, too, and they
asked me to warm myself in the kitchen, which I was

glad to do. They put a bench for me on the hearth; the whole crowd of peasants stood around and warmed themselves also. I took my throne grandly among the crowd, all with broad hats on, and rattling away in their unintelligible dialect, and having a most suspicious look; then I made them cook my soup under my own eyes, and gave some wholsome advice about it (yet it was not eatable after all). Then I begged to have some conversation with my subjects on the hearth, and they showed me a little mountain in the distance, from which flames were continually shooting up, a very peculiar spectacle in the night,—the name of the mountain is Raticosa; and at last they took me to my chamber. The host, putting his hand upon the linen sheets, said, ' very fine goods;' then I went to sleep like a bear, only saying to myself, before I dropped off, ' Now you are in the Appenines.' The next morning, after I had taken breakfast, my driver asked me, in a friendly fashion, how I was satisfied with my treatment in the hotel. Then he began to put forth no end of talk about the present condition of France, cursed his horse in German because it came from Switzerland, and spoke French with the beggars who surrounded the carriage, while I took occasion to give him a lesson or two on his accent."

Very bright and vivid, too, is Mendelssohn's picture of his approach to Florence and his entrance into the city; for the benefit of those of my readers who have not his "Letters of Travel " at hand, I will recite the passage.

" The driver pointed to a place between the hills where a blue cloud lay, and said, ' *Ecco Firenze* !'. I looked quickly thither, and saw the round dome in the mist before me, and the broad valley in which lies the city. The spirit of travel came again to me when I beheld Florence.

I saw what looked like a number of willows by the side of the road, and the vetturino said: ' *Buon' olio,* ' calling my attention to the fact that they were olives. An hour's walk from Florence, he says, the beauty of the land commences; and it is true, Italy really begins to be beautiful at that point. There are country houses on all the hills, old walls are decorated, roses and aloes on the declining slopes, grapes above the flowers, and above these the olive trees or cypresses, or the broad pines, all delineated sharply upon the sky; add to this the handsome, square-cut faces, life everywhere in the streets, and, in the distance down the valley, the blue town. You may imagine, then, that I drove with comfortable feelings down into Florence; and, although I was rather dusty and shabby, as a man should be who comes from the Appenines, yet I did not think much of that; and passed between all the fine carriages, out of which the most dainty English ladies' faces peeped, and thought to myself, ' Perhaps by-and-by it will come to my shaking hands with my driver, whom I now so look down upon, — only a little clean linen and the like between us.'—I did not have any shame about passing by the Batisterio, went on to the Post, and was regularly jolly after getting three letters from you. A happy man now was I indeed; and, as I went along by the side of the Arno to Schneider's Hotel, the whole world seemed to me vastly beautiful. "

While in Florence Mendelssohn does not seem to have come into very close contact with the fine circles whose existence he had espied in the carriages above mentioned. Nor do we find any traces that he heard or produced any music there, his time in Florence being doubtless entirely occupied in looking at the works of art in which the city is so rich, and in the enjoyment of the beautiful country around. Yet, of a visit to the so-called Tribune, the holy of holies, in the Uffizi palace, he writes characteristically : " Now I will go to the Tribune, and be serious. There is a place where I like to linger. You see directly before you the little ' Venus de Medici, ' and above it that of Titian ; and, if you turn a trifle to the left, there hangs Raphael's ' Madonna of the Goldfinch, ' a great favorite of mine, which seems to me to be a twin to the lovely ' Jardiniére ' in Paris ; you see the ' Fornarina ' also, which has not made a very strong impression upon me, because, in the first place, I knew it in the copper-plate exactly as it is, and, in the next place, the countenance is not thoroughly agreeable, and is indeed a little common. But when one looks away to the two Venuses one falls into a better mind. It is as if the two great spirits which could produce such great works as these were flying through the air, and grasping me. Titian was a mighty man, and delighted in portraying life in his works ; yet the ' Medici ' is not to be despised ; and then the divine ' Niobe, ' with all her children, about which I do not find words to speak. I have not yet been in the Pitti palace, where are the St. Ezekiel,' and Raphael's ' Madonna of the chair. ' "

Respecting the vast collection in the Pitti palace Mendelssohn says nothing further in his letters, to our great disappointment. He speaks of the visit to the Boboli garden which belongs to this palace : " Yesterday I visited in the sunshine, the garden of the Pitti palace. It is magnificent, and the countless cypresses and thick myrtles and laurels make a rare impression upon one ; but if I should say that I found the beeches, oaks, limes, and pines, ten times fairer and more picturesque than all

this beauty, Hensel will cry out, 'O, you northern bear!'"
But we say, "Thou true German heart! it is natural
that the oaks, the beeches, the limes, and pines of thine
own country, should speak more to thine heart than this
distorted park in the old French taste, with its many
statues, under this Florentine sky : it is the same genuine
love of nature which made thee prefer Switzerland, with
its green alpine meadows, to the famed beauty of Italy ;
the same feeling which incited thee to the composition
of the song, "Wer hat dich du schöne Wald ;" the same
patriotic feeling which, at the close of this pilgrimage,
caused thee to write to thy father that thou hadst chosen
the land in which to live and labor, and it could only be
Germany."

The last letter from Florence is dated Oct. 30. It
breathes of his delight in the sky and the beautiful
scenery around him. "After the warm rain of yesterday, it has become so warm and comfortable that I am
sitting at the open window writing ; and certainly it
does not injure the prospect, that the people are passing
to and fro with their baskets of flowers, and offering me
fresh violets, roses, and pinks. Yesterday I was all
tired out with statues and vases and museums, and so
at noon I resolved to take a walk through the whole
afternoon. I bought a nosegay of narcissus and helio-
trope, and so mounted the hills between the vineyards.
It was one of the most delightful walks that I have
ever taken. Refreshed and renewed was I in spirit ; a
thousand merry thoughts came to me on the way."

After bidding farewell to the Pitti and the Uffizi
gallery, and seeing his "Venus" once more, he set out
for Rome on the 30th of October, under military protec-
tion. He went by way of Sienna, and arrived on the

morning of the 1st of November, in the clear moonlight, entering the city over the Ponte Malle.

With his stay in Rome, which continued unbroken from Nov. 1, 1830, to April 6, 1831, begins the third stage in our young artist's life. In the letters written not only to his family in Berlin, but also those to Devrient and Zelter, we learn with pleasure how actively he used all this time in the production of his musical works. Several important compositions were ended here, several begun ; for example, the Luther " Hymns,'' the A-minor symphony and the " Walpurgis Night," owe their origin to this stay in Rome. In a letter dated Nov. 5, he gives expression to the influence of the city upon his mind. " I cannot describe to you what a peace and joy of spirit have come to me here. What it is that produces this expression I can myself scarcely tell. Probably the great Coliseum and the cheerful Vatican and the pleasant air, the spring and the friendly people, and my comfortable room, all combine to produce this result. I have not felt myself so well and happy for a long time ; and I am filled with a perfect impatience to write, so that I presume that I shall accomplish even more than I have set before myself to do. If God only grants me a continuance of this happiness, I foretell one of the richest and most delightful winters of my life."

We shall, of course, be interested in becoming acquainted, under Mendelssohn's own direction, with the place which was to be the cradle of so many of his works.

" Imagine to yourself," he writes in the same letter, " a little house with two windows, No. 5 Piazza di Spagna, having the sunshine the whole day ; and the chambers in the first story, where stands a good piano,

and on the table some portraits of Palestrina, Allegri,
and others, with their scores, and a Latin psalm-book,
to help me compose 'Non nobis' [German, "Nicht uns
Herr," etc., Psalm 115, for chorus, solo, and orchestra,
appearing as Opus 31, the first important work written
at Rome]. This is my home. It was too far to be at
the Capitol, and I was afraid of the cold air, from which
here I have nothing to fear, even if I stand in the morning and look out over the Square, and see everything
distinctly in the clear air. My host was formerly a
captain in the French army; the daughter has the most
beautiful contralto voice that I know; over me lives a
Prussian captain, with whom I talk politics; in fact, the
place is a good one. When I come down early in the
morning to the room, and the sun shines brightly upon
my breakfast (you see I am dropping into poetry again),
you have no idea how comfortable I am; for it is late in
the autumn, and with us we are not expecting warmth
and pleasant skies and grapes and flowers at this time of
year." . . . "Among the other comforts of my life," he
goes on to say, "is this, that I am reading for the first
time Goethe's 'Journey to Italy;' and I must confess to
you that it gives me great pleasure to know that he
entered Rome at the same time of the year that I did;
that he went to the Quirinal at the outset, and heard the
requiem; that he, too, was impatient in Florence and
Bologna; that when he reached Rome he got a quiet,
and, as he called it, a 'solid' spirit for everything.
What he experienced I have experienced too, and that is
pleasant."

In the same letter he goes on and tells us of the
manner in which he employs his time.

"After breakfast comes work, and then I play and

sing and compose until noon; then all Rome lies before
me as something to enjoy.   I go out very deliberately,
and choose each day something new and of universal
interest; sometimes I walk on the ruins of the old city,
and another time to the Borghese Gallery, or to the
Capitol, or to St. Peter's, or to the Vatican.   That gives
a charm to every day, and makes every impression
stronger and more sure.   When I am at work in the
morning I feel as though I never wanted to stop; but I
say to myself, ' You must see the Vatican, too; ' and
when I am there I feel as though I did not want to leave
it again; and so all my occupations give me the purest
delight, and one paves the way for another.   When at
last I have filled up the day in this thorough fashion,
twilight has come, and it is past.   Then I look up
acquaintances and friends, we talk over what we have
each done; i. e., what we have enjoyed; and we are
well pleased with one another.   I have been mostly at
Bendemann's and Hubner's, where I meet German
artists, and sometimes I go to Shadows."

In general he did not find much to praise in the
German painters whom he saw in Rome.   In his letter
of the 10th of December, he paints them in the following terms: " They are dreadful creatures, as I find them
sitting in the Café Greco; I seldom go there, because I
dislike them and their favorite resort so much.   It is a
little, dark room, some eight paces wide, on one side of
which you may smoke and on the other you may not.
There they sit on the benches all around, with their
broad-brimmed slouch hats on, and their huge mastiffs by
them; their necks and cheeks, indeed, their whole faces,
covered with hair; they make a terrible cloud, especially
on the smoky side of the room; they say all manner of

coarse things; the dogs make good provision for the dissemination of vermin; a necktie and dress coat would be novelties among them; what the beard leaves, their pipes and spectacles hide. And so they drink coffee, and talk about Titian and Pordenone as if they were sitting by and also wore beards and slouch hats; and, besides, they make such sickly Madonnas, such weakly saints, such milksops of heroes, that one has a great desire to slash fearfully at all of them."

Further on, in the same letter, he says: "These unfriendly critics have no respect even for the picture of Titian in the Vatican, about which you enquire. It has no meaning, they say; and it does not occur to any one of them that a master who has occupied himself so long with such a picture, giving to it his whole love and devotion and time, saw no more than they with their colored spectacles; and, if I do nothing more in my life, I will at least cry down with my whole heart the men who have no respect for the great masters. In that I should certainly be doing a good work." Then follows an exhaustive description of Titian's great picture, which, according to the analogy of Raphael's "Transfiguration of Christ," may be called "The Glorification of Mary." Of all these letters of Mendelssohn from Rome, may be summed up in a word what Goethe said to Zelter about them: "They are the tenderest and the fullest of letters, and they give the clearest idea of this admirable young man." I cannot refrain from urging the readers of this biography not to content themselves with the extracts which I make from Mendelssohn's correspondence, which serve the purpose of simply connecting the events of his life, but to make themselves fully acquainted with the well-known volumes, containing his rich and delightful epistles.

I cannot refrain from quoting here another of Mendelssohn's criticisms upon the musicians, on whom he passes nearly as severe a judgment as he did upon the painters. He says, in a letter to his father: "It makes me angry to my inmost heart, when men who have no special direction or talent take upon themselves to condemn others who wish to accomplish something, even though it be but small. I have lately expressed myself roundly in a little company to one of the musicians here. He wanted to pass his judgment upon Mozart; and, because Bunsen and his sister love Palestrina, he tried to ingratiate himself in their favor by asking me what I thought of the good Mozart and his sins. I replied, 'I would gladly exchange my virtues for Mozart's sins; but, of course, I venture no judgment on the extent of his virtues.' They all began to laugh at this, for it evidently pleased them; but how shocking that people have no respect for a great name!"

The first thing that Mendelssohn saw of music in Rome was the German work, "The Death of Jesus," by Graun, the text of which had been admirably translated by the Roman abbate, Fortunato Santini. Mendelssohn expresses his delight at this work in his first letter from Rome: "The music of this heretic, with the translation, has already been sent to Naples, where, in the course of the winter, I am told it is to be brought out with grand solemnity; and I hear that the musicians are delighted with the work, and that they are attempting it with great enthusiasm. The abbate is longing with impatience, I hear, to see me, and wishes to know my opinion on several points in German music. He hopes, too, that I shall bring with me the score of Bach's 'Passion.'" What a delight must this have been

to him, who a year and a half before had called this
great work back, as it were, into existence! One understands the deep meaning of his words, "You see there
is progress always, and the thing is as certain as the
return of day. If it is misty now, it is only the sign
that the brightness is to come, for come it must." The
acquaintance with this abbate, whose library was extremely rich in Italian music, and which was freely
opened to Mendelssohn's use, was very delightful to him.
In the third letter from Rome, dated Nov. 16, he says
regarding him: " Old Santini is always kindness itself.
When, in company evenings, I praise a piece or do not
know it, the next morning he taps lightly at the door,
and brings it to me, done up in his blue handkerchief; I
in return accompany him home in the evening, and we
are very fond of each other. He has just brought me
his 'Te Deum' for eight voices, and begged me to
correct some modulations in it. It is too monotonously
in the key of G-major, I perceive. I will see whether
we cannot introduce something of A-minor or E-minor."
 In the meantime he had been very active in his own
compositions. At the close of the same letter, Nov. 16,
he writes to his sister Fanny: " The gift, dear Fanny,
which I have prepared for your birthday [Nov. 15,] is
the Psalm for chorus and orchestra, ' Non nobis Domine '
[the one already alluded to as Psalm 115, Opus 31, in
the German books]. You know the words already.
There is an aria in it which has a good ending, and the
whole chorus will please you. I hope I shall have an
opportunity to send it to you next week; if so, I will do
so, with some other new music. I have finished the
overture [to the " Hebrides "], and, please God, will
take hold of the symphony [he refers to the Scotch, or A-

minor symphony]. A concerto for the piano, which I should like to write for Paris, already begins to stir in my head. [This is the incomparably beautiful G-minor concerto, already alluded to, which indeed he did bring in complete form to Paris, but which he played first in Munich]. God grant success, and we will yet enjoy a great deal together. "

How grandly was this wish fulfilled! Had Mendelssohn written nothing else than the three overtures " Midsummer Night's Dream, " " Meeresstille," and the " Hebrides, " the A-minor symphony, and the G-minor concerto, these alone would have sufficed to make his name immortal.

Although not strictly in the line of Mendelssohn's musical activities, yet I cannot refrain from alluding to a passage in a letter under date of Nov. 22, to the dear brother and sisters, in which he advises them how to deal with their father's growing impatience and excitability ; an example not only of extreme tenderness, but of equally admirable psychological insight. The close of the letter is noticeable : " Do not reply to me, for it will take four weeks to receive a letter, and by that time you will have something new to tell me ; but, in a word, if I have been stupid in this advice I do not want you to cudgel me for it ; and if I have been wise in it, why simply follow my instructions. " In a continuation of this letter written on the 23rd, he takes up again his progress in musical work : " The choral, ' Mitten wir im leben sind, ' is now done, and I think it is one of the best Church pieces that I have written. After I complete the ' Hebrides, ' I propose to take up Handel's ' Solomon, ' and to prepare it for some future representation, with abbreviations ; then I contemplate writing the Christmas music to ' Vom Himmel

hoch' [Christmas hymn for five voices, not published
until after Mendelssohn's death], and the A-minor symphony; perhaps also some things for the piano, —a concerto, etc.    But I greatly miss here some one to whom I
can communicate my thoughts, who could look at my
score, who would know how to sing a bass solo, or play
the flute; when I have written anything, I have simply
to lay it aside in a drawer, without having any one to
share my joy in it.    You see I was spoiled in London;
such friends as I had there I do not expect to find again.
Here I can only express about half of what I feel, and
keep the other half to myself; while there I only had to
express the half, to have the rest immediately understood. "

At the end of this letter he speaks of his first appearance as a pianist before a large circle in Rome.    What
he says about his extemporizing is especially interesting;
"Yesterday, at Bunsen's, was music by Palestrina, as
there is every Monday there; and for the first time I
played *in corpore*, before the musicians of Rome.    I
know exactly what to expect of myself when I begin to
play before people in a foreign town.    At first I am a
little constrained, and I was so yesterday.    The papal
singers had already finished with their Palestrina, and
now I was to play something; what was brilliant was
not seasonable, and of what was earnest they had already
had more than enough.    I asked the director, Astolphi,
to give me a theme, and he touched lightly on his piano
a few insignificant notes, and smiled.    The black-robed
abbati gathered around me in great merriment.    This I
perceived, and it just moved me to do my best; in the
end it came out well.    They all clapped furiously, Bunsen thought that I had confounded the clergy,—in short,

the thing was splendid. With regard to public playing, the outlook is poor; and so I have nothing on my hands but society, and that is fishing in troubled waters."

In the letter of Nov. 30, he tells us further of his musical undertakings: "I am extremely glad to hear that Mantius [a celebrated tenor singer], likes to sing my songs. Remember me to him, and ask him why he does not keep his promise and write to me. I have written to him several times, especially in music; in the 'Ave Maria,' and in the choral, 'Aus tiefer Noth,' there are passages written expressly for him, and he will sing them with effect. . . . Rietz, too [Edward, the violin player, Mendelssohn's intimate friend], is silent, and I long to hear the violin and his deep spiritual playing, that always comes back to me when I see his dear, delicate handwriting. I am working almost every day upon the 'Hebrides,' and I shall send it on as soon as it is completed. It is a piece for him; it is exactly in his style. I will tell you about my way of life next time; I am very busy and very happy. . . . Yesterday I had to improvise again before the papal singers. The rascals had thought out the most complicated of all themes for me, for they wanted to drag me on to the smooth ice; they call me 'The Insuperable Professor,' and they are, to speak the truth, very nice and kind."

Although not directly, yet in an unquestionable manner, Mendelssohn gained advantage from two eminent artists then living in Rome, Thorwaldsen and Horace Vernet; he met these two at a ball given by Polonio, as he tells us in a letter of Dec. 20. He afterwards entered into very close relations with them: "My piano playing has secured me here a pleasure and delight. You know how Thorwaldsen loves music, and I sometimes play to him in the morning when he is working; he has a good instrument in his studio, and when I see the old man standing there kneading away at his fine brown clay, touching an arm here, and fining off a bit of drapery there, in short, when he is at work on that which afterwards is to fill us all with amazement, it delights me to be able to give him a bit of pleasure. As for my work, I am full of occupation. The 'Hebrides' is done at last, and is a curious thing. A piece for nuns' voices I have in my head. [The commencement of the three motets for women's voices, with organ, and three-voiced chorus for the nuns of Trinità de' Monti, which first appeared in 1828, somewhat modified, as Opus 39]. For Christmas I propose to write Luther's choral, ' Vom Himmel hoch. ' This I shall have to do all alone, a pretty serious piece of business; as, indeed, will be the anniversary of the silver wedding, on which I shall light up a lot of candles for myself, play the ' Vaudeville,' and look at my English baton. After that I will take hold again of my instrumental music, write some more things for the piano, and perhaps another and second symphony; for there are two rattling around in my head. [He refers to the Scotch in A-minor, and the Italian in A-major, of which the last seems to have been done the first.]

What Mendelssohn says in his letter of Jan. 17, 1831, about his exchange of art ideas with Horace Vernet, is very attractive. Vernet had already told him that Don Giovanni was his favorite; especially the duel and the commendatore at the end: " So I dropped into preluding on Weber's ' Concertstück, ' and passed unmarked into a free improvisation, thinking that I should do him a pleasure if I should come back to those themes; and for a while I played wildly enough. I never saw a man

so delighted with music as he was with mine, and we became friends at once.    Afterwards he came to me, and
whispered that we must make an exchange, for he had a
knack at improvising.    I was very curious, as was natural, and he gave me to understand that there was a secret in the matter.    But he is a mere child, and cannot
hold anything a quarter of an hour; so he came to me
again, and took me into the next room, and asked if I
had any time to lose; for he had a canvas already
stretched, and would like to take my picture for a souvenir.    I might send it to you, or keep it to myself, just as
I preferred.    I, of course, said 'Yes;' and I cannot
describe to you what a pleasure it afforded me that he
took so much delight in my playing.    Pleasant evening."
    The whole letter is so full of fine comments upon the
miserable Italian music and the beautiful Italian scenery,
that I must beg the reader to look up and read the whole
letter.    Respecting the above composition for the nuns
of Trinità de' Monti, Mendelssohn writes very amusingly
to his friends in Berlin, Dec. 20, 1830: " As the sun declines, the whole landscape changes and takes on new
color; as the time for the Ave Maria approaches, we go
into the Church of Trinità de' Monti.    The French nuns
sing there, and it is delightful.    I am becoming extremely tolerant, and am hearing bad music with edification;
but what can I do?    The composition is ludicrous, the
organ playing still worse; but it is twilight; the little
church is full of kneeling men, on whose faces will fall
the rays of the setting sun, as soon as the door is opened;
the nuns who sing have the sweetest voices in the world,
extremely penetrating and touching.    Add to this that
the singers cannot be seen, and you will understand what
a queer resolve I have made to myself; I will compose

something for their voices (the register I have noted carefully), and will send it to them through channels known to me. They will sing it, I am sure; and will it not be pleasant to have people whom I shall never see sing what a man has written for them whom they will never see, and a barbarous German, too? I am delighted with the plan. The text is in Latin, a prayer to Mary, — do you like the idea?"

He does not seem to have carried out this little whim, but he does appear to have written, in consequence of this impulse the text of the motet which we now possess in Opus 39, " Veni Domine et noli tardare, " " Laudate pueri—sit nomen Domini benedictum," " Surrexit pastor honoris, " with the duet " Tulerunt Dominum meum." These have no direct relation to the Virgin, but they are flowing, singable, and yet in churchly style; I think them, especially the third, among the best things which Mendelssohn has composed. Reissmann has happily characterized them in his " Biography of Mendelssohn : " " In these motets we meet everywhere the effort to unite the traditional music with that of the newer period; to blend the one with the other, so as from both to gain a new and appropriate ecclesiastical style. If the two forms can be distinguished in this piece, and the fusion is not complete, we can all the more distinguish the mutual effect of the one style upon the other." Almost the same thing could be said of his greatest works of ecclesiastical music, the oratorios " St. Paul" and " Elijah. " Whether the three motets were ever sung by the nuns of San Trinità, we do not know from his letters; but they have become favorites with the most cultivated singers in Germany.

The most important fruit of his stay in Rome, indeed,

one of the greatest productions of Mendelssohn, in which the most mature results of his genius are joined with the freshness of his youth, is his music to Goethe's "First Walpurgis Night." This poem is called by its author a cantata, and is a portraiture of the great sacrifice offered by the ancient Germans to Wodan on the 1st of May, at the time of the final struggle against the encroaching power of Christianity. It is a dramatic work, full of life ; in form alternating between solos and chorus ; the lines pure, flowing, and melodious, and admirably adapted to musical composition. Goethe wrote in words which Mendelssohn has made famous by quoting them as the introduction to the piano score of the music ; they occur first in a letter to Mendelssohn, dated Dec. 9, 1831. "The principles upon which this poem is based are symbollic in the highest sense of the word. For, in the history of the world, it must continually recur that an ancient, tried, established, and tranquillizing order of things will be forced aside, displaced, thwarted, and, if not annihilated, at least penned up within the narrowest possible limits, by reason of innovations. The intermediate period, when the opposition of hatred is still possible and practicable, is forcibly represented in this poem, and the flames of a joyful, undisturbed enthusiasm, once more blaze high in brilliant light." It is not to be denied that the poet has succeeded in fully expressing this high symbolic intent, although he allows his idea of Christianity to play a rather sorrowful role, in contradistinction to the fearful power of superstition. The whole comes to its culmination in the closing chorus of the druids : —

> "Unclouded now, the flame is bright !
> Thus faith from error sever !
> Though foes may cloud or quell our light,
> Yet thine, thy light, shall shine forever."

It is not to be concluded that these words of Goethe's, in the letter cited, caused Mendelssohn to undertake this composition; for, in a letter written from Isola Bella, July 24, 1831, he says to his friends in Berlin: "The ' Walpurgis Night' is finished, and the last touch given; the overture also will soon be ready.   The only man who has heard it yet is Mozart [Carl Mozart, the oldest son of the great composer, whose friendship Mendelssohn had made in Milan], and he took a great deal of pleasure in it.   He even wanted me to put it to press."   We are sure, therefore, that it could not have been Goethe's impulse which led him to this work, but that he found his way to it of himself alone.   The story of the origin of this most admirable work of his youth, and of its completion, is told us so clearly in the letters of Mendelssohn, that I shall secure the gratitude of my readers by simply establishing the chronological order of its composition.   The first conception and the stimulation to its development came to him unquestionably in Vienna, and was the work of his beloved sister Fanny. She had written to him from Berlin that she wanted to strengthen the Sunday concerts by some more pretentious productions, with chorus and solo, also by trio and string quartets, with the best musical talent in Berlin. The brother caught this idea with all the fire of his artistic nature.   He wrote from Rome, Feb. 22, 1831; "I cannot tell you, dear Fanny, how much your plan about the Sunday musicals pleases me.   It is a brilliant conception; and I beg you not to let it die, and not to stop urging your wandering brother to write something new for you.   The man will be glad to do it, both for your sake and for the sake of your idea.   You must tell him what voices you have at command.   You must call in your subjects to counsel you in the case; for even the people have their rights, dear Fanny," etc., etc.  He goes on to give her some very useful practical directions, and then continues: "I think that one piece will owe its origin to these Sunday musicals of yours.  I was thinking what I could write for you, and all at once an old plan flashed again into my head, but so complete that I want to make it over to you.  Hear, and be astonished! I have half written music for Goethe's ' First Walpurgis Night' since I left Vienna; till now I have had no courage to transcribe it; but now the thing has taken new form, has grown to be a grand cantata, with complete orchestra; and merry enough it is, for in the beginning there are songs and the like; then, when the watchmen come in, with their

"Come with torches brightly flashing,"

there is a great chance for fairy and witch frolics, and you know I have an especial foible for them.  Then come the druids, with their sacrifice, — trombones in C-major; then the watchman again in terror, where I introduce a light, tripping, and uncanny chorus; and the whole winds up with a grand sacrificial hymn.  Do not you think that would make a new kind of cantata? Of course, I have an instrumental accompaniment, and the whole thing is lively enough.  I think it will be ready soon.  The composition is going on with all its might."

It is remarkable how clearly this work formed itself in his mind at the outset, and how unchanged substantially it remained to its completion.  We find Mendelssohn's next allusion to it in a letter from Rome, March 29, 1831: "My work goes on poorly in these last days. The spring is here in all its bloom; the warm blue sky is without a cloud, just as we only dream of it in Germany; and the journey to Naples is in every one's thoughts. Of course I have not the quiet that I need for writing. From April 15 to May 15 is the finest season of the year in Italy. Who can wonder that at such a time I cannot transpose myself into the clouds of Scotland? And so for a time I have put aside my Scotch symphony, and am going to work upon the 'Walpurgis Night.' Now, if I can have two or three days of bad weather, I shall get on famously; for even the weather is too good, too seductive. There is lacking yet a bit of introduction; if that occurs to me, I can finish the whole thing up in a day or two."

It does not appear that the hoped-for bad weather came to him in Rome; for from Naples, April 27, he writes: "The bad weather which we have been having for some days was good for my working, and I plunged with all zeal into the 'Walpurgis Night.' The thing grows more and more interesting to me, and I employ upon it every free moment I have. In a few days it will be done, I think, and a jolly piece it will be. If I remain in the humor in which I now am I shall finish my Italian symphony [the one in A-major], and then I shall have something to show for my winter's work."

After some remarks about the Italian singers, Fodor, Tamburini, and others, as well as about Italian music, he goes on: "I must now get back to my witches; pardon me if I stop for to-day. This whole letter seems to me to be in a kind of mighty mood of uncertainty; or, rather, I am hovering in uncertainty whether in my music I shall use the bass drum or not.

"Come with torches brightly flashing,' etc.

really drives me to the big drum; but moderation coun-sets otherwise. I am certainly the only man who has ever presented the Brocken without piccolo music, and I have had some concern about the bass drum; but, before Fanny's advice can come, the whole 'Walpurgis Night' will be done and packed, and I shall be going through the country; and who knows what will be in my mind then? I am convinced that Fanny will say 'Yes,' and yet I am undecided about it; we must have a great noise, in any event."

And the composer did indeed have "a great noise." The big drum (*il gran tamburo*), reinforced by cymbals and piccolos, is admitted into the great chorus, No. 6: but it is the most delightfully musical noise that was ever made.

On the return journey Mendelssohn takes up the subject again in his letter from Milan, July 14th. "This week has been one of the happiest. First I got a small piano, and then pegged away at the everlasting 'Walpurgis Night' in order to put an end to it. To-morrow it will be finished, at any rate, excepting the overture, about which I have not decided whether I shall write a great symphony or a short introduction, in which the idea of spring shall appear." Fortunately he did neither; the material was not adequate for a symphony, but he wrote a brief delightful overture in A-minor with a short conclusion in A-major as a transition to spring. Respecting this happy thought, he says: "the end has come out better than I dreamed; the spectre and the bearded druid with his trombone, in imagination, stand behind me and twit and make no end of fun for me, and so the morning goes merrily by."

Mendelssohn mentions the "Walpurgis Night" in that delightful letter of July 14th and 15th to his friend

Edward Devrient in which he defends himself against
the unmerited reproach that he is now twenty-two years
old and has done nothing to make his name immortal,
because he has written no opera. He says in this letter:
"I have since then composed a great work which I may
eventually make public: the first 'Walpurgis Night'
of Goethe. I began upon it because I liked it. it
interested me. About the representation I have not
thought, but now that it is done I see that it is suitable
for a great concert piece, and in my first appearance in
Berlin after my return, you must sing the part of the
bearded druid. I have written it for your voice. although
I have before learned to my sorrow that things that are
done expressly for people do not always suit them best.
I write this that you may see how practical I have
become; but what has music to do with practicality?
Music is the most unpractical thing in all the world: it
is just as if one should make love in lines all rhymed to
order." How far was this genuine artist removed from
all that false straining for effect which is the leading
characteristic of our modern great opera writers!

From Paris Mendelssohn writes again in his letters
about this composition. In one addressed to Fanny, Jan.
21, 1832, he says: "Do you ask why I do not compose
the Italian A-major symphony? Because I am composing the A-minor overture with which I am going to introduce the 'Walpurgis Night' in order that the piece can be
properly played in the aforesaid Berlin concert and elsewhere. In the following letter of Feb. 4, in which he
speaks of the loss of his beloved friend Edward Rietz,
the violinist, he says: "The news of Rietz's death made
me so sad that I could think of nothing else and could do
nothing. To-day I have compelled myself to labor and

have finished my A-minor overture." On the 13th of Feb. again he says: "My A-minor overture is done. It is a picture of storm and disagreeable weather; the introduction, which represents the approach of spring, was ended some days ago, and so the days of this piece are counted; the seven numbers want to be touched a little, and then good-bye to it. I think it will please you."

After having glanced at the workshop of the artist it will perhaps please my readers to look at the work itself a little more closely. At the outset it is of course to be said that we have here to deal with a thoroughly classical work, i. e., with one where the form exactly answers to the contents. Mendelssohn's work consists, as already said, of the overture and nine numbers, in which the composer has skillfully woven together thirteen different stanzas of the poem without changing or omitting a single word.

The overture represents, as before intimated, not merely a season of stormy weather, but also the last obstinate struggle of the winter with storm, frost, and snow and rain, against the gentle spring-time which at last with its warm breath and sunny smiles gains a decisive victory. It begins with an *allegro con fuoco* in A-minor, the outset being a protracted chord of four measures of flutes, oboes, clarionets, horns, and trumpets, while at the same time, in the middle of the second measure the stringed instruments intone the theme, which is carried on with great contrapuntal skill, in A-minor and its kindred keys. Later in the overture appears for an instant a new theme in F-major, intoned by the bassoon and horn in C, as a herald's call announcing spring, which shortly before passing into the *allegro vivace non troppo* is again repeated in A-minor. With this *allegro vivace* played by

flute, clarionets, bassoon, first and second violin, violoncello, and double bass, the victory of spring declares itself
in a clear joyful A-major.

No. 1 opens in the same *tempo* and in the same key,
in a noble tenor solo which the druid sings : —

> Now May again
> Breaks winter's chain,
> The bud and bloom are springing,

and this is repeated by a chorus of four women's voices.
The druid sings further : —

> No snow is seen,
> The vales are green,
> The woodland choirs are singing:

The chorus repeats this and closes with four voices : —

> Now May again
> Breaks winter's chain.

Then the druid takes up the song : —

> Yon mountain height
> Is wintry white ;
> Upon it we will gather;
> Begin the ancient holy rite,
> Praise our Almighty Father.

Then follows a tenor solo *allegro assai vivace* : —

> In sacrifice the flame shall rise ;
> Away, away,
> Begin the ancient holy rite,
> Praise our heavenly Father.

These last words are set to a beautiful melody.  A chorus of druids, bass and tenor, follows : —

> In sacrifice the flame shall rise,

and the sopranos and altos come in with: —

> Thus blend our hearts together,

The same words are taken up again with a constant

interchange of parts and in the close are intermingled solos and chorus : —

> Thus blend our hearts together,
> Away, away,
> Thus blend our hearts together.

No. 2 stands in effective contrast to this : an alto solo. This stands in Goethe's text, "An old woman from the people," which Mendelssohn changes to "one of the people," the only alteration which the composer has made in the words.  The aria warns and wails in D-minor : —

> Know ye not a deed so daring
> Dooms us all to die despairing?
> Know ye not it is forbidden
> By the edict of our foemen?
> Know ye spies and snares are hidden
> For the sinners called the heathen;
> On the ramparts they will slaughter
> Mother, father, son, and daughter.

A chorus of women, soprano and alto, repeat the lamentation : —

> On the ramparts they will slaughter
> Mother, father, son, and daughter.

Then the alto solo : —

> They oppress us,
> They distress us;
> If detected,
> Nought but death can be expected;

which is repeated by the chorus : —

> Nought but death can be expected;
> On the ramparts they will slaughter
> Mother, father, son, and daughter.

The chorus closes with the alto solo : —

> If detected,
> Nought but death can be expected.

This alto solo, although uniform with the expression of the whole number, is, nevertheless, not at all monotonous, but has a certain melodic charm of its own.

Delightfully restful, after these tones of lament, comes No. 3, *andante maestoso* in A-minor. The high priest (baritone solo written for Devrient) reminds them in tones of solemn earnestness of their duty : —

> The man who flies
> Our sacrifice
> Deserves the tyrant's tether;
> The woods are free;
> Disbranch the tree
> And pile the stems together.

The chorus of druids, basses and tenors, the high priest's voice leading, repeat these words. Then follows in a quieting tone the solo, *andante tranquillo* in E-minor : —

> In yonder shades
> Till daylight fades
> We shall not be detected;
> Our trusty guides shall tarry here
> And ye will be protected;
> Conquer with courage slavish fear,
> Show duty's claim respected.

The chorus takes up these last two lines again, the high priest's voice being heard singing : —

> With courage conquer slavish fear,
> Show duty's claim respected.

This is completed by a short recitative solo in E-major.

> Disperse, ye gallant men,

The chorus of druid watchmen follows with No. 4, *allegro leggiadro*, likewise in E-major ; —

> Disperse, ye gallant men,
> Secure the passes round the glen;
> In silence there protect them
> Whose duties here direct them.

The words " In silence " are repeated *piano* by all the
four parts, but with breadth and beauty of tone.

The bass solo recitative ushers in No. 5, a watchman
uttering this cry in A-minor :—

> Should our Christian foes assail us,
> Aid in schemes that may avail us,
> Feigning demons whom they fable
> We will scare the bigot rabble.

Then follows a solo in G-minor : —

> Come with torches brightly flashing,

which forms the transition to the chorus of the druid
watchmen accompanied by bass viols, violoncellos, kettle-
drums, bass drums, (yet *pianissimo*, and without cymbals : afterwards, horns in D are added). This chorus
is, as it were, the prelude to No. 6, the grand culmination
of the whole musical drama, great chorus, *allegro multo*
in six eighth measure ; first the tumultuous outcry already announced in No. 5, given with all the resources
of music, yet always within the limits of good taste. We
have bass drums and cymbals, kettle-drums first in D,
G, then in E, A, alto, tenor, and bass trombones, and
trumpets and clarionets in C, horns in D, piccolos, flutes,
oboes, bassoons, and all the varieties of stringed instruments. From the voices are heard, first the tenors with
a united cry of " Come ! " then after sixty measures of
the instruments, the chorus breaks forth again first with
basses and tenors : —

> Come with torches brightly flashing,
> Rush along with billets flashing ;
> Owls and ravens
> Howl with us, and scare the cravens.

This passage gradually passes into a grand chorus of
the watchman, the druids, and the heathen populace,
strengthened by the women and girls. The original

theme in A-minor is modulated through all possible allied keys, E-major, G-sharp minor, B-minor, and again back to A-minor, and the whole chorus closes with a sustained and united : —

> Come, come, come, come.

After this musical and yet charming tumult we come to No. 7, in two fourths measure, a pleasing transition in E-major to *andante maestoso* again in A-minor. The high priest sings in a voice half sorrowful, and yet full of dignity, the comforting solo : —

> Restrained by might,
> We now by night,
> In secret here adore thee.
> Till it is day
> Whene'er we pray
> And humbly bow before thee.

These words are repeated by the chorus of druids and of the heathen populace. The priest strikes in again with the solo : —

> Whene'er we pray
> And humbly bow before thee.

This is repeated by the basses and tenors. Then the high priest's solo : —

> Thou canst assuage
> Our foemen's rage,

which the whole chorus repeats, but *pianissimo*. The priest continues : —

> And shield us from their terrors,

which the chorus gives in its turn. The passage is full of a mighty yet uncanny power. The priest then sings : —

> The smoke retires :
> Thus clear our faith from errors ;
> Our customs quell'd,
> Our rights withheld.

Chorus repeats : —

> Our customs quell'd,
> Our rights withheld, etc.

The grand effect of this number can hardly be surpassed, but in order to make the drama complete it is necessary to portray the effect of this incantation upon the Christian watchman.   This is accomplished in No 8, *allegro non troppo*, tenor solo in C-minor : —

> Help, my comrades ! see, a legion
> Yonder comes from Satan's region.

The dull horror of their mind is expressed by a transition from D-sharp minor to C-minor ; then follows the alternating strain, between the solo and chorus, of the Christian watchman : —

> See yon group of witches gliding
> To and fro in flames advancing ;
> What a clattering troop of evil !
> Let us, let us quickly fly them.

And after the whole terrified crowd had been put to rout, we come to the splendid conclusion of the whole piece : No. 9, *andante maestoso*, given with all the splendor of instrumentation and beauty of harmony and melody in the clear resonant C-major to which the basses and celli lead the way ; then follows the splendid four part chorus given by the druids, priest, and people : —

> Unclouded now the flame is bright,
> Thus faith from error sever,
> Though foes may cloud or quell our light
> Yet thine, thy light shall shine forever.

These words are repeated by the high priest, and with the expression " Thy light, thy light," given with indescribable charm, the whole comes to its worthy and splendid conclusion.

I trust that this analysis of the work will lead my readers to a more intimate acquaintance with it, for it is not too much to say, that it is one of the noblest of Mendelssohn's productions, and one which is eminently suitable to be given not only in the concert hall, but also on the stage, for which, indeed, it has been prepared by Mendelssohn's friend Devrient.

It only remains, to complete my account, that I should make some brief mention of the changes wrought in it after its first draft had been completed, and before it was left in its present state.

Its first public performance, as Mendelssohn determined it should be, was in Berlin, not long after his return from his great journey. Devrient gives us an account of it in his Recollections: "Mendelssohn gave four concerts in the small hall of the theatre in Berlin, between Nov. 1832 and Jan. 1833, in which, among other things, he gave us the 'Walpurgis Night' for the first time. He has altered it considerably since he came home. I cannot fail to be impressed with the power which this cantata must exercise when thrown into dramatic form, and when I spoke to Felix about this, he answered, 'Very possibly, you try it.' · 'That will I,' replied I, 'as soon as a stage is put at my control.' It was in May 1860, that Devrient, then director of the theatre at Carlsruhe, placed the 'Walpurgis Night' in his standing repertoire.

Respecting the gradual changes in the work, Mendelssohn wrote to his friend Klingemann, in London, Nov. 18, 1840, from Leipsic "You have much to answer for with your admirable title [Mendelssohn refers to his well-known Lobgesang, or Hymn of Praise, written as a symphony cantata for the anniversary of the discovery of printing], for I not only am sending this piece into the world, but I am strongly tempted to finish up the first ' Walpurgis Night, ' print that, and so get rid of it. It seems strange to me that when the idea first seized me that I would compose a symphony with chorus, I afterwards lost my courage, because the first two movements were too long to serve as an introduction ; yet, I always kept the feeling that there was something wanting besides a mere introduction, and now I am going to arrange the movements according to the old plan. Do you remember it? I fancy that the thing is suitable for concerts, and I like to work at it."

To his mother, he wrote also in two letters from Leipsic, the first of which was dated Nov. 28, 1842 ; " the ' Walpurgis Night' I should like to make into a symphony cantata, which was indeed my original plan ; it fell through only for want of courage. " Also under date of Dec. 11, 1842 ; " on the 21st or 22nd we give here a concert before the king ; in the second part my ' Walpurgis Night' is to come to the light, certainly somewhat differently clothed from what it was ; before it was a little too warmly lined with trombones, and rather scantily habited for voices, but I have written the whole score out from A to Z, have added two new arias, not to speak of other tailoring upon it. If it does not please now I give you my word to abandon the thing for the rest of my life. "

This letter is all the more noticeable as being the last which Mendelssohn's mother received from him, as she died only the next day, after a brief struggle. Perhaps, for this reason, the " Walpurgis Night " was not given in the proposed concert, before the king. Instead of this, the Eroica, the overture to the " Midsummer Night's Dream, " and Mendelssohn's " Forty Second Psalm " were given ; yet, before the end of the year 1842, Men-

delssohn took up the "Walpurgis Night" again. Under
date of Jan. 13, 1843, he wrote to Klingemann: "In
the days before Dec. 11, I had undertaken what, indeed,
I had long proposed to do: to transcribe my 'Walpurgis
Night," and had gone so far as to finish the voice parts;
then I was summoned to Berlin, and after a long interruption I began to work in my little chamber, with its
pleasant outlook into the country, and undertook the
writing out of the instrumental parts; I could hardly tear
myself from the table, so fettered was I with my well-
known old oboes, and violins, and the like, which will
live a great deal longer than we all shall, and which become like good friends. I had no heart for new composition but this mechanical driving and pegging away was
my consolation in those times when I was alone, and
could not look at wife and children, with their dear faces,
whose presence makes me forget music, and only remember that the first duty of my life is to thank God for all
the goodness which he shows me."

It is impossible now to know what changes Mendelssohn made in the work, since, unfortunately, the original
score no longer exists. They can scarcely have been important, for unquestionably he retained the first conception, both in its structure and in the development of the
orchestral and vocal parts. The work now lies before us
as Opus 60, having first been published by Friederich
Kistner, without date; but it is now in the well-known
complete collection of Breitkopf and Härtel. We may
conclude that in its last form it satisfied its author, from
the fact that it was given for the first time in Leipsic,
Tuesday, Feb. 23, under the direction of its composer,
and on the evening before his thirty-fourth birthday.
The first part of that concert was made up of a symphony

by Haydn, an aria by Mozart, " Deh per quest' istante ; "
Beethoven's " Fantasie, " for piano, chorus, and orchestra. [The piano part played by Clara Schumann, the
violin by Henselt]. Overture to Euryanthe, and chorus,
and Von Weber's " Lyre " and " Sword. " A true bouquet of classical music. In the second part, the " Walpurgis Night. " I had the pleasure of being not only a
witness, but a coöperator on this grand occasion.

The picture which Fanny gives us of the first performance of the " Walpurgis Night" in the Mendelssohn
house at Berlin is exceedingly interesting. It was communicated in two letters to her sister in Rome, under
date of March 2nd and 18th; in the first she writes:
" On Aug. 1st and 2nd Felix is to direct a grand music
festival in Zweibrucken, at which, among other things,
the ' St. Paul' and the ' Walpurgis Night' are to be
given. The last I rehearsed yesterday for the second
time ; Sunday it will be sung. It went splendidly ;
Decker, Augusta Löwe, and our new basso, Baer, did
wonders in the solos. You can imagine how beautiful
the music is, and how indescribably amusing ; the
rehearsals afforded the greatest pleasure." And under
date of March 18th, she continues : " Last Sunday we
had the most brilliant musicale that we have ever had,
not only as respects to the public but also the performance. Twenty-two equipages in the court, Liszt and
eight princesses in the hall. The repertoire consisted
of a quintette by Hummel, duet from Fidelio, variations
by David (played by the splendid little Joachim, no
phenomenon, but a wonderfully gifted child), two songs,
one of which, " Lass die Schmerzen dieser Erde," was
given from memory by Felix and Fräulein Decker ; then
followed the ' Walpurgis Night,' for which my public

had been eagerly waiting for four weeks, and which went extremely well. We had had three rehearsals, at which the singers amused themselves so much that they would have liked to have had the whole thing over again. They wanted to have Felix lead, but he declared, once for all, he would not; he did, however, consent to play the overture with me, and at various places struck in now in the bass, now in the discant, so that a kind of improvised four-handed arrangement came out of it which made a good effect."

Hensel relates two pleasant incidents as occurring at the performance in Berlin. A very quiet gentleman belonging to the higher aristocracy was pleased to commend what he considered the very "satisfactory tone" of the closing chorus, where the good spirits get the victory over the heathen and drive them from the scene. In Austria, on the contrary, the Censor, instead of being pleased with this passage, did not allow the words

Feigning demons whom they fable

to remain, but caused the passage to stand

Feigning demons, feigning demons

In Austria it appears that demons do not belong to the realm of fable.

From Soden Felix writes, July 19, 1844, to his brother Paul, in Berlin: "My stay in England was delightful. I never in my life have been received with such universal kindness as this time, and have played more in these two months than I have elsewhere in two years. My A-minor symphony, twice; 'The Midsummer Night's Dream' overture, three times; the 'St. Paul,' twice; the trio in D-minor, twice; and on the last evening that

I spent in London, the 'Walpurgis Night,' with indescribable jubilation," etc.  Finally from Frankfort, March
24, 1845, he writes to his sister Rebecca in Florence:
"To-day, for the first time, that pleasing air outside that
you know well, in which all the ice and coldness of
winter melt away, and everything grows mild and warm
and joyful."  Then follows a beautiful description of
the passing of the ice down the river, as viewed from
the bridge over the Main, and then Mendelssohn pro-
ceeds: "In Düsseldorf they are announcing for the
second day of the Musical Festival, 'The Requiem,' by
Mozart, *my* 'Walpurgis Night,' and finally Beethoven's
symphony with chorus: 'O tempora! O mores!'"

A passage of tragic interest was connected with the
last performance of the "Walpurgis Night" in Mendelssohn's father's house at Berlin.  On Friday afternoon,
May 14, 1847, Fanny, who was believed to be in perfect
health, was having a rehearsal for the next Sunday's
music.  While sitting at the piano she experienced a
dull sensation in her hands, and had to surrender the
instrument to her friends.  They were then working
upon the choruses of the "Walpurgis Night."  She
listened to them from her room, the doors being opened
which connected her with the hall, while they bathed
her hands with hot vinegar.  "How delightfully it
sounds," she said joyfully, and thinking herself entirely
well again, was on the point of returning to the hall,
when a recurrence of the attack took place and she lost
consciousness.  That evening at 11 o'clock, she breathed
her last.  How wonderful, and yet how sad that this rare
and gifted woman, who lived only to art, closed her life
while occupied upon the music which her brother, so
truly beloved, had written under her impulse and for her

special joy! The world has never seen an instance of a nobler and purer life, nor such a perfect and unbroken mutual understanding as existed between this brother and this sister. Felix himself did not outlive this severe stroke long. He had just returned from England where he had enjoyed his triumph with the "Elijah," given his music to "The Midsummer Night's Dream" in the Philharmonic concert, and played Beethoven's "G-major concerto" with the constant enthusiastic applause attending him, when, returning to Frankfort, he found his wife and children, and learned the news of his sister's death. He lived from that time as it were under the drawn sword of the angel of death. On Nov. 4th of the same year he was united with his beloved sister.

Thirty-six years after, Nov. 3, 1883, I heard the "Walpurgis Night" in the Leipsic Theatre for the last time, and as I experienced afresh the power of this great work, I thought with sadness and regret of what greater things he would have been capable, had his life been protracted to the ordinary age of man. From this long digression respecting the "Walpurgis Night" we return to the delineation of his life.

Respecting the stay in Rome, I may add the following, which he communicates in a letter to Fanny, Feb. 21, 1831: "With composing, things are going on again quite brightly; the Italian symphony is making great progress, it will be the maturest thing that I have done, especially the last movement, *presto agitato;* for the *adagio* I have not thought out anything definite; I believe I will reserve that for Naples. 'Verleih uns Frieden' is done, and 'Wir glauben All' will soon be. Only the Scotch symphony seems to be beyond my grasp. I have had some good ideas lately for it and will take hold of it directly and bring it to a close."

Respecting his conscientiousness in the matter of using time, the beginning of the letter dated March 1st, gives us an interesting report: "As I write this day I am reminded how rapidly time is flying. Before the month comes to an end, Holy Week sets in, and after Holy Week I shall have been in Rome a very long time. As I think over whether I have used it all well, I find many wasted moments. If I could only grasp one of the two symphonies! The Italian I must retain until I have seen Naples, for that must play a part in it, but the other escapes me the nearer I come to it. The more closely I approach the end of this quiet time in Rome, the more hurried I become, and the less successful in my work. It seems to me as though I never should have such a quiet comfortable time again as here, and so I want to do all that is possible, but I fail in the attempt; only the 'Walpurgis Night' goes bravely on, and will, I hope, soon be completed."

Very interesting, too, is the account Mendelssohn gives us of the performances of Holy Week, especially those in the Sistine chapel, and the impressions which are made upon his mind. He grasps them in a large sense, taking up the conception of the whole without being disturbed by mere external trifles. The most effective in its working and on his mind were the "Miserere" by Allegri, and the so-called "Impropreria" by Palestrina. His letter to his friends in Berlin, written in April 1831, gives us a good account of his impressions. This letter is so complete in its delineation that I will only refer the reader to it, but should a more musical account of Holy Week be desired it will be found in his letter to Zelter, under date of June 16, 1831. I will content myself with the following: "The Nocturnes began on Wednes-

day at half past four ; the psalms are sung alternately by
two choirs, yet always in the same tone, at one time
bass and at another tenor ; and so hour after hour you
hear the most monotonous music; only once are the
psalms interrupted by the ' Lamentation,' and that is the
first time in the long passage when you hear again a
complete chord.   This chord is given very softly, and
indeed the whole passage is sung *pianissimo*, whereas,
the psalms are shouted out as strongly as possible, the
words being rolled out with the greatest rapidity, and at
the end of each verse a cadence makes the only discrimi-
nation between the various melodies.   It is no wonder
that the gentle strain in the first ' Lamentation ' in G-
major sounds weak.   The music continues then in the
same monotone.   At the close of every verse a candle is
extinguished, so that at the end of an hour and a half
the fifteen around the altar are out.   There remain then
only the six great ones over the entrance.   The entire
chorus with altos, sopranos, etc., intone, *fortissimo* and
in unison, a new melody, the song of Zacharias, in D-
minor.   This is given very slowly and solemnly while the
darkness closes in ; the last candles are then extinguished,
the pope leaves his throne, throws himself before the
altar upon his knees, as do all with him ; they then
repeat the Pater Noster, *sub silentio*, i. e., there is a
pause during which you know that every one is repeat-
ing the Lord's prayer, and immediately after this the
' Miserere ' begins *pianissimo;* this is to me really the
grandest moment of the whole.   What follows afterwards you can imagine, but you cannot imagine this.
The rest of the ' Miserere,' by Allegri, is a simple suite
of chords established either by tradition, or, which is
more probable, the work of a clever maestro, brought

out first as embellishments for some fine voices, and especially for a very high soprano. These embellishments pass again into the same chords which we heard before, and as the whole thing has been well thought out and arranged for the voices, it is a delight to hear them. I have not been able to find anything wonderful or superhuman in this whole performance; it is enough for me that it is comprehensible, and of the earth in which we live. . . . It was entirely dark in the chapel; when the 'Miserere' began, I climbed up a great ladder which happened to stand there, and had the whole chapel full of men, the kneeling pope with his cardinals, and the music, all below me; that made a magnificent effect. Friday morning the chapel was stripped of all its ornaments; the pope and cardinals appeared in mourning; the 'Passion,' following John's account, and composed by Vittoria, was sung; then followed the 'Impropreria,' by Palestrina, during which the pope and all the rest removed their shoes to go to the cross and pray. In the evening was Baini's 'Miserere,' which was sung best of all. On Sunday the pope held mass in the Quirinal, and gave his benediction to the people, and so it came to an end. It is now Saturday, the 9th of April, and to-morrow I take my seat in the carriage, and a new beauty will come to me. . . . My journey is towards Naples, the weather is becoming clear, the sun is shining again for the first time for several days, the passport is ready, the carriage is ordered, and I am eagerly looking forward to the spring."

In this happy humor our Felix remained during the whole of his journey, as well as during his stay in Naples. He was accompanied thither by the painters, Bendemann, Hildebrand, and Karl Sohn, with whom he visited the

islands, Ischia, Capri, Procida, then across sea by way
of Velletri, where they spent the first night; then through
the Pontine Marshes, via Terracina, Fondi, and Itri, as
far as Molo di Gaeta, where they spent the second night;
then by way of Capua to Naples. The account of this
journey is one of the finest things which Mendelssohn
has ever written. His letter to Rebecca on her birthday,
April 13, gives testimony as to his happy state of mind :
" If you do not gather from the heading of this letter,
you certainly must from its tone, that I am in Naples. I
have not been able to come to any regular quiet thought
since I arrived. It is altogether too jolly on every side of
me. It simply invites to doing nothing and thinking
nothing, and the example of so many thousand men
around me is irresistible. I fancy myself that the humor
will change, but the first days must certainly run out into
idleness, that I already see; I stand for hours on my
balcony, and gaze at Vesuvius and the bay. " This is
the true *dolce far niente*, which, after his assiduous labors
in Rome, we may gladly accord to our friend. He
lived, as every traveller does who can, in Santa Lucia.
" I live here, " he says in his first letter, " in Santa Lucia
as in heaven, for, in the first place I have Vesuvius, and
the mountains as far as Castellmare, and the bay before
me; and in the second place, the house is three stories
high. Unfortunately that rascal of a Vesuvius does not
even smoke, and looks like any other handsome mountain; in compensation for it they sail on the bay with
torch-lighted boats, darting hither and thither to catch
sword fish; it is a pleasant sight. " Mendelssohn chiefly
delighted in the charms of the country around him. He
went on long walks, and his favorite points were those
which were quite unknown to the Italians; besides, he

found pleasure in looking up all the musical people who were in the city. Yet he found their performances beneath criticism, worse even than in a small German town. Of productive work, with the exception of the little on the " Walpurgis Night, " he did nothing in Naples.

In a letter written to his parents, June 6, he says: I take all pains to make the acquaintance of the musicians who live in Naples; we play a good deal together, but I do not care for their flatteries. Fodor is almost the only artist whom I have met in Italy; in any other country I should not have cared much for her singing, but I did enjoy everything which she sang, because one can tell that it is real music, and, after hearing no good music for a long time, hers was a comfort.

The most southern point reached by Mendelssohn was the temple of Ceres at Paestum. He would have been glad to visit Sicily, for he wanted to see a real volcano, but his father was unwilling to allow him to go, perhaps out of fear that his son would be robbed; and so the obedient Felix, to whom his father's wishes were as commands, struck this from his route. Goethe, who heard of this loss through Zelter, wrote to the latter, June 28: " Mendelssohn's father was wrong in not allowing him to visit Sicily. He must have read in my Sicilian or Neopolitan letters what a disagreeable impression this island made upon me."

After taking a hasty run by way of the Grotto of Posilepo to Pozzuioli, and then around the bay of Baiae to the lake of Avernus, he visited the islands of Ischia, and Capri, and the Blue Grotto, and at the beginning of June turned back to Rome, whence he wrote to his parents the letter already cited. At this time he found the city engaged in the celebration of Corpus Christi and witnessed the daily processions.  It made a great impression upon him to find the change which had come over all the streets with the advent of summer; everywhere booths and ice-water, all the people in light clothing, the windows open, and the jalousies closed; although he missed no special friend, no one in fact whom he particularly knew, yet he experienced the old emotions in seeing again the Piazza di Spagna, and the familiar names of streets.  After making an excursion to the mountains on the occasion of the festival of the Infiorati, he wrote to Zelter a very full letter, describing the Passion week.  This letter, to be found in his collection of Letters of Travel, deserves to be mentioned with great praise; for, if the parting from Rome was a trial to him when he went thence to Naples, how much more was it when he left it without the hope of seeing it again.

On the 25th of June we find him again in Florence. The journey thither by way of Perugia, appears to have been quite disagreeable; he had for company, three Jesuites, a dissatisfied Venetian lady, and a Roman vetturino.  He writes regarding these things to his sister: " Such a journey as mine from Rome to Perugia and hither is certainly no jest.  Jean Paul says in the ' Flegeljahre, ' that the presence of a hateful being is oppressive, and hard to bear: such a being, however, is my Roman vetturino.  He permits one no opportunity to sleep; he allows one to hunger and to thirst; in the evening when he ought to provide the supper, he knows how to arrange matters so that it shall be midnight before one can get to bed, and indeed one is happy to find a bed at all.  In the morning at a quarter past five he is off, and takes his five hours siesta at mid-day without fail, but always in some low tavern where nothing is to be

had.    He gets over about six German miles in a day, and
journeys *piano* when the sun burns *fortissimo.*"

In Chiesa, a half day's journey from Florence, he came
to a decisive contest with the vetturino, whose bad tem-
per was no longer to be endured, and so, taking his goods
into his own keeping, he bade the fellow go.    After having a fracas with the hostess, who was also post-mistress
of the post and demanded four times too much for the
horses, a respectable man procured for him a light carriage ; delighted at this change Felix hastened on to Florence, and richly compensated himself the next day by
his enthusiastic joy in the treasure of art which the galleries furnished him.    From Florence he went to Genoa,
and thence back to Milan.    We have no full account of
the impression which Genoa la Superba made upon him.
It is to be hoped that he was advised to go by way of
Pisa and the Riviera di Levante, Massa, Carrara, Lerici,
Spezzia, Chiavari, and Rapollo ; this road is one of the
finest in all Italy, and is to be compared with that from
Rome to Naples.    It passes now into the mountain land,
and anon to the shore of the beautiful Mediterranean.
The vegetation is completely southern ; mighty aloes
border the streets, avenues and groves of orange trees are
frequently seen.    At the present time the railway has deprived this road of a large part of its charm.    That he
visited Venice, we learn from a letter which he wrote to
Frau von Pereira, in Vienna, dated July 1831, without
giving the day.    He declines in this letter a proposition
which she made him to compose music for Zedlitz's
" Nächtliche Heerschau," and justifies his refusal in his
spirited and interesting way.    In Milan, he made two
very agreeable acquaintances : first, the Baroness Dorothea von Erpman, the well-known favorite of Beethoven,

with whom he stood in intimate relations, and to whom
he dedicated his A-major sonata. 'He also became acquainted with her husband, General von Erpman; the
latter he met accidentally in the royal palace, as he was
arrayed in evening dress, for the purpose of paying his
respects to the General's wife; he had thought out some
very appropriate words to say as he should be presented,
when, in a very beautiful arched ante-room in the lower
story and among a troop of soldiers, he met an old man
in a nankeen jacket, whom he asked whether General
von Erpman lived there. The man replied: "I am he,
what is wanted?" Mendelssohn named his errand, but
the General did not appear especially edified by it, yet
when Mendelssohn mentioned his name, he became very
polite, and named two o'clock in the afternoon as the best
hour for his visit to his wife. Frau von Erpman received
Mendelssohn at the appointed time in a very friendly
manner, and played to him at once Beethoven's Sonata in
C-sharp minor. The old General appeared also, but this
time in a splendid gray military coat with many orders,
was in a very good humor, and even wept with delight
to see and hear his wife play again. When the talk fell
upon Beethoven's B-major trio, which Frau von Erpman
could not recollect, Mendelssohn played it by heart. Thus
a league of friendship was formed between them, and
Mendelssohn passed with the aged and cultivated couple
the most delightful hours which can be imagined. The
whole account is given in one of his "Letters of Travel."
In the same circle he made another delightful acquaintance
to which we have already alluded, that of Carl Mozart.
Mendelssohn speaks in full regarding this in a letter from
Isola Bella, under date of July 24th. "Herr Mozart, an
official in Milan, is really a musician in every sense of

the word.  He must have the greatest similarity to his father in his nature; for such things as are very touching in the letters of the father come to the surface immediately in the *naivete* and frankness of the son, and win one's affection in a moment.  I was delighted to find that he is as jealous of the honor of his father as if he were a young musician of our time; and one evening at the Erpmans' when they were playing a good deal of Beethoven's music, the Baroness suggested softly that if I would play something of Mozart's it would greatly please the son; and after I had given the overture to Don Giovanni, he began to thaw out, and then asked me to play his father's Zauberflöte overture and showed the delight of a child in it!  One must love such a man. "

That this Mr. Mozart of Milan, was the only man to whom Mendelssohn showed his " Walpurgis Night " when it was completely finished has already been mentioned.

He also enjoyed some other agreeable days, although the weather was not favorable, on the Borromean Isles, in which he was reminded of his youthful journey thither in the year 1821 over the Simplon.  On reaching this pass now, the weather cleared up and became as beautiful as possible.  He then went down the road as far as Martigny, and from there journeyed on alone, his cloak upon his shoulders; afterwards with a thick peasant boy, who was at once guide and porter, over the Col de Balme to Chamouni.  In a strain of perfect delight he writes to his parents respecting the view of the whole Chamouni valley, Mount Blanc, and all the glaciers which sank away before him in the glory of the evening sun. " From time to time I must write you a letter of thankfulness for this wonderfully beautiful journey, and after doing so once I must again, for more glorious days than I have had on the whole way thither, and am now having, I never experienced in my life.  To my joy you know the valley, so I do not need to describe it; indeed how would it be possible to describe it?  Only this I will say, that nature has never come out so clearly in my view in its grandeur as here.  Even the first time when I saw it with you my impression was not as strong as now.  And as one would give thanks to God for having given him the ability to grasp and take in all this greatness, so I must also thank you who have enabled me to enjoy it."

From Chamouni our wanderer went first a little way into the so-called Allée Blanche in order to study Mount Blanc from the south side; and from there he journeyed on to Lake Geneva; thence, over the Col de Jaman, which Lord Byron describes as " beautiful as a dream," and onward to the Chateau D'Oex and the valley of the Saanen.  Up to this time the weather was tolerably favorable, but from that time on it grew steadily worse and worse; in Boltigen there was no room in the hotel, and he was obliged to sleep in a neighboring house where he passed a wretched night.  To the discomforts produced by the filthiness of the place and the crying of a child, was added the terror of lightning, and of thunder, and unceasing rain.  By noon of the next day he arrived at Zweisimmen, and was entertained in a house entirely in contrast to that where he had passed the night.  Thence, he journeyed on to Interlaken, and giving his bundle of clothing to the post to be expedited, he made up his mind to journey on through the country with the simplest possible provision.  But the pitiless Jupiter Pluvius entirely broke up this plan; the rain poured in streams, daily growing heavier.  On the 8th of Aug.

Mendelssohn writes from Wimmis: "*Prosit Mahlzeit* (Hurrah for good luck)! it is growing too severe for anything. My plan to go on to-day to Interlaken I must give up: it is not possible to carry it out. For four days it has been pouring as if the clouds were squeezed dry; the roads are as soft as feather beds; of the mountains you only see a trace or two, and that seldom." Even his little note book he had to hide under his waistcoat, for an umbrella was of no account. Still this misfortune did not prevent him from taking an exceedingly interesting sketch of Weissenburg which he incorporated in the letter from Wimmis. In Spiez they would not take him in, and he was compelled to turn back to Wyler. With great difficulty he got on as far as Unterseen, whence he writes in the evening: "My jest has become bitter earnest; the weather has raged fearfully and has done great harm; the people cannot remember a worse storm and more rain for many years, and it has been so very rapid withal." The next day the rain began to subside, but at 9 o'clock it renewed itself with more violence than ever. By good fortune he was able to find a small boat and be carried over to Neuhaus. He says of his condition when he arrived there: "I looked as if I were wearing top boots over my light trousers: my shoes and stockings, and all as far as the knees, were dark brown, then came a saturated blue overcoat; even my note book, which I carried under my vest, was moist." It is very easily understood that with this appearance he did not have any too welcome a reception at the hotel at Interlaken: in fact, that he was not received. He was compelled to turn back to Unterseen where he was provided with a fine room, which was all the more agreeable because there was an excellent piano in it,

which reminded him of the small one in his room in
Berlin.　After receiving from the daughter of the landlord two very delicate sheets of note paper, he sat
himself down to compose.　He writes : " I have two
songs now in the works, dear sister, one in E-major,
' Auf der Reise.'　It is very sentimental."　[He refers
to the one already mentioned " Bringet des treuesten
Herzens Grüsse," Opus 19, No. 6, in fact, one of his
finest.]　" I am now making one that will not come out
well, I fear, but when we three take hold of it it must go
well, for it is very well meant ; the text is by Goethe.　It
does not go at all to music, but I find it so divinely
beautiful that I had to sing it to myself."　He refers to
the wonderfully fine song " Ein Blick aus deinen Augen
in die meinen," which Goethe made out of a letter of
Bettina to him.　The composition is just as delicate and
spiritual as the poetry itself.　On the following morning
Mendelssohn wrote further : "The song which I composed
yesterday is now done.　Also some things for the piano
are getting bravely on."　The following remark is worth
quoting : "I have, unfortunately, no opinion at all about
my new productions. . . . I do not know whether they
are good or bad, and this because no one of the people
to whom I play them do anything but exclaim, ' How
very beautiful !'　I only wish that some one would be
reasonable in this, or, to speak more fairly, would praise
with discretion.　In the meantime, I must get on as
best I can alone."　As a thank-offering to the landlord's
daughter for the notepaper, he wrote three waltzes on
what remained of it, and gave them politely to her.

The weather improved meanwhile, and Mendelssohn,
who had already once gone to Interlaken, began to take
up the thought of undertaking the Bernese Oberland.

He went first to Lauterbrunnen, whither the road, only passable on foot, had become more than wildly romantic by reason of the excessive rains. The whole of that familiar way had been so flooded that frequently the bare trunks of trees were seen half submerged in the river bed. From the Wengern-alps he sends greeting on the 14th of Aug. to his friends. The mountains were then without clouds and in their most gorgeous array, and in his joy he writes from Grindelwald : " I believe that the face of God looks as this landscape does to-day. Whoever does not know Him cannot have eyes for the beauty of his works. And what shall I say besides of the delightful freshness of the air which invigorates one when he is weary, and cools one when he is hot? "

From the Wengern-alps Mendelssohn, accompanied by an old peasant, ascended to a point a thousand feet higher than the little Scheidegg in order to be present at an alpine festival, and here he gained a wonderful and glorious view.

He ascended the Faulhorn on the 15th of Aug. and again experienced the reverses of the weather : " Oh, I am freezing, it is snowing outside powerfully ; the storm rages and howls. We are more than eight thousand feet above the sea ; we must be above the snow line. Nothing in the world can be seen ; the weather has been fearful the whole day." And during his further journey over the great Scheidegg, Grimsel, and the Furca, and even as far as Lucerne, the same unfortunate weather attended him. Still he did not allow it to disturb his pleasant humor, but wrote : "And yet, whenever we can be a half hour without rain it is too beautiful. Journeying on foot through this country, with weather even as it is now, is the most charming thing that can be imagined.

With pleasant weather it must be too fine for any expression." He was compensated for so many misfortunes by a few days in Engleberg, where he found a comfortable tavern and had a magnificent view of the meadows and the snow-covered Titlis, and the rocky crags of the Great and Little Spannörter. The weather was delightful while he was there, and he enjoyed greatly reading again Schiller's " Tell," which he found in the convent library. He formed a close friendship with the monks of this convent which was founded in the twelfth century, played upon their beautiful organ, and even officiated as organist on the occasion of a great festival; he also played in the afternoon a number of new organ pieces.

As a little memorial of Felix' stay in Engelberg, there is to be seen in the letter of Aug. 23rd, a very pretty pen sketch from his hand, which represents the convent and the grand mountains that stand behind it. I hope that every one who visits this charming valley will recall the happy days which Mendelssohn passed here.

A letter from Lucerne to William Taubert, in Berlin, who accompanied him to Milan, is especially worth noting here as containing his thanks for several songs, which Taubert had sent him: " How delightful it is to find one musician more in the world who is striving for the same end, and travelling the same road with oneself. What this is you can hardly tell, especially to one who is coming, as I am, out of a country where music no longer lives among the people; it would be indeed a strange thing if there could be music where there is no spiritual capacity." In the same letter there is also a very strong expression aimed at the haughty disdain and hostile cynicism of those who speak lightly of Goethe

and Shakespeare, and find Schiller altogether too trivial
for their taste. "Are you not of one mind with me," he
writes, "that it is the first qualification of the artist to
have respect for real greatness, and bow down before it,
and not seek to put out its great flames in order that his
own little candle may shine the brighter?" Truly
memorable words, which ought to be committed to
golden tablets by those who speak to-day of rising above
Mozart, and who call Mendelssohn weak. After a visit
to the Rigi of which he gives a very interesting account,
he went again, in storm and rain, over the Hoken to the
convent of Einsiedeln; then to Wallenstadt and Sargans,
in which two places he practised on the organs, such as
they were, by reason of the steadily pouring rain; and
at last came by way of St. Gallen to Lindau where, after
an absence of almost a year and a half, on the 5th of
Sept. he again set foot on German soil. Here he found
a very fine organ on which he played to his heart's
delight, 'Schmücke dich O liebe Seele.' From Lindau
he went another short day's journey by way of Mem-
mingen and Augsburg to Munich. . . . If the reception
which Mendelssohn had when he first visited Munich
was enthusiastic, much more did it deserve that name
when he came thither the second time. He was here
more than a month, and we have but two letters as the
record of the time; a proof, even in their limited extent,
that he was greatly occupied by the calls of society,
and by the practice and the duties of his art. A great
concert which he wanted to give in behalf of the poor
of Munich was postponed in consequence of the October
festival; and the completion of his own G-minor concerto, which he desired to play on this occasion, engaged
him exclusively; but he took great delight in this occupa-

tion. "It is a grand feeling," he begins his letter of
Oct. 6th, "when one awakes in the morning and has to
instrumentalize a big piece of *allegro* with oboes and
trumpets, while outside the weather is magnificent, and
invites one to take a long walk; and this has been my
experience now the whole week. The agreeable impression which Munich made upon me the first time has
been even heightened now. I scarcely know any other
place where I feel so much at home as I do here. It is
a great delight to live among pleasant people, to feel
oneself one with them, and to recognize almost everybody whom one meets on the street."

One can read Mendelssohn's varied nature in these
words; can recognize his delight in his profession; also
in nature and in the fresh invigorating air, and also in his
intercourse with the cheery and agreeable men by whom
he found himself beloved.

Respecting his life in Munich in other regards, he says,
among other things: "I live on the lower story, in a
room that was once a shop, so that I can go with a step
into the street, when I take down the shutters before the
door. Whoever goes by peeps in at the window and
says, 'good morning.' Near me lives a Greek who is
learning the piano; he is horrible. But the landlord's
daughter who is very slender, and wears a silver trimmed
cap, is all the prettier. Every week I have music in my
room three times, at four o'clock in the afternoon. There
are Bärmann, Breiting (the well known and admirable
tenor), Staudacher, and young Poissl and they make a
musical picnic for me. I am also becoming acquainted
with the operas which unavoidably I have never yet
seen, such as Lodoiska, Laniska, and Medea, all by
Cherubini; also Preciosa and Abou Hassan. We get the
scores from the theatre."

There follows a very entertaining account of a musical *soirée* which was given in Mendelssohn's room as the result of several lost wagers. The apartment was very limited; a list of thirty was made out to be invited and several came without being invited. They had to place some upon the bed, while some good naturedly went into the little sleeping room. People were so anxious to hear that they took their places above stairs, some in the street and in the passage ways; the whole performance was indescribably animated and successful. Mendelssohn played first, his B-minor quartet, then Breiting sang "Adelaide," then one gentleman executed variations on the violin. Bärmann played Beethoven's first quartet arranged for two clarionets, bass horn, and bassoon; then came the aria from " Euryanthe " which was applauded without end; and, to conclude, Mendelssohn was compelled by a fearful storm of calls to improvise, although he had nothing in his head as a theme, except wine glasses and chairs, and cold and roast ham. The jolly company remained together singing and drinking healths till half past one. That evening came the compensatory performance: Mendelssohn was summoned to play before the Queen and the court. Everything there was polite and prim; on every side one encountered an excellency; the most polished and finished forms of address were current in the rooms, and he, a simple burgher, was in it all with his citizen's heart, and his aching head. " I made as short work of it as I could, but in the end I was compelled to improvise, and was much applauded. It pleased me most that the Queen said to me after the improvisation : ' That was wonderful, you just carry one away with your playing;' on which I begged to be excused in consequence of my approaching departure. Mendelssohn has some very interesting words in the close of the letter about his daily organ practice. In Munich he had found an instrument whose register enabled him to play Sebastian Bach's "Schmücke dich O liebe Seele." He speaks of the scope of this register in touching terms : "The choral is drawn out so still and penetratingly as if it were the voices of men far away singing from the heart," etc. The whole letter from which this is taken is so well worth reading that I refrain from quotation, only asking that it be perused in full.

In a letter to his father he depicts the preparations they were making for the concert above mentioned, and the concert itself. The rehearsals occurred in the time of the October Festival. Mendelssohn went to a general rehearsal in which the whole personnel was assembled, and he must submit to a task which was hard for him ; namely, inviting in polite terms, the whole orchestra of the theatre to coöperate with him. This he accomplished without any difficulty, stepping before the prompter's desk, and extending his invitation, which was responded to with shouts of encouraging applause. On the following day he had sixty names upon his circular : even the oboeists, whom he was obliged to enlist in place of the bass horns and trumpets, would take not a penny of pay, and he had at least eighty in his orchestra. It afforded particular delight also to Mendelssohn that the chorus sent one of its directors to him with the proposition that if he would allow them to sing a piece written by himself, they would all gladly sing it without compensation. Mendelssohn was unwilling to have more than three pieces of his own in the concert, but this active spirit of coöperation rejoiced him greatly. The first rehearsal was not satisfactory, he was obliged to work for two hours on his C-minor symphony ; the G-minor concerto would not go well ; the " Midsummer Night's Dream " overture had to be rushed through in all haste, and he was inclined to withdraw it from the programme ; to which, however, Bärmann would not give consent, but later on the general rehearsal was a success, and the concert itself all that could be desired.   He says of it : " In the evening when I heard the sound of the carriages I began to recover my spirits and to be in excellent humor ; at half past seven the court came, and I took my little English baton in hand, and directed my symphony ; the orchestra played splendidly, with an enthusiasm and a fire, such as I have never seen under my direction before ; the *forte* was given grandly, and the *scherzo* was very fine and light.   It pleased the people immensely, and the King constantly applauded.   Then my stout friend Breiting sang the A-flat major aria from " Euryanthe, " and the public cried *da capo*.   Breiting was happy, sung with spirit and with great beauty.   Then I came to my concerto which was received excellently, the orchestra accompanied well and the composition went lively enough ; it gave the people evident pleasure : they wanted to call me out afterwards, as the custom here is, but I was shy and did not come.   In the *entr' acte* King Louis took hold of my shoulders, praised me very much, and asked all sorts of questions, whether I was related to the Bartholdy into whose house he always went at Rome, because it was the cradle of modern art, etc.

The second part of the concert began with the " Midsummer Night's Dream" overture, which went very finely and made a very good impression.   Then Bärmann played, after which came the Finale in A-major from " Lodoiska " given with the whole strength of the opera ;

but Mendelssohn had no ears for this, for he was preoccupied in the waiting-room, having been ordered to produce as a Finale to the concert, a free improvisation for which the King had given, as a theme, the *Non piu andria*, from " Figaro's Wedding. "   He gained great applause by this ; the Queen said very pleasant things to him, and the people would not end their clapping of hands ; but he himself was not pleased with it.   He did not like the custom of improvising on such occasions, considering it inappropriate and senseless.   " This was my concert on the 17th, " he writes :   " and it already lies behind me.   There were 1100 persons present, and the poor people can be happy.

Your ever faithful, Felix. "

Another token of honor which Mendelssohn received in Munich was a proposition which came from the management of the Royal Opera House, that he should compose an opera expressly for it.   He would have been glad, as we know, to have carried this into execution, but we also know that he was very particular in the choice of a text.   " He could and would compose nothing which he might not undertake with his whole soul. "   In like manner, he frequently expressed himself in his letters to his friend Devrient :   " Give me a good text for an opera and I will compose it upon the spot ; I desire nothing more earnestly. "   But his demands for such a text were high and he would compose no " mish mash " of art and nonsense, as Mullner called the opera, but he demanded material which should lay claim to deep human interest.   In this vein, for example, he once wrote to Devrient from Milan while he was on his travels :   " You exact that I write only operas, and you blame me for not having done it long ago. I reply, produce a good opera for me and in a few months it is composed, for I long every day anew to write an opera: I know I can produce something fresh and bright if I only find it; but the words are lacking, and I am not able to compose a text that will inspire me. If you can name a man who can produce an opera, name him to me for God's sake, I desire nothing better; but till I have a text shall I do nothing? My writing church music has been a necessity to me, just as one oftentimes feels driven to read some book, the Bible, or something else, and finds himself very well employed in the occupation. If my work has a resemblance to Sebastiah Bach, I have written it just as it came to me: if I have fallen into the same mood and method as the good old master, I am so much the more glad, for you cannot suppose that I keep him in forms and not in substance. If I could, I could out of sheer emptiness bring no piece to an end. " And further on the same subject he writes to Devrient: " I am going now to Munich where they want an opera of me, in order to see whether there is a man there who is almost a poet, for I need a man who is a poet of talent and facility; it is not necessary to have a giant, and if I find no one there I am going to make the acquaintance of Immerman; if he fails, I shall try my fortune in London, and lay the matter directly on Klingemann. You see, what I want is the right man; but where shall I look for him, and what shall I do to find him? Certainly he is not living in the Hotel Reichmann. Although I believe the dear heavenly Father provides everything, even opera texts, as soon as we need them, yet we must do our miserable duty and look around to provide ourselves, and I would the text were already here; meanwhile, I write as good things as I possibly can. "

In like manner Mendelssohn writes again to Devrient, from Lucerne, on the 31st of August: "If you succeed in securing, not singers and decorations and situations, but men and nature and life, I am persuaded that you will write the very best operas that we can have; for if one knows the stage as well as you do he cannot possibly write anything undramatic. I cannot imagine why you find fault with your verses; for if there is a genuine feeling for nature and music, the verses will be rich, beautiful, and musical, even if they go haltingly in the text book; write then, for my sake, prose; we will put the music to it. Then if it must be so, it will not be hard; but if the verses are musical in sound and not musical in thought, if we have merely on the outside fine expressions, and a want of true life within, then you are right in saying that that is a pinch from which no man can extricate himself."

In like manner Mendelssohn writes on this subject, June 28th, 1853, from Leipsic, to Devrient, who had sent him the text of an opera and asked him his opinion about it. "Atterbohm's 'Insel der Glückseligkeit' contains no true material for an opera, according to my opinion. Magic and wonders do not make an opera, as I understand it; it is the real human, the ennobling and the inspiring qualities which are, in my judgment, the essence of the matter, and these I have not yet found."

I have not been willing to curtail these extracts, because they contain fruitful hints for the writers and composers of operas even now. Devrient had meanwhile written for Märschner the text of "Hans Heiling," and for Taubert "The Gipsy;" he had also laid before Mendelssohn a sketch from the "Peasants' War;" but Mendelssohn found in all too obvious echoes of "Freyschütz " and " Preciosa." Once more he wrote to Devrient from Frankfort, April 26th, 1845 : " See if you cannot give me counsel. The work, as you see, I must do myself, but the ground work—that is my trouble ; it must be German, and it must be noble and cheerful ; be it a Rhenish folks legend, or any national event or tale, or a strong type of character as in ' Fidelio ; it is not ' Kohlhas,' and it is not ' Blue-beard ' ; it is not 'Andreas Hofer ' or the ' Lorelei '; and yet it might have something in common with all of these. Can you make out really what I want? I wish you would help me to it. "

As Mendelssohn did not find the poet whom he sought in Munich, he went on to Düsseldorf to meet Immerman whom he was sure would be the man he needed. Immerman entered directly into the matter, and proposed as a theme for an opera Shakespeare's ' Tempest, ' a proposition which was acceptable to Mendelssohn. He promised the text by the end of May, at the latest; but the event proved that Immerman was not the man for the occasion : he had neither the gift of writing musical verses, nor could he grasp his matter so as to produce something fanciful, vivid, natural, and holding human interest. On the 7th of Dec. Mendelssohn's father advised him to turn rather to a French poet; but, in the first place this counsel came too late, as Mendelssohn had already entered into relations with Immerman ; and, besides, he had not inclination for it. His confidence in Immerman was still entirely unimpaired. He wrote to his father, from Paris, on the 19th of December : " From all that I know of Immerman I have reason to expect a capital *libretto* from him." Further development of affairs showed that Mendelssohn completely deceived himself in this expectation. Immerman was a thoroughly unlyrical nature. Devrient was compelled to agree with Mendelssohn in the rejection of the text which Immerman offered. And yet, in the course of time the connection with Düsseldorf was to bring forth excellent fruit, as we shall see hereafter.

We find Mendelssohn then at the beginning of Dec. in Paris. He went thither from Munich by way of Stuttgart, Heidelberg, Frankfort, and down the Rhine to Düsseldorf. In a letter from Zelter, written from Paris, Feb. 15th, 1832, he speaks of his great satisfaction with musical affairs in Southern Germany. He was not particularly delighted with music as it was in those days at Frankfort. He says: " It is on a large scale, and is conformable to the style of a great city, but is not true music ; " but he was charmed with the " Cecilia Society, " which was one of the great musical attractions of Frankfort at that time.

After expressing himself in terms of thorough appreciation respecting Schelble's influence on the taste for good music in Frankfort, he closes with the words : " At the same time Philip Veit is there and is painting his pictures, which are as simple, beautiful, and pious as the work of the old masters ; there is no excessive ornamentation and affectation in his work, as there is with the German artists in Rome, but an upright, sound, and artistic nature. When Mendelssohn was speaking as he did of his satisfaction with the ' Cecilia Society,' he little thought that in the summer of 1836 he should take the place of his friend Schelble in the direction, and thus experience the purest and most complete happiness of his life.

From Frankfort Mendelssohn went down the Rhine to Düsseldorf, as we have intimated, in order to conclude his negotiations with Immerman respecting the presentation of Shakespeare's ' Tempest. '   Although the result of his interviews was unsatisfactory for the time, yet they led to the formation of ties which afterwards brought him into very close relations with the management of the Düsseldorf Theatre.   Besides this, Mendelssohn felt himself greatly attracted by the artistic spirit in Düsseldorf in respect to both painting and music.   In the letter already cited from Paris to Zelter, he writes regarding this: " And then one comes to Düsseldorf, where Schadow is director of the Academy of Painting, and is at work with all his might: something should come out of it; Lessing, meanwhile, is engaged with his drawing ; there is a small orchestra able to give Beethoven's symphonies," and so on.

From Düsseldorf Mendelssohn went to Paris in order to make the acquaintance of that city in its musical, political, and art life.   He remained there from the middle of Dec. 1831, to the middle of April 1832, met his old friend Ferdinand Hiller, and entered into close relations with all the distinguished musicians there, and other eminent men, living a life of great joy and youthful freshness.   His " Letters of Travel" and the " Letters and Recollections " of Ferdinand Hiller give a satisfactory account of this Paris episode.   The orchestra of the conservatory under Haverneck's direction pleased him very greatly, especially by reason of their manner of treating Beethoven's symphonies.   A humorous incident occurred in one of the concerts of this conservatory, in which Mendelssohn played a leading part.   Hiller tells it in his " Recollections : " " Through Haverneck and his orchestra Mendelssohn came into contact with the great public. He was playing the D-major concerto of Beethoven, and with what success can be seen in his own 'Letters of Travel.' The overture to the 'Midsummer Night's Dream' also was brought forward and received with great applause; I was present at the first rehearsal: the second obeist was absent, a loss that was greatly to be felt; but as they were just on the point of beginning, it was discovered that the place of the kettle-drum was also unfilled. To the amusement of all Mendelssohn sprang forthwith to the orchestra, took possession of the sticks, and rattled away like a drummer of the old guard."

We have a much higher proof of his musical skill, and especially of his amazing memory, in the account of a great Musicale given by Abbé Bardin, a clergyman who was extremely fond of music. Hiller had previously played the E-flat major concerto of Beethoven, and there was a great desire to hear it again. The orchestra was represented by the stringed instrument players, but the wind instruments failed to appear. "I will undertake this," said Mendelssohn, taking his seat at a small piano which stood by, and from memory completed the orchestral parts so perfectly that I do not think that a note even · of the second horn was omitted; it was all done so simply and in the best taste; just as if it could not possibly fall out otherwise."

In like manner he once was playing to his musical friends the air from Haydn's Seasons, "Hier steht der Wanderer nun" (Here stands the wanderer, confused and full of doubt). He played this without the omission of a note between the alternating figures of the violin. It sounded like a genuine piano piece, and we looked on a good while, "confused and full of doubt." Of the distinguished musicians with whom Mendelssohn came in contact I mentioned the aged and famous Cherubini whom Mendelssohn visited from time time, the distinguished violin players, Baillot, Paganini, and Ole Bull; subsequently he made the acquaintance of Chopin, Franz Liszt, Meyerbeer, Kalkbrenner, and Henri Hertz. We have already mentioned that Liszt astonished Mendelssohn beyond measure by playing at sight a G-minor concerto from manuscript. On the other hand the jealousy between Kalkbrenner and Hertz amused him much. He did not stand on the best terms with Meyerbeer; it displeased him to find that every one perceived a great resemblance between them, and, in order to make this less visible, he caused his hair and beard to be clipped short. Meyerbeer in his unbounded good nature took the thing as a joke. The French musicians spoke of Mendelssohn in terms of the highest respect: " Ce bon Mendelssohn, quelle talent, quelle tête, quelle organization! " were expressions which were often heard from them.

Mendelssohn was an accomplished chess-player; a good deal of time was given to this amusement, and his adversaries, the poet Michael Beer, brother of Meyerbeer, and Dr. Hermann Francke, could only occasionally get the advantage of him. The latter would not admit that he was the weaker player, and Mendelssohn was compelled to say, after every victory: " We play exactly equally well — exactly equally well — only I play a trifle better. "

Mendelssohn does not appear to have produced much new music in Paris. Besides the manuscripts of the " Walpurgis Night, " the " G-minor concerto, " and the " Hebrides, " he brought out the first " Song without Words " in E-major, which was composed in Switzerland. This he played to Dr. Francke and Hiller, and gave to it at that time the name which since then has been so much misused.

More important than all else which Mendelssohn's stay in Paris called out (a fact not yet known to all the friends of Mendelssohn), is that here he first conceived the plan of writing his " Oratorio of St. Paul." We learn this from a letter of Mendelssohn to Devrient, dated March 10th, 1832. "I have something to ask you about, Edward: answer me directly. I am to write an Oratorio for the Cecilia, and, as I cannot in any event begin my opera before July, I have, from the next month on, a full quarter of a year's time, and I should like to make use of it and write at least a part of my Oratorio, as I have already thought out many good things for it. The subject is the Apostle Paul: he will be introduced in the first part; the stoning of Stephen and the presecution will occupy the second part; the conversion will be the theme of the third part, in which I shall introduce Christian life and preaching, and either the death of the martyrs, or Paul's parting. The words I should like to take mainly out of the Bible and hymn book, and then have some small things: for example, some hymns and chorals; the defence of Stephen I will take from the Bible. But I cannot bring this altogether myself. Will you undertake it? You know the Bible better than I do, and you know exactly how to do it, and it will cost you less time. You are the very man for it; therefore, reply at once, and we can correspond further, for there is very little time to lose in the matter."

Devrient did not feel himself qualified to undertake this honorable task, and referred Mendelssohn to two friends whom he had known from youth, Bauer, and Schubring, the latter of whom prepared the text, and won not only great honors for himself, but accomplished a work of the highest value in a musical sense.

In Paris Mendelssohn received several painful tidings, among them, that of the death of his friend Edward Rietz, and of his great friend Goethe; respecting the latter he says in a letter home dated March 31st: "Goethe's loss is news that makes one feel so poor. How changed does the whole country seem now. It is one of the things that have come to me which will always be connected with the name of Paris in my memory, and the impression of which, in spite of all the friendliness and of the whirl of merry life here, will never be lost by me."

After successfully escaping from a light attack of cholera, Mendelssohn went to London where new honors awaited him. Arriving there April 22nd, he had the most affectionate greeting, not only from the old friends, Moscheles, Klingemann, and Rosen, but also in all musical circles. He writes regarding this in his letter of April 27th: "I wish I could tell you how merry I am here, and how pleasant everything is, how delighted I have reason to be with the kindness of the old friends, Klingemann, Rosen, and Moscheles; I have joined myself as closely to them as if we had never been separated; they form the centre of my life here. We see each other every day, and it is charming to find myself again among good, earnest men, and true friends, against whom I do not have to guard myself. Moscheles and his wife exhibit a touching kindness to me, which is all the more delightful to me that I love them so much."

Respecting his reception by musical people, he gives the following example in his letter of May 11th: "Saturday morning was rehearsal at the Philharmonic, in which, however, nothing of mine could be given, because my overture to the Hebrides was not written out. After Beethoven's Pastoral Symphony, during which I was in the box, I wanted to go into the hall in order to greet some old friends.  Scarcely, however, had I come below than some one cries out from the orchestra, ' There's Mendelssohn ! ' and at once they began to clap and to call in such a manner that I at first did not know which way to turn ; and as soon as that was through, another cries out, ' Welcome to him ! ' and so the noise began again, and I was obliged to climb up into the orchestra and express my thanks.  That is something which I shall never forget ; it showed that the musical people loved me, and that they are glad that I have come, and it has given me more happiness than I can express. "   His stay in London, of scarcely more than a month, gave him an opportunity to display his astonishing musical abilities in a manner that was simply astounding.  On the 14th of May the overture to the " Hebrides " was given by the Philharmonic Society under his direction for the first time.  Mendelssohn, writing to his father May 18th, says : " It went splendidly, and produced a rare effect, placed as it was between a good many things of Rossini's. The people have taken up me and my piece with uncommon kindness.  On May 28th he played, likewise at the Philharmonic, his G-minor concerto for the first time, and on June 18th, for the second time.  On May 26th, he produced in the Morris Evening Concert for the first time publicly, his newly finished Rondo, brillante in E-flat major.  On the 1st of June he played in Moscheles' concert, and with him, Mozart's concerto for two pianos, and directed his two overtures to the " Hebrides " and to the " Midsummer Night's Dream. "   On the 5th of June he rehearsed with Moscheles a four-handed arrangement of the latter overture ; on the 10th he played in St. Paul's Cathedral, and, to the amazement of all hearers, fugues for the organ. On the 21st he improvised in a *soirée*, after Paganini had played, taking as his theme a glee by Horsley. Amid all this activity the sad tidings reached him of the death of his old friend and teacher Zelter, an event which moved him scarcely less than the death of Goethe. While under the weight of this affliction he sought a brief refreshment at the home of his friend Attwood, in Norwood, Surrey, and at the end of this brilliant season in London, on June 23rd he returned to Berlin.

———————

# PART III.

### MENDELSSOHN'S ACTIVE LABORS IN DUSSELDORF AND LEIPSIC, FROM 1833 TO 1841.

In spite of all the impressions which he had received in foreign lands, and his magnificent successes, especially in London, yet Mendelssohn expressed himself repeatedly in his letters to his father as decided in his choice of Germany as his future home and the scene of all subsequent labors. In which city he should live, however, he had not yet determined. At the very moment when he returned to Berlin there seemed to be an opening for his best activities there in his own city. He would have been glad to remain with his family in Berlin, although the unhappy influence of Spontini on musical taste in Berlin, and the many unhappy coteries in the city, would not have been pleasant to him. Through the death of Zelter, the post of Director of the Singacademie was made vacant. This position was occupied by Rungenhagen, a very zealous musician but of moderate talents, entirely without eminence as a composer. He was aided by Zelter's pupil, Edward Grell. Mendelssohn himself would not become an applicant for the post, but declared himself ready to accept if the choice should fall on him. He even went so far as express a willingness to undertake the direction in connection with Rungenhagen, a step which, however, did not please the latter. The first meeting of the male members of the Singacademie which was called to consider this affair took place August 19, 1832, but after dragging along for six months amid all kinds of crooked and low intrigues, finally on January 22, 1833, the choice was determined, Rungenhagen receiving 148 votes; Mendelssohn 88; and Grell 4. It is said that this result was due to the influence of some old ladies who took exception to Mendelssohn's Jewish extraction. What a pitiful prejudice against a young man of whom, of course, they must have known that he had been baptized and educated as a Christian; who not four years before had conducted, with their co-operation, "The Passion" of Bach, and had written in Rome music to the most beautiful of Luther's hymns! At all events, it was the work of the *Dii minorum gentium*, people who had their little spites against Mendelssohn, and who were small enough "to make faces at him," as he himself says in a letter written to Moscheles in 1839. The Singacademie of Berlin condemned itself by this action, as Devrient says justly, to a long series of years of insignificance. Aside from the bitterness of feeling which this affair created in the Mendelssohn family itself (they all withdrew from the Singacademie), Felix passed a happy winter in the circle of his friends and relatives. Besides the reading of Jean Paul and Hegel, also of dramas in which the parts were distributed dramatically, he took up his earnest musical occupations, laboring upon the "Walpurgis Night" in its new form, also on the "A-minor Symphony," which he intended to bring out in the spring at London, and putting his hand to the first part of "St. Paul." Between November and January he gave in the Concert Room of the theatre four concerts in which he produced, among other of his own compositions, the overture to the "Hebrides" and the "Walpurgis Night." He does not appear to have given his "G-minor Concerto;" at least, I find no trace of it in the records at hand; he played the piano, however, as a soloist, repeatedly. Respecting his playing at that time, Devrient makes the following remarks: "Felix' piano playing had now reached a point of supreme excellence, and had taken upon itself the character of his own individuality. It was not as virtuoso; not his astonishing technique and endurance, his precision and energy, which held the hearer spell-bound; one forgot the instrument, one perceived only the interpretation of the piece in hand — he played, of course, only the best music — he gave a real musical revelation, it was the speech of mind to mind. By reason of the depths of his thought and the skill of his forms the public had reason to regret that he did not improvise more frequently, but he called it a folly to do so; to use his own words, it was as if one should say, on such and such an evening and at such and such an hour I am going to have fine thoughts. His playing," Devrient goes on to say, "made a great sensation in Berlin, and produced a very great impression, although perhaps not as much as in other cities. His compositions, too, did not meet with the same favor there that they found in all other places; his musical eminence was recognized in his own city only too late."

Under such circumstances, the invitation to Düsseldorf was doubly welcome, where he was asked to take the direction of the local Musical Festival. This came to him through the instrumentality of his amiable and gifted friend, Mr. Von Woringen. The festival was to be held in Düsseldorf, Whitsuntide, from May 28 to 31, 1833. Mendelssohn went thither towards the end of April, and from there to London, whither he returned after the close of the festival at Düsseldorf.

With his stay in this city a new period of his life

begins. The first we may call that of preparation or of youth; the second the period of travel; and the third we may indicate as the period of baptism by fire. He went through it victoriously so far as to preserve always his loyalty to his calling, while he was always held within limitations by it. It was the period when he encountered opposition not only from musical people but also from others; while it was, on the other hand, a happy piece of good fortune that he entered from the very beginning a circle of intimate friends. For here were living and laboring the painters with whom he had already wandered through the Hesperides, and the whole circle, William Schadow being the centre of all, bade him welcome as an old friend and artist of equal birth with their own. To the end of his life he remained in the most intimate relations with them. Here, too, under the direction of the painter Schirmer, to whom he dedicated his 114th Psalm, he made advances in the art of drawing and painting, and produced a number of water colors of admirable quality.

Before, however, we accompany Mendelssohn into his new field of activity, we must briefly go with him to London. He went thither April 25, and in two days produced with Moscheles variations for two pianos on the Gipsy March from "Preciosa." This was afterwards played by both artists in Moscheles' concert. Their mutual understanding went so far that oftentimes the two would improvise on two pianos, in which, of course, there must have been an identity of musical thoughts as they took their themes from one another. On the 13th of May Mendelssohn directed in the Philharmonic for the first time his "A-major Symphony," which, as already indicated, he refers to in his letters as the Italian, and which he had

composed with special reference to the Philharmonic
Society.   He began this work, which is full of the youthful spirit of joy, when he was under the impressions of
Italian scenery and Italian life, whose traces it distinctly
bears, but he finished it in Berlin.   After its performance
in London, where it was received with great applause,
Mendelssohn seems to have laid it aside, for it only appeared after his death as " Symphony No. 4,'' Opus 90,
and No. 19 of the posthumous works.   In Leipsic he never
produced it during his direction of the Gewandhaus concerts.   I myself heard it for the first time two years after
Mendelssohn's death, November 1, 1849, when it was
given from manuscript, but since then I have frequently
heard it.   Although this symphony in grandeur, depth and
careful treatment falls below its sister symphony which
was completed later, the ''A-minor Symphony,'' yet it
bears the mark of so much geniality and unquestionable
freshness that it always leaves a most delightful feeling
upon the hearer.   It consists of four movements all in the
closest connection.   The first, allegro vivace, written in
A-major, leads out in a cheerful strain full of spring time
and of love, and with the most charming alternating
motives ; not at all as Reismann tells us a paraphrase of
of the so-called hunting song in the first group of songs
without words, with which it has only the key in common, but rather with suggestions of the overture to the
'' Heimkehr aus der Fremde ;'' the second movement andante con moto in D-minor is a somewhat slowly moving
strain, said to have been a processional hymn and probably giving the name of '' Italian Symphony'' to the whole.
I cannot discover that the piece bears any mark of a
decided Catholic character, for if I recollect rightly I once
heard Moscheles say that Mendelssohn had in his mind

as the source of this second movement an old Bohemian Volks Lied. The third movement, without any other indication than con moto moderato, in A-major, has the form of a charming minuet with a beautiful little trio in E-major, and with the suppressed horns in E, produce a lovely effect; the final movement, Saltarello, the Neapolitan National Dance, presto, in A-minor, is decidedly Italian, full of glow and Southern life. After the two artists Mendelssohn and Moscheles had played the variations on the Gipsy March from "Preciosa," Mendelssohn returned to Düsseldorf in order to direct the Musical Festival there.

He found here the most hearty welcome possible not only from the musicians but also from all friends of music. His father, who had come to Düsseldorf in order to be at the first great public rehearsal of his son, and who had been received into the home of Mr. Von Woringen with what appeared to him a really incredible friendliness and a truly unique hospitality, writes to the mother on the 22nd of May: "Felix was just commencing the rehearsal as I arrived. Woringen had hastened to announce to him with special triumph that I had come, which Felix refused to believe. After some time he came himself, and I will not deny to you that in his joy he kissed my hand. He is looking very well and, if my eyes do not deceive me, he has improved much within a short time; his features are more sharply drawn, and, therefore, stand out more than before, the eyes have the same appearance, and this taken altogether produces a very peculiar effect. Such a face I have never beheld. I have never seen a man so popular on all hands as Felix is here; he cannot praise enough the zeal of all who take part in the festival, he cannot say enough of their confidence in him, and best of all, by his playing he sets them all into enthusiasm, and by his memory he excites their highest amazement. It so happened that he changed a Beethoven symphony which had been announced and which had already been played once here, and put the 'Pastoral Symphony' in its place, and as therew as no time for special rehearsal and no score for him, he directed it from memory alone and sang the parts of the instruments that were lacking."

Mendelssohn had the good fortune to discover the original score of Handel's "Israel in Egypt," and so the presentation of this immense work formed the central feature of the festival; in addition there were given the "Pastoral Symphony," the great Leonora overture in C by Beethoven, the Easter cantata by Wolff, and the "Power of Tone" by Winter; to these were added the "Trumpet Overture in C-major" by Mendelssohn, and he himself played Weber's "Concertstuck." This musical festival, adorned by the coöperation of the distinguished singer Frau Decker, née Von Schatzel, was received with such favor that after both of the chief days had closed a third concert without rehearsal was improvised in which the majority of the pieces already given were repeated amid thunderous applause on the part of the public.

As Mendelssohn was descending to the floor at the close of the concert he was overhelmed with a shower of flowers, and one of Von Woringen's daughters brought upon a velvet cushion a wreath of laurel with which, nolens volens, he was compelled to be crowned.'

After the concert there was a brilliant soirèe and ball at Schadow's, where Mendelssohn received new ovations. Some one struck up on the piano "See the conquering hero comes!" and Mendelssohn was obliged to place his garland again upon his head and march two or three times through the room at the head of a procession. Afterwards there began the wildest waltzes and galops. Mendelssohn was compelled to play for these at first but afterwards he danced merrily with the rest. Madam Decker supposed that Felix did not dance, that he was altogether too earnest and busy with other things, but he soon convinced her to the contrary, and she said to his father when he was resting for the first time, "Felix dances extremely well."

The committee of the festival honored Mendelssohn with a seal cut in stone after a pattern given by Schadow. This was perserved by him as a souvenir, and kept in daily use.

Much more important, however, than these tokens of homage was the offer of the Düsseldorf magistracy requesting him to take the post of Musical Director to the city, and offering him six hundred thalers* as salary, and a yearly vacation of three months. His duty would be to provide the music in the Catholic churches and the winter concerts, and to direct the vocal and instrumental societies existing in Düsseldorf. Mendelssohn accepted this position for three years. Before entering upon his duties, however, he went in company with his father to London again. On the 10th of June he gave at the Philharmonic concert his overture in C-major, the same one which had been already given in Düsseldorf. Mendelssohn's father had the misfortune to encounter a similar accident to that of his son some years before, and during the time of his convalescence, Felix, as the father himself confesses, nursed him with touching fidelity and care, and meanwhile wrote for Moscheles a four handed arrangement to his

*About 450 dollars of our money.

septet. He also played his overture to Melusina to Moscheles from the original manuscript score. According to
common report the first conception of this overture came
to him at sight of a picture in Düsseldorf which represented Melusina as a fisher wife ; but the oddest account of
the origin of this charming piece of the music Mendelssohn himself gives in a letter to Fanny, dated Düsseldorf,
April 7, 1834 : "I have written this overture to the opera
by Conradin Kreutzer which last year about this time I
witnessed in the Konigstadt Theatre. The overture was
desired da capo, yet it displeased me extremely ; afterwards the whole opera was wanted again, but the singer
Hahnel, who took the part of Melusina, was not wanted ;
but she was really very lovely, and especially in the song
where she presents herself as a mermaid ; she was so
charming in this, that I conceived the idea of writing an
overture. This the people have not cared much for, but
it pleased me greatly in the writing, and chimes well with
the subject of the story ; and so in short, my overture
came to the world, and this is the history of its pedigree."

Moscheles produced this overture for the first time in the
Philharmonic concert on the 7th of April, 1834, where I
must confess it met with only slight recognition, but afterwards on the 8th of May, being repeated, it pleased much
better. At this latter concert he also played from manuscript the "Rondo in E-major," dedicated to him by Mendelssohn. It is possible that the failure of the Mendelssohn
overture at the first performance may have come from the
want of the right instrumentation, especially in the use of
the clarionet, but later, when it succeeded, Mendelssohn's
joy was complete and he expressed it in his heartiest manner. He needed this kind of cheering because he always
doubted himself. He says in jest that this applause is

more welcome to him than three orders. To his sister
Fanny he wrote later in Leipsic, January 30, 1836:
"Of the Melusina, many people here say it is my best
overture, at any rate it is the one that comes most from
the heart; it is the one that deals most thoroughly with
red corals, green sea monsters, and fairy palaces and deep
seas. This all excites even my own astonishment."

On the 29th of August, 1833, Mendelssohn, having
closed a series of extraordinary performances with great
success, left London and did not see it again for a considerable period. At first he accompanied his father to
Berlin, where he passed several very delightful days with
the family, and then entered definitively on his new labors
in Düsseldorf. On Sunday the third of October he directed his first mass. He writes concerning it to his sister
Rebecca in Berlin, October 26: "The choir was fully
packed with singers and singeresses who had adorned the
whole church with green twigs and with tapestry. The
organist rattled tremendously up and down, the mass by
Haydn was scandalously jolly, yet the whole effect was
good. Then came the procession with my solemn march
in E-flat, where the bass repeats the first part while the
treble goes straight on; but that does no harm in the
open air, and as I met the procession later they had
already played the march so often that it went very well.
I reckon it as an honor for myself that the musical people
connected with the fair have asked me to compose a new
march for them."

Then follows in the same letter a touching account of
a "tragical-comical" scene whose close does great honor
to Mendelssohn's tenderness of heart. The chaplain of
the church had complained to Mendelssohn that the music
was altogether too poor. The Catholic Burgomaster

would march in the procession only on condition that the music should be improved. " An old sorrowful looking musician with a shabby coat was introduced to me and said to me that he wanted and would have no better music than we now have; if we wanted better we might go somewhere else; he knew very well that this is a time when there are very great claims made. Everything must be very fine now, and he believed that real music was just as good in his time as it is now. I hated to say no to him and also hated to assert that we had better than they had had formerly, but at the same time I could not help thinking within myself that if in the course of fifty years I should be called to the Rathhaus and a little fellow should snub me and my coat should be as shabby I should equally fail to make out why things are better then than they are now — and so I confess my heart sank."

Mendelssohn discovered to his sorrow that among all the music at his command there was not a tolerable mass, not one that had any earnestness of character, nothing of the old Italian school, but mere modern trash. He undertook, therefore, a tour of discovery as far as Elberfeldt, Bonn and Cologne, and returned richly laden with his spoils. The "Improperia" of Palestrina, the "Misereres" of Allegri and Bai, also the score and voice parts of "Alexander's Feast;" six masses by Palestrina, one by Lotti, one by Pergolesi, and Psalms by Leo, &c., &c., were the treasures which he discovered in the libraries of the above-named cities. Contemporaneous with these activities occurred the visit of the Prussian Crown Prince, afterwards Frederick William IV., for whose reception great preparations had already been made in the roads through which he should pass. On the day of his

arrival, the Crown Prince gave a dinner to which
Mendelssohn was invited; the Prince was very gracious
towards him, expressed his lively regret that he had left
Berlin for so long a time, called him " my dear Mendelssohn " and treated him in a manner which was very
grateful to Felix' loyal heart. The whole artist world
of the city united its talents to give the Prince a reception
worthy of his birth.

The concerts which Mendelssohn directed seem not
to have been received at the outset with the applause
which was hoped for, for we find that between November, 1833, and May, 1834, only three were given, yet the
fault, if fault there were, is certainly not to be ascribed to
Mendelssohn, who made complete preparations for them
and appeared twice personally in them, playing the
violin.

In the meantime a light cloud began to appear in the
relations hitherto so affectionate and intimate between
Immerman and Mendelssohn. We have already seen
that Immerman had wished to write for Mendelssohn the
text of an opera based upon Shakespeare's " Tempest; "
the rejection of this on Mendelssohn's part had always
vexed Immerman, yet it had had no apparent influence
upon their mutual relations; on the contrary, they
seemed somewhat more affectionate than before, they
always addressed each other as " thou," and in spite of
the matter of the " Tempest" and his sensitive feeling,
Immerman appears to have been devotedly attached to
his fellow director.

The presence of two men so distinguished, their
number soon to be increased by the eminent Von
Uechtricz, caused an immediate improvement of the
stage in Düsseldorf; Immerman, Mendelssohn and

Uechtricz were all ready for this. Between December, 1833, and the end of March, 1834, there were so-called "model performances" to indicate what their purpose was. The first of these which Mendelssohn directed was "Don Giovanni." We need not enter into the painful history of the manner in which this was rejected by a part of the public and applauded by another part, nor need we portray the excited state of feeling which pre- . vailed not only in the management of the theatre but also in the public at large; the Düsseldorf papers of that time indicate that the city was deeply stirred, and, of course, it could not fail to be one of the causes of a subsequent breach in the harmony of Mendelssohn and Immerman.

The next performance of this character was in January 1834; it was Egmont with Beethoven's music. Respecting the first rehearsal, Mendelssohn writes in an ironically jovial manner to his family: "I have just come from the Egmont rehearsal, where I have witnessed for the first time in my life a score of music split in two . . . . . . . . . . . . . . . yet in spite of this it has in so far given me pleasure that I am now hearing something from Beethoven here for the first time; but in the performance I must confess I have not been greatly pleased; there are only two passages that have gone exactly to my satisfaction. The third performance was that of the 'Steadfast Prince' by Calderon, and the fourth and last of these pattern performances was Cherubini's 'Wasserträger.' They were afraid on giving this that the stormy scenes of 'Don Giovanni' would be repeated, but fortunately they were not, and the whole affair passed quietly by, winning the greatest applause from the public."

As a result of these performances a company was formed with a large capital, a new theatre was built bearing the name of The Dnsseldorf Municipal Theatre. The management consisted of eleven persons; Immerman and Mendelssohn were members and at the same time leading directors, one for the drama and the other for the opera. Mendelssohn, who was unwilling to give his entire time to the enterprise, induced his friend Julius Rietz, even then a distinguished musician, to come to Düsseldorf. They had become acquainted originally in Berlin, were of nearly the same age, and Mendelssohn had for a period given instruction to Rietz on the piano. On the 28th of October, 1834, the new stage was dedicated with Henry Von Kleist's "Prince of Homburg," and with a prelude written expressly for the occasion by Immerman. Unfortunately this theatre became only a source of discomfort between the two directors; they both had unquestionably the best intentions, but they were far apart from each other in their views regarding the whole subject of management. Immerman was glowing with the idea of establishing a really National theatre to which he would dedicate his life, whereas to Mendelssohn the opera was only a side issue; what he wanted was to dedictate his life to the composition of new works. He had neither talent nor inclination for such tasks as the engaging of singers, the arranging of salaries, and the like; everything of that sort was thoroughly contrary to his nature. He expresses this very plainly in letters to his parents and other members of his family, still more to his friend Devrient. He ought indeed to have considered this before he accepted his post, but we must bear in mind that he had had no experience in such affairs, and we must also remember that the mutual relations of the directors were not so completely sundered but that the duties of one occasionally entrenched upon those of the other. Out of this state of things first came reproaches, then the interchange of words and sharp letters, and finally complete estrangement. "In short I have taken my resolve that in three weeks after the opening of the theatre I will give up my post as manager and be a man again." He did in fact withdraw after having twice given Weber's "Oberon," and never re-established relations with Immerman again. It must be said that Abraham Mendelssohn as well as Devrient did not approve the violent sundering of the relations of the two men. The theatre sustained itself with great difficulty up to the spring of 1837.

But we must pass from this somewhat unhappy incident of his life and speak of our composer in his true and great musical career as Director and as Composer. The concerts and the Musical Society both flourished in the winter of 1834–5, in their finest bloom. There were seven public concerts in which, among other things, were given the "Messiah" and the "Seasons," but the event of the greatest interest to Düsseldorf was the composition of the largest part of "St. Paul," respecting whose gradual progress Mendelssohn gives information in his letters not only to his family but also to his friends. For example, to Louis Spohr, he writes on the 8th of March, 1835: "I began about a year ago an oratorio which I expect to end in the course of the next month, having for its subject St. Paul; the words have been collated for me from the Bible, by some friends, and I think that the subject as well as the manner in which it is put together is very well adapted to music and thoroughly solid; at any rate I have taken the greatest possible delight during its composition." Besides the "St. Paul," Mendelssohn wrote in this period the three Capriccios for the piano, Opus 23, a fugue in A-flat major, several songs with and without words, among them, "Auf Flügeln des Gesanges," and among the latter those of the second book; also the three Volk Songs by Heine, bearing the collective title "Entflieh mit mir und sei mein Weib," in the first collection of his songs for soprano, alto, tenor and bass, Opus 41 : and in addition to these the overture to the " Fair Melusina " already spoken of. Besides these he was not at all sparing of himself in rendering his personal assistance at various concerts; in Elberfeldt and Barmen he directed; in the spring of 1834 he visited the musical festival at Aix la Chapelle, where he met Ferdinand Hiller and Chopin; and it must be confessed that in spite of his comparatively light work in operatic matters his stay in Düsseldorf shows an amazing activity.

In the spring of 1835 he was requested to direct the musical festival at Cologne, which he did. There were given the festival overture by Beethoven in C, Handel's " Solomon," Beethoven's " Eighth Symphony," Milton's " Morning Hymn," set to Reichardt's music ; the " Overture to Euryanthe," the " Sacred March and Hymn" by Cherubini. It is observable that Mendelssohn practised the self denial of bringing nothing of his own forward; the recognition which he found there was extraordinary; the committee of the festival honored him with a copy of the great London edition of Handel's Works in twenty-three stout folios bound in the most solid English fashion, in green leather, bearing not only the title of the work but also the words " To Director Felix Mendelssohn Bartholdy, from the Musical Committee of the Festival of 1835 in Cologne." Besides this there was sent to him a very friendly letter signed by all of the committee and a parchment roll containing the signatures of all the members of the society, about six hundred in all.

In the meantime the attention of the city of Leipsic had been directed to Mendelssohn, and a wish was expressed to secure him as the head of the musical life in that city. Some of the most distinguished members of the university had cherished the thought, at the outset, of founding a professorship of music, and hold Mendelssohn, whose general culture was known to be so high and even scientific, as the most suitable man to fill this place. Inquiries were addressed to him respecting it, to which he replied with thanks, declining giving lectures, for which he said he had no talent at all. In the meantime the desire to have him live there grew more and more urgent, and the direction of the Leipsic Gewandhaus concerts was proposed as the means to win him thither. Mendelssohn had already a year before become acquainted with the musical life of Leipsic, which at that time had assumed importance. In September of 1834 he had tarried in Berlin for some weeks, and had gone back to Düsseldorf by way of Leipsic and Cassel. On the 1st of October he came to the city and took up his abode at the house of his friend, Francis Hauser, whose name may be recalled by the readers of this narrative as having become Mendelssohn's friend as early as the brief visit to Vienna years before. On the first of October he trod the floor of the Gewandhaus hall for the first time, was present at a rehearsal of his own "Meeresstille," and witnessed the great skill of the admirable orchestra, under the guidance at that time of the energetic and clever Matthai. The admirable performance was certainly no hindrance to his accepting the task which was laid upon him, and the negotiations came to a happy conclusion in April. Mendelssohn made only two conditions, the first of which was that his predecessor should not be forced to resign because of his coming, and that he himself should at least receive as much salary as he had received at Düsseldorf. It was voted that for the first two years he should receive six hundred thalers, and for the four following years a thousand thalers (a thaler being about seventy-five cents of our money). He had reserved the right to close his Düsseldorf contract at the end of two years; he did this, and having given a great concert there on the 2d of July, to the profound sorrow of his many friends there he left that city on the 30th of August and arrived in Leipsic, taking up his abode in the first story of a building abutting upon Reichel's garden.

Leipsic, the venerable home of the muses, ever rejuvenating its countenance with the years, and at present brought into the circle of great cities by its lines of splendid buildings; Leipsic which unites at once eminence in trade and in letters; whose people have always been equally renowned for their cosmopolitan spirit and thoroughly German patriotism; hostile to all that is stiff and pedantic, sensitive to all that is good in science and in art, embracing many noble patricians, many most accomplished men, and especially famous for its skill in and love of the noble art of music, this city was indeed the place where more perhaps than any other the genius of Mendelssohn could attain to its freest development. In addition to this, he could not forget the special devotion which had been shown in this city for two hundred years to the art of music. Here it was that the great cantor of the St. Thomas School, John Sebastian Bach, had as early as 1729 produced his Passion music, trained his magnificent choir, and produced his works as a constant and in-

tegral part of divine worship on all Sundays and festival
days; where from 1729 to 1736 he had also given public
concerts, having had as a rule two every week; here
where from 1743 to 1778 what had before been given in
private, assumed the form of a great public entertainment, and in 1781 had expanded to the dimensions of the
hall of the Gewandhaus. The "Gewandhaus" concerts
dated from this beginning. The hall, originally used, as
the name implies, for the storing of cloth, with its wooden
floor and with its wooden ceiling, was so admirably
adapted to music that its equal could hardly be found in
the world. Above the orchestra there stood even then
the beautiful device, " *Res severa est verum gaudium*,"
a motto which has been maintained with truth from the
beginning to the present day. From 1781 to 1785 J. A.
Hiller was cantor of the Thomas School, from that time
to 1810 J. G. Schicht; J. P. C. Schultz followed them
up to 1827, and from 1827 to 1835 C. A. Pohlenz. When
Mendelssohn took the post he found not only a thoroughly
trained orchestra which could play Beethoven's works in
tolerable perfection, and besides the Thomas School, he
found also a Vocal Academy, the admirable student chorus of the "Paulines," the Ossian Society composed of a
mixed chorus, and a number of skillful *dilettanti*; besides these there was also a well-established opera. On
a soil so thoroughly prepared, an accomplished director
could bring Leipsic to a position of eminence not only in
Germany but even in all Europe. Mendelssohn, but
twenty-six years of age at that time, was received with
open arms. He writes in a letter to his family, October
6, 1835: "I cannot tell you how satisfied I am with this
beginning and with the whole way in which my position
here is settled. It is a quiet field. The Institute has ex-

isted for fifty-six years, and the people are very friendly to me and to my music; the orchestra is good, thoroughly musical, and I think it will improve in six months, for they accept my hints and directions with such readiness that in both rehearsals which we have had thus far it has been really touching to see it.  There are indeed some deficiencies in the personnel, but they will soon be made good, and I think I can look forward to a series of agreeable and satisfactory performances."

With Mendelssohn's stay in Leipsic, which lasted almost without interruption from September, 1835, to 1844, and from 1845 to the end of his life, begins the fourth period of his career, an epoch full of the richest, freest, and most manifold activity, and at the same time an equally brilliant period for Leipsic itself which could only be continued with equal splendor by the greatest exertions on the part of those who should follow him. He directed the Gewandhaus concerts continuously from 1835 to 1841, accomplishing a great deal of his best and most finished work during this time and also thoroughly apreciated by his public; he knew how to use the rich materials which he found before him with the greatest skill, with constant power and patience, and in this way to reach the best effects.  He did not limit his activity at all to the more classical concerts of the Gewandhaus; he gave an impulse to all that was best in the life of the city. He established not only concerts that brought out the greatest works of the greatest men but also those which exhibited the historical development of music, and brought the noble writers of the past into honor.

The fourth of October, 1835, was the day that was to be so full of meaning in the history of music in Leipsic, for on this day Mendelssohn appeared as conductor of his

first concert at the Gewandhaus. The public journal of
the time says that the hall was crowded and on the appearance of the young conductor the most unmistakable
signs of applause were freely expressed. The universal
favorite of Mendelssohn, the Meeresstille, was conducted
in a manner which could not be surpassed. The other
pieces at the same concert were a scena and aria by
Weber, Spohr's violin concerto No. 11, the introduction
to "Ali Baba" by Cherubini ; the second part of the concert was devoted to Beethoven's " B-major Symphony,"
which was given with a precision hitherto unknown in
Leipsic. Mendelssohn had studied this in the most careful
manner and brought in some improvements which were
new and at the same time most natural and appropriate.
Up to that time the symphonies had always been directed
by the first violinist standing at the desk, but with Mendelssohn came a new epoch in which the director assumed no care save that of his direction. Of course, there
was a gain in shading and in the exact use of every
instrument under this system of careful supervision, of
which before they had had no conception. It may be
remarked that Mendelssohn always was famous for the
admirable manner in which he directed this his favorite
symphony ; with every new performance he brought out
some new beauty and threw some new light upon it, so
that the hearers could say at the close — so complete
have we never heard it till now.

In a letter addressed by Mendelssohn to his own family
on the 6th of October, he says : " I wish you could have
heard the introduction to my Meeresstille ; there was a
quiet in the hall that allowed one to hear the finest touch,
and they played the whole adagio in a masterly fashion ;
I admit that the allegro, accustomed as they are to a slow

tempo, dragged a little, but the finale they gave magnificently, the violins led off with such a force and rush that I myself was almost frightened, but the public were delighted. The other pieces by Weber, Spohr and Cherubini did not go so well; the one rehearsal was not sufficient, and the music was occasionally shaky; but on the other hand the 'B-major Symphony' by Beethoven, which composed the whole of the second part, went superbly; the people applauded loudly after every movement. There was an eagerness and an attention in the whole orchestra the like of which I have never seen. After the concert I received a mass of congratulations, first from the orchestra, then from the Thomas boys; they are wonderfully exact and I have promised them an order already; then came Moscheles and the crowd of dilletanti, &c., &c.''

On the 9th of October, Moscheles, who had come to Leipsic to visit Mendelssohn, gave an extra concert, and for weeks the festivities assumed a character such as may be readily imagined with such a man as Mendelssohn, and with such coöperation as he had from his admirable fellow workers and the applause from his host of new friends.

But amid all these jubilations and delights there came a stroke of the greatest severity and of absolute suddenness on the 19th of November, which brought him the tidings of the death of his father. Abraham Mendelssohn had for a long time been suffering in his eyes, and finally had become completely blind, but had taken great delight in Moscheles' visit to Berlin, his own son being there also and the two often playing together, to the great joy of the father. In his want of sight he continually confounded the playing of one with the other and only at the close was he aware of his mistake. Mendelssohn had returned to his work again and had celebrated his mother's birthday on the 14th of November. On the 18th of that month she was awakened during the night with the tidings that her husband was unwell. It was supposed to be a stroke, but the sick man was in complete possession of his senses; the physicians declared the condition of affairs not dangerous and refused to allow Felix to be summoned to Berlin. This was at ten o'clock in the morning; the invalid turned himself over and said he would sleep a little, and yet half an hour later he was dead. So gentle was the end that no one of the children gathered around his bed were aware of the precise moment when his decease occurred. Fanny gives us this beautiful account: "So fair and with such changeless peace expressed upon his countenance that we looked upon it not only without fear but with the true exaltation of love; the whole expression was so calm, the forehead so pure and beautiful, the hands so gentle; it was the end of a just man; a fair and enviable ending; I pray God to give me the like, and so long as I live I will strive to merit it as he merited it. It was the most reconciling and beautiful picture of death." I have in another passage already alluded to Fanny's desire that she herself might come to a similar end, which indeed she did. William Hensel took extra post at once and drove to Leipsic in order to prepare Mendelssohn for the news; two days later, on Saturday morning, they both entered Berlin again. Felix' condition was pitiful; he was as one crushed in body and soul, weeping but little indeed, but in the deepest distress. No son ever mourned a father more than he; he lost in him his best friend, one to whom he had always looked up to with childlike reverence, without whose counsel he had never been willing to enter upon any important enterprise, whose correct judgment, even in musical things, with all his want of technical knowledge, was always a subject of wonder to his son. How sore his loss and how great was Mendelssohn's sorrow is exhibited among other tokens by the two tender letters which he wrote to his friend Schubring, pastor in Dessau, and Bauer, pastor in Belzig, on the 9th of December: "You have already heard of the dreadful stroke that has afflicted my life. It is the greatest sorrow that could occur to me, and a trial from which I shall never thoroughly rise. It is now three weeks since I felt this pain for the first time, but it has not diminished at all; it will never cease; I shall bear it to the end of my life . . . . . . . I was ten days in Berlin in order to comfort my mother, but what days you can judge and I need not tell you; you have certainly thought of me in this dark time." In a somewhat milder tone, but just as much from the heart, he expresses himself in his letter to Bauer: "I received your letter on the very day when the baptism was to take place with you, just as I came back from Berlin where I had been to comfort my mother in the first days of her sorrow; so I received the tidings of your good fortune at the very moment when I was entering my empty room and experiencing for the first time what it is to live through the bitterest and most painful hours of life. It has always been my wish not to outlive my father, and I do not know how I can possibly continue my life without him. He was my one friend and my best friend in all these last years; he was my teacher in all that pertains to art and to life."

With the loss of his father, Mendelssohn set before him

two resolutions, the first of which was to finish the
"Oratorio of St. Paul" as soon as possible and to make it
as good as possible. He writes to Schubring: " I am all
the more zealous about this work of ending the ' St. Paul'
in that the last letter of my father urged me to it and
looked very impatiently forward to the completing of
this work ; and now it seems to me as if I must employ
all my faculties to make it as good as possible and to
fancy to myself that he is taking an interest in my work."
The second resolution was to found a family for himself.
It had long been the wish of his father to see Felix
happily married, and now he perceived that the most
natural cure for his heavy sorrow lay in that. His
mother encouraged him in this desire and in this decision,
a decision which was fulfilled in the course of the next
year.

It was an especially kind arrangement of Providence
that at this time of his great grief he again enjoyed the
society of Ferdinand David, the friend of his youth,
and his fellow student in Munich. This man, born in
the same house with Mendelssohn, and scarcely a year
after him, had chosen the violin as his favorite instrument, had enjoyed the best of instruction, and was now
established in the Konigstadt Theatre of Hamburg, where
he was enjoying the special favor of the public and of
his directors. The time had now come when he was
open to a proposition to remove to Leipsic, which he
accepted on the 10th of December, playing two of his
own compositions there and receiving a full meed of
applause. Matthai, the deserving leader, died soon after,
and David was immediately chosen to his place. Since
1843 he has been, next to Mendelssohn, the most celebrated teacher of the Leipsic Conservatory. He directed

the Gewandhaus concerts himself alternately with Gade in 1852-53, and in 1853-54 he had the exclusive management.

I will not weary the reader with a full account of all the musical performances during the ensuing winter ; enough to merely indicate the most important of them and what in them was completely new.  It may be remarked that Mendelssohn favored and introduced a revival of interest in Haydn's music, which at that time had lost favor with the public, and he succeeded in causing the freshness and naivette of the old master to  delight again  the hearts of nearly all lovers of music in Leipsic. ˙ No less successful was he with Mozart's work, and that not only as director but as performer.  In the fourth subscription concert given on the 28th of January, he played Mozart's concerto for the piano in D-minor just as the master wrote it and not according to the modern transcription.  In a letter to his sister he gives an interesting account of this concert and especially Mozart's number.  From the close of this letter I will quote these words : " And so during the whole winter I have had no day which has brought me any vexation ; scarcely have I heard a word regarding my position but what gave me great delight ; the whole orchestra, which is made up of very clever men, seeks to anticipate my every wish, makes the most incontestable progress in fineness and clearness, and is so devoted to me that it often touches me."

The concerts given this winter under Mendelssohn's direction called forth a recognition of an entirely different character from the popular applause and the special favor of his fellow musicians.  The Philosophical faculty of Leipsic University, inspired to the step by the Rector, at that time Dr. Gunther, gave him the degree of Doctor.

of Philosophy, honoris causa, and in the eulogium pro-
nounced on the occasion, it was stated that the reason
was, *ob insignia in artem musices merita.* The Rector
Magnificus himself accompanied the diploma with a
personal communication. The reply of Mendelssohn is
too characteristic of his modesty for me to deny myself
the pleasure of inserting it here : " Your Magnificence
has accompanied the memorable mark of honor which
the University has been so kind as to confer upon me
with such words of favor that I beg to acknowledge what
I cannot myself worthily express to those who have
granted me this distinction. The more keenly I feel
that in all that I have done I have failed to reach what I
had set before me, the more grateful I am for the act on
your part, which I regard not as a reward for tasks so
much as a stimulus for the future. As such it is in-
estimable, leading me as it does to fresh hopes of making
my art serviceable to mankind ; and as showing me, too,
that with all that has stood in my path thus far of dis-
couragement and hindrance, I have not fallen into error
in my main intent. A grateful confirmation is it, too, of
my efforts, that your act evidences that others share with
me on my own secret aspirations ; as a mark of confidence, therefore, reaching back into the past and
forward into the future, permit me to say that your
undeserved kindness entirely surpasses my power to
utter my thanks."

The noble modesty which this communication of
Mendelssohn breathes must receive all the higher honor
that at this time his first great work, the " Oratorio of St.
Paul," had been finished about a year, and now lay before
him, in the course of two months to have its first public
presentation at the great Rhenish festival held in Düssel-

dorf.   Should one of the newer composers be selected as
a suitable follower of the great creators of the lyrical
sacred drama, Bach and Handel, it was assuredly Mendelssohn.   He had from his earliest youth thoroughly
studied the works of both of these great masters, and he
it was who, while but a young man of twenty, had summoned the " St. Matthew Passion " again into life after its
sleep of a hundred years.   In this young man there were
united the three admirable qualities which fitted him
especially to become the composer of oratorio music :
deep religious feeling, reverence and love for the Bible as
the Revelation of God and the true source of a worthy
text, and an overflowing creative power.   However
much that was great and excellent he accomplished in
other departments of music, the towering height of his
activity, in which he stands above all other composers
since Bach and Handel, even above Haydn in his "Creation," is unquestionably the oratorio.   It is true in the " St.
Paul " he had not yet reached his perfect independence ; in
the grouping of his materials, in dividing them into recitatives, arias, choruses and chorals, he is a very close
follower of John Sebastian Bach, yet in his second and
last great work, the " Elijah," which is thoroughly original,
he seems to me to stand nearer to Handel.   In the " St.
Paul " there is a near approach to Bach in the splendid
instrumentation and thorough mastery and application of
counterpoint, and this, not developed with a hard and
repellent harmony, but everywhere with a solemn and in .
suitable places, even a cheerful and attractive melody ;
and this not in the parts which stand alone, but in the
great choruses of Jews, Heathen and Christians.   The
leading thought of the whole oratorio is the struggle and
victory of Christianity in its advance to the position of a

world religion, represented in the person of the great
apostle to the Gentiles. We must regard the choice of
exactly this material as so far a progress, that no one of
the great German artists with the exception of Heinrich
Schutz had ever before selected the history of Paul as
the subject of a musical composition. Taken as a whole
it was entirely new. We must, therefore, concur with
what Bitter says in his spirited and impartial judgment
on Mendelssohn as a composer of oratorios : " With this
work Mendelssohn has brought the oratorio back to us
and into this our time, freed from the blemishes of the
former age and with a purity of conception and a matured
grasp of form that makes it seem like a new creation.
Whenever and wherever the ' St. Paul' has been given it
has always had a welcome which is granted only to
works of high grade. He has fully accustomed us also
to own our great and manifold obligations to the composers of the past, without whose pioneer work we should
have striven in vain to reach the completeness of the
present time."

We have on another page quoted from a letter of
Mendelssohn to Devrient, written as early as 1832, in
which he mentions that even in Paris and amidst its
diversions he was actively engaged in working out a plan
of an oratorio on St. Paul. The first sketch comprised a
three fold division ; first the martyrdom of Stephen ;
second, the conversion of Paul ; third, his life and
preaching to his martyrdom ; but had he carried this out,
it would have become tedious in the development and the
impression would have been weakened. The work as it
stands consists of only two parts, the first of which embraces the death of Stephen and the conversion of Paul ;
the second, the departure of the apostle from the Church

at Ephesus, and the indication of his death then immi-
nent.    It is true that the stoning of Stephen and the
conversion of Saul are each very important events taken
by themselves, but their union in the same part of the
oratorio is justified by this, that the death of Stephen was
the immediate cause of Saul's conversion; without this
background the splendid penitential aria No. 18 and the
Song of Praise No. 20 would be psychological impos-
sibilities.

We are not informed as to the precise time when Mendelssohn laid his hand to the work, but it is certain that
the larger share of it fell within the epoch of his labors
in Dusseldorf; with what extreme care he wrought upon
the text, and how he himself always resorted to the words
of the Bible as most suitable, are shown clearly in his
two letters to Julius Schubring, his friend, the pastor in
Dessau, and to J. Fürst in Berlin.    Respecting the gradual progress of the composition, he says among other
things to Schubring: "I have finished half of the first
part, and I think that some time in February I shall complete the whole."    On the 6th of August, 1834, he writes
to the same: "The first part of my 'St. Paul' is almost
done, and yet I stand before it and cannot bring it to an
end. . . .    What is wanting is the overture, and a tough
piece of work it is."    Afterwards he found the key to
his difficulty; he began the overture with the first four
strophes of the choral, "Sleepers, wake, a voice is calling," carried on as a theme into a symphonic movement
in the manner of one of Bach's fugues, and thus the overture comprised within itself the foundation thought of
the whole First Part, the awakening of Paul and the taking him out of his blindness into higher light.    Fanny
Hensel writes, after hearing the overture at the first or-

chestral rehearsal in Düsseldorf: " The overture is most
beautiful.    The idea of making use of the choral, ' Wake,
sleepers, wake, a voice is calling,' as the introduction to
the whole of the ' St. Paul,' is magnificent in execution."
Mendelssohn, in his letter to Schubring, thinks that the
finest passage in the whole First Part is the great chorus,
" Rise up, arise and shine," and I think that all who have
ever heard the " St. Paul " would agree with him.    This
chorus, introduced with gentle tones and afterwards swell-
ing to almost thunderous proportions, followed by the
choral, " Sleepers, wake, a voice is calling," is one of
those passages which always, when played with Mendelssohn's instrumentation, produces an irresistible effect.

Mendelssohn, in a letter of the 4th of November to his
mother, says : " In the ' St. Paul ' I am now at the point
where I should like to play it to some one, but the right
person is not here.    My friends are almost beside themselves with delight, but that does not prove much.    The
cantor is wanting with the thick eyebrows and the critical
judgment.    (He refers to his sister Fanny.)    The second
part I have almost complete in my head up to the point
where they take St. Paul to be Jupiter and wish to offer
sacrifice to him ; here there ought to be some good choruses, but I have not yet the slightest conception of what
they shall be.    It is hard."    Every one knows how beautifully he in due time hit upon the choruses for this place,
breathing the most delicate fragrance of classical hellen-
ism.    He writes later to Fanny Hensel : " To-day I have
sketched the overture to ' St. Paul,' and have thought I
might perfect it, but it is too much to do ; . . . but I
am at work hard at it, am living at peace with all mankind, and am leaving the future to God, in the hope of
having my oratorio complete in March, and of compos-

ing a new A-minor symphony and a concerto for the piano." To Rebecca he writes, December 23, 1834: " To-day I have composed a whole chorus for the ' St. Paul.'" In a later letter to the same, from Frankfort, he writes, when the " St. Paul " had already been given in Düsseldorf: " The whole time that I have spent here I have worked upon the ' St. Paul,' because I want to produce it in the most perfect state possible ; and I know thoroughly that the beginning of the first and the end of the second part have been made at least three times as good ; it often happens to me that with subsequent labor I can make myself more clear and complete in the minor parts of my work ; but in those which are the leading features I cannot change them, they must stand as they first came to me. I have been working for now more than two years on my oratorio ; . . . this is indeed a very long time, and I shall be only too happy when I come to correct it for the press and can begin something else." In a letter written to Ferdinand Hiller, February 26, 1835, Mendelssohn writes : " My oratorio will be entirely finished in a few weeks, and in October it is to be given by the Cecilia Society, as Schelble writes me ;" and, in like manner, to his father, April 3, 1835 : " My oratorio is to be given for the first time at Frankfort in November." Mendelssohn wished to be present as a spectator at the time of its rehearsal, but it was not to be. Perhaps Schelble was even then too feeble. The first performance of it in fact took place at the musical festival on the 22d of May of the next year, after Mendelssohn had already been eight months in Leipsic.

After the completion of the work, the chorus numbers were engraved by Simrock in Bonn and sent to Düsseldorf. The work caused the very greatest admiration and when Mendelssohn reached Düsseldorf on the 8th of May, he found the whole music thoroughly studied. Mendelssohn's sister Fanny, who had come to the first performance, writes regarding the rehearsal: "The choruses go stirringly, the solos were not sung yesterday. When, after the chorus ' Rise up, arise and shine,' there was a tumult of applause followed by a flourish of trumpets, I thanked the God you, dear mother, are not here, for, if I can judge by the impression of this first imperfect rehearsal as to what the full performance will be, I am sure you could not endure it." Mendelssohn had only one regret in his own heart, that was not granted to his father to be present at that which he had so greatly desired to see. The performance was on Whitsunday, May 22, 1836. The reception of it was most brilliant.

After this great event, Mendelssohn made so many changes in the work that the whole voice score became entirely unavailable. Ten numbers he left out entirely, and the first great aria of St. Paul in B-flat minor he reduced to one-third. On the other hand he composed a little soprano aria in F-major: " Let us sing of the grace of the Lord," No. 27, in the second part, not to speak of countless smaller changes.

After this festival, Mendelssohn went on the 4th of June to Frankfort in order to direct the concert of the Cecilia Society, in place of his friend Schelble who was then visiting the sea baths of Scheveningen. His acquaintance with Schelble dates from his youth, Mendelssohn having met him in 1822 on his return journey from Switzerland. This acquaintance was renewed in 1827, on which occasion Mendelssohn witnessed the production of an oratorio of Handel conducted by Schelble, and again the two friends met in Frankfort in 1832. Mendelssohn had been delighted with this city when he had passed through it as a child and now on later experience it pleased him extremely ; he felt himself so comfortable there that he expressed himself jestingly in one of his letters that if he should remain longer in Frankfort he should certainly become a zealous gardener.    While in this cheerful mood he discovered the fairest of flowers, thereafter to adorn the garden of his life, Cecile Jean-Renaud, the younger daughter of the former pastor of the Reformed French church in Frankfort, who was then living with her mother and sister, an older sister, in the house of her grandfather, a rich gentleman of one of the old families of Frankfort. Mendelssohn had already been introduced into this house by a friend, and now, renewing his visit, found himself irresistibly attracted by the beauty and loveliness of Cecile.    Edward Devrient, in his Recollections, gives us the following admirable sketch, which, from personal observation, I can confirm in its main truth, saving the too emphatic allusion to the tokens of her early death : "Cecile was one of those sweet womanly natures whose very presence exerts a tranquilizing and beneficial effect on every one ; a slender girl, with features of dazzling beauty and delicacy, hair of deep blonde and eyes blue and large, she showed even then signs unfavorable to a protracted life.    She spoke very little and that little very softly, having that voice which Shakespeare so praises in woman, and that charming silence which Shakespeare, in the utterance of Coriolanus, extols no less highly than does Lear Cordelia's soft low voice."    All Mendelssohn's friends had good reason to expect that this gentle being would exert a most tranquilizing effect upon his excitable nature and stimulate him to a calm and fruitful activity.    Hensel in his "Mendelssohn Family" completes this picture on its spiritual side: "It was not the presence of strong and marked peculiarities which made her so lovely : — rather it was the absence of these, — the harmony and complete roundness and balance of her character. She was not especially brilliant, not wonderful in her wit or learning, or in any particular gifts — but she was refreshing as a breath of autumn air or a draught of pure cool water ; it seemed as if this woman was created for Felix. No one could have been better adapted to his temperament, no one could have secured him such unbroken joy."

Ferdinand Hiller in his Recollections of Mendelssohn also speaks of Cecile : "If in this period Mendelssohn spoke but little with her, all-the more did he talk about her in her absence ; lying in the sofa in my room, he spent evening after evening in extolling her beauty, grace and loveliness. Intemperance in praise was not his way in anything, and so it was in a bright, airy vein that he talked, even with laughter: never anything sentimental or pathetic or passionate tones ; but how thoroughly earnest he was in the matter could not be concealed for an instant ; be the theme of converse what it would, he could not keep it long away from her. I did not know Cecile then, I had to take the part simply of a sympathetic listener."

Although Mendelssohn's feelings respecting this lovely woman were then permanently settled, yet he wanted to give them the test of a final trial. He went, therefore, on the advice of his physician, and before he had declared himself to her, to the sea baths of Scheveningen, in order to benefit his excitable nerves. It is natural that his letters to Hiller at the time of his stay there should be full of a humorous pretence of raging at the pain of absence and of longing to see again the object of his love.

The first letter, written August 7th, and indeed all the following are delightful tokens of his state of mind. " If you do not answer this letter, and do not devote at least eight pages of it to Frankfort and a certain gate of that city [in the neighborhood of which Jean-Renaud's family was living] it is very possible that I shall become a cheese merchant here and never come back any more."

Soon after his return to Frankfort, on the 9th of September, the engagement took place, and directly after it, at the close of the day, this incomparable son wrote to his mother : " In the very moment of entering my room I cannot refrain from writing to you first of all, and telling you that I have just become engaged to Cecile Jean-Renaud. My head swims even now with what I have done to-day ; it is late in the night—there is nothing to be said but simply to write to you. How rich and happy I am ; to-morrow, if it be possible, I will write you in full — and perhaps she will too ; your letter is before me, open but not read : I just glance at it to see if you are all well. Farewell, and think always of me. Felix."

Mendelssohn was unable to enjoy many weeks in the presence of this beloved girl ; as early as the end of September he was compelled to return to his duties at Leipsic. On the 2d of October we find him again at his director's stand in the Gewandhaus hall. He opened the first subscription concert with the newly discovered "Overture to Leonora," and with the finale from Cherubini's "Wasserstragër" and "Beethoven's A-major Symphony."

Meanwhile the opportunity had arrived for testing Mendelssohn's ability as a director in still more honorable manner than ever before, and at the same time to bring into play the whole strength of the musical resources of Leipsic. " Israel in Egypt," that great work of Handel, whose chief strength lies in its choruses, was studied. To these choruses Mendelssohn brought all his wonted energy and fidelity and with immediate results of the happiest character ; he restored the work to the complete shape in which Handel originally wrote it. How confidently he looked forward to his success in the work may be clearly seen indicated in a letter to Hiller on the 29th of October : "Do not boast too much of your Cecelia Society ; we Leipsic people are now working at 'Israel in Egypt' and are going to make a success of it which cannot be surpassed. I have over two hundred chorus singers, besides the orchestra and the organ in the church ; in about a week we shall be all ready to bring it out." On the 7th of November, 1836, it was given in the church of St. Paul in a masterly manner.

Of the other performances of this winter which were given under Mendelssohn's direction, I will only mention one, interesting in its personal character. It was the last concert of the year 1836, and had been set back from Thursday to Monday in order to gratify Mendelssohn's longing to go to Frankfort. After Beethoven's "E-flat major Concerto" had been played in the first part, the second began with the "Meeresstille" overture, which was followed by some solo performances, closing with the second finale of "Fidelio." At the close of the chorus :—

"Whoe'er has won a lovely bride
Let him chime in with our jubilant strain."

Mendelssohn was called by a storm of applause to the piano, took his place and played variations upon the theme in a most astonishing manner ; the whole assembly were animated and excited to the highest degree, for everybody knew that he was going to visit his beloved in Frankfort.

It is perhaps worthy of remark that during this winter a distinguished English musician visited Leipsic, whose personal performances on the piano as well as his own compositions gave great delight, Sir William Sterndale Bennett. He came for the purpose of qualifying himself still further under Mendelssohn's guidance.

The time had meanwhile arrived when Leipsic might try its matured forces upon that great and newly completed work which should ere long carry the fame of its composer into many lands. The "Oratorio of St. Paul" began to be studied. As early as February, 1837, the first rehearsals were held and all the zeal and thoroughness which had been previously given to the great work of Handel was devoted to this in even enhanced measure. The magnificent chorals and choruses, although accompanied only by the poor piano used for such work, did not fail of their full effect upon all who took part, and were sung with constantly increasing enthusiasm. Most powerful of all was the choral, "Sleepers, wake, a voice is calling," whose thrilling trombone accompaniment could be imagined even from the slender tones of the piano. Powerful, too, in effects, even in this meagre presentation, was the chorus, "Rise up, arise and shine," and no less the thrilling call from Heaven, "Saul, Saul, why persecutest thou me?" Not less impressive were the numbers which bore the character of joy, renunciation and trust; chief of all perhaps the opening triumphal chorus, "Lord, thou only art God;" hardly second, the choral full of love and humble submission to Christ, "To Thee, O Lord, I yield my spirit;" grand also in their massive power were the two choruses so tenderly sad and yet so beautifully consolatory, "Happy and blest are they who have endured," and — "The Lord He is God; he

shall dry your tears and heal all your sorrows : " the first
one of which, celebrating the death of Stephen, with a
tender flow of underlying, and as one may say wave-like,
melody, culminating with the words, " For though the
soul shall live forever," touched every heart in its deepest
recesses.   But speaking in general, there was not a single
chorus which we did not take pleasure in singing (the
writer took part in this whole series of rehearsals), and
Mendelssohn understood as no other director has how to
enlist his singers' whole enthusiasm ; it was owing to his
splendid leading that we accomplished such marvels in
the crescendo, diminuendo, whispered tones and the like.

After such a thorough preparation, of course the performance of the oratorio, which occurred March 16, 1837,
in the church of St. Paul, could not fail to be brilliant.
The choruses consisted of three hundred voices, with a
corresponding strength on the part of the orchestra.
Regarding the impression produced by the whole, I can
speak less decisively, as I myself had the pleasure of
being a coöperator.   But the leading critic of that day
says in the chief musical journal : " Under the splendid
direction of the composer, the orchestra and the chorus
were handled in the most thorough and energetic manner,
and gave a specimen of work so fresh, so strong, so
round, so exact and finished in its shading, that its equal
I have never seen or felt.   Whoever had the pleasure
of witnessing this presentation must admit, that taking
for granted the admirable material at his command, the
main praise must lie with the director and composer of
the work."

This would not be the place to enter into any extensive
or exhaustive criticism of a work which has now become
the possession of the world.   A few hints, however, may

not be without their value with reference to what, from a
strictly æsthetical point of view, may have its weaknesses.
Unquestionably, in the first part, the personality and activity of Paul are subordinate to the martyrdom of Stephen;
and the second part of the work is inferior to the first in
dramatic interest; but the idea which runs through the
whole work is a higher and broader one than can be connected with any single person; it is the glorification of
Christianity in its humility, in its joy of living and dying
to the Lord, as set over against the stubborn obstinacy of
Judaism, and the bright, sensuous view of life of the
classical world. It is the encounter of both these latter
currents with the first, and the victory through the revelation of eternal light and the direct working of the divine love. This idea is incarnated in the persons of
Stephen, Paul and Barnabas, and it concentrates itself in
the point which is in fact the centre of the whole oratorio, the conversion of Paul. Mendelssohn has been re-
proached with putting the word of the Lord in the mouths
of a chorus of females, or, as may be said, of angels. It
has been claimed that he ought to have indicated the voice
of the Lord by a mighty sound of a trumpet; but exactly
this medium point between the hard, strong voice of a
man and the delicacy of even softer tones, seems to me
to be a most happy conception of the artist, for in this
way he gives a supernatural conception of the occurrence
without leaving the actual earth on which we live. It
seems to me that all reasoning must yield to the powerful
impression which this angelic chorus makes upon every
hearer, however slightly sensitive to music. Who is
not always overcome with a sense of the omnipresence
and the omniscience of God? And then how greatly is
this impression increased by the powerful chorus, "Rise

up, arise and shine," which flashes into the earthly darkness like a glance from Heaven.  What a mighty warning to turn in his course of persecution, in the solemn
choral, "Sleepers, wake, a voice is calling!"  What a
triumph of the victory to come, and also of the judgment about to come, in this majestic series of trombone
tones, which remind one of the glory of the ancient Zion
illuminated with the light of the new covenant!  How
vividly in the choruses are expressed the contrasts of the
Christian, Jewish and Heathen elements of thought!  Let
one compare the choruses, "Happy and blest are they who
have endured," No. 11, and "Oh, great is the depth of
the riches," No. 32, with the two Jewish choruses, "Now
this man ceaseth not to utter," No. 5, and "This is
Jehovah's temple; ye men of Israel help;" and then
again with the choruses Nos. 3 and 35, "The Gods
themselves are mortals," and "Oh, be gracious, ye im-
mortals," and one will confess how characteristically
these three modes of religious thought are rendered.  A
remarkable peculiarity and a beautiful grace of the oratorio is found in the choral, which is always introduced
at the most fitting places.  If in these the purest expression of Christian feeling is concentrated, their power also
is greatly enhanced by the artistic addition of the most
charming harmonies.  Certainly many a hearer must
have had the beauty of these angelic hymns come to
him as a new revelation while hearing these chorals.  It
may indeed be that this effect has been copied from Sebastian Bach, but we must not deny to the composer who
followed him by more than a hundred years that he has
used all the original depth and strength of feeling even
enhanced in expression by the later appliances of modern
art; and although the strength of the oratorio consists in

its choruses and chorals, I must be careful not to speak
lightly or imply the least depreciation of the great beauty
of the solo parts.    The recitatives are in every instance
noble in character, and the two arias of St. Paul, the
great one, " Consume them all, Lord Sabaoth," and the
penitential one, " Oh, God, have mercy upon me," cannot
be conceived of as more dramatic and at the same time more
adapted to a classical style.    In like manner in the soprano
aria, " Jerusalem, thou that killest the prophets," in the
arioso for the alto, " But the Lord is mindful of his own,"
and in the aria of St. Paul, " I praise Thee O Lord, my
God," assuredly are exhibited the depth and vitality of
of Christian feeling in its most complete musical form.
The whole oratorio is, in a word, " unto edification," and
that, too, in the highest sense : it strengthens, it exalts, it
enobles the spirit by the happiest portraiture of the religious feeling in the garb of the beautiful.    Wherever the
eternally true and the eternally fair extend their hands to
each other, there is reached the highest point to which
art can attain.

Decorated with fresh laurels which the performance of
his " St. Paul " not only accomplished in symbol but in fact
(upon his director's desk lay a laurel wreath), Mendelssohn hastened to Frankfort in order to unite the garland
of glory with the myrtle of matrimony.    On the 28th of
March, 1837, his marriage with Cecile Jean-Renaud took
place in the French Reformed Church.    Respecting the
ceremony, Ferdinand Hiller, who was present, writes:
" There was something odd in hearing a man so genuinely German pronouncing French words at this solemn
moment, but the simplicity of the service and the attrac-
tiveness of both the parties enchained and touched all
hearts."    Hiller had composed a wedding song for the

reception of the newly married couple in the house of Cecile's grandfather, and it was executed in excellent style by a chorus led by Hiller himself. Mendelssohn and his charming wife were touched at this expression, and all the members of the family showed themselves in the happiest light. His wedding journey was taken to Freyburg in the Breisgau, that most delightfully situated town, where they passed some weeks. Mendelssohn writes, respecting their stay there, to Fanny on the 10th April: "You remember, perhaps, how, when we were on our return from Switzerland, we ran from the rain into the cathedral and admired it with its dark painted windows, but we could not see the situation of the city then, and I confess I have never met anything so lovely, nor do I think I ever shall again; so peaceful and beautiful on every side, rich valleys, and the mountains near and far; villages wherever the eye falls, and well clad men; waters rushing from the mountains in every direction; and in every valley the first green and on the mountains the last snow. . . . You cannot imagine how soothing this all is; and if I walk leisurely the whole afternoon with my Cecile in the warm sunshine, and stand here and there and look around and speak of the past and the future, I can well say 'What a happy man I am.'" The journey from Freyburg went slowly on to some valleys of the Black Forest and the upper Rheingau, and a letter to Devrient, written in Lörrach in Baden the 3d of May, shows the same happy frame of mind and heart. "You know that I am now here with my wife, my dear Cecile, that this is our wedding journey, and that we are an old married pair of six weeks already. . . . I have really so much to tell you that I cannot make a beginning; I will only say that I am altogether too happy

and merry, and, what I certainly had not expected of myself, not beside myself, but as calm and wonted to it as it
were always so.  You ought to know my Cecile."  These
words of the young husband give us the key to the psychological riddle that even in the time of his first happy
love he did not diminish the flow of his productions but
employed the wedding journey for the composition of
one of his most perfect works; the composition of the
"Forty-Second Psalm," not to speak of other works.
Even in the letter to Fanny already cited, Mendelssohn
expresses his determination to be industrious.  "I should
like to bring all sorts of new things to light and make
regular progress; but it seems to be necessary to go on
first with all the old matter which I have heaped up, and
that I will do during the summer; and what is not done
by winter I will simply leave as it is.  I have composed
three organ preludes in Spire, which I think will please
you; a book of songs without words is also ready for the
press [among which the one in A-minor, Opus 38.].  I
am thinking of undertaking even greater matters yet; I
have almost finished a violin quartet [E-minor, Opus
44, No. 2] and will then begin a second one.  I am
thoroughly happy in my work."

In explanation of the fact that Mendelssohn could compose the "Forty-Second Psalm" upon his wedding journey, Hiller remarks appositely: "I was astonished when
he showed me what he had accomplished on his wedding
tour, the 'Forty-Second Psalm,' but I did not remain
long with him before I saw how he had written it, for the
tender longing which expresses itself in some parts of that
psalm rests entirely upon a basis of the happiest and most
blessed trust in God; and the quiet and deeper feeling
which prevails in the largest part of the work cannot be

separated from the heartfelt happiness in which he then was spending every hour."

Arriving at Frankfort with his young wife again, and entering the distracting duties of social life with which, of course, the young couple were overwhelmed, he yet finished the above-mentioned beautiful string quartet in E-minor.

Early in July he left Frankfort, following a rash impulse, to spend some weeks at Bingen on the Rhine. Undoubtedly it was the necessity of escaping the manifold distractions of Frankfort and of passing the time undisturbed with his wife and his muse. Here he was engaged in active composition, although he found it difficult in this entirely Catholic and unmusical town to procure two things which were absolutely indispensable, a bible and a piano. He composed here the greater part of his "D-minor Concerto" (Opus No. 40), which he afterwards finished in Hochheim. In addition to this, he was occupied, as we learn from a letter to his friend Schubring, in laying his plans for a new oratorio to be called "St. Peter." It was to be divided into two parts, the first, from the leaving of the fisherman's nets to the words: "Ju es Petrus," the second to be confined to the great Pentecostal Festival, from the address to Peter after Jesus' death on to the outpouring of the Holy Ghost. Fortunately he gave up this plan, probably on the instigation of Schubring; it assuredly is not a subject capable of dramatic treatment, scarcely indeed of lyrical. Mendelssohn himself felt this, as we see from his speaking of it as "symbolic." In the place of the "Peter," there occurred to him in November of the following year, the subject of Elijah, one far more dramatic than even the "St. Paul." He carried this thought with him for a long time, and it was only in 1846

that this oratorio, decidedly the most powerful and best of
his works, was completed.

From Bingen, Mendelssohn went in the beginning of
August, in the company of his young wife, her mother
and sister to Düsseldorf, and received the heartiest welcome from all his immediate friends with the single exception of Immerman. Mendelssohn was extremely popular in Düsseldorf; according to his own expressions, his
visit to that city were the most delightful moments of his
life. He was unconstrained, jovial, free to grant all
claims upon his time and talents, and unwearied in giving
himself to his friends. The " St. Paul " was given under
the direction of his friend Julius Rietz, in his honor, while
he was there. He himself could delight them with the
fresh fruits of his activity, including the " Forty-Second
Psalm," the piano " Concerto in D-minor," and a violin
quartet in E-minor. But now the time was at hand when
a greater work was before him, even if it also brought
greater honor. He had pledged himself to conduct the
musical festival in Birmingham from the 19th to the 22d
of September, and a programme of unsurpassable richness had been prepared for this festival. On the first day
Mendelssohn was to play the organ ; on the second he was
to direct the " St. Paul," on the third he was to play the
piano, and at the close of the fourth he was again to play
the organ ; besides, it was contemplated to give his new
psalm, and the music to " The Midsummer Night's
Dream." In addition to this, Neukomm was to produce
his "Ascension," there were to be several passages of
Bach's music, besides the whole of the " Messiah," and
at every concert a symphony and an overture. One can
imagine how Mendelssohn who had parted from his young
wife with so heavy a heart was called into the very height

of his activity by this colossal programme, and indeed he did by his efforts earn all the honors which he received. He himself writes to his mother on the 4th of October : "I dare not try to describe the musical festival of Birmingham ; I must only say to you, because I know it will please you, that I have never had such brilliant success in my life, and I probably never shall have again. The applause and the recalls when I allowed myself even to be seen would not cease, and indeed it was to me a little ludicrous. I can only say that I see distinctly that all this favor is given to me because it is not my first concern what people want and what they praise and what they pay for, but that which I myself consider good, and that I cannot be led out of my way by any other considerations ; this success is, therefore, all the more precious to me, and I now know that it is genuine, inasmuch as I have not done the least thing meretricious to win it and never will." After Mendelssohn had played the last chord on the magnificent organ in Birmingham, he instantly took the Liverpool mail coach to London, where he arrived about midnight. Here his friend Klingemann met him and introduced him to the committee of the Sacred Harmonic Society, which presented him with a massive silver snuffbox with an inscription. At about half-past twelve he took his place in the mail again and was, at nine o'clock in the morning, at Dover, where, without a moment's delay, he was obliged to take the steamer. After a bad passage, in the course of which he was compelled to land, not at Calais but at Boulogne, he drove on through the night in the diligence to Lisle, aud thence still on to Cologne, where he arrived at ten o'clock in the morning ; at eleven he took steamer again. On he went through the night, but at two o'clock in the morning the boat came to a stand, being checked by the fog; so he landed and took a well-known footpath to Hochheim and thence to Coblentz, where he took stage again, and at last, after six days and five nights, reached his friends in Frankfort. Without delaying, and with the company of his wife, he was obliged to hasten on to Leipsic, where, after three days more of journeying, he arrived on the second of October at two o'clock, four hours before the concert which he was to direct. Wonderful indeed was it that this delicately sensitive body could endure such a great strain after the tremendous efforts at Birmingham, for we, with our facile communications by rail, have no idea what it was to travel in those days; but he and his young wife, while receiving in Leipsic the most hospitable welcome, were amply repaid for all their toils upon the way. He writes at the close of his first letter from Leipsic to his mother: " It is altogether too delightful here; the whole day and every hour is to me in my new housekeeping like a festival, and whereas in England, in spite of all the honors and joys, I had not a single thoroughly happy moment; every day here is a succession of delights, and I am now for the first time in my life thoroughly at rest."

Directly after his resuming the baton and being received with the applause which was so cheerfully given, Mendelssohn devoted himself at once with renewed energy and delight to his profession. The "Jubilee Overture" of Weber, the chorus by Haydn, "Des Staubes eitle Sorgen," Beethoven's " C-minor Symphony," an aria from " Freischutz," and a new concerto by David, opened the series of the musical performances of the winter in a most worthy and attractive manner. Not to weary my reader with all the delights which followed, I will only speak of one feature of the winter which I cannot forget as a very agreeable result of Mendelssohn's journey to England. We owed to this the presence with us of the beautiful singer, Clara Novello, daughter of a musical publisher in London, for whom Mendelssohn had already written in 1832 a "Morning Service." Her bell-like, silver voice, her perfect method and charming bearing won all hearts. The concerts were more thronged than ever.

The year 1838 brought us a new product of Mendelssohn's muse, the "Forty-Second Psalm," which, as we have already seen was the finest product of his wedding journey, was produced for the first time on January 1st, and was at once recognized as an unique and thoroughly complete work. Never, perhaps, has the pious yearning of the soul for God been uttered in music with more depth than in this production. After the chorus had given expression to this longing in the magnificent passage, "As panteth the hart for the water brooks, so panteth my soul after thee, O God," the soprano solo utters the same cry, but with yet greater emphasis and strength. A chorus of women takes up and enlarges the same thought in the passage which tells of the myriads who hasten to keep their holy day in the house of the Lord, and this strain which, with its march-like movement, might suggest a joyful pilgrimage to the temple, ushers in the noble chorus of men's voices, "Why art thou cast down, O my soul? Trust thou in God." This is naturally followed by the complaining voice of a woman who, being thus reminded of the delightful service of God in his temple, breaks forth, "My soul is cast down within me, all thy waves and billows are gone over me," and what should still these laments but the consolatory tones of a beautiful quartet of male voices, accompanied with cellos, "The Lord will command his loving kindness in the day-

time, and in the night his song shall be with me, and my
prayer to the God of my life." Again that plaintive cry
mingles with this note of joy and trusting confidence,
until it is lost in the final burst of all the voices, male and
female, in the grand chorus of praise to the God of Israel.
The whole is really a religious drama expressed in music.
Yet if one has not heard the Psalm sung, or taken part
in its singing, he can draw from my sketch a very meagre
conception of its character. But those who have sung it
under the leadership of the composer himself will need
no words of mine to convince them that it would be hard
to find an example of nobler harmony and sweeter melody and more appropriate expression than are afforded in
this work.

Mendelssohn passed from this to a series of historical
concerts   On the 14th of February the course began with
works by Sebastian Bach, Handel, Gluck, and Viotti. A
suite by Bach was followed by Handel's hymn, " Great is
the Lord ; " then a sonata by the same master in E-major
(No. 3, for piano and violin), played by Mendelssohn
and David. The second part was made up of the overture and introduction to the first scene from Gluck's
" Iphigenia in Tauris," followed by a concerto· for the
violin by Viotti. The second of these concerts brought
to our notice works by Haydn, Cimarosa, Neumann and
Righini. The repertoire is so interesting that I cannot
resolve to exclude it: "Overture to Tigranes," the aria
from " Armida " by Righini, overture to " Il Matrimonio
Segreto " by Cimarosa ; trio for piano, violin and cello by
Haydn, introduction, recitative and last scena of the first
part of the " Creation " by Haydn. The second part of
the concert was a quintet and chorus from Neumann's
" Pelligrini," the so-called " Abschied Symphony "

(Parting Symphony) by Haydn, written when Prince
Esterhazy was compelled to dismiss his orchestra, —
the story runs that he was so moved by this symphony
that he could not part with his company. Mendelssohn
writes regarding this performance: "At the close we
gave Haydn's 'Abschied Symphony,' in which, to the
great delight of the public, the musicians really blew out
their lights and departed till the violinist at the first desk
remained alone and closed in F-sharp major. It is a
curiously melancholy production." The third of these
concerts brought out works by Mozart, Salieri, Mehul,
and Andreas Romberg. Among other things was the
hitherto entirely unknown quartet from "Zaida" by
Mozart, and an ensemble from Mehul's "Uthal," an
opera which he had composed at Napoleon's command
on a subject taken from Ossian, entirely without violins.
The most brilliant feature of this concert was Mendelssohn's own playing of Mozart's "C-minor Piano Concerto ;" but scarcely less was the overture to the "Magic
Flute," which opened the concert. The programme of
the fourth and last of these contained Abt Vogler's
overture to "Samori," Von Weber's overture to "Freischutz," the "Hunters' Chorus" from "Euryanthe,"
Beethoven's great violin concerto and the "Pastoral
Symphony." That these concerts not only brought
about a better understanding of the older masters, but that
they aided much to the cultivation of the musical taste in
Leipsic, need hardly be said. At the close of this season,
Mendelssohn produced his own particularly interesting
serenade, "Allegro Giojoso," Opus 43, regarding which
he writes to his friends in Berlin: "This evening is the
concert given by Botgorschek ; an admirable contralto
singer has begged and begged me to play something, and

I have at last yielded; trying to think what I had that I could play at short notice, but finding nothing at hand, I resolved to compose a Rondo, of which the day before yesterday not a note was written, and which I am to give this evening with the whole orchestra; we have had one rehearsal this morning; it sounds merrrily enough; but how I shall play the gods alone know, and they scarcely, for at one place I have fifteen measures of rest in the accompaniment and I have not the slightest idea what I shall put in there, but one who plays *en gros*, as I do, makes everything go through."

Thus passed a winter of the greatest musical delight, owing chiefly to Mendelssohn's manifold activity; but during the summer which followed he granted himself no rest, going again to assume direction of the Cologne Musical Festival. The chief feature of this was to be Handel's " Joshua," which he had formerly arranged for the organ, as he had also the " Solomon." The festival was not one of the most successful; the separation from his wife and his first child and son came very closely home to him; he was rather melancholy, but in spite of this he played on the 3d the serenade " Allegro Giojoso."

Scarcely had he returned to Leipsic when the expression met him on every side of the desire that the " St. Paul " should be repeated. Mendelssohn undertook this gladly, and conducted the rehearsals with his wonted fidelity. After it had been given this time, it was never repeated but once during his lifetime. It may be said, parenthetically, that no work has ever found universal recognition in so short a time as the " St. Paul." The two years 1837 and 1838 might be called, in the history of music, the " St. Paul " years. In Germany, in Tyrol, Switzerland, Denmark, Holland, Poland, Russia and

America the " St. Paul " was given, and in many cities
two or three times.   The next event of interest in Mendelssohn's life was the writing of the overture to " Ruy
Blas," concerning which he says, in a letter to his
mother, written March 18th, 1839 : " You wish to know
how it has gone with my overture to ' Ruy Blas.'   Merrily enough.   Between six and eight weeks ago the request
came to me to write something for the performance connected with the Theatrical Pension Fund, a very excellent
object, for the furtherance of which they were going to
play ' Ruy Blas.'   The request came to me to write an
overture, and in addition they besought me to compose a
Romanza, because they thought the thing would succeed
better if my name were connected with it.   I read the
play ; it is really of no value, absolutely below contempt ;
and I told them I had no time to write an overture, but I
did compose the Romanza.   Monday (a week ago), was
to be the day of the performance.   On the Tuesday before,
the people came, thanking me warmly for the Romanza,
and said they were sorry that I had written no overture,
but they saw perfectly that for such work time was needed,
and next year would be more thoughtful and give me a
longer time.   They stirred me up ; I took the thing at once
in hand that same evening, and blocked out my score ;
Wednesday morning was rehearsal, Thursday was concert, and yet on Friday the overture was ready for the
copyist ; Monday it was given three times in the concert
room, then rehearsed once in the theatre, and in the evening was given in connection with the wretched play, and
has made me as much fun as anything I ever did in my
life.   In the next concert they are going to repeat it ' by
request.' "

No one who is not familiar with the above would have

the slightest idea that this work, with its strength and fine movement, had such an ephemeral source. It is a genial conception, admirably instrumented, lively and bright and full of charming and original themes, especially in the middle passage, and is heard with pleasure in concerts even now.

In the spring of 1839, Mendelssohn directed the Düsseldorf Festival in connection with Julius Rietz. The occasion was one of the most brilliant. Handel's " Messiah" and Beethoven's " Missa in C" were given as the chief works. Of his own compositions, the " Forty-Second Psalm " was sung. On the third day he played his own " D-minor Concerto," and accompanied many songs on the piano.

From the strain of this festival, Mendelssohn went for some weeks to Frankfort. In his honor they made a feast for him there, a kind of a musical picnic in the wood, which he describes in a letter to his mother in the happiest vein : " The most beautiful thing which I ever saw in my whole life, so far as a social gathering of people is concerned, was a festival in the forest here, which I must describe, since it was unique of its kind. The place was a retired spot some quarter of an hour's walk from the road, and so shaded by trees as to have only glimpses through them of the rest of the wood : a very slight footpath led to it, and as soon as one came within a short distance, the white figures of the people were to be seen beneath a little group of trees hung with flower wreaths. This represented the concert hall ; how delightfully the voices sounded as the soprano trilled and the sweet bird-like notes rose on the air ! What a hush, a charm and delight there was in it all I cannot express. I had by no means anticipated the possibility of it, and upon their singing my song ' Ihr

Vöglein in den Zweigen,' the tears really stood in my eyes. It was more than magic, it was pure poetry, and when they had sung the whole group through, and three new songs (the last my ' Lark Song '), it had to be repeated twice amidst a perfect hurrah of fun and enjoyment."

In the winter of 1839–40, Mendelssohn again conducted the Gewandhaus concerts and with the same care and large coöperation as before, sustaining them at the high point to which he had brought them in the winter previous. Many new treasures were brought out to us in the course of this season. The concert in honor of the Reformation was opened with a piece of Mendelssohn which we have not heard, the " Verleih uns Frieden Gnädiglich," by Luther. The deep prayerful tone which is expressed in the words has been thoroughly reflected and retained in the music. I have already mentioned that Mendelssohn set several of Luther's hymns to music while he was in Rome, and thus defended himself most successfully from that sensuous charm of the Catholic worship to which so many German artists in Rome succumbed. I must confess, however, that the piece was received coldly.

The year 1840, one of the most important in advancing Mendelssohn's constantly increasing fame, brought us even at its outset a new and striking work. It was the " Hundred and Fourteenth Psalm," " When Israel went forth out of Egypt," composed for chorus and orchestra. This was given for the first time at the New Year's concert, and while entirely different in conception and execution from the " Forty-Second Psalm," was nearly as great a work. The choice itself of this sacred hymn, one of the most beautiful examples of Old Testament lyrical compositions, was one of the composer's happiest thoughts, and how admirably has he in his music caught the tone of the original and reflected the glory of God! In a grand sweep of inspiration, calmly yet majestically, the double chorus continually ascends in power until it reaches the height of its dramatic effect in the words " What ailest thou, O thou sea that thou floodest, thou Jordan that thou turnest back." This strain is answered with kindred sublimity, " Tremble thou earth at the presence of the Lord," and the final hallelujah peals as if in the very presence of God. If one can imagine an assemblage of the ancient Israelites in which the Levites, aided by all the modern devices which add fullness and strength, sounded forth the full volume of their praises, one can feel what our modern composer attained in this great work, whose fidelity to the ancient religious spirit and whose modern perfection of form are in perfect accord. In this respect it is a classic.

The third new work which came from the master's inexhaustible mind this winter was in an entirely different domain; it was the charming trio in D-minor for piano, violin and cello, No. 49. It was first played by Mendelssohn, David and Wittman on the 1st of February, and from the first movement displayed that fire and passion which has been the characteristic of the modern composers, but the andante con molto tranquillo which follows, is touched with the inimitable charm of true sentiment, as it depicts both the longing and the joy of the soul; the scherzo follows and flings its attractive grace over us, giving way to the finale which, with its allegro appacianato, hurries on and leaves us at last in the realm of contentment and delight. The whole was a true picture of Mendelssohn's depth and abandon, the fruit of his happiest inspirations, and with all its apparent freedom, an example ot his complete mastery of form.  It was given, I need not say, in the most perfect manner, and was received with tumultuous applause.

I might say much respecting the musical delights of this winter, but I must confine myself to one, namely, that in the month of January there were given under Mendelssohn's direction Beethoven's four overtures to "Fidelio."  If it was a most interesting thing for every lover of art to enter, as it were, into the very workshop of this greatest of composers, and follow the growth of his thought from the rougher stages to its last crowning completion, no less a delight was it that such a work should be given to the public in a manner commensurate with its merits.

We now hasten to the time which may be regarded as an important epoch in the career of Mendelssohn.  The four hundredth anniversary of the invention of printing was to be celebrated in most of the larger cities of Germany on the 25th of June, 1840.  Naturally, in Leipsic, the centre of this industry, the celebration would attain to large proportions.  The musical part of the commemoration was intrusted most cheerfully to Mendelssohn, who undertook this task with visible delight.  Of course it was necessary to choose a suitable text for a composition to be composed with reference to the unveiling of the statue of Gutenberg in the market-place. This must be of a popular character and well adapted to music.  The selection resulted in the choice of a song by Adolphus Prolls, teacher of religion in the Freyburg Gymnasium, whose composition united all the desired qualities.  Mendelssohn set this to music and arranged a choral for men's voices, with trombone accompaniment.  When it was heard at the first rehearsal in the

Gewandhaus, I well remember what enthusiasm, almost bacchanalian in its tumultuous acclaim, greeted this composition; anything so popular, strong, cheerful and free had not been heard for a long time. It was very entertaining, while the rehearsals were going forward in the garden of the Schutzenhaus and they were endeavoring to ascertain how the music would sound in the open air, and at what distance the singers and trombonists should be separated from one another, to see Mendelssohn springing around with that slight and graceful body of his. During the festival there were two choruses, removed some distance from one another, one of which was led by Mendelssohn and the other by David. They began with the choral above mentioned, which was followed by the Gutenberg hymn; then a tenor passage, allegro molto, " The Lord said, Let there be Light," and then another choral set to the melody, " Nun danket alle Gott." This work is one of those which bear no opus number, but it appears in the collective edition of Breitkopf and Härtel. The Gutenberg hymn has also appeared arranged for single voices, and, aside from its special end, it deserves to be known in every part of Germany. Yet I must confess that the impression of this music was by no means so powerful as had been expected from the character of the composition. In the large open space the sound was not heard to advantage; in order to have done justice to it there should have been at least a thousand voices.

But all this was, as it were, only the prelude to the great work, the true ornament of the festival, which was to edify and delight all hearers in the highest degree. The " Lobgesang," or " Hymn of Praise," a great symphony cantata, was composed by Mendelssohn expressly

for this festival and was given on the 25th of June, in the
afternoon, in St. Thomas' Church, before a very large
assembly.   The first part of the concert was made up of
Weber's " Jubilee Overture " (" God save the King "
at the close played by the organ with wonderful effect)
and the " Dettingen Te Deum " by Handel.   Although
the effect of both of these works was great, that of Mendelssohn surpassed it.   How, the reader will ask, had he
grasped his conception?   What he wished to do was to
exhibit the grateful joy which must be felt at the victory
of light over darkness.   Of course, with his pious and
believing nature there was no conception of any other
victory than that of the divine light over the hostile power
of earthly darkness which loves the world more than it
loves light.   Thus was suggested the most manifest relation to the Gutenberg Festival as a memorial of that
discovery which gave the divine light its widest and
quickest course, and which, therefore, must be especially
regarded as the gift of God.   It was in this sense that the
pious artist grasped his work, and how magnificiently
did he execute it!   I do not share the opinions of those
who suspect that the three movements composing the
first part of the work were already in his hands, and all
that they required was the additional vocal music; the
whole piece bears the stamp of the freshest spontaneity
and unbroken unity.   Just as little can I agree with the
critics who find in the " Lobgesang " only an imitation of
Beethoven's " D-minor Symphony," for, so far as concerns the inner character of both of these great works,
they are as unlike as an Alpine landscape in its bright
sunlight is to chaos after the creation, illumined by
the first ray of the divine light; as unlike as Michael
Angelo's " God the Father " to Raphael's " Sistine

Madonna" or the "Transfiguration of Christ." They have, indeed, this in common, that they both end with a vocal movement, which in Mendelssohn's "Lobgesang" comprises the half of the work; so that the first three symphony movements and the vocal really divide the work into two parts which, however, stand related in the closest manner. Beethoven, on the other hand, uses the human voice only as an accessory in order to bring into harmonious relations that painful struggle after joy which has characterized all the previous portion of the work. He seems in his mind to have been thinking more of angelic than of human voices, and, therefore, he was compelled to have recourse to the only vocal help which lay at his hand. Mendelssohn, on the other hand, seems to have wished to use on a large scale vocal music as a means of praise for so great a gift as the art of printing. Hence the name "Symphony Cantata" is completely justified. The main thought of the work appears in the very first movement in a clear delightful B-major, repre- sented by trombones and trumpets. This is immediately repeated by all the instruments and carried on in artistic involutions, but always with the same tumultuous and joyful acclaim. Even at that stage before the words, "All that have life and breath, sing to the Lord" have been announced, the instrumental music has really uttered it so completely that its joyful inspiration must have been felt in advance. This is allegro maestoso è vivace. As a necessary contrast to this, there follows immediately an allegro agitato passage, which pictures the struggle for light in a strain of mediæval romance, as it were, which reminds one inevitably of chivalry and monastic life. The pain of the soul thus wrestling for existence, is immediately stayed by an adagio religioso, which seems to indicate the

yearning after divine help and the entrance of divine
light into the world of earthly darkness, and which
thereby leads fittingly to the last movement, which, in a
magnificent vocal chorus, takes up the first animating
theme. In this, one distinctly hears a lovely soprano
solo ; this is followed by a lyric dramatic picture and, as in
the "Forty-Second Psalm," a voice is heard warning the
others not to repress their cheerful joy in the help of the
Lord, "Sing ye praises all ye redeemed of the Lord ; "
this is followed by a beautiful duet by two female voices,
spiritual and deep, at the same time lovely and most
graceful : " I waited for the Lord, he inclined unto me,
he heard my complaint ; O blessed are they that hope
and trust in the Lord." A wailing penetrating tenor
thereupon takes up the theme and pictures the fearful
condition before the divine help came ; " The sorrows of
hell had closed all around me and hell's dark terrors had
got hold upon me." The thrice repeated and soul-
moving question, " Watchman will the night soon pass?"
which follows this, is one that no one can forget. It is
answered as with a voice from heaven like that of an
angel : " The night is departing," and immediately the
whole choir takes up " The night is departing, the day
is approaching," closing with the pious prayer, " Therefore, let us put off the works of darkness and let us gird
on the armor of light." This double chorus which alter-
nates in singing the words, " The night is departing, the
day is approaching," is perhaps the grandest of its kind
that has been written in modern times, and in powerful
effect can only be compared to the chorus in Haydn's
creation : " Let there be light," or with Mendelssohn's
chorus in " St. Paul ; " " Rise up, arise and shine."
This is appropriately followed by the choral accom-

panied by all the instruments: " Let all men praise the
Lord " (" Nun danket alle Gott ") in which the unison
in the second verse has a specially powerful effect; the
text of this verse is as follows :

> " Praise to the triune God,
> With powerful arm and strong,
> He changeth night to day ;
> Praise him with joyful song."

and now, in order to give the work a suitable, beautiful
ending, and at the same time one worthily musical, there
follows this a charming duet, " My song shall always
be thy mercy, singing thy praise, thou only God," and
then the whole force of voices and instruments takes up
the closing number, " Ye nations, ye monarchs, thou
heaven and whole earth, offer to the Lord glory and
strength," and so, suitably and majestically, the piece
closes.   The whole of the text was chosen by Mendelssohn himself out of the Bible, and it deserves to be mentioned that it was done without any assistance from his
theological friends.   I cannot control the judgments of
others, but to me the " Lobgesang " seems to be one of
the greatest and most delightful of Mendelssohn's works,
in which he has shown himself free from any constrain-
ing influences produced by earlier composers, and has
brought his whole individuality into action in the most
spontaneous manner.   One does not know how to praise
most, the clear delineation of the themes and the pious
and spiritual delight in God, or the charming harmony
and melody of tone in this work.   The difficulty is the
greater, perhaps, that each of these features is perfect in
its kind, and all together make the great work it is admitted to be.

The first presentation of the cantata was brilliant in the

highest degree, the choruses and the orchestra admirable
as always.   The work called forth the highest enthusiasm
from all hearers, although, of course, this was not expressed by audible tones, it being given in the church.
But after the first beautiful duet a light murmur, ran
through the crowded edifice which indicated the pleasure of the whole assembly.   On the following evening
Mendelssohn was greeted by a torch-light procession
coming to his house and serenading him there.   He
was visibly pleased with this mark of honor.   "Gentlemen," he said, in his neat and kindly way, with that
peculiar and touching pliancy of voice so characteristic
of him, " you know it is not my manner to use many
words, but I thank you heartily."   A three times three
from us all, was our answer.

Scarcely had he completed this great work, when he
passed at once with his unquenchable energy of spirit to
another task, the erection of a monument to his great
master and precursor in the Thomas School, John Sebastian Bach.   This man, whose influence as cantor at Leipsic had been so fruitful, was now, after this long round of
years, again to appear before the world in visible form.

Mendelssohn resolved to erect a monument to him out
of his own means, and for this purpose brought all the
musical resources of Leipsic together to study the works
of the great master.   He gave several concerts, the pe-
cuniary results of which were to be devoted to the Bach
monument, and in these concerts only Bach's works were
given.   He himself announced them with a statement of
the object, and under his own signature, in the " Leipsic
Journal."   The first of these was an organ concert given
on the 21st of July, and then repeated on the 6th of
August.   He alone played, choosing the most beautiful

and the most difficult things of Bach, especially the magnificent fugue in E-major, fantasia upon the choral, "Schmücke dich O liebe Seele!" Prelude with fugue in A-minor, the so-called "Passacaille" in C-minor, with its twenty-one variations, the "Pastorella," and the "Tocata" in A-minor, closing with a free improvisation on the choral, "O Haupt voll Blut und Wunden." This performance was all the more astonishing that it had been a long time since Mendelssohn had touched an organ.

Respecting this concert, he wrote under date of August 10th, to his mother: "On Thursday I gave an organ concert here in the St. Thomas Church, from whose results old Sebastian Bach is to receive a monument placed before his own Thomas School. I gave it solissimo, and at the close a free improvisation. Bach made the entire programme. Although I went to considerable cost in in the performance, I yet realized over three hundred thalers clear. In August, or in spring, I will repeat the joke, and then shall have money enough to raise a suitable stone. I have been practising on this thing more than a week incessantly and now can hardly stand upon my feet, and when I walk on the street I seem to be doing nothing but executing pedal passages."

When we think of the greatness and variety of Mendelssohn's activities during a single year, we can only wonder that his tender body endured the strain upon it, and it is not surprising that he was ill not long after this organ concert. Scarcely was he restored from this, however, when he prepared himself for a journey to England. He had given his promise that in September he would direct the musical festival in Birmingham and bring out his "Hymn of Praise" there; on the 11th of September he had not arrived in London, and so the first rehearsal

had to be held without him. But on the 18th of the
month he reached London; on the 20th he journeyed
with Moscheles to Birmingham, and on the 23d the performance of the "Hymn of Praise" took place. I need
not say that it was accompanied with the most brilliant
success.

In the company of his friend Moscheles, Mendelssohn
left London and returned to Leipsic. On the 19th of
October he gave a soiree in the hall of the Gewandhaus,
at which both the overtures to "Leonora" and the
"Forty-Second Psalm" were performed. Moscheles
played his "G-minor Concerto," and then with Mendelssohn his "Hommage à Handel."

But one of Leipsic's most delightful and perfect
musical days was to come on the 3d of December, for
the "Lobgesang" was to be given in the Gewandhaus
for the first time. The ample display of flowers upon
the director's desk, the storm of applause with which he
was received, indicated to the composer in advance the
gratitude of a delighted public. I need not mention in
detail the programme of the first part of the concert, but
the second was devoted entirely to the "Hymn of Praise;"
never have I heard the opening soprano solo given more
beautifully than upon that occasion; indeed the highest
praise must be awarded to all, singers and instrumentalists; the enthusiasm of the hearers knew no bounds; in
the German fashion they would have been glad to have
taken the composer, decked him with flowers, and have
borne him triumphantly home.

This well deserved triumph was soon to be followed
by another, more quiet, indeed, and yet, perhaps, more
brilliant and full of honor. The Saxon king, Frederick
Augustus, the discriminating patron of science and art,

came to Leipsic on the 15th of December, and expressed a wish to hear the "Hymn of Praise;" it was given on the 16th. It was interesting to see the two kings, the earthly monarch and the monarch in the realm of thought and spirit, confronting each other and yet having so much in common. The assembly listened in breathless silence to the music and watched to see the impression which it made upon their beloved ruler. At the close of the concert, the king hastened from his seat and advanced rapidly through the middle aisle to the orchestra where Mendelssohn, David and the other performers were standing. He uttered his thanks with few words but in the most friendly manner. Mendelssohn accompanied the king back for some distance and doubtless there came into the minds of many of the hearers and observers the lines of the poet:

"Ec darf der Sänger mit dem König gehen,
Sie beide wandeln auf der Menscheit Höh'n."

The year 1840 closed with still another incident which I must not omit, the proposition made to Mendelssohn to establish a Conservatory at Leipsic. He wrote, under date of April 8th, a very full and clear letter to director Von Falkenstein in Dresden, in which he laid down the ground, why he thought that Leipsic was admirably adapted as the seat of a school of music, and begged him to ask the king to allow the legacy of twenty thousand thalers left by a distinguished official of the name of Blumner to be devoted to this end. We shall see later to what important results this letter led.

The year 1841 was a year of unusual activity with Mendelssohn. Besides those concerts in which works characterized by special beauty were given, there were also historical concerts, in which he displayed the same taste and enterprise and energy as in the series previously noticed in these pages. At each of these concerts he generally gave the music of one master, and never of more than two. In the first he played Bach's "Chromatic Fantasia," and a theme with variations by Handel, written in the year 1720; in the third he gave the "D-minor Concerto" and the accompaniment to songs, by Mozart; in the fourth he accompanied Madame Schröder-Devrient in "Adelaide," and directed the "D-minor Symphony." This last was received by the public with more delight than ever before, the performance indeed was an exceedingly animated one; Mendelssohn's keen eyes had discovered new beauties, and these he developed in such a manner that gave a new life to the whole symphony; but the interest of the season was by no means confined to these historical concerts; at every one of those which followed, Mendelssohn brought out something that was of special interest, and oftentimes works that are so, to us, as his own productions. In the seventeenth, for example, we had the beautiful song, "The Hunter's Departure," "Wer hat dich du schöne Wald;" this is, perhaps, Mendelssohn's most popular composition, and has already made the circuit of half the world. In the twentieth concert Madame Schröder-Devrient sang "Ach um deine feuchten Schwingen," that wonderful composition of Mendelssohn's, so perfectly harmonizing with its words. When recalled by a storm of applause she gave Mendelssohn's own song, "Es ist bestimmt in Gottes Rath," and by turning to him at the close she indicated that she had in her mind the contemplated parting of Mendelssohn from his beloved Leipsic friends. It was already known that negotiations were on foot respecting his transference to Berlin.

After all this success of Mendelssohn in every department, it would hardly have been deemed possible that he
could advance to higher honors and to a larger unfolding
of his genius, and yet this was possible; the greatest
proof of his power was yet to come.   About the middle
of February, 1841, he began to study with a numerous
chorus of *dilletanti* the numbers of Bach's "Matthew
Passion," a work which, in spite of the skill of the Leipsic
singers, was yet a herculean task; yet our director possessed the spirit of a Hercules, dwelling, however, in a
very delicate body, whose endurance during the rehearsals was simply amazing.   What endless pains and
patience he expended upon this double chorus with its
frequent great and perplexing difficulties!   At the very
first rehearsal there was a comical division of the singers,
in spite of Mendelssohn's efforts to keep them together;
he could not withhold his own laughter at the serious
break, but he did not rest until he brought every difficulty
under control and had made his choir all it could become;
when at last they had reached the point of singing the
whole thing mechanically perfect, he passed to the study
of the inner meaning of the work.   He laid especial
stress upon the chorals; they must be sung with the
greatest piety and delicacy of feeling.   When, at the last
rehearsal, the soloists were present, everyone was delighted with the depth and the grandeur of the work.
We believed that at last the day had come when this
greatest of all oratorios could be comprehended.   The
performance took place on Palm Sunday, April 4, 1841,
in the illuminated St. Thomas Church and for the benefit
of the Bach Memorial Statue.   It had never been heard
in Leipsic since Bach himself, on Good Friday, 1729,
had directed it in the same church.   The impression

upon the audience was certainly powerful, although of course not intelligible to all; yet everyone felt the grandeur and dignity of the work. Since then it has become one of the great favorites in Leipsic, and on Good Friday it is invariably performed.

If this year was abundant in labors it was also rich in honors. In June, 1841, the king of Saxony nominated Mendelssohn to be his Capellmeister. He desired that Mendelssohn should remove to Dresden, but was obliged to content himself with the promise that he would now and then, at the king's command, give a concert in Dresden. King William Frederic the Fourth of Prussia, who had just then mounted the throne, and who was endeavoring to draw all the great talents of his time into his immediate neighborhood, had cast his eye upon the former resident of his capital and endeavored to secure Mendelssohn to himself almost contemporaneously with the call to Dresden, naming him as his own Capellmeister and offering him a salary of three thousand thalers. The king purposed to establish in Berlin an Academy of Fine Arts and to divide it into four classes, painting, sculpture, architecture and music, and to appoint a director of every class; and Mendelssohn was to be director of the fourth class. As early as November, 1840, Von Massow, Frederic William's minister in charge of those matters, had turned to Mendelssohn's brother Paul, endeavoring to ascertain how Felix could be won to this enterprise. The musical class was in reality to consist of a great conservatory, and it was proposed to have this connected with the Royal Theatre and thus to give public concerts, partly of a religious and partly of a secular character; but attractive as the plan was to Mendelssohn, he yet missed in it that sphere of practical activity which had become so precious to him in his Leipsic life. He expressed strong doubts, not so much as to whether the plan *could* be carried out as whether it *would* be carried out ; and the result justified his doubts, for the idea of such a conservatory completely vanished, and so long as Mendelssohn lived, never came to anything feasible ; whereas the establishment of a similar one in Leipsic appeared to become more probable every day. The fact was, Mendelssohn's heart was in Leipsic, although he found it hard to resist the extremely honorable proposals of King Frederic William the Fourth. At last, after long negotiations, Mendelssohn resolved to ask for a year's absence from his position in Leipsic. After meeting the minister Von Massow and others, and speaking with them at length respecting the music school which was to be formed in Berlin, he left Leipsic with his family, yet without breaking off his nominal residence there or announcing his plans. On the evening of his departure his friends serenaded him ; when they had sung the hymn, " Es ist bestimmt in Gottes Rath," he stepped forth among them and in a firm clear voice said, " Auf wiedersehen." The direction of the Gewandhaus concerts for that winter was entrusted to his friend David.

## PART IV.

Although King Frederick William the Fourth of Prussia had no immediate special field of activity for Mendelssohn in his capital, nevertheless he had ideas manifold and great, which would fully occupy the talents of the composer. The music of Sophocles' trilogy, " Oedipus," " Oedipus at Colonos," and " Antigone," the complete music of the " Midsummer Night's Dream," as well as to Racine's " Athalie " followed in rapid succession, and Mendelssohn eagerly entered into their composition.

The first thing which resulted from the king's musical ideas was the composition of the overture, choruses and melodrama to Sophocles' " Antigone." This task he took up with all the fire of his genius. In his youth he had already become familiar with the distinctive character of Grecian poetry ; he had studied this very play of Sophocles and knew it thoroughly. Ludwig Tieck had proposed this to his royal master, and in the preparing of the play for the stage it was his counsel which was enjoyed every moment. With what delight and what fine intelligence Mendelssohn gave himself to the task appears in a letter which he wrote October 21st, to his friend David : " I am glad to hear that you read the ' Antigone ' at once. I knew, of course, perfectly well, that it would please you if you should read it, and it was just that impression which the reading of it made upon me which is the real reason why I undertook the thing; everybody talked about it, and no one would begin it, and so the thing went on and on till at last I felt the peculiar power of the piece so strongly that I laid hands on good old Tieck and said to him, ' It must be now or never,' and he was very kind and said, ' It shall be now,' and so I set to work with all my enthusiasm upon it, and already we have had two rehearsals, and the choruses go in a manner that would delight you ; the task was one just after my heart, and I have wrought at it with perfect joy.   It is to me remarkable that art itself is a thing so little subject to change ; all the various thoughts expressed in the choruses are so genuinely musical even to-day, and are so different from one another, that no one could desire anything more beautifully adapted to composition.''

At the outset, it was a question with Mendelssohn whether he should have his choruses entirely recitative and in unison ; and whether the solo parts should be accompanied only by instruments similar to those in use when Sophocles lived ; but he soon rejected this view ; he would not compose antique music ; what he would compose was that which should be a mediator between the ancient play and modern thought.   Very rightly says Fanny Hensel in her diary : '' There is no question that my brother's music has contributed much to the understanding of the whole.   If Felix had adhered to his intention of composing simply rigidly antique music, that and the piece, instead of being brought together, would simply have parted company.'' That Mendelssohn grasped the real character of the work is perhaps best estimated by the praise which he received from the eminent Berlin philologist, Professor Bockh, who pays high tribute to Mendelssohn's accuracy in grasping the ancient Greek spirit and life as set forth in Sophocles' work.   Bockh says further that Mendelssohn has so utilized the modern resources of art as to retain the character of the ancient poetry and at the same time to give the most beautiful musical expression of it. . Devrient says also, respecting the same work : " The sensation which it produced was very great : the powerful impression, the realization of the ancient tragedy amid our modern life promised to mark an epoch in art ; it purified the very air of our stage, and certain it is that Mendelssohn has accomplished a very great work in this undertaking."

He composed the music in the incredibly short space of eleven days.   On the 9th and 14th of September, after Tieck's first reading of the " Antigone," Mendelssohn deliberated with Devrient on the conception of the work ; on the 25th and 26th, he showed him the sketches and talked over the melodrama ; this he completed on the 28th ; in the first days of October the study of the choruses could begin ; on the 10th of October, Mendelssohn accompanied the melodrama, at the rehearsal, on the piano, and was making so much advance with the instrumentation that on the 22d of the same month the first rehearsal with scenery could take place in the concert room of the theatre in Berlin ; on the 26th of October, general rehearsal was held in the private Royal Theatre of the new palace at Potsdam, where a stage was built in the Grecian fashion, and on the 28th the performance took place in the presence of a most distinguished audience, gathered by invitation, from Berlin.   Fanny Hensel, who was present with the other members of the Mendelssohn family, says, respecting this performance, " The aspect of the little house was surprisingly beautiful, and I cannot tell you how much more worthy I found this arrangement

than our paper stage decorations and the tasteless row of
lamps.  The falling of the curtain even, which brings
the faces of the performers into view before their feet, is
a great improvement on our method of making acquaintance first with the ankles; the whole rendering of the
piece was to me the most interesting thing that I have
seen on the stage for a long time, and the intentness of
attention, and the grasping of the meaning of the work
by all who have not given up all seriousness of purpose
in theatrical matters, was to me a source of great delight."

The miscellaneous public did not enjoy this piece for a
considerable time; Leipsic put it off for a long period,
although it was the production of her great favorite, and
it was only brought out under Mendelssohn's personal
direction on the 5th, 6th and 8th of March, 1842.  Berlin
followed on the 13th of April in the same year.

The main employment of Mendelssohn in the capital
during the first half of the winter was the direction of
several grand concerts, of which it is not necessary to
speak in detail.

In the winter of 1841-42, Mendelssohn, being then in
Leipsic, displayed an extraordinary activity, although the
season was broken by several journeys to Berlin.  He
had divided the direction of the concerts with his friend
David, and everything was continued in the spirit of the
master.

On the 3d of March, at the nineteenth subscription
concert, appeared the new work which had long been
looked forward to with great interest, Mendelssohn's
" Symphony in A-minor."  It was the third which he
wrote, but the first which attained to universal recognition in the musical world.  His first " Symphony in

C-minor " was a youthful production on which he himself laid no special value, the second in A-major, of
which I have already spoken, was written for the Philharmonic Society in London, and had never been heard
of much beyond England.   But in the third he first made
his mastership evident to all, and showed that he had
attained to the highest reach possible in instrumental
music.   We have already seen that the first conception
of this symphony occurred to him on the occasion of a
visit to the old and partially ruined palace in Edinburgh,
where the singer Rizzio, the lover of the light minded
queen Mary Stuart, was killed at the instigation of her
rough-handed husband Darnley.   This thought imparted
to the so-called Scottish symphony a certain dark and
melancholy character.   Mendelssohn began to work upon
it as early as the winter of 1830–31, but it was impossible
for him, amid the cheerful influences of a southern sky
and climate, to continue, and therefore he preferred to
work upon his other " Symphony in A-major," which he
produced in London in the year 1832.   Several other
important compositions, among them the " St. Paul,"
intervened to hinder the continuation of the " A-minor
Symphony."   It was completed only at the beginning of
1842, in Berlin, and on this account, when first given, it
was from manuscript.   In this work he remained true to
his character as a composer ; it is a fine, thoughtful work,
breathing a gentle air of sadness, and although not in the
least seeking after great effect, yet by the simplest possible
material finds its way straight to the heart.   Mendelssohn
produced it at first as a complete work without breaking
it up into movements.   This method of representation
was not favorable to the understanding of the piece ;
on that account he divided it later and indicated the

movements as introduction and allegro agitato, scherzo assai vivace, adagio cantabile, allegro guerriero and finale maestoso; the first of these, a rather long drawn out movement, after a short introduction in A-minor, introduces certain themes which sound like sad folksongs; there follows, as the second movement, a delightfully joyous scherzo, which works like a refreshing bath; then follows the adagio and again introduces tones of sadness, yet also of reconciliation. Beneath the allegro guerriero, which again moves forward in a minor but somewhat constrained rhythm, one could fancy the last struggle which gave to Queen Elizabeth her complete victory over her unfortunate rival, and in the short but noble finale maestoso, in a brilliant A-major, the sun seems to rise after a stormy night over the wildly moving waves and announces a brighter future. Without this reconciliation and conclusion, the heavy air of sadness that fills the work for the most part were scarcely to be borne, yet the symphony as a whole was received with favor, although the charming and thoroughly delightful scherzo and the deep and spirituelle adagio found the greatest applause from the public. It was repeated at the following concert by universal request. In June of the same year, Mendelssohn produced this his latest work in the Philharmonic concert in London, where it was received with enthusiastic applause, and as soon as it appeared in print as the Scottish symphony, it was dedicated to Queen Victoria, who received it with the most gracious thanks.

Leipsic had occasion to be all the more thankful for this gift, inasmuch as it was coupled with a second and, if possible, a more valuable gift still. On the 5th of March, Mendelssohn gave before a crowded house the "Antigone" of Sophocles, set to music by himself. This, which was

repeated on the stage of the Leipsic Theatre, was directed by the composer himself, and was received with
immense applause.  Respecting the relation of the music
to this ancient tragedy, I have already cited Fanny Hensel's apt and admirable judgment.  Mendelssohn was so
thoroughly interpenetrated by the spirit of the tragedy,
that he was able to give to it an interpretation which
brought it nearer to the hearts of men than it had ever
come before.  This was admitted even by the German
philologists, for at their session in Cassel in the autumn
of 1843, they sent a communication to Mendelssohn ac-
knowledging the great assistance which he had rendered
in awakening an intelligent interest in Greek tragedy.
With us who took part, as perhaps everywhere else, the
Eros chorus, thrilling as it does with the divine omnipotence, and the Bacchus chorus, joyfully swinging the
thyrsi and praising the son of the maiden of Cadmos, are
among the most delightful passages of all, but scarcely
less so are the melodramatic portions where Antigone
descends into the bridal death-chamber, and where Creon
bears away the body of his son.  The impression produced by the whole play was certainly very powerful.
It was with amazement that our modern world perceived
the power of the ancient tragic muse, and recognized the
greatness of fate which exalts man while it crushes him.
In breathless silence the assembly watched the melodious
flow of words and followed with eager interest the unbroken course of the drama.  Thanks to the experienced
skill of the Nestor of philologists, Professor Gottfried
Hermann, the stage had been conformed with exact
fidelity to the ancient methods.  The choruses were not
simply sung well, they were given with rare intelligence,
and the parts of the special performers were so repre-

sented as to leave little or nothing to be desired; certainly no hearer left the hall without an experience of great satisfaction and exaltation at being brought into such close contact with the exalting and purifying spirit of the ancient drama; even people of a common type were heard to speak of the splendid language of the piece, although, of course, they were not competent to measure the whole excellence of it. It was given on three occasions, and always before a crowded house and amidst the most unmistakable signs of applause. At the close of the first representation, the composer and the chief actor were called out. A year later the tragedy was again brought upon the stage before a full house. In Berlin, the "Antigone" was produced on the 13th of April with Mendelssohn's music; the impression, as Devrient informs us, there was so decidedly favorable that within three weeks six representations had to be given.

With the approach of Whitsuntide, Mendelssohn again visited his favorite Düsseldorf in order to take charge of the festival there in conjunction with his friend Julius Rietz. He was favored with the most delightful weather, and the musical resources placed at his control were numerous and brilliant. Over five thousand players and singers, among them the first in the land, took part in the various performances. I must mention that, at the third concert on the day devoted to salon music, the violinist Ernst, of Weimar, who was prevented by sickness from being present, created a break which was only filled by Mendelssohn playing without rehearsal Beethoven's "E-flat major Concerto." A gifted critic wrote this notice respecting Mendelssohn's performance: "His appearance after so many famous artists, reminded us of the Egyptian Magi with whom Moses had to contend.

So far as concerns technique, finish and touch, there was no palm to be won over his, but the artist was not content with this; he strove to reproduce the very meaning which Beethoven had at heart, and he completely gained his end; everyone was astonished and confounded. Mendelssohn so clearly showed the difference between one man's playing and another man's music, between the piano in his own hands and the piano in the hands of another, that there were few present who did not see clearly the difference between the spirit and the letter, between a truly interpretative and a merely mechanical skill." After the " E-flat major Concerto," Mendelssohn delighted the assembly by some of his " Songs without Words," and closed with a free improvisation, in which he rehearsed nearly all the most striking passages during both of the previous days.

As a testimonial of the recognition of Mendelssohn's remarkable and undeniable merit at this festival, he received a new token of the royal favor. In June the journals announced that the king of Prussia had made him a Knight of the Order of Peace, founded by Frederick the Great, and restored by Frederick William the Fourth, *pour la merite.* With the beginning of the same month, Mendelssohn, in company with his wife, went to England, where old friends and new triumphs awaited him; musical enjoyments in the circle of his friends, especially in Moscheles' house and with his coöperation, alternated with distinguished public performances; on the 13th of June, Mendelssohn directed at the Philharmonic concert his " A-minor Concerto," which was received with great applause, and this was followed by many others which I will not recount in full. But I must not omit to speak of the special and unique occurrence during this visit of Mendelssohn in London, namely, his visit to Queen Victoria, who, on the 20th of June, invited him to Buckingham Palace. Mendelssohn has given very full accounts of this in two letters to his mother and Hensel, in his "Mendelssohn Family," has also detailed it *in extenso;* I will merely indicate those passages and not repeat them here, save that I will mention the account of it which I have had from Mendelssohn's own lips. Her gracious majesty, as well as her royal husband, being herself a distinguished virtuoso in music, received the composer in the most confidential manner, that is, in the presence of Prince Albert and a prince of Gotha, all being in her own living room. When Mendelssohn entered she begged his pardon for finding the apartment not in complete order, and endeavored to put it to rights, Mendelssohn assisting her. After this she begged him to play something, and then, at his request, sang several songs, among them "Schöner and Schöner," really written by Mendelssohn's sister, although appearing under his name. Yet before she sang she said, "I must carry this parrot out, otherwise he will cry louder than I can sing." The prince of Gotha said, "I will take it out," but Mendelssohn exclaimed, "That you must permit me," and himself bore the great cage out to the amazement of the servants in the ante-room. When the queen had sung, she was not completely satisfied with her performance, and expressed herself jestingly that Mendelssohn must ask Lablache, for she could sing better, only she was afraid of him. After this, Prince Albert, who had already played from memory a choral upon the organ standing in the room, giving it so clearly and neatly that many an organist could learn something from him, sang the song, "There is a Reaper whose name is Death;" at the close of this, Mendelssohn was called upon to extem-

porize upon the choral which the prince had played and
the song which he had sung ; and this he did, weaving in
both the songs which the queen had sung.   He told me
that the improvisation succeeded with him better than
common.   When the queen had withdrawn for a moment
(she was just on the point of leaving on a journey to
Claremont), Prince Albert gave him, at the command of
the queen, a little étui containing a beautiful ring on which
was engraved " V. R. 1842."

As an indication of the enthusiastic reception which
Mendelssohn received at this time in England, a passage
from a letter written on the 22d of June to his mother will
suffice : " A little while ago I went into a concert in Exeter Hall, with which I had nothing to do ; I was loung-
ing at my ease with Klingemann — they were already in
the middle of the first part — there was a matter of three
thousand persons present, and as I was just entering the
door, a shouting and clapping of hands and standing up
began of such magnitude that I could not believe that it
concerned me ; but when, coming to my place, I saw Sir
Robert Peel and Lord Wharncliffe close by me, and also
applauding, I was obliged to make my acknowledgments.
I was extremely proud of my popularity in Peel's presence.   When I went away after the concert, again they
followed me with their hurrahs."

On the 12th of July, in the company of his wife, he
again left London, and found his refreshment in Switzerland, the country which had formerly been so dear to
him.

Returning thence, he went with his family to Frankfort, where he spent sixteen days.   Here he found his
friend Ferdinand Hiller married to an attractive Italian
lady possessing a fine voice ; the time spent in this city was

filled with all kinds of musical enjoyments and festivities. Mendelssohn was at the height of his spirits; " Never," says one who saw him at that time, " have I seen a happier man than Mendelssohn was." On the 25th of September he went by way of Leipsic to Berlin.

Meanwhile, in the Saxon city, a great change had occurred, — great in its relation to the musical life there. The hall of the Gewandhaus, which had long been insufficient to contain its hearers, had been enlarged by breaking it in the middle and supplying it with galleries. It had become somewhat smoky and sooty in the course of time and now was restored with brightly colors, and the dim lamps had given way to the more brilliant ones of gas. Unfortunately the paintings on the wall had suffered. Many supposed that with the change in the old hall its spirit would be found to have departed, a fear which, however, was never justified. The motto upon the hall remained, "*Res severa est verum gaudium;*" the admirable acoustic properties had not suffered in the renovation. On the day of the dedication, there was one man whose presence was considered absolutely necessary, and Mendelssohn was called from Berlin to direct the first concert. The enthusiasm of the assemblage at his appearance surpassed that which Weber's "Jubilee Overture," with all its splendor of performance, could excite. After this concert, Mendelssohn returned for some weeks to Berlin, in order to direct the symphony soirees, and at the same time negotiations were renewed with Frederick William the Fourth regarding his position and sphere of activity in Berlin. This ended with this result: that Mendelssohn should give up half of his salary, leaving it free to the king to summon him whenever he needed him and accepting freely the task of composing music to the

"Athalia," "Midsummer Night's Dream" and "Oedipus at
Colonos." In a farewell audience which the king granted
him, he was most graciously dismissed, and went at the
end of October again to Leipsic, where, with his family,
he took up his old quarters in their comfortable fashion.
He had already promised to be in Berlin in order to celebrate Fanny's birthday, but he was unable to keep this
promise, because he was needed at that time at Dresden,
in order to make arrangements respecting Blumner's
legacy to the Leipsic Conservatory. He writes to Fanny:
"This is all done now, and I am free to go on with my
work without any complications with matters here or in
Berlin." And it would appear, indeed, that although
subsequently the king promised him the title of General
Music Director, and entrusted to him the charge of all the
ecclesiastical music in the kingdom, especially the direction
of the service in the cathedral in Berlin, Mendelssohn
preferred to remain in Leipsic.

On the 12th of December, his mother died in almost as
peaceful a manner as her husband had before her. Mendelssohn lost in her his true protector and one whose care
for his bodily and spiritual concerns had been unfailing,
and who was also his first teacher. He bore this loss,
which cut him to his soul, with his usual manly composure. He soon turned back to his regular work in Leipsic, where so many tasks were awaiting him, knowing
well that the best cure for such a pain lies in constant
activity.

The year 1843 brings to view an important musical performance in the neighboring city of Halle. Here, in the
beginning of January, and under the direction of the well-
known Robert Franz, happily living to our time and full
of honors as he is of years, — the man whose name is con-

nected forever with the great works of Bach and Handel — a great performance was arranged in connection with the erection of a statue of Handel, the programme consisting of the overture to the " Herbrides," a part song of Schubert, Mozart's " D-minor Concerto " and Mendelssohn's " Hymn of Praise."

In Leipsic, on the 16th of January, 1843, there appeared the current programme of the new school of music, proposing to give instruction in composition, piano, violin and voice, together with scientific lectures on the history of music, esthetics and practice in playing together, and chorus singing. The teachers were Moritz Hauptmann, Robert Schumann, Ferdinand David, C. A. Polentz and K. S. Becker. The number of applications at the outset was forty-six ; in July it amounted to sixty-eight, of whom forty-two were received, among them two Germans, an Englishman and an American. On the 3d of April, the conservatory was formally opened in the name of his majesty the king. In the middle of this month, the complete programme of instruction was published. Mendelssohn had exercises in solo singing, instrumental playing and composition ; Hauptmann, the theory of harmony and counterpoint ; Schumann, the piano, and the examination of private compositions ; David, the violin, and Becker the organ. Money began to flow into the institute, as well as substantial gifts, but especially interesting is the spirit with which Mendelssohn devoted himself to this enterprise. He was not only its founder, but also its most efficient co-worker. He displayed, in a manner which he had scarcely ever done before, his remarkable talent for musical instruction. How valuable his mere hints as he examined compositions, how stimulating the hours spent in piano practice and solo singing were, will never be forgotten by any of his pupils. He used to take part in the private rehearsals of the single classes with the greatest zeal ; even in the lower classes he was present often, and no one will forget his hints regarding modulation, his bright flashing eye, his fine ear. The timid he used to draw out, and whenever he had occasion to reprove for immoral misconduct, he knew how to do so by saying the right and effective word. I have known him to pass half a night in order to attain a correct result in awarding cer- tificates of progress. Of course he could not take this active interest and continue in his creative work, but as long as he undertook this role he gave himself entirely to it in word and deed, with body and soul. With all this, he refused in noble modesty to be called anything but one of the six teachers ; he would not be recognized as the director of all. It was his great delight that Moscheles responded to his invitation, and came to Leipsic and joined him in the care of the institute. From the year 1846 to the year 1870, Moscheles thus fulfilled the wishes of one who had formerly been his pupil and was now his friend.

I have in the earlier pages of this book made such full report of the rise and progress of Mendelssohn's "Wal- purgis Night," that I need not enter further into that mat- ter save to say that it was never given in Leipsic till the 2d of February, 1843, but I will append here the judg- ment of Hector Berlioz, who heard it at that time, upon this work : "Truly I may say that I was, at the first movement, quite beside myself at the beauty of the vocal part, the skill of the singers, the exactness of the orchestra, the rhythm of the words and the splendor of the composi- tion. I think this the most admirable work that Mendels- sohn has thus far produced ; one must hear his tones in

order to estimate what an admirable use he has made of
Goethe's poem. His score is perfectly clear, despite its
constant involutions; the instrumental parts cross each
other continually and in the greatest seeming confusion,
yet with such skilful management and such power, that
the effect is the highest perfection of art. I must indicate
as special examples the excellence of two styles quite unlike each other, the dim and mysterious strain during the
setting of the guards, and the finale where the voice of the
priest is heard distinct and calm above the raging of the
whole rabble of witches and demons. I do not know
which to admire the most, the orchestra, the chorus, or
the mighty rush and whirl of sound which sets the whole
in movement. A true masterpiece."

We cannot refrain from fully and cheerfully subscribing
to this judgment.

I pass over several performances which followed, in so
far as they have nothing especially new to offer us. But
I cannot refrain from mentioning with some detail the
important musical event connected with the unveiling of
the Bach monument, already referred to. The concert
which celebrated this took place on the 23d of April in
the hall of the Gewandhaus. Mendelssohn endeavored
to honor the memory of the great master in the most
worthy manner, and had collected a rich and varied programme from his chief works. It was as follows: Suite
for a full orchestra, consisting of overture, ariosa, gavotte,
trio and finale; and the double chorus motet, "Ich
lasse dich nicht du segnest mich denn" ("I will not let
thee go unless thou bless me"). Then followed a concerto for the piano, and orchestral accompaniment played
by Mendelssohn, the aria with oboe obligato from the
"Passion" music, "Ich will bei meinem Jesu wachen"

("I will watch with my Lord"), and an improvisation
on themes from Bach by Mendelssohn.   The second part
consisted of a cantata given in honor of the election in
Leipsic in 1723, prelude for the violin alone, by David,
and Sanctūs from the "B-flat minor Mass" for chorus
and orchestra.   Mendelssohn, although not well, accomplished all that he promised.   Directly after the concert,
was the unveiling of the statue.   A choral by Bach
opened the festivities.   Councillor Dalmuth gave a short
and appropriate address, and the solemnity, at which a
grandson of Sebastian Bach was present, closed with the
great motet, sung by the Thomas choir, "Singet dem
Herrn ein neues Lied" ("Sing to the Lord a new song").
The memorial stone, modelled by Bendemann and Hubner and put into stone by Knauer, is certainly no brilliant
specimen of genius, but it accomplished its object, which
was to remind succeeding times of that great master who
wrought on this spot and whose piety and devotion well
deserve remembrance.   It stands on the left of the Thomas
gate, not far from the old Thomas' School.   But, in addition, the city, grateful for the services which Mendelssohn had rendered it so long and the honor which he
had conferred upon it by his labors, gave to him the
right of citizenship.   His letter of reply accepting the
honor was so much in the spirit of his acceptance of the
honorary title conferred upon him previously by the University, that I will not give it here.   It was like that, full
of his own modesty, his sense of his discontent with any
supposed accomplishment of his ideal work in life, and a
noble and enthusiastic purpose to continue steadfast to
the end in rising to that ideal.

    After conducting a public performance of his "St. Paul"
in Dresden, he seems to have had leisure for some rest;

at least, to have not allowed himself to be driven as before. Neither in England nor on the Rhine did he direct any great festival. It is probable that he devoted the most of his time to his new creation, the Conservatory ; and it is certain that in this summer, on the immediate instigation of the king of Prussia, he composed the additional music for Shakespeare's " Midsummer Night's Dream." He made one public appearance in Leipsic, at a concert given on the 19th of August, when he played with Clara Schumann an andante for two pianos, composed by Robert Schumann. During the same month his "Antigone" was performed, with great applause, on the stage at Mannheim. On the 14th of October, the first performance of Shakespeare's charming play took place in the new palace in Potsdam ; the rehearsals began on the 27th of September, in the upper story of the royal palace in Berlin, because that room, being lofty, permitted the use of scenery much higher than that ordinarily found in the theatres. Ludwig Tieck showed his customary skill in putting the piece upon the stage. He had purposely divided the play into three acts, but, as he had not informed Mendelssohn of this, the latter had composed the music with reference to the original division and was obliged to exercise an uncommon degree of skill in so weaving the themes together that Tieck's division should remain and yet the whole of Mendelssohn's music be given. It was admitted that every note was so beautiful that no one could be spared. The reception given by the public to the piece was extraordinary ; Fanny's and Felix' account may be found in the letters.

The preparation of the piece for the public was very exhausting to Mendelssohn, but he could not rest and recover from this strain, for the king laid new commands upon him, and he was even bidden to present, as soon as the 19th of October, the music to his "Antigone" at the new palace at Potsdam.

Indeed, with the removal of Mendelssohn to Berlin, his life began to be one of almost abnormal activity. The king had now given him a definite sphere of action, entrusting to him the care of the music in the cathedral, six great concerts in the Singacademie, and the symphony concerts of the Berlin Capelle. Ferdinand Hiller was appointed his successor at the Leipsic concerts for this winter.

It may, perhaps, be mentioned that on the 30th of December his great and charming work, the "Midsummer Night's Dream" music, was given for the first time in Leipsic. He, indeed, could not be there to direct it, yet we had, as it were, his representative in his music. Although the presentation of this piece was by no means brilliant, yet it was agreeable and tasteful, the skill of the performers sufficing to atone for many deficiencies in the stage setting. Still, as a whole, the piece was given heavily and with too energetic and massive a touch; we were conscious of the great beauty of the music to which we were listening; we saw clearly enough the masterly skill of the composer, and we enjoyed the delightful play of his genius over the fields of fairy life which he illuminated with his gentle, playful grace. We saw with him how the trivialities of life yield at last to the power of poetry and of love. The music was no new creation, it must be confessed, it was only an unfolding of those charming themes with which we had already become familiar in the overture. The delightful elfin gambols on leaf and flower in the moonlight, the awkward jesting of the clowns, the laments and yearning of disappointed love, the power of the heroic strains, the festal pomp of the princely wedding: all this had been suggested in the splendid tone picture overture, written almost twenty years before; all that remained was for the composer, with his perfect tact and his thorough comprehension of the poem, to seize upon these and bring them out on a more extended scale. The new numbers were the charming scherzo, No. 1, allegro molto vivace, in B-major; the delightful slumber song of the fairies over Titania, No. 3, A-major; the intermezzo allegro appacianato in A-minor, No. 5; the beautiful notturno in E-major, No. 7, and the magnificent wedding march, No. 9, C-major; and by way of contrast, the ludicrous burlesque in No. 10, the funeral march of Thisbe, to be played simply on the kettle-drum, trombone and clarionet. I must not omit to speak of the very effective music of the melodrama in No. 2, B-major, No. 6, E-minor, and No. 12, E-major. Respecting the relation of Mendelssohn's music to Shakespeare's piece, Fanny says, in a letter to Rebecca: "We have grown up from childhood in the 'Midsummer Night's Dream,' so to speak, and Felix has really made it so entirely his own that he has simply reproduced in music what Shakespeare produced in words, from the splendid and really festal wedding march, to the mournful music on Thisbe's death, the delightful fairy songs and dances and entr'actes —all men, spirits and clowns, he has set forth in precisely the same spirit in which Shakespeare had before him." To which I might add, certainly not in contradiction, that it might be too much to say that the play has gained by Mendelssohn's music; a play of Shakespeare admits of no improvement, but this is certain, that the popular comprehension of the play has made a very great advance; the music has translated it, has brought it out of

its darkness into the light of the day, and permitted even
prosaic spirits, which are always demanding what is
earthly in poetry, to see what Shakespeare meant by this
wonderful work.

In the summer of 1844, Mendelssohn led an extremely
active life. After a brief visit to Leipsic in February, in
which he delighted us by appearing at a concert and listening to the production of his "A-minor Symphony,"
and again, after having made us a brief second visit, during which he took part with David and Servais in playing
Beethoven's B-major trio, he went by way of Frankfort
to London, where, after his arrival on the 8th of May, he
displayed the most exhaustless activity. Almost on the
day of his arrival he rehearsed with Moscheles a new
work, variations in B-major for four hands. On the 13th
of May he conducted, at the Philharmonic concert, his
symphony in A-minor; and on the 14th he displayed his
music to the "Walpurgis Night." These may be considered examples of his almost daily exertions during his
stay, which, as usual, was thoroughly stimulating and delightful. The correspondent of the Leipsic "New Journal of Music" says, respecting this visit to London:
"Mendelssohn's appearance at the fourth Philharmonic
concert, as well as the rehearsal, gave occasion for that
indescribable tumult of jubilation with which the English
people always greet him. But who could have refrained
from applauding to the echo this charmingly sympathetic
and finely sensitive man and great artist? His conducting
produced an immediate change in everything. Upon the
orchestra he exercised the most decided and yet favorable
influence; his performance attained to a certain grade of
perfection which had never been known before." Another
correspondent adds: "Mendelssohn has already won for

next year the conducting of the concerts for the Philharmonic Society.   It is true this does not give pleasure to some gentlemen of great note, because it disturbs them in their slumbers, but as soon as his magic staff has animated the drowsy spirits of the orchestra his harmonious notes penetrate all the spaces, untroubled by any whisperings in the corners."   Klingemann says, in a letter written on the 18th of May to Rebecca : "As an artist, never has a foreigner had such applause as Felix.   His clear, pure and noble spirit, yet his strong, calm will, bore him securely above all the dust and smoke ; even the Philistines felt this and respected him.   It would do your sisterly heart good to be here and see how he is received. Take the last Philharmonic concert, for example, which he directed ; all, hearers and players alike, caught the charm. They gave the ' A-minor Symphony' more beautifully than ever before, and the listening was more eager and, as I may say, devout ; the applause more enthusiastic ; it was as if an enchanter were there and had thrown his charm over them all."

On the 10th of July, Mendelssohn left London, but only to engage at once in new activities.   He had promised to direct at the musical festival of the Palatinate, which was to occur on the 31st of July and the 1st of August.   The programme embraced for the first day his " St. Paul," on the second Beethoven's " B-major Symphony," the "Walpurgis Night," and Märschner's " Bundeslied."   His skill in directing awakened in his hearers everywhere the greatest enthusiasm.   He himself describes his work at this festival, in a very spirited and graceful way, in a letter to Fanny, written at Soden on the 15th of August.   In September he was at Frankfort with his friend Moscheles, and they two gave together the " Hommage à Handel."

We find Mendelssohn in Berlin during the month of October, directing in some symphony soirees. At the first of these Beethoven's B-major, and Haydn's " E-flat Symphony " were given, as well as the overtures to the " Magic Flute " and to the " Waterbearer ; " a second soiree, which was held on the 14th of November, had for its programme Spohr's " Symphony No. 2," D-major, Beethoven's in C-minor, and the overtures to " Coriolanus " and " Euryanthe." He won great applause in the capital by his perfect leading, yet he did not enjoy Berlin ; there was that in the air which seemed to fetter and to limit him, and in the middle of November he asked for leave of absence. This was granted him by the king in terms of the highest deference and favor, he retaining his title of General Music Director and a large portion of his salary, which the king forced upon him with the condition that from time to time he should come to Berlin and bring out something there. Respecting this proposition, Mendelssohn expresses himself to his friend Devrient, at that time in Dresden, in the following terms : " My position here has assumed a new status within the last few days, and is now just what I could wish. I remain on the old footing with the king, so far as musical composition is concerned ; I shall receive only a moderate salary, however, but so far as concerns all obligations to Berlin in musical matters, being in the city and the like, I am to be perfectly free ; in a short time I purpose to return to my family in Frankfort, and then to come to Berlin on visits as often as I like, but never to remain. I shall enjoy the companionship of my brother and sister all the better even, that I do not have to live in the capital ; and so everything has fallen out as I could wish, and as I could hardly have expected."

The last act of Mendelssohn's career in Berlin during this winter was the production of " St. Paul," which he gave at the request of the king, on the 25th of November, in the Singacademie. He then withdrew to Frankfort, passing through Leipsic, in order to have a long rest; at least, so far as to abandon public performances and to give himself to his calling as composer. Whoever has followed the course of his varied and busy life down to this time must gladly grant him the right to take this step. Of his productive work this year, it remains to be said that, at the command of the king of Prussia, he produced a portion of the music of Racine's " Athalie," the overture in D-minor, and the march of the priests, F-major. He composed the choruses in 1843 ; in addition, during the year of which we speak, he wrote the music to the hymn, " Hör, meine Bitten," four sonatas for the organ, two psalms, the Forty-Third and the Twenty-Second, for eight voices, the fifth collection of the " Songs without Words," and several selections of songs for two and four voices ; also for men's voices and for a mixed chorus. Certainly one must admit that this was a fruitful season. Nor must we refrain from adding that at this time occurred the conception and the beginning of his oratorio " Elijah," which had really been suggested to him in the year 1838 : also the music to the " Oedipus at Colonos ; " and, finally, the composition of the three trios in C-minor, Opus 66. It is a curious fact, which I must not omit to mention, that the king of Prussia, Frederick William the Fourth, desired that he should set Aeschylus' " Oresteia" to music, namely the Agamemnon, the Choëphoroi and the Eumenides. He did, indeed, begin to think about writing music to the last, afterwards he contemplated the possibility of bringing the three into

one protracted representation; but no one who knows
Aeschylus' rough and ungainly language, and his massive
thoughts, will wonder that Mendelssohn declined the
undertaking. The king at first was very much disturbed,
but afterwards became reconciled.

In the winter of 1845-46, a new step forward was to be
taken in Leipsic under the leadership of our great composer. As early as spring the report went out that Mendelssohn and Moscheles were now devoting their united
powers to the Conservatory. At the beginning of August
he arrived again within our walls, to the great joy of the
city, and we ventured to hope that he would take up his
permanent abode with us. The concert season promised
to be brilliant in the highest degree; Mendelssohn and
Gade were to be united in conducting the concerts, Miss
Dolby and Jenny Lind had been secured also as coöpera-
tors. I should be glad to detail the pleasures of this winter, but my limits will not allow; suffice it to say that
Mendelssohn was one of Jenny Lind's admirers; he rejoiced in the enthusiasm of the public over her, and delighted to have us express it. "Yes," he once said in a droll
and quiet way, " Yes, she is a very excellent person; " but
this quiet remark, which contains nothing in itself, veiled,
as we all knew, the admiration which he had for the
purity and modesty and deep moral earnestness which
Jenny Lind brought into all her work and life. She was,
indeed, a kindred spirit to his own. On one occasion, on
hearing a very enthusiastic person expressing himself in
terms of almost limitless praise, which many thought excessive, Mendelssohn simply said, " It is not too strong."

In Berlin appeared, meanwhile, two very important
works of Mendelssohn which he had composed at the suggestion of the king of Prussia, the music to the "Oedipus

at Colonos " and that to "Athalie." They were, indeed different works in their matter and nature, the one from the legends of classic antiquity, the other from the history of the Old Testament. He had been at work upon them at various places between 1842 and 1845, closing them in March of the last year. We find an allusion to the beginning of the "Oedipus" in a letter of Mendelssohn to Klingemann, written in Leipsic, November 23, 1842; later, he says to his mother : "The 'Midsummer Night's Dream' and the 'Oedipus' are waltzing in my head swifter and swifter every day." In a letter to his brother Paul, July 21, 1843, he says : "I ought to have explained at once how far I have gone upon the 'Oedipus;' I have given my answer (to Von Massow, the minister of the king) that I have worked upon the 'Midsummer Night's Dream' conformably to Tieck's wishes ; that I have written choruses to 'Athalie' at the special command of the king, and that I have postponed the choruses of the 'Oedipus' because I am told that another Greek play has been determined upon." In another letter to Privy Counsellor Müller, who had urged him to write music to Oeschyls' "Oresteia," Mendelssohn wrote in 1845 : "I beg you to convey to his majesty that at his command I have ready the 'Oedipus at Colonos' of Sophocles, Racine's 'Athalie,' and Sophocles' 'Oedipus the King.' The first two of these are complete in score and nothing remains excepting the assigning of the parts to the singers and players. The last is fully sketched." It seems to have remained in this form simply as a sketch. We have no information of his having ever done more upon it. To his sister he writes from Frankfort, on the 25th of March, and after telling in a very merry fashion about the representation of "Antigone" in Covent Garden Theatre in

London he says: "Despite all this, they have the bold-
ness to ask me when they can give the 'Oedipus;' as to
which I have referred them to the king of Prussia."

On the 1st of November, 1845, the "Oedipus at Colonos, with music by Felix Mendelssohn Bartholdy," was
given for the first time in the new palace in Potsdam, and
on the 10th of November in the Royal Theatre at Berlin.
In Leipsic we never heard it during Mendelssohn's life;
it was first given there, under Julius Rietz' direction, in
February, 1850.

Much more allied to our understandings and feelings is
the second work which Mendelssohn undertook at the
command of the king of Prussia, and to which he imparted a still higher charm than the author himself could
give — Racine's "Athalie." In this work we are no
longer in the realm of the mythical and legendary, but
upon biblical and historical ground, fully detailed in the
Second Book of Kings, chapter 11, and Second Chronicles,
chapters 22 and 23. Athaliah was the daughter of Ahab,
king of Israel, and of the Phœnician princess Jezebel,
who, as will be remembered, played her tragical part in
the life of the prophet Elijah. Athaliah was, like her
mother, a woman full of passion, blood-thirsty and devoted to idolatry. When her husband, Joram king of
Judah, died of an acute disorder, and his successor, her
son Ahaziah, had been killed by Jehu king of Israel,
in consequence of his idolatry and his bloody deeds,
Athaliah destroyed the whole of the progeny of the royal
house and mounted the throne, which she held from 884
to 876 B.C. A child of tender years, Joash, Ahaziah's
youngest son, was saved alone of all the children by his
aunt, the royal princess Jehoshebah, wife of the high-
priest Jehoiada, and during the six years of Athaliah's

reign was secretly reared by them in the temple. In the
year B.C. 876, Jehoiada restored the worship of Jehovah,
and proclaimed Joash king of the Israelites, armed the
Levites and procured the destruction of Athaliah. This
is the theme of Racine's work. It is a religious drama
with an undercurrent of tragedy, yet it is more conformable to our modern devotional feeling than the ancient
tragic drama, which, notwithstanding, seemed nearer to
the mind of Racine and caused him to introduce the
chorus of the ancients for the first and only time into
French dramatic poetry. The chorus consists of pious
Israelites of both sexes, allowing the composer the fairest
opportunity for mixed four-part songs as well as for
charming soprano and alto solos, duets, trios and even
choruses alternating between male and female voices.
Racine wrote his "Athalie" for a female seminary in
St. Cyr, and the work has, therefore, a certain weak, not
to say sentimental, tone, and is not free from a touch of
pious phraseology. The composer has, however, reinforced this by the power and fulness of his music.
One might say that over the whole there shimmers now
a kind of Oriental cloud of fragrance, and the free use of
the harp as an accompanying instrument reminds one of
the temple service and the psalms, and gives to the work
a unique charm. The king had already previously as-
signed the subject to a man of minor talents who had
composed music for it, but of an entirely inadequate
character; so much so that the king and all the critics
were dissatisfied with it. It was, therefore, given to
Mendelssohn. He undertook it gladly, but he did not
compose the work in a consecutive series of days; he
worked at it gradually, writing the choruses in Leipsic
during 1843, at the outset only for female voices with

piano accompaniment ; in 1844 he composed the overture
in D-minor and the war march of the priests in F-major ;
in 1845, the instrumentation and arrangement of the
choruses for soprano, alto, tenor and bass ; and the work
was given with great applause on the 1st of December,
1845, in the royal theatre of Charlottenburg. I do not
discover whether it was performed publicly in the theatre
in Berlin. In Leipsic we heard it for the first time after
Mendelssohn's death ; it was received with great applause
and given several times. Should we select any portion
as of especial excellence, it would unquestionably be the
overture, which stands by itself as one of Mendelssohn's
masterpieces. It was written in London during July,
1844, at a time when he was engrossed with perplexing
business matters. It opens with eighteen measures, consisting of chords produced by wind instruments and the
viola ; this is followed by a harp passage, whose effect is
delightful. This passes into a pianissimo on the violin,
con arco, and then, after a number of agreeable themes,
the close of the overture is ushered in by the recurrence
of the opening maestoso, the violins playing in *ff*, the
harp leading, and the whole orchestra crowning all with
their brilliant and resounding strains in D-major. The
chorus then opens the vocal portion with the splendid
and joyful passage in C-major, which utters defiance to
the prevailing idol worship, and is the key-note to the
whole work. Then follows a beautiful alto solo, which
again is succeeded by a soprano solo, taking up the first
theme again and closing with the chorus and the full
tutti ; then, after the first and second soprano and the
first alto have sung the praises of the omnipotence of God
and glorified the law as the highest, purest and best, the
chorus again utters its solemn strain in recollections of

the giving of the law on Sinai, which is reinforced by a soprano and alto solo, closing again with a magnificent chorus in praise of the Holy Law and the Divine Grace. The piece closes with an andante maestoso and with a similar strain of praise to that with which the work opened.   I will not enter into a closer analysis of the work, lest I may weary my readers ; I will merely refer to some of the chief beauties ; a difficult selection indeed, where all is so beautiful.   I name first, however, No. 2 after the andante quasi recitativo of the sopranos, altos, tenors and basses, which expresses the joy of the people at the first view of the royal child : " Oh how happy is the child that the Lord has taken into his care."   This is answered by the full chorus : " Oh happy, happy days of childhood."   The celebrated alto solo, with the chorus which follows, is one which will impress itself upon every hearer even with the first performance of the piece : " Thou art silent, O Zion, thou art silent," and in like manner the beautiful solo of the first soprano in B-major : " How long yet, O Lord, how long ? " which the chorus takes up and carries over into a solemn and choral-like number : " We sing to Thee, O God," in full chorus. No. 4 begins with a wonderful eight voice chorus in E-major, accompanied throughout by the harp and pro-ducing a really beautiful effect : " Let us listen to the holy words of the Highest."   After the soprano solo had uttered the warning words : " Cease from your fear, await in patience," a four-part chorus replies, " We wait in patience," and then a lovely trio of the first and second sopranos and first alto follows : " A heart full of peace has rest in every moment," which is repeated by the chorus of male and female voices.   Lastly comes the splendid march of the priests, a number full of power

and freshness, penetrated throughout by the holy glow of
battle, which, if not so brilliant, is scarcely inferior to the
celebrated wedding march in the " Midsummer Night's
Dream." After the victory over the perverse Athaliah
has been announced, the whole closes, as it began, with
the splendid chorus in C-major. In this sketch I have
by no means exhausted the list of the beauties of this
work, which seems to me ought to rank in the first
class ; it is musically even higher than the " Oedipus at
Colonos ; " it seems as if it were created in a single impulse of genius, and one feels that Mendelssohn here was
moving in the sphere best fitted to him. It is no true
oratorio, it is rather a religious drama, and yet the effect
upon the mind is precisely that of an oratorio, edifying
and quickening ; and now that we have the words of
Devrient connecting the various parts together, we have
no longer any special need that it be given on the stage
with scenery, and the music is of such a character that it
might well be given yearly as a part of the repertoire of
our great concerts.

We now glance for a moment at Mendelssohn's round
of activities in Leipsic. On the 22d of January, 1846,
we had the pleasure of hearing in the Gewandhaus hall
the music of his " Midsummer Night's Dream " under his
own personal leading. Our fine orchestra, electrified by
the baton of its beloved leader, seemed even to surpass
itself ; the fairy passages, especially the scherzo, were
given with the faintest breath. The vocal solos were
splendidly sustained, and the concert was one that can
never be forgotten. I will not specify further other concerts in which Mendelssohn took an active part, but all
of them were of an especially high character.

Notwithstanding his activity as a director, his productive work was meanwhile going forward with renewed ardor, and in the silence of his own study he was engaged with great enthusiasm upon a work which had already occupied him for years; it was his "Elijah," which he had promised to produce at the great festival of Birmingham in August, 1846. We have already seen that as early as 1838 he was busied with the thought of this oratorio. He conferred frequently with his friend Schubring respecting the text, and the reader of Mendelssohn's letters will easily recall one which he wrote to this clergyman November 2, 1838, in which he pictures his own conception of the character of Elijah. He grasps him as a man entirely in contrast with the effeminate spirit of his time; a man strong, resolute, gloomy even, capable of wrath, eager and zealous, and yet, with all this, born above the world as if on angels' wings. The reader will also recall Mendelssohn's stress on the dramatic element which he proposes to give to the character, and also his desire that Schubring should select opposite passages of scripture to be used for this work.

Respecting the dramatic element, he expresses himself again in his letter of December 6, 1838; and especially noteworthy is a passage in Ferdinand Hiller's Recollections in which he speaks of meeting Mendelssohn in Leipsic during the winter of 1839-40: "One evening I encountered Felix in his room with his Bible open upon his knees, 'Listen to this,' he said, and he read to me with his gentle, yet moving and sympathetic voice, a passage from the First Book of Kings which contains the words, 'Behold the Lord passed by,' (Kings 1st, chap. 19, 11 and 12 vv.) 'Would not this be magnificent for an oratorio?' he cried. It was a suggestion of the 'Elijah' that was to be." On the 16th of December, 1832, Mendelssohn writes again to Schubring : "I send you herewith, in accordance with your indication, the text of ' Elijah,' so far as I have read it.   I beg you to help me bravely on with it, to make all manner of marginal notes, references to Bible passages and the like.   In one of your early let- ters you have made the most discriminating mention of the chief difficulty which I have to encounter in the text, namely, a certain vagueness in the expression, a kind of universality of tone in the most forcible passages ; but bear in mind that I am not proposing to make a biblical ' Wal- purgis Night.'   I have indicated with Latin letters where I see a lack, and I beg you to put in words which have more definite and sharp dramatic force."

I must beg the reader, if he is interested in this matter, to turn to the appropriate passages in Mendelssohn's letters where he discusses the value of the dramatic element in oratorio at considerable length.   The last letter which Mendelssohn wrote to Schubring respecting the work is dated Leipsic May 23, 1846.   He commences as follows : " Dear Schubring :  I come once more to get your help in my ' Elijah ;'  I hope for the last time.   I hope, too, that the day will come when you will find some pleasure in reaping the fruit of your labors.   How happy I shall be then, too !   I am now just closing the first part ; and of the second, Nos. 6 and 8 are already on paper.   What I am needing now is a lot of Bible passages which shall help me out, and I beg you to choose them for me.   There is no hurry, for I am going down the Rhine for three weeks, but when I return I want to put my hand at once to my work, and so I beg you to have them here — a great quantity of nice verses.   You have no idea how much you have helped me thus far ; and I shall tell you only by word of mouth.   Now be a good fellow and help me out again in making the second part as beautiful as the first."

It would be interesting to cast a glance on the process of development in this work, but who is able to enter the secret laboratory of the artist? We only know that for the most part Mendelssohn had composed and completed this work before the end of the spring of 1846. In June it was so far ended that he was able to give out the voice parts. The text, which was brought together from the 16th, 17th and 18th chapters of the First Book of Kings, was translated into English by Mr. Bartholomew, a man who had much skill in this kind of work. The oratorio began with Elijah's prophecy of the famine, which is followed by the lamentation of the sufferers; then comes the removal to a distant land of the prophet, and the awakening to life of the widow's son; the destruction of the priests of Baal, the opening of heaven by means of Elijah's prayer, and then the splendid chorus of thanksgiving follows, which indicates the pouring down of the streams of water. Here ends the first part. The second comprises the persecution of Elijah, his flight into the desert, his ascension and the prophecy of the Messiah. I shall speak later on of the musical value and significance of the work.

Busy as Mendelssohn had been during the previous year, his labors appeared now to be even doubled and trebled. He undertook the direction of not less than three musical festivals following each other in quick succession. The first was in Aix la Chapelle, where Jenny Lind gave her great assistance. From this place, his friend Julius Rietz begged him to come to Düsseldorf to take part in a soiree projected by him. On this occasion Mendelssohn played the piano parts of Beethoven's B-major trio, his own sonata in B-major, with cello (Opus 48), with Rietz,

and three songs without words. Thence he went to
Liege, where he was to produce his " Lauda Sion " on
the occasion of the six hundredth anniversary of the establishment of Corpus Christi day. This great work demands
more than an allusion. We did not hear it in Leipsic
until after Mendelssohn's death, when it was given on the
22d of March, 1849. The half legendary, half historical
origin of the Corpus Christi celebration, a festival of prime
importance in the Catholic church, is as follows : At the
beginning of the 13th century, according to the legend,
Christ appeared in Liege to a nun as she slept, and said to
her : " You Catholic Christians have many noble festivals,
but you have forgotten the best : the transformation of the
host into my body and my blood." The archdeacon living there, to whom the nun communicated this dream, at
once received permission from the pope to celebrate this
festival, and as he himself was afterwards pope under the
name of Urban IV., he naturally confirmed the permission which had previously been made to him. The festival was celebrated in Liege, June 11, 1246, and extended
thence over the whole of Catholic Christendom, and with
especial rapidity after it had been sanctioned in 1311 by
Clement V. And now that, in 1846, the sixth hundreth
anniversary of this festival was to be observed in Liege,
of course it was a matter of prime importance for all Bel-
gium and the Rhineland. No less a person could be invited to compose a suitable musical work for this occasion
than the greatest of the then living artists.

Although at that time busy with the completion of his
" Elijah," yet Mendelssohn grasped this subject in his remarkable way and produced a work which was not only
entirely in conformity with Catholic feelings, but also was
a proof of his extraordinary artistic objectivity. Although

written in the most rigid ecclesiastical style, yet the work
is not without great grace and variety, showing the master's hand in every line.   He .skilfully divided the long
sequence of twenty-three three and four line stanzas into
eight tolerably uniform sections, in which choruses alternate with solos and with quartets.   After a short introduction, an andante maestoso in the solemn C-major, in
which the subdued trombones produced a very fine effect,
there followed in the same key a simple, clear and joyful
chorus, '' Lauda Sion Salvatorem.''   This is connected
with the chorus, which announces the true object of the
festival, at first alternating between the basses and the
tenors, then the sopranos and the altos ; later, the whole
chorus united.   The key is the mysterious and sad C-
minor.   No. 3 is a charming soprano solo and chorus
in A-flat major and F-minor respectively ; the first a full
clear note of praise leading on with its joyful jubilation to
the chorus which is a noteworthy recitative unisono quasi
parlando, of the basses and tenors, gives the theme, ''For
the solemn day is Come.''   This chorus closes in a very
striking way in D-major and glides over to the fine quartet, No. 4, in G-major, which announces the victory of
the new Paschal feast over the old, the light over the darkness, and then adds the command of Christ to keep this
supper in memory of Him.   The chorus following, No.
5, '' Docti sacris institutis,'' in A-minor, the two first
verses unisono, the last in harmony, expresses the confidence of the Catholic faith in the dogma of transubstantia-
tion, and reveals in the last clause the great mystery
which lies hidden under the form of the bread and wine.
Then follows a soprano solo in F-major, exceedingly
beautiful and spiritual, which expresses the joyful confidence of each soul which receives the bread as the body,

and the wine as the blood, and so incorporates into itself the unbroken Christ. In No. 7, the unison again appears, confirming the unshaken faith of the soul, and expressing the various ways in which participation in the sacred body influences the believer, bringing death to him who is evil, and life to him who is good. This chorus has some points of real greatness, and is suggestive of Mozart's " Tuba mirum spargens sonum." Especially powerful is the " Fracto demum sacramento " in the clear B-major, in which chorus and alto alternate in short passages, and scarcely less so the finale, " Ecce panis angelorum," which brings the work to a close with wonderful beauty, indicating Christ as the Good Shepherd defending his own and bringing them safely to the eternal home.

I trust that I have indicated in this brief account enough to show in what a peculiar, yet interesting, manner Mendelssohn grasped the material which was before him, the instrumentation, as will be easily seen, being completely adapted to the work, rather sparing in movement, and of appropriate effect. I have no doubt that the piece was heard with the greatest interest by the Roman Catholic assembly when it was sung, and even in the concert room it makes an agreeable impression upon the minds of all hearers, of whatever religious persuasion. The work belongs to the best of that which Mendelssohn has written. He was not the director when it was first given ; he was simply a hearer.

From Liege, Mendelssohn went first to Aix la Chapelle, and then via Düsseldorf to the first German and Flemish musical at Cologne. He had set to music Schiller's " Festgesang, An die Künstler," commencing with the words, " Der Mensche!t Würde " ; certainly a very noble and comprehensive text, which, in Mendelssohn's hands, and sung by three thousand voices accompanied only by wind instruments, could not fail of producing the most imposing affect. In my judgment this composition belongs to the most admirable of Mendelssohn in a field in which he cannot be surpassed. The harmony flows forth like a mighty stream, and yet with a delicate and gentle current. After the opening, there occurs a passage in the first two lines beginning with the unison of basses and tenors, but again weaving in a charming melody, and in the last passage rising to a splendor and glow and force that must have charmed every ear. In one word the music is classic, for text and composition cannot be separated.

In addition to the " Festgesang," Mendelssohn directed in Cologne some other pieces, for example, his Bacchus chorus from the " Antigone," a " Te Deum " by Bernhardt Klein, and " O Isis and Osiris," from the " Magic Flute." After this festival, he returned to Leipsic. I had the pleasure of an interview with him at that time ; he seemed very well pleased ; the massive character of the musical resources had greatly impressed him, and the patriotic element, the sympathy between the Flemish and Germans, had been very gratifying to him. In a musical respect, " O Isis and Osiris " had pleased him the most. He was in a very cheerful mood, and he spoke appreciatively of the Düsseldorf music festivals, promising to let us know if anything very remarkable should be given there. Alas ! that this promise was never fulfilled ; he was not permitted to see his beloved Düsseldorf again.

In the middle of August, Mendelssohn went to England in order to direct his " Elijah " at the great festival to be given from the 25th to the 28th of this month in Birmingham. The programme was composed of masterpieces by Handel, Haydn, Beethoven and Cherubini.

There was the greatest eagerness in the anticipation of Mendelssohn's new oratorio. It was given in the forenoon of Wednesday, the 26th of August, in the magnificent hall devoted to these festivals. A place had been made for him between Haydn's " Creation," which was given on Tuesday, and Handel's " Messiah," which was to be given on Thursday ; on Friday, Beethoven's " Missa Solemnis " in D was to be sung. Respecting the first impression of the " Elijah," the London correspondent of a leading musical journal writes :

" How shall I describe this day in the Music Hall? After such an excitement, it is indeed difficult to utter one's feelings in cold words. It was a great day for the festival, a great day for the artists, a great day for Mendelssohn, and an epoch for art. Four da capos in the first part, and an equal number in the second ; eight encores, and at the close of the ' Elijah,' the calling out of the artist, are important matters when one remembers that it is the strict regulation of the committee that there shall be no applause at all on the part of the public ; but the enthusiasm of the occasion put to rout all such orders ; when the heart is full the mouth must speak. It was a grand sight, the hall crowded with men, the galleries filled with ladies decked in their beauty like beds of tulips, to which must be added the effect of the magnificent music, and at the close the thundering bravos."

This was the first impression in England, and although given by a German correspondent, what was said in Germany of the work? In Leipsic we were not so fortunate as to hear it during Mendelssohn's life under his direction ; the chorus rehearsals were going on in the autumn of 1847, when the brief sickness and death of Mendelssohn occurred. We heard the work for the first

time on the 3d of February, 1848, at the celebration of
his birthday. It was a sad evening for Mendelssohn's
friends in Leipsic which brought to them the long
wished for pleasure of hearing the great and closing
work of the beloved departed artist. The hall was
suitably decorated, the motto, " *Res severa est verum
gaudium*," never was more true than then, and Mendelssohn's bust, crowned with fresh evergreen, looked
down upon us from above. A more suitable way of
celebrating his birthday could hardly be suggested than
this, in which his own genius seemed to live again
among us. What a magnificent and imposing theme his
" Elijah," the representative of the patriotic spirit in the
ancient dispensation ; this bold proclaimer of a theocracy
over against the tyranny of kings ; this powerful zealot
for Jehovah arrayed against the sensuous worship of the
idolaters ; this strong and, perhaps one may say, even
stubborn hero of God, yet not without many truly human
features, as for example, in the beautiful scene with the
widow of Sarepta and the touching end of his life in the
wilderness, when he says, " It is enough." To all this
must be added the brilliant apotheosis and ascension to
heaven. No other subject but Moses could have surpassed this in the Old Testament, no other could have
given such splendid material for an oratorio. It is said
that he would have written an oratorio in honor of Moses
had he not been betrayed by another to whom he communicated his plan ; but in the " Elijah," with what
skill are those scenes in which a more common mind
would find only loose and scattered materials woven together into a complete whole ! With what fine and deep
religious feeling ! with what knowledge of the scrip-
tures ! with what comprehensive insight into the meaning

of prophecy are the passages chosen from the prophets
and psalms and woven together ! — a work in large part
accomplished, it is true, by his friend Schubring, and yet
completed by Mendelssohn's decisive judgment.   It is a
great advantage to the piece that the materials were
drawn from the Old Testament, if we regard the work
from a dramatic point of view, for it is unquestionable
that the Old Testament is much more dramatic than the
new, and although the new may have a deeper and
higher religious value, yet in strength and richness of
poetic imagery certainly no one can compare the two.
One who is familiar with the Bible must see at a glance
with what fine skill he has brought together his materials,
and with what genius he has poured into them all the
glowing fire of his art.

The question has been raised whether " Elijah " is an
advance upon the " St. Paul."   There can be no question
regarding this.   " St. Paul " is indeed more ecclesiastical,
but " Elijah " is as a musical work greater, has more
originality, greater wealth in invention, a more powerful
delineation of situation and character.   There is not the
slightest trace of any falling off of power in this work ;
on the contrary, it marks the highest point reached by
the composer's creative genius.   If it be true, as has been
said by the authorities in Berlin, that the special mark
of greatness in Mendelssohn is the invention of melodious
passages, where in all his productions is there such a
fulness of those which cling to the ear and cannot be forgotten ?   It is enough to recall as instances of this merely
the air of Obadiah, " If with all your hearts ; " the theme
in the double quartet of the angels, " For he shall give his
angels charge ; " in the chorus, " Blessed are the men
who fear him ; " in the prayer of Elijah, " Lord, my God,

O let the spirit of this child return ; " the Baal choruses,
and the beautiful solo of Elijah, with the chorus, " Open
the heavens and send us relief," the leading theme of the
closing chorus in the first part, " Thanks be to God,
he watcheth over Israel ; " the aria of Elijah, " It is
enough ; " the alto aria of the angel, " O rest in the
Lord," and the trio of the angels, " Lift thine eyes."
The choruses are not only powerful but they are delightful
and new ; everywhere there is the charm of the blending
of melody and harmony ; the two parts into which the
work is divided keep the hearer in a frame of inter-
changing eagerness and anticipation.  The first part is a
bright dramatic picture with constantly shifting scenes,
all of them handled in the most delicate and apt manner.
The recitative, which is freely used, gives new power to
the work.  The true overture of the piece may be said
to be the passage which indicates that the prophet Elijah
broke forth as a fire and his words burned like a torch.
The instrumental overture is rather a mediatory passage
from the opening utterance of Elijah to the mournful cries
for help for a land suffering under the divine wrath.  In
the further course of the first part we distinguish three
characteristic groups, all of them underlain by the sense
of the divine power as connected with the prophet ; the
raising from the dead of the son of the widow of Sarepta ;
the struggle and the victory of the servants of Jehovah
over the priests of Baal, and the opening of the gates of
heaven by reason of the prayers of the prophet.  Over-
wise critics have found fault with the scene with the
widow's son as too dramatic, and have wished to ex-
punge it from the oratorio.  But ought such a passage be
slightingly treated ?  Should it be removed from the piece ?
— a passage which, perhaps, more than any other indi-

cates the power of the prophet? The extraordinary vivid
and dramatic music must interest every hearer. The
first part is perhaps the most full of incident, but the
second part is a more vivid picture of mental and spiritual
frames. The work advances in its development more
and more to the deepest mystery of God's nature ; the delightful trio of angels, the chorus, " Holy, Holy," affords
views into another world such as could only be granted
to a man divinely quickened as Mendelssohn was. In
the second part there may be said to be three groups ; the
appearance of the prophet taking his place in opposition
to the king ; the flight and the miraculous sustaining of
his body in the desert ; the glorification upon Mount
Horeb, and the ascension. In conclusion we may only
say in one word, the " Elijah " is unquestionably Mendelssohn's greatest work. I have already quoted the
language of a German correspondent whose glowing style
took no exception as to the manner of its presentation ;
but in a letter which Mendelssohn wrote, on the 31st of
August, to his friend Frau Dr. Livia Frege, he criticised
sharply the leading soprano ; he expressed perfect satisfaction with the tenor and the bass, but the soprano voice
he called simply pretty, not pleasing, but entirely destitute of soul and of intelligence.

A little incident may be related respecting Mendelssohn's quickness and aptness in case of need. On the
last day of the festival, the so-called " Anthem " of Handel
was to be given. The concert had already begun when
it was discovered that the recitative which was printed
in the books was lacking in the music. The directors
were in perplexity. Mendelssohn, who at that time was
in the foyer of the hall, heard of the trouble, and said :
" Let me help you out," and sitting down, instantly

composed a recitative, had it transcribed, passed round the papers while they were still wet with the ink, and the passage was sung prima vista. The inspiration of the moment worked upon the artist as it did upon the composer, and it went splendidly.

It is scarcely a matter of wonder that after so stirring a life and such almost incredible exertions that Mendelssohn, on his return to Leipsic, should find himself overstrained. He did, indeed, take part in the direction of the subscription concerts, sharing it with Gade, and was especially effective in bringing out Beethoven's symphonies, especially those in B-major and in F-major, which, perhaps, were never heard so admirably given. He also assisted in introducing to the world the new symphony of Robert Schumann in C-major; but of his own new compositions he produced nothing in Leipsic, and was very reserved in bringing forward the earlier ones. In the whole cycle of concerts under his direction, we had nothing from him with the exception of the " Scene and Aria in B-major," Opus 92, the overture to the " Meeresstille," and the " A-minor Symphony ; " yet the selection for music in the concerts was admirable, consisting almost exclusively of classical masterpieces. In the historical concerts, which began with the seventeenth of the subscription list, he included nothing of his own, contrary to the universal expectation. Playing in public was denied him by his physician on account of his excitability ; he often complained of severe headache, and it was with difficulty that he was persuaded to undertake the direction of the last rehearsals of " St. Paul," the performance of which occurred on Good Friday, 1847, in the illuminated St. Paul's Church — the last under his direction. He justified his withdrawal from public performances by telling his intimate friends that he must make use of such time as yet remained to him to compose. Up to his fortieth year he would labor; then he would rest. He doubtless referred in this only to his productivity in regard to new works. Yet conformably to a promise given directly after the performance of the " St. Paul " in Leipsic, he went to England in order to bring out his " Elijah " in Exeter Hall, London, at the request of the Sacred Harmonic Society. This association was a rival to the great kindred association of Birmingham which a year before had brought the work to the light for the first time. Near the end of April the " Elijah " was given three times in Exeter Hall under Mendelssohn's direction, and always with great applause. After the first performance the prince consort wrote the following words in the text-book which he had used, and sent it to Mendelssohn as a souvenir : —

" To the noble artist, who, when surrounded by the Baal worship of the false, has, like a second Elijah, employed his genius and his skill in the service of the true ; who has weaned our ears from the senseless confusion of mere sound, and won them to the comprehension of all that is harmonious and pure — to the great master who has held in his firm control and revealed to us not only the gentle whisperings of the breeze, but also the majestic thunderings of the tempest. In grateful remembrance,
" Buckingham Palace. ALBERT."

Certainly a noble testimony from the hand of a prince admirable in character and deeply skilled in art — a testimony equally honorable to the giver and to the receiver. Between the three performances in London, Mendelssohn was present at an admirable presentation of his work in

Manchester on the 11th of May.   In the presence of the
court, he produced his music of the " Midsummer Night's
Dream," played Mozart's " G-major Concerto " with improvised cadenzas which remain unforgetable in the
memories of the delighted hearers.

Unfortunately the deepest shadows were about to fall
upon this supreme moment of elevation and joy.   On his
return to Germany, and in Frankfort, where he delighted
to find himself with his family, there came to him, like a
thunder-clap out of a clear sky, the news of the death of
his beloved sister Fanny.   She died, as we have already
said in a previous chapter, a genuine artist's death, while
engaged in conducting the rehearsal for her next Sunday's
musicale.   Mendelssohn was fearfully shattered by the
news ; the contrast between the cheerful scenes in which
he had played a leading part in England and this sad
event, could not but work most unfavorably upon him.
We know how he had shared his finest feelings with this
sister from his earliest youth ; how there had always been
an interchange of thought between them ; how highly he
himself rated her counsel and assistance.   At the first tidings of Fanny's death, he is said to have uttered a loud
cry.   It was not simply a mental but also a physical pain
which seized him so severely ; as the nerve of his spiritual
communication with his sister was sundered by this sudden event, there was, in the opinion of his physician, a
rupture of an artery in the brain, which caused the intense
headaches which he suffered and which, after repeated at-
tacks, induced his death.   And so, according to this view,
the loss of his sister may have been the immediate cause
of his own death.   And yet, I am of the opinion that he
would, had his health been firmer, have struggled against
and have risen superior to this severe and dreadful blow.

"Pearls," says Lessing, in "Emilia Galotti," "are the expression for tears;" but tears can also be transformed into pearls," and the two letters which Mendelssohn wrote to Hensel and Hensel's son Sebastian after Fanny's death, are genuine pearls.   It is with regret that I abstain from citing those letters at this point, but they are to be found in the well-known book of Hensel, "The Mendelssohn Family;" they are the picture of a sympathetic heart which in its own pain does not forget the grief of others. They are the reflections of one of the noblest and purest of men.

He was indeed bruised and broken, and for a long time he could not command himself; yet the strongest ties of friendship and love bound him to his home and to his friends, and doubtless he would still have continued to do his work on the earth.   In my judgment the real cause of his premature death lay not so much in any such physical cause as was conjectured by his physician, as in his restless activity through which he prematurely exhausted his whole vitality and the force of his nervous system.   I find a proof of this in the circumstance that towards the last months of his life he was not able to hear music without weeping.   But can we blame him for the energetic manner in which he forced himself to labor so long as he had strength?   To his wife, who often endeavored to check him, he used to say, " Let me work on, there will soon come a time to rest," and to his other friends he used to say, with a premonition, as it were, of his coming death, " I must employ the time that is granted me; I do not know how long it will last."

It is evident that he sought alleviation for his grief in creative activity.   At first he did not succeed in producing new music; he wrote in a letter, during the first weeks

after Fannys, death : " I can only labor mechanically ; "
and by reason of this he forsook his tasks and rested for a
season with his family in Baden-Baden ; thence he went to
Switzerland, and there, in the contemplation of the majestic beauty of nature, he regained tone and power of his
mind.   He had at first contemplated going to Vevay, on
Lake Geneva ; but, in consequence of the disturbed political conditions there, he retired to a quiet corner in
Switzerland, in beautiful Interlaken, and there, in com
pany with his brother Paul and his family, at the old hotel
Interlaken, under the great shade of the walnut trees, he
remained a long time.   Here he labored whole uninterrupted days, alternating with frequent walks up and down
the mountains.

Two works which engrossed him chiefly here were his
new oratorio of " Christus " and his opera of " Lorelei,"
for which Emanuel Geibel had written the text ; of the
oratorio, he completed only the passage relating to the
birth of Christ, consisting of the recitatives, " When
Jesus was born in Bethlehem in Judea," which was
followed by a trio of three male voices, bass, tenor and
baritone, accompanied by cellos ; " Where is the new
born king of the Jews? we have seen his star in the
East," followed by the chorus, " There shall a star arise
from Egypt," and lastly the choral, " How beauteous
shines the morning star," an admirable piece of Christmas
music, which is even yet often given in our churches ; in
addition to these, there are only a few choruses representing the Passion.   The work was planned on a grand
scale ; it was to be divided into three parts, comprising
the earthly pilgrimage, the descent to the dead, and the
ascent to Heaven.

Of the opera " Lorelei," we possess only a beautiful

Ave Maria chorus, with solo; then an extremely dramatic finale, in which Lorelei is deceived by her lover and is surrendered to the water sprites who should avenge her, and who declare her to be the bride of the Rhine. In addition, there are also a grand march with chorus and the beginnings of three other pieces. The effect of the finale one could judge on the 4th of November, 1884, when it was magnificently rendered on the Leipsic stage. In addition to these works, Mendelssohn wrote in Interlaken also two string quartets, in F-minor and D-minor, and some motets and songs, among them a splendid "Night Song" of Eichendorf, "Departed is the light of day" (Opus 71, No. 6), in which he unquestionably had in mind his departed sister. On the 18th of September he returned to Leipsic; he seemed to be tolerably bright and cheerful, but he said the Leipsic air oppressed him. The journey subsequently to Berlin, and a stay of eight days there with his family amid so many painful recollections, opened the wound afresh; yet even after this he was able to renew his work; he contemplated visiting Vienna for the purpose of directing the "Elijah," and, subsequently to this, he proposed to give it in Leipsic, and began to make preliminary preparations for rehearsal. Still the end was drawing near. As an esteemed friend was singing to him some of his songs, and among them Eichendorf's "Night Song," he suddenly became pale, and fell in a swoon. He was able to return to his home in the Königstrasse, but there was a recurrence of the same trouble, from which he was with difficulty brought back. On the 13th of October he took a short walk with his wife and ate his dinner with a good appetite, but after this his symptoms appeared with increased severity. The physicians declared it to be a nervous prostration;

the sick man lay for a long time unconscious; when, subsequently, he came to himself, he complained of bitter pains in his head, yet his condition improved somewhat and the physicians did not appear to give up all hope. The tidings of the danger in which this precious life was hovering speedily communicated itself throughout the city, and awakened the most tender and heartfelt sympathy. Wherever one looked or wherever one went there could be seen anxious faces, and heard anxious questionings. His consciousness came back to him on the 3d of November. A slight circumstance, such as may often occur in the sick room of a nervous patient, so disturbed him that he never came fully to himself again; he uttered a loud cry, as if called forth by some sudden stroke of pain, and fell back upon the pillow. From that time on he said nothing but a faint " Yes" or " No," save that to Cecile he uttered the words " Weary, very weary," and so he slept quietly till the next day, Thursday the 4th of November, when at half past nine o'clock in the evening his breath ceased and he breathed out his soul. His features immediately assumed a transfigured aspect; he was so like one asleep the day after his death that many of his friends thought it was not truly death, a deception which often comes to those who greatly mourn. His friends Bendemann and Hubner, who had been summoned from Dresden, took a copy of the glorified face, and Knauer afterwards produced from it a bust.

The mourning over the loss of this beloved man was boundless. It appeared as if the city had encountered a universal misfortune. Hundreds of sympathizing friends hastened to the dwelling in order to view once more the endeared features, and the family were not disposed to hinder their approach. Mild and peaceful he lay there in

his narrow bed, like one who joyfully anticipates the day
of account, adorned with the tokens of his well-earned
youthful fame, the branches of palm and laurel with which
his friends decorated his remains, although his glory
needed no coronation. Gradually his nearest friends
were obliged to constrain themselves to composure in
order to prepare a worthy burial for him. It took place
on the 7th of November, at four o'clock in the afternoon,
in the illuminated church of St. Paul. Four black
draped horses drew the coffin, richly adorned with palms
and laurels and flowers. The pall was borne by his
friends Robert Schumann, David, Gade, Hauptmann,
Rietz and Moscheles. Before the coffin, went the members of the orchestra and the various choirs of the city, the
teachers and the male pupils of the Conservatory ; directly
after the coffin the nearest relations, among them the
brother of the deceased and his brothers-in-law, Hensel
and Dirichlet, then the clergy and officials of the city and
University, officers in uniform and the innumerable train
of friends and admirers of the deceased, all marching with
measured step to the church to the solemn strains of military music. Moscheles had arranged his " Song without
Words," in E-minor, from the fifth collection, to music
for wind instruments. Arriving at the church, the coffin
was placed on a catafalque and draped in black and surrounded with six wax candles, while upon the organ was
played a prelude from " Antigone," the passage where
Creon bears in the body of his son Hemon. A pupil of
the Conservatory laid a laurel wreath of silver at the foot
of the master, whereupon the chorus gave the verse " Remember me, my Savior," in which the whole assembly
joined. Then followed the noble choral by Mendelssohn
from " St. Paul," " To Thee, O Lord, I yield my

spirit," upon which Pastor Howard of the Reformed Church gave a modest but worthy address, which he based upon the words of Job, " The Lord gave and the Lord hath taken away," and closed with an impressive prayer. Then was heard from the chorus, accompanied by instrumental music, one of the finest of the passages in " St. Paul," " Behold we count them happy who endure," and after this the beautiful passage from the " Passion " music :

> " We sit beside thy grave in tears,
> And say our last farewell ;
> Rest sweetly, sweetly rest ! "

There was no one who was not deeply moved and edified and comforted by this solemn service. When the whole assembly had left the church, a stately figure in deep mourning entered, knelt at the grave and prayed. It was she who brought the last offering of her love to her husband.

The coffin with its precious contents was borne in the night, by a special train, to Berlin. When at midnight it reached Köthen, it was received by the local chorus there with a choral. In Dessau, at half-past one o'clock in the morning, the venerable Nestor of music, Frederick Schneider, received it with uncovered head, and, surrounded by his pnpils, showed the last mark of honor to his beloved master by leading in a song expressly composed for the occasion. When the coffin with its wealth of flowers and palms had reached the Anhalt Station in Berlin, it was borne in the hearse to the house, while the chorus sung the choral, " Jesus my confidence ; " the cathedral chorus repeated the same choral as the funeral procession, illuminated by the first rays of the rising sun, reached the Trinity churchyard before the Halle gate, and the preacher Berduscheck, who was an intimate friend of the Mendelssohn family, gave a touching address, at which no eye remained without tears.   After this, the Sing-academie, under the direction of Rungenhagen, sang the song, " How peacefully they rest," to which, as with angels' voices, a hymn, composed by Grell, was given as if in response.   The coffin of Mendelssohn was placed beside his sister in the family vault.   The last time Mendelssohn had been in Berlin, Fanny had reproved her brother for not having celebrated her birthday with her for a long time.   " Depend upon it," replied he, " the next time I will be with you."   He kept his word.   And so the brother and sister sweetly sleep together awaiting the day of resurrection.

There has, perhaps, never been in modern times a death more deplored throughout the entire world than this ; it can only be compared with the loss of Raphael as it has been recounted to us by Vasati.   Throughout all Germany solemnities were held in his honor.   In Berlin, at one of the last symphony soirees, a funeral march from Beethoven's " Eroica " was given ; a Kyrie followed, then Mendelssohn's " A-minor Symphony," the overture to the " Midsummer Night's Dream " and the " Hebrides."   The closing part consisted of a psalm a Capella and the song, " Es ist bestimmt in Gottes Rath."   William Taubert arranged this admirable programme and conducted.   The Singacademie would not be behind, and gave " Elijah " almost for the first time in Germany.   The solemnities in Vienna were on a very grand scale ; on the 5th of November the first performance of " Elijah " occurred, which Mendelssohn had been expected to lead.   The numerous soloists were clothed in deep mourning ; the ladies of the chorus in

white, with a band of black upon the left arm. The
desk at which Mendelssohn would have stood was hung
with dark cloth, a roll of manuscript and a fresh green
laurel wreath lay upon it. Seidl, the director, stood at
another desk. In London the Sacred Harmonic Society
produced the "Elijah" in his honor; all present were in
black; the concert was opened with Handel's "Dead
March in Saul," the whole assembly standing. This
society wished to erect a monument to Mendelssohn in
London, to which Queen Victoria and Prince Albert contributed fifty pounds sterling. A commemoration scarcely
less important took place in Leipsic; on the day when
Mendelssohn died a concert was to take place, but no one
would play, and probably no one would have been willing to attend. The programme of the next concert,
which was on Thursday, the 11th of November, bore at
the top, "In recollection of the departed Mendelssohn
Bartholdy." The first part contained the following compositions of Mendelssohn: prayer by Martin Luther,
"Verlieh uns Frieden gnädiglich" ("Graciously grant us
peace"); overture to "Melusina;" the "Night Song" by
Eichendorf, "Departed is the light of day," motet a Capella, "Lord, now lettest thou thy servant depart in peace,"
written in Switzerland, and the overture to "St. Paul."
The second part was given to Beethoven's "Eroica";
and thus the whole life of the deceased was worthily represented; his pious aspirations to things above, his purest
earthly love, his surrender to the will of God after he had
fulfilled his whole duty, and the voice which called him
to a joyful resurrection. In Beethoven's "Eroica" we
see the love which this man bore to the greatest master
of his art, and the place which he would afterwards fill
on earth in our hearts. The hall, which was crowded

with hearers, seemed like a house of mourning, the assembly like a great family weeping for a departed friend. There was no applause, but the hush of a perfect silence ; it was as if the spirit of Mendelssohn hovered in the room and touched each heart.

In like manner the cities of Cologne, Bremen, Lübeck, Frankfort on the Main, Mayence, Breslau, Altenburg, and many others, according to their resources, celebrated the memory of this beloved man.   Even crowned heads did not stand behind their subjects in showing their regard. Queen Victoria and the kings of Prussia and Saxony sent their tributes of respect to the widow of the departed. The great German artists at Paris sent a communication of sympathy.   There was but one exception : the crown prince of Hesse, afterwards elector, denied his Capellmeister, Louis Spohr, the privilege of holding ceremonies in honor of the departed friend.   Therein appeared the brutal, tyrannical spirit which afterwards drove him from his throne and his land ; but Spohr could comfort himself with the thought that, although denied this privilege, throughout all Germany every heart that glows with admiration for what is holy and high, and not every heart in Germany alone but throughout the world, forever will cherish this man with love and veneration.

## PART V.

### MENDELSSOHN AS MAN AND ARTIST.

It is impossible for the reader to have followed me thus far without receiving a very distinct impression of the amiability of character and of many marked traits in Felix Mendelssohn. And yet I cannot close my life of a man so rich in talents and in opportunities without completing my sketch of his career by a view of the man himself. He was of moderate stature, somewhat neglectful of his bearing but graceful in his walk and demeanor. His head, framed in its black and slightly curling hair, his forehead large and high and the worthy home of his rich thoughts, the features of the countenance distinct and sharp but noble. An eye unspeakably expressive; when filled with anger, or searching your face with care, scarcely to be borne; when glancing with friendliness, extremely beautiful and winning; the nose striking and a little bent, almost Roman; the mouth firm, and, when closed, with something of a magisterial character, yet capable of a delightfully mirthful expression. In this delicate and well built figure lived not only a lofty spirit but also the noblest heart. To sum up in a word what was most striking in his character, he was an Evangelical Christian in the fullest sense; he knew and loved the Bible as few did in his time; and from this intimate acquaintance came the assured belief, the steadfast piety, without which it would have been impossible to create works of so deep and strong a spiritual character as he wrought.  But also the principle of the true gospel life, love, was equally strong in him ; love as a son, love as a brother, love as a husband, and love as a friend ; in all of these was to be seen the great central sun, the divine love.  In all that concerns the human heart and the human life, Mendelssohn is an unsurpassable example. With what gentle reverence he clung to his father ! how he honored him as his best friend and counsellor !  Our previous pages have given touching testimony of the story of his deep pain and regret at his loss ; how, as a faithful son, he bore his mother in his arms, as it were, and trusted her not only with the sacred affairs of his heart but also with the details of his artistic career, are declared in his letters to her, of which the reader will find a rich collection in the volumes that bear his name.

Of that tender and touching relation in which he stood to his sister Fanny, of that strong tie which bound him to Rebecca, of the assured bond of tried friendship in which he was related to his brother Paul, we have already given sufficing examples in these pages.  With what love, tenderness and care he cherished his beloved wife belongs to that sacred region which may not be revealed to the profane glance of the observer.  But how happy he was in his household life, how he found in it the complete complement of his own being, we have already recounted in our quotations from his letters.

In spite of his constant activity, he devoted himself as much as he could to his five children, and found in his intercourse with them, in the observance of their peculiarities and fostering of their gifts, his truest delight and his best consolations in his seasons of grief.  In a word, his family life was the happiest possible.  Even to his servants he extended a gracious care, as is seen in the

letters to his brother and to his friend Klingemann.
Whoever did not know him nearly enough to perceive in
him how skilfully and carefully he avoided all disturbing
influences, would perhaps not imagine that his heart was
exceedingly open to friendship and formed for it ; but the
large number of those with whom he stood in the most
intimate correspondence, the openness with which he
declared himself to them, his deep sympathy in their
experiences and trials, especially his intimate relations
with his friends in Berlin, Düsseldorf, London and Leipsic, the rich stores of communications which every one of
his intimate friends could exhibit, proved the contrary.
A man like him could naturally not give his heart to
every one whom he met ; he was in a similar condition
with Goethe, only that he was a man of more warmth
and communicativenes than Goethe.  A peculiarity of
Mendelssohn was his almost morbid shyness respecting
the publication of everything that concerned his person.
From principle he read almost nothing that was written
about him, and he never would permit that anything
from him and regarding him should be printed, musical
matters alone excepted.  Enthusiasm which, of course,
met him in great force, was contrary to his nature ; he
had seen too much of it manufactured to believe readily
in its reality, yet a delicate and appreciative word of
praise delighted his heart.  That he was sometimes ex-
asperated by blame, that he was capable of being thrown
into an ill humor, no one who came into close relations
with him could deny, for a spirit so sensitive and fine
could, of course, easily be untuned, and whoever carried
round in him such fulness of thoughts might well claim
the right to oftentimes walk, as it were, by himself.  In
accordance with his education and the surroundings in

which he had moved from his childhood, he, of course, possessed the tone and the manners of fine society. In larger companies he was exceedingly reserved, especially where it did not seem worth his while to open his heart, but when once the silence was broken, often word followed word and he spoke with great rapidity ; it was not always easy to follow the blazing track of the spirit which, by reason of its universal culture, moved with such ease over the leading courses of human knowledge and human art. In the circle of intimate friends where he felt himself at home and had no fear of being misunderstood, he was often merry to the highest degree ; larger circles, too, he often animated with his art, and in Leipsic the singing societies of men, and a circle composed of the most select ladies and gentlemen, remember his delightful presence with constant gratitude. In especial, his charming four-part songs afforded us the greatest pleasure. In the rehearsals of these, he was stimulating and amiable to the last degree.

Through the inheritance direct from his own parents, through his wife, and the profits of his works, he was a rich man, but he constantly made the noblest use of his wealth. He remembered well the words that true religion consists in visiting the widows and the fatherless in their affliction, and he followed it out to the letter. His threshold was familiar to the needy of all kinds, his benificence knew no boundaries, and the tender grace with which he imparted his gifts often increased their worth far beyond the material value of them. Instances might be quoted, numerous and striking, of the aid given to needy students in music ; and to men in desperate need of musical assistance and supplied with meagre funds, he proved his liberal heart and generous hand. I may perhaps be permitted to say that to the members of the orchestra of the Gewandhaus, whose members were poorly paid, Mendelssohn frequently gave twenty thalers each, or fifteen dollars of our money, yearly, and gifts of this character were constant with him.

But what was more striking still, in connection with his affluent circumstances, was his restless activity in his calling. Many productions of the German muse have been children of need, and without external pressure would perhaps never have been produced. In many a man, talents which are fostered and which become eminent in time of poverty, are quite extinguished as soon as the Goddess of Fortune smiles; but he, born in luxury and reared in affluence, never gave himself idly to the enjoyment of his wealth; he used it only that his genius might labor undisturbed in its course; he did not produce in order to live, but he lived in order to produce. It must, of course, be admitted that this impulse to action was in him a natural endowment. For him to be idle was impossible. Even while the scholars of the Conservatory were endeavoring to solve theoretical tasks, he used to employ the time in drawing, and in this way often produced charming sketches which he collected and carried home. He was a man who could not be easily disturbed in his labors. Where he wrote was to him indifferent. He always composed while on his numerous journeys, and as soon as he came under a roof he called for a table and set himself immediately to work in writing music.

His relations with other artists form a peculiar feature in a sketch of his character, especially towards those whose course deviated from his own; that he was on terms of personal intimacy with such artists as. Mos-

cheles, David, Gade, Taubert, Franz and others, whose
views harmonized with his own, would not, of course,
be accounted a merit, and no one would have wondered
if, with the purity and nobility of his own striving, with
the sacred earnestness with which he treated art, with the
rigid upholding of his own ideas, he had been cold and
distant with those who did not pursue the same course as
himself. But this was very seldom the case. In his
judgment on the performances of his contemporaries, he
was very cautious, yet oftentimes his play of countenance
was a good barometer of his feelings. The crowd of virtuosi whose merit lay only in their mechanical skill, was
endured with much patience ; and if this mechanical skill
was extremely great, he did not refuse a certain recognition of it, although the mistreatment of great masterpieces
in their hands often pained him to the heart; yet when
real taste and appreciation were joined with mechanical
skill, he was the first to express his astonishment, and
oftentimes gave to such artists his immediate support. A
few examples may indicate this. In January, 1840, Franz
Liszt came to Leipsic for the first time and gave a concert. His manager had pressed his claim in a somewhat
too mercantile fashion, and had made some unexpected
changes in the arrangement of the hall, and thereby had
prejudiced the public in a manner against him. When
Liszt took his place at the piano, he was not greeted with
applause ; indeed a few hisses were heard ; Liszt glared
upon his audience like a lion, and began to play quietly
and in such a way that at the end of the piece there was
indeed a murmur of applause, yet there was a fatal breach
between the public and him. Now what did Mendelssohn
do? He gave in the hall of the Gewandhaus a brilliant
soiree to Liszt, to which he invited half the city and

furnished the entertainment, not only music, but also refreshments. It was a family party on the grandest scale, in which he and his wife took the part of host and hostess in the most attractive and charming manner. The beautiful Cecile, arrayed in a simple white dress, and decked with diamonds, flashed hither and thither in her easy graceful motion like a fair apparition from Heaven. Music of the best was furnished, and as complete as perhaps Liszt in his life had ever heard before. At his request they gave Schubert's newly discovered " C-major Symphony," the " Forty-Second Psalm " and some numbers from" St. Paul." At the close, Mendelssohn, Liszt and Hiller played a triple concerto by Bach. The public was completely reconciled to Liszt by the great skill with which Mendelssohn had managed the matter. The guest played afterwards amid storms of applause.

A second example I may cite from the year 1843. In the beginning of January of that year Hector Berlioz came from Weimar to Leipsic; knowing well that the character of his music diverged widely from that of Mendelssohn, he feared a cold reception from the latter. Capellmeister Chelard nevertheless encouraged him to write to Mendelssohn, and the reply which he received was as follows : —

" My dear Berlioz :

" I thank you heartily for your good letter and that you still remember our friendship in Rome. I shall not forget it all my life and I shall be delighted to tell you so by word of mouth. Everything that I can do to make your stay in Leipsic pleasant I shall do with pleasure and as my duty. I believe I can assure you that you will be pleased with the city, that is, with the musicians and the public. I beg you to come here at once, as soon as you leave Weimar. I shall be delighted to give you my hand, and say welcome to Germany. Do not laugh at my bad French, as you used to do in Rome, but remain my friend as you were then, and as I shall always, your devoted, FELIX MENDELSSOHN BARTHOLDY."

Berlioz came to Leipsic just at the time when the "Walpurgis Night" was in rehearsal, and admitted the greatness of the work, as we have seen on a previous page. He reminded Mendelssohn of their meeting in the baths of Caracalla, and begged Mendelssohn to give him his baton, which he consented to under the condition that Berlioz would give him his own in exchange. Although Mendelssohn was nearly exhausted by the protracted rehearsals of the "Walpurgis Night," and was in no condition to play the part of the host, yet he helped Berlioz to arrange his concerts and treated him in all respects like a brother.

One of the most delightful pleasures which Mendelssohn arranged for th comfort and entertainment of one who was allied to him in art, was the soiree arranged on the 25th of June, 1846, in honor of Spohr. He chose productions from this master's compositions exclusively; the overture to " Faust," aria from "Jessonda," violin concerto in E-minor (played by Joachim), two songs with clarionet accompaniments, and the symphony, "Consecration of Sound." It must have been for Spohr a rare pleasure to hear his works produced in such completeness under such direction. To see these two great masters together was indeed a delight. At the close, Spohr mounted the podium of the orchestra and directed, in order to give testimony to the musicians with what youthful delight he rejoiced in the two last movements of his symphony.

What gave Mendelssohn so great a compass to his

musical activities was the union, in the highest perfection, of three gifts which are usually granted only singly to men in the measure with which he commanded them. He was great as a conductor, as he was a virtuoso and composer. When once his fine, firm hand grasped the baton, the electric fire of his soul seemed to stream out through it, and was felt at once by singers, orchestra and audience. We often thought that the flames which streamed from the heads of Castor and Pollux must play round his forehead, and break from the conductor's staff which he held, to account for the wonderful manner with which he dissipated the slightest trace of phlegm in the singers or players under his direction. But Mendelssohn conducted not only with his baton, but with his whole body. At the outset, when he took his place at the music stand, his countenance was wrapped in deep and almost solemn earnestness. You could see at a glance that the temple of music was a holy place to him. As soon as he had given the first beat, his face lighted up, every feature was aflame, and the play of countenance was the best commentary on the piece. Often the spectator could anticipate from his face what was to come. The fortes and crescendos he accompanied with an energetic play of features and the most forcible action, while the decrescendos and pianos he used to modulate with a motion of both hands, till they slowly sank to almost perfect silence. He glanced at the most distant performers when they should strike in, and often designated the instant when they should pause by a characteristic movement of the hand, which will not be forgotten by those who ever saw it. He had no patience with performers who did not keep good time. His wondrously accurate ear made him detect the least deviation from the correct tone in the very largest number of singers and players. He not only heard it but knew whence it came. Once, during a grand performance, when there were about three hundred singers and over two hundred instruments, all in chorus, in the midst of the music he addressed a young lady who stood not far from him, and said to her in a kindly way, "F, not F-sharp" (F liebes Fraulein, nicht Fis).

To singers his rehearsals were a constant enjoyment. His praise was always delightfully stimulating; his criticism not chilling nor disheartening. By throwing in all kinds of bright and merry words, he knew how to rouse the most indifferent and idle to the best performance they were capable of, and to keep the weary in good humor. Repeated and perverse carelessness would provoke him, but never to a coarse or harsh word; he had too much knowledge of the world, and too much character for that; the farthest he went was to a dash of sarcasm. "Gentlemen," he once said to a number of men who insisted on talking together after the signal had been given, "I have no doubt that you have something very valuable to talk about; but I beg you to postpone it now: this is the place to sing." This was the strongest reproof that I ever heard him give. Especially kindly was he when he praised the singing of ladies. "Really," said he once, when a chorus went passably well at the first singing, "very good for the first, exceedingly good; but, because it is the first time, let us try it once again;" on which the whole body broke into a merry peal of laughter, and the second time they sang with great spirit. All prolonging of the tones beyond the time designated by the written notes he would not suffer, not even at the close of the chorus. "Why do you linger so long on this note, gentlemen? it is only an eighth." He was just as averse to all monotonous singing. "Gentlemen," he once said at a rehearsal, "remember this even when you sing at home : do not sing so as to put any one to sleep, even if it be a cradle-song." The pianos could not be played too softly for him. Did the chorus only sink in a piano passage to a mezzo-forte, he would cry out, as if in pain, "Piano, piano, I hear no piano at all!" It was one of the remarkable features of his leading to hear the largest choir sink at the right places into the faintest breath of sound. Mendelssohn's unwearied patience at rehearsals was all the more remarkable as his frame was so delicate and his ear so sensitive ; but it made the result, when *he* was satisfied with it, as perfect as any work can be in the hands of human performers.

Mendelssohn's skill as a virtuoso was no mere legerdemain, no enormous finger facility that only aims to dazzle by trills, chromatic runs, and octave passages ; it was true, manly, *virtus*, from which the word virtuoso is derived, that steadfast energy which overcomes all mechanical hindrances ; not to produce noise, but music, and not satisfied with anything short of exhibiting the very spirit of productions written in every age of the musical art. The characteristic features of his playing were a very elastic touch, a wonderful trill, elegance, roundness, firmness, perfect articulation, strength and tenderness, each in its needed place. His chief excellence lay, as Goethe said, in his giving every piece, from the Bach epoch down, its own distinctive character ; and yet with all his loyalty to the old masters, he knew just how to conceal their obsolete forms by adding new graces in the very manner of his playing. Especially beautiful was his treatment of Beethoven's compositions, and the adagios most of all, which he rendered with unspeakable tenderness and depth of feeling. The soft passages were where his strength lay in his performance upon the piano-forte, as they were in his leading of a great choir; and in this no man has surpassed him, I might say no one has approached him. His skill on the tenor-viol has already been spoken of. He possessed a pleasant but not strong tenor voice; but he never used it, excepting at the chorus rehearsals, or, at the practice of a soloist, to indicate a tone-figure, or an interval, or, at the most, to sing a brief recitative.

To speak more at length of Mendelssohn as a composer is hardly necessary, as I have already detailed the history of about all his more important productions. These works speak for themselves; and if they do not, no analysis of mine can speak for them. But, in fact, they stand in need neither of approval nor defence. The most audacious critic bows before the genius of their author; the power and weight of public opinion would strike every calumniator dumb. What so universally affects and pleases, must be true and beautiful. But what has made Mendelssohn's a classic muse? Foremost of all, the master's pure and lofty aspiration, which set for itself only the purest ideal, and did not bow before any throne, not even that of the world; his moral energy of will, which did not ask what pleased the multitude, but, listening only to the inspiration from within, broke for itself a victorious way through all obstacles. Then his universal culture, which made him at home in a great variety of spheres, enabled him to enter deeply into the nature of any given subject, and choose that form of representation which best harmonized with it. Music was to him utterly plastic; first the transparent clearness of his understanding allowed him to conceive of his object with noon-day distinctness, and

then his mastery of art gave him a matchless power of expression.   He always knew what he wanted to do ; and,
when he had once grasped his subject, he did not rest till
the musical delineation perfectly corresponded to the idea ;
and his light hand wove all the graceful fabric with
almost magical skill, and with the speed of light.   It is
true, in all his greater works, his style is earnest, I might
say severe, throughout — true to his models, and always
worthy of his subject — but never wearisome and heavy.
Whether Mendelssohn treated a religious, a romantic, a
lyric, an epic or a dramatic theme, he always transported
the hearer to the situation, transferred his own feeling to
him, and held him to the very close in perfect satisfaction
and unabated interest.   The main thought was manifest
at once ; and it was invariably one which it was worth
while to follow, through which heart and soul were
mightily moved.   Thus in " St. Paul " the noble choral,
"Awake, a voice is calling," discloses the entire burden of
the piece ; so in the " Hymn of Praise " the wonderful
theme, " Let all things that have breath praise the Lord,"
running through the whole first movement, and reappear-
ing in the mighty chorus which ends the work ; so, too,
the first measures of the overture to "Antigone," pervaded
by the deep earnestness and fire peculiar to the antique
tragedy.   To all these genuine artist-gifts, there was
added the most needed one of all — a fancy teeming with
images, and able to present each thought in that ideal,
characteristic dress which made it unmistakable.   The
finest instances of this are his descriptive overtures, with
their sumptuous tone painting, always perfectly intelligible, yet never going too minutely into details.   Thus
in the overture to " The Hebrides," there are seen the
moist, heavy fog, the gray, strange-shaped clouds ; there

are heard the simple song of the old bard, the dull crash of battle, and the maiden's lamentation, as she stands by the sea-shore and waits for her lover, for whom she shall wait in vain.   And in the wave-like "Melusina" overture, does not the sea-nymph lift herself bodily and offer herself in love to the brave knight?   Even more characteristic and life-like in tone color are the other two overtures of which I have previously spoken in some detail.   Only a hearer utterly without fancy can fail to see what the artist meant to embody in music.

The last element of power that I will speak of in Mendelssohn was the depth of soul, the kindling fervor of his feeling, the profound and almost romantic melancholy, the tendency to revery, the light and airy sportiveness, the last of which appeared especially in his smaller pieces, his trios, quartets, sonatas and songs with and without words, and which equally pleased and amazed the listener. In the "Songs without Words," Mendelssohn has created a new department of music, in which it is not wise for everyone to be an imitator.   It was a necessity with him to throw into artistic form the fulness of charming melodies with which his soul teemed, and to which there were no words at hand to wed them.   The number of songs which he wrote from this need of expression is a lasting proof of the rich world of tone in which his spirit lived.   The text to his songs must be not merely musical in its flow, it must be thoroughly poetical to correspond to the feelings to which Mendelssohn gave expression when he wrote his "Songs without Words;" for when he had chosen his theme, he poured out a wealth of fantasy and feeling, of sympathy with nature, of noble aspiration, of thanksgiving and praise.

www.ingramcontent.com/pod-product-compliance
Lightning Source LLC
Chambersburg PA
CBHW020938030726
47496CB00005B/1254